Gods of IMAGO

Greg Belliveau

Published by Rogue Phoenix Press, LLP
Copyright © 2023

Names, characters and incidents depicted in this book are products of the author's imagination or are used fictitiously. Any resemblance to actual events, locales, organizations, or persons, living or dead, is entirely coincidental and beyond the intent of the author or the publisher. No part of this book may be reproduced or transmitted in any form or by any means, electronic or mechanical, including photocopying, recording, or by any information storage and retrieval system, without permission in writing from the publisher.

ISBN: 978-1-62420-742-6

Credits
Cover Design: David Sladek
Editor: Sherry Derr-Wille

"Swerve me? The path to my fixed purpose is laid with iron rails, whereon my soul is grooved to run. Over unsounded gorges, through the rifled hearts of mountains, under torrents' beds, unerringly I rush! Naught's an obstacle, naught's an angle to the iron way!"

— Herman Melville, *Moby-Dick* or, the Whale

Dedication

To Patricia, Kaitlin and Meghan

Part One

The Mendel Fragment

Gods of IMAGO

Chapter One

    She woke as he woke, a mirror image, a shadow, silent like him, and like a shadow just out of his view, something taken for granted. The gray haze of the morning had not yet appeared, so the darkness cloaked her. It also allowed her the space to dress quickly and follow him toward the Meeting House. It was so cold this morning, her legs and arms, though wrapped in her many layers, remained stiff and numb.

    She watched him with his thick-furred hat, his eel-skinned leggings, and fur-lined boots, watched him tall and secure in his own arrogance, those confident strides with that confident crunch of fallen leaves beneath his confident boot soles. He deserved what he got, this one. Hawthorn was right. Didn't it say to observe the world and see. Well, she was observing now, wasn't she? She observed the daily hoarding of this scrap of cloth, that small crumb of cracker or discarded and putrefying eel flesh. Yes, Hawthorn was right, right about it all. It started with this one. But how? This was the question. How and where?

    As she watched the High Priest, alone with his Acolytes, his special position—as he liked to call it—as she watched him pull apart the newly baked bread, the steam escaping, his assured nature, she suddenly doubted her resolve. She was so close—wasn't she? Hadn't she obtained access, stood knocking at the very doors of power? Not even knocking. The door had been opened for her...by him...the High Priest himself. She watched as he sipped from the small cup, the ceremony of it all, the pouring just a drop, maybe two of the Thunsae Myrrha with the wine, the blessing. Watching it all now unfolding before her, she doubted her own confidence. Could she really trust the Hawthorn? It had been nearly a year. He was a schemer, she knew that, and his conspiracy theories!

The blessing of the day complete, the High Priest of Widorexiton gathered his satchel and, together with his armed acolytes, walked from the Meeting House and down toward the outskirts of town to the stables. She followed, silent, the settling fog making it harder and harder to keep them in sight. The rolling wooden wheels pulverized the layers of scattering, swirling leaves, a vellum of broken, stiff biological detritus drifting, then exploding in a vortex of panic—this sound concentrated her mind, and she realized they were now very far indeed. Moving from tree to tree, she pushed on, head down against the cold offshore breeze.

By the time she arrived at the docks, the guards and the merchants were loading the barrels of eel oil onto the ship for its delivery to the mainland. Then it would be exported around the Black Mountains, through the Forest of the Dead and to the mysterious city called Kyrnunos, an outpost town at the very edge of the known world. At least this is what Hawthorn told her, but who knew. Kyrnunos, Cogstin, these where mere letters, syllables, placed side-by-side without meaning, mythological nonsense from a delusional and untrustworthy source. No, what was true, what was hard, as real as the bone handle knife at her side was simply, the High Priest was up to something, and she needed to find out. She crept forward to the edge of the woods and crouched, the hood of her coat pulled back slightly from the stiff, biting wind.

The *Intruder* was a two-masted hybrid schooner—wind and boiler, a blending of natural, thaumaturgic, and mechanical engineering with a deep hold perfect for transporting the eel oil across the open expanse of ocean to the mainland. She knew the ship well, for it was the only one that ever docked at Widorexiton. She watched the dockhands load the rope netting, hoist barrel after barrel up to the deck, before they lowered down into the hold. She watched as Captain Robert escorted the High Priest with ritual and pomp up the plank to his quarters, the guards straggling behind. She had time. Patience was needed now. This was the first of many trips to the mainland in the next few weeks. *How easy it would be to lie in wait, scurry aboard..?*

Her thoughts scattered, suddenly, a hand, thick and calloused over her mouth and nose.

"Not a word," he whispered close to her ear, pulling her back so that she lost her balance and fell into him. "What will the High Priest say to this, I wonder?" He pulled against her resistance. "Not a word."

She felt his body cup her own, a great span of coat and arms. She knew that a multiple of options now stood before her.

"Look at her," he said in her ear. "Look at her beautiful lines, and that hold. The way she accepts her cargo willingly." He moved closer, legs parted, pulling her further back. "You can almost feel the stiffness of those masts, straight, hard, reliable in any season."

She sighed, pushed the hand away and stood staring at the ordered chaos on the schooner. "So now you're following me?" Her voice was without malice.

"Somebody's got to keep you from trouble."

Roman was tall for a Thunsi, his body more muscular than most, strong as steel cable, notorious in the city of Widorexiton for feats mythical during the great eel hunts. And those eyes! Set deeply in the skull, dark and shadowed. She felt a surge of desire as their night together settled back into her memory. "A trouble that is none of your business."

He pulled her around to face him. "Maybe, but trouble is

trouble." He reached up gently to her face and cupped her cheeks with his hands. "You left early."

"I had some business."

"That is obvious."

She turned back to the docks, noting for the hundredth time the procedures, the spaces between the patterns. *Yes, it could be done.* She felt him move up to her, arms swooping around her chest and waste.

"Lara, seriously, this is no place to be. Why give them any reason? They catch you here, and how long would it take to expose us. What happens then?" He reached in his pocket and pulled out a small leather sack, opened it and handed her several small, dried licorice root. "Here."

"This doesn't fix everything," she said, but took it greedily, shoving it into her mouth, chewing it to pulp, the bitter aftertaste a relief to the nearly forgotten hunger pains.

She saw the sadness in Roman's eyes, those beautiful eyes. Yes, so much was at stake, so many serious moments to come. She once again realized the severe collateral damage with every new choice from this moment forward.

Chapter Two

    Lara had known Roman all her life. Their families forged into the classes by routine and ritual. Every year they would head to the coast, along with the whole town of Widorexiton, board the multiple ships and journey the forty miles for The Begetting Festival. Year after year. This ritual created multiple shared experiences, formed deep relational grooves. Indeed, it was on one of these very coastal visits that Lara met Hawthorn. That one dreaded day, mothers, and fathers, rushed and frantic, searched for their Thunsi children, dragging, holding, running to the ships that remained. Class and status evaporated on that day. It was only survival that mattered. It was that day that the families of Roman and Lara boarded the *Endeavor* together, huddling in the large hold with other survivors, mothers murmuring praises to the Horned God for his deliverance from the Blodetan—Blood Eaters. Nobody knew back then what they were. As the survivors buttressed the swells, the wooden hold leaking seawater, the eel oil lantern above swaying violently with every pitch and roll—as every family wrestled down the memories of the slaughter—Lara found her hand clasped in Roman's, those deep-set eyes shadowed, a sense of calm, even after so much carnage.

    Twenty years had passed. Their relationship grew from the soil of that tragedy, like intertwining shoots, merging, separating, merging again, separating, always within reach, the forbidden nature of the thing pushing to an inevitable conclusion never in question. But then last year's Begetting changed everything. The Horned God had spoken. The High Priest proclaimed it.

    Lara stood in the crowd at the end of the fall festival, her belly full of licorice root pie and eel blubber, the white foam from the tide gathering on the slick rocks behind her, her thoughts distracted from her chance meeting with Hawthorn a week earlier. The High Priest finished the liturgy of the Gathering, and in a droll, monotone voice spoke the names of the chosen Thunsi. Those who were to enter the Year of Purity and preparation for the Horned God. She was obviously too old to be called, her family part of the serving class, irrelevant for such a privilege. But then the Priest spoke her name. All the sorrow, terror, and elation suddenly exploded within her.

    That was almost a year ago, and now she found herself once again in the forbidden arms of Roman. Nearly once a week, Lara would sneak out early from the Purity House, walk through the cold leaf-blown world of forest and ocean to the outskirts of Widorexiton to the small wooden shack Roman called home. A fire blazed in the large iron stove, a red glow emanating from the oval glass door. Their skeleton bodies fused like two corpses twisted together from a storm. Lara lay on Roman, her head to his osseous grooved chest, humped and scarred flesh the only remnants of terror she could only imagine. She felt the soft touch of his calloused fingers as he played with her shoulder blade, drifting down her spine and to her protruding ilium. She pushed ever so slightly upward to encourage the motion. He rolled his own licorice root cigarette, breathed in the aromatic smoke. He now lay contented in the smell and warmth of pleasure.

    She looked up, grabbed the cigarette, and inhaled deeply, blew out smoke. She laid her cheek to his rising chest and stared at the familiar room. It was small for one in his class, like the cabin, but lined with bookshelves which were in turned lined with books. Each title an iconic monograph in the world of Thunsi Thaumaturgy. There were books on the biological mathematics of eels, books on creating cell generated electro thaumaturgical interactions, books on oceanic chemo-mathematical elements, even books on nautical and geological alchemy. Roman was a hoarder of spell casting. Since he chose to live outside the village and forged his personae by killing the great eels—nobody knew the severity of his obsession. Oh sure, there were whispers about the green and blue lights emanating from his cabin on occasion, but most excused it as preparation for the eel hunts.

"You can't survive as long as he has out in the great blue desert without a little help from something!"

Roman created a Demi-god mythos about him, a Thunsi of such greatness and courage—Eel Slayer they nicknamed him, impervious to water and tooth. Lara knew better. She saw, like now for instance, how intimate and gentle he could be.

"Old Bony Root has returned," Roman said without emotion. "The Couplings will be posted today or tomorrow." He glanced down at her. "You need to be prepared."

"Which is your favorite," she said with nearly a whisper, a trapped thing trying to release.

"I'm serious. You need to be ready. That's all I'm saying."

"I'm serious," Lara said. "Which one?"

"Hmm?" He smoked the cigarette to the nub and put it out in the ashtray.

"Out of them all," Lara said now on her elbows, anchoring on the words the more she thought about the question. "Which one would you take. Say if this place was burning to the ground?"

They both sat up now, interested in such a hypothetical, like a philosophy professor positing an ethics question to a class, and stared at the many volumes.

"Burning to the ground, you say?"

"Hot flames everywhere," she said.

He touched her lips. "As hot as these?"

"Nothing's as hot as these," she said. "Be serious. This reveals everything."

"Everything, hmmm. I better choose wisely." He rolled another licorice root cigarette and played with the ash. "Well, none of them actually." He breathed in the hunger-suppressing narcotic of the smoke.

She slapped him playfully on the chest. "Come on, be serious. It was a serious question. A book tells a lot about the person."

She mocked like she would slap him across the face this time, and he mocked a defense.

"I like them all, so I would take them all...or burn with them."

"You would burn with your books?"

"You're right," he said scratching his hair, "this is a revelation."

Lara got out of the bed and walked naked to the shelving. Her hips were plumper than a Thunsi woman's hips, her chest ribbed, breasts nearly flat, her spine pressing tightly against her skin, knobbed and slender like the mountains on a topographical map. Her legs, bulbous at the knee and elbow were typical of all Thunsi. She grew to like the fleshy part of herself, and she half expected this was why the Horned God chose her. She pulled a book from the shelf and paged through it.

"This one?"

"Let it burn."

"This one?"

"Burn them all."

She stood before him and pouted. "I'm serious."

"So am I," he said. "Now come back to bed. We haven't got much time."

She watched him as he lay there, his scarred flesh

strangely erotic. "No dessert until you have your medicine," she teased.

"I told you. Let them all burn. They are all important...or completely irrelevant."

"You know why I come here?" she said.

"For this," he said pointing at his crotch.

"Well, yes, but that was not the correct answer."

"What else could there be?"

"You have never lied to me," she said. "That's why I am here. No matter what, you always speak truth."

He sat up, a serious look on his face, the moment of excitement suddenly evaporating. He stared at her, sucked in the narcotic again and breathed the smoke through his nose.

"Left bookcase, fourth shelf down, fourth book from the left."

Lara hesitated, staring at him, then with glee she danced over to the bookcase and followed the instructions. She pointed to the title, *The Oceanic Thaumaturgic Chemical Periodic of Anguilliformes*.

"That's it. Open it."

She pulled the spine out and caressed the cover, plain with a slight engraving in the cloth board. She opened it, then looked up with a start.

"You asked."

"I don't understand."

Roman put out his cigarette and motioned her to bring it to him. He gently took it from her hand and pulled out the pane of glass, like two large microscope slides sealed together. The book had been carved out and replaced with a foam boarder, pages only a facade, a secret hidden safe bound in cloth. He held the glass up. Pressed between the panels was a scrap of yellowed paper. On that paper was scribbled as if in a hasty, arthritic hand, several thaumaturgic expressions. "It's the only surviving example of Quantum Alchemic Thaumaturgy. I have never shown this to anyone. You asked what I would enter a burning building for, what book I would risk everything for...? Well, this is it. Doctor Cornelius Mendel copied this down, this shard, this scrap, this...this masterpiece."

"Where's the rest of it? Why don't you have the whole thing?"

Lara sat beside him. The undecipherable equation scrawled in pencil in uneven lines. She noticed the stains of fingerprints covering the glass surface.

"Well, it is said that he alone was the only one to see the full book, and that was only briefly, time only for this...a hasty copy of a half page."

"Where did you get it?"

"Eel oil is not the only thing traded at our port, Lara. Where do you think all these books came from?" He stared at the glass, then gingerly placed it in the foam, closing the cardboard cover like the lid of a jar. "It came from Cogstin..."

She laughed, an unintended burst of sarcasm, then covered her mouth. "I'm sorry. I didn't mean...

"Cogstin is real, Lara." He said this defensively. "This is proof. This page proves the myths true."

Lara screwed up her face, staring at Roman, trying to parse any hint of sarcasm. No, he was a true believer. "I'm sorry, but you don't *actually* think there *actually* was a Christopher Dante who wrote a special book in a ruined city called Cogstin...and this is...this is *actually* from that?"

Roman turned his head. He was smaller in her eyes, frail, a puffed, feathered thing suddenly deflated. He walked it to the bookcase, sliding it back into anonymity.

"I didn't say I believed it," he said to her, his tone suddenly changing back to his confident personae, Roman the Eel Killer.

He sauntered back to the bed and stroked Lara's thigh.

She withdrew, an unintended revulsion, apologized, and began the smoldering process of artificial lovemaking. Her head swam in doubts of character, of what if's, of assertions and assumptions built on sand. When Roman rolled off her, she counted in her head to ninety, sat up, apologized, hurried out of the cabin and down the trail to the town.

First Hawthorn, she thought, *now Roman.* She did not believe in coincidences. *Although he had an artifact, an actual artifact. Hawthorn would know about this, could validate this. I must get to the mainland.*

She entered Widorexiton as it stirred from its slumber, her head swirling with the unshakeable revelation that the world she understood to be solid may in fact only be shadows on a cave wall.

Chapter Three

What defines a community? Perhaps it is the landscape, an outside geological force pushing and pulling, eventually forming generation after generation. Perhaps it is the religious practices over time, proved paths like the ancient elephant searching for watering holes. Whatever the case, it was indeed ironic that a people, the Thunsi of Widorexiton, who had almost no body fat, a skeleton race of solid bones, bones as strong as stone or metal, unbreakable—it was indeed some trick of fate that this tribe of people should live in the bitter cold of the North. The Thunsi were a special race. They thought themselves special, because their bones were strong, because their blood was like antifreeze, special because the Horned God pronounced it so.

They were born and bred for the North, for the sea. This northern living controlled every aspect of their lives. They were a people of daily survival and hourly tasks intricately intertwined with problem solving of a very rudimentary type. How do I control my hunger? Do I have enough Licorice Root for today? What is my store of eel blubber? What is the tide and weather...always the weather...always the sea. Of course, tying all of this together was the Horned God and his religious cycles. When the sunlight faded and the leaves fell, the chill sweeping across the Salty Sea from the North—the season of The Begetting. When the great thaw started, the emerging of flora, fauna and Thunsi, a season of new life, new hope—this began The Gathering. Between these two immoveable religious festivals were the cold and ice, the waiting, the haunting time of surviving. The snows came. The Ice crusted and thickened over every surface. The Salty Sea began to freeze—a seemingly eternal isolation, intolerable, desperate but manageable. Do we have enough licorice root? Can I control my hunger? Do I have eel Blubber? Can I make it to the thaw? The Thunsi were made for this, prepared for this by ancestral lore, a nearly genetic symbiosis of legend and biology passed down since the beginning.

What was the beginning? Most Thunsi as stated earlier, save for the High Priests, did not even consider this. This would take archival astuteness, a curiosity. More importantly a space and time to consider, research, write and create codices of genealogy. Who had time for such things? Even though there was no time, there were guesses and a considerable amount of evidence to support the Theory of 400 which most Thunsi took for granted. Four hundred years ago, the Proto-Thunsi crossed the Black Mountains or crossed the Great Salty Sea from the North. Whatever the actual event, someone entered the caves in the Black Mountains and drew their story on cave walls which was the first depiction of the Horned God. As every Thunsi has been taught since their childhood, it was the Horned God who introduced the barks, sailing on the Salty Sea which led them to settle on the small island of Widorexiton. There they learned to kill the giant eels.

The narrative had issues, a chicken or egg problem with the Thunsi. That was made more complicated with each succession and generation of High Priest. Which came first, the Horned God or the Thunsi? Did the Horned God create the first Thunsi...or did the Thunsi create the Horned God into existence, invoke him, so to speak. Again, who had time to ponder such things? As the Thunsi saying goes, "Four elemental truths walk with you between your rising and your setting, The Horned God, Licorice Root, the great eel, and the Salty Sea."

Widorexiton was an Island, an arrowhead land mass three miles wide and fourteen miles across. It was wind-swept and rocky, with trees and freshwater springs, serval ridges jutting up with some cliffs on the western side. The town itself was nestled on the edge of the island directly in the center of the two sweeping wings of land. These wings created a natural barrier from the always unpredictable open blue. The Bay of Widorexiton and the town itself stared southerly at the coastline of the continent forty miles away. This was the port where Lara watched the High Priest and Captain Robert board the *Intruder*. The crossing to the mainland was never easy, nothing ever taken for granted. Once on the coast...well, those horrors and savagery hid, rooted deep in every Thunis's imagination.

Lara, being from the peasant class—identified by the first letter of her name—cared as little as possible of existential things and cared even less for those who discussed them. She was a utilitarian, a practical mind, keen on observation, and yes, at times, swept up with the religious festival zeal that occasionally ravished all Thunsi.

Now her head was filled with other things. Primarily that was Roman and Hawthorn and getting back to the Purity House without notice. She hurried to the entrance of the town, being careful of potential observing eyes, and made it to the back door without incident. She rushed down the hallway adjacent to the dining hall and turned the corner when she heard that voice.

"Well, finally. You're back."

She stopped, closed her eyes tightly and calmed herself, the path for the morning obviously now obstructed. She chose a new path, a new story, reset and headed down the new ever-narrowing route filled with traps.

"Good morning," Lara said, walking past Raya to the brewing licorice root coffee steaming on the black iron stovetop.

She took a copper cup from the rack and poured the bitter liquid into it, hand slightly shaking. Raya stepped up and stole it, sipped it, and stood imposingly before her.

"I've been waiting for quite some time for one of *your kind* to come."

Lara reached up, took another cup from the rack, desperately trying to subdue the ingrained subservient triggers now screaming in every muscle of her body.

Raya pulled out a paper packet of licorice root cigarettes, walked elegantly to the plush table and cushioned chair and sat down, legs crossed, arm cocked upward holding her lit fag, lips an annoyed straight line. "Where were you?"

"What do you mean?"

Lara sat down at a nearby table and sipped from the cup.

Raya just stared, her smug confident self. She was tall, perfectly thin, Thunsi gorgeous thin, generational breeding thin with each bone curved and angular. She wore her coat and winter attire open to expose the beautiful, sculpted torso, being sure to wear her tailored eel skin under garments as tight as possible. Her face was long, long chin, high cheek bones, lips thin with jowls pronounced, her hair wispy thin and pulled straight up atop her skull to show its gossamer qualities. Her eyes were set deeply, so deeply in fact that her nearly imperceptible nose was pronounced. The dark shaded lines around her sockets enhanced this feature perfectly. With each moment in Raya's presence, Lara saw the chasm between her world and the world she had now entered expand...Raya and Roman now only a sightline.

"I walked past your empty room," Raya said. "I wonder what Ruth will say."

Lara pulled out a pack of cigarettes and lit one, trying desperately to steady her ever increasing tremors. "I don't care what Ruth says. My morning is my business."

She sucked in the licorice root smoke, holding it there, allowing it to calm her muscles and growing appetite.

"Is that so?"

That was when Lara entered the first trap set for her. Too late.

"Everything is my business," said a cackling, strained voice from the doorway.

It was the Chief Acolyte to the High Priest—Ruth. She was dressed in her usual heavy coat and large hood. She had been part of the ruling class for so long, the generations before her all Acolytes one after another that she cared little for demonstrations of any kind. Class was class. Those who are, are. Those who are not—well—they are not. She was firmly in the camp that Lara's choice for the Begetting was indeed an abomination, one more artifact in a long line of evidence that the current High Priest was losing favor with the Horned God.

Ruth pulled her hood down and waved ceremoniously to Lara to fetch her coffee. "...and my dear, you most certainly should *care* what I say."

She hovered for a moment for effect, then glided to her official seat off to the side of the room and sat. Her face was a bag of loose skin, translucent and folded about her chin and neck, lined, and creased across her forehead and cheeks as an old, folded map. Her lips were drawn in from her missing teeth, and her eyes nearly vanished in the recesses of her sockets. "Routine. Preparation. Did you have your Prayers? If I asked for the Begetting Psalm, I wonder if you could repeat a single line."

She smirked, mumbled something else, fading into herself then coming to as Lara brought her the cup. Ruth waved her away, a bothersome fly.

Raya smiled and pressed out her cigarette in the ashtray. At that moment several other young Thunsi women sauntered in, all with the features of Raya, all giddy and excited. Young, and innocent, in awe like belles at the ball groomed to be chosen by the Horned God. There was Rebecca, Rachel, Rita, Raelynn, Regina, and the youngest at fifteen—Renilda. They swooped and swarmed, separating like a flock of birds, chirping and pecking at each other, huddling around Ruth, scattering, then finally gathering together at two tables intensely drinking the coffee and eating cut portions of eel blubber.

Lara sighed, put out her cigarette nub and stood up.

"Oh," Raya said, voice higher and more pronounced for effect. "I almost forgot."

She pulled out another licorice root cigarette, rolled it in her hand, then lit it. Breathing out the smoke she said, "The High Priest posted the list." She smiled wanly. "Poor dear. Well, what does one expect. It does seem, however, Roman and I...well..."

The young Thunsi Rita, Rachel and Renilda huddled close, heads turned toward Lara, hands to mouths. Rebecca and Roberta, friends with Raya since babies—watched with delight as Ruth opened her mouth, gulping the air, staring at Raya, then to Lara in complete astonishment.

It was the second trap, and Lara walked right into it. She should have anticipated the move. Roman had said as much. "I see," Lara said in a whispered voice.

Raya sipped her coffee, her hand steady as the granite cliffs of Widorexiton. She hesitated, as light and airy as if speaking of the tides, "I'm sure you and old Bony Root will..." She tapped her ash into the tray. "Roman and I had such a laugh over it all."

Lara gathered herself and walked, steady, calmly. The story in her head once again shifting, another extremely dangerous path stark and bold before her. When she was out of view, she raced down the hallway and out into the cold of morning to find the posting, the dining room exploding in a cacophony of laughs and chortles.

Chapter Four

It was evening when the old Thunsi knocked on his door. She was expected, and the conversation to be had—delayed for obvious reasons—now increasingly desperate. The High Priest adjusted his coat, fluffed out the gilded sleeves and hood, like an exotic bird ready to mate. He smirked with the thought of Ruth and him in the act of coitus, lips souring, like a rotted piece of eel blubber mistakenly chewed. He heard the knock, soft and feeble, Ignored it again. Good to make her wait. And in his standard authoritative High Priest voice said, "Enter."

Ruth hobbled through the door, pulling her hood down, her wrinkled face reminding him of the ancient breeds of mythical dogs he fastidiously studied so many years ago.

"It's late and cold," she said in her faded voice.

"Good for the bones," he replied, delighting in her discomfort, but very much aware that his body also was resisting the warmth, and the hunger more pronounced than ever. "There is coffee, tea, something stronger if you would like."

He saw her eyes widen with that last statement, and he rung the small bell on the table next to him. An acolyte entered. "Bring the 35 reserved, please."

The acolyte bowed again and left the room. The High Priest gathered his pipe, a reddish briar with a slight bent stem. He pulled dried licorice root from a glass container, pinched, and rubbed it into the bowl, delighting even more in his slow, glacier delay.

"We had agreed it was to be last week," Ruth said. "I'm

assuming..."

The acolyte came in, served the Thunsae Myrrha Reserved 35 into polished copper tumblers. The High Priest interrupted her by toasting the air. "To the favor of The Horned God and success to the coming hunt."

She smiled at him, then gulped the rich liquor down, closing her eyes.

Was it remembrance? Prayer? What was behind those eyes of the petrified turd? "More?" he asked.

She looked up, but before she could answer he bid the acolyte pour another round. This one without ceremony, his intentionally untouched on the table as a show of power and confidence as he fiddled again with his pipe. *That should blunt the fangs of the old bat.*

"What news from the coast?" she said. "Your recent trip was unexpected."

"Unexpected in its timing, but not unlooked for."

"The church calendar is quite emphatic on when..."

The High Priest drifted off to that unexpected and unlooked for journey to the coast. The timing was indeed off. The threat of sinking from waves or eels was so high, he almost did not believe the calling. Better to fade out then to drown or be eaten in the sea. The calling was real, and his presence summoned. He tried to muster as much thaumaturgy as he could, a stability hex around the *Intruder*. His powers had so diminished by then, that he knew it was a futile gesture which made it doubly precarious and anxious. He did make it, and he did travel without incident through the forest to the Grove of the Horned God, to the Black Mountains, to the Cave of the Horned God. The terror of entering was still palatable, the absolute—how does one articulate the experience—obliteration? He shivered with the absence of memory. Yet, what resonated in his brain, pounded in his thoughts was simply, COME. COME. EXPECT

SOMETHING WONDERFUL. So, he did. He would go every week. He would stay and wait. He would expect the wonderful. On the third trip, the last trip, only two weeks ago to this very day... "If you refuse to explain your journey, and if nothing has changed..." And with a sudden and ferocious voice, "Ralph! For the love of the Horned God! Are you even listening to me."

Ralph raised his eyes. *Yes, yes, yes, I am listening to every dried, ruined, and crumbling word you say, you horrible little shrew of a woman.* Instead, he said, "Now, Ruth. We have been friends for what now...?" He puffed his pipe to life, breathing in the acrid calming smoke. "Fifty years at least. You know as well as I do that a summons can come at any time."

"So, you *were* summoned? The Horned God *Summoned* you...all those times?"

"Indeed, I was. Indeed, he did."

Ruth's visage screamed doubt and cynicism. He could feel those dark, hidden eyes probing him for signs, signals of weakness. They both knew the stakes of this game. The Horned God only called or summoned the High Priest if he (the Horned God) was pleased with the fruits of the Begetting. It was a precarious position, for if he was not pleased... The High Priest calmed himself and closed his eyes. *No, he called me. What else could that be? Was I not there? Did I not come and pray before the cave paintings? Did I not see the blessing? Well, maybe I didn't see it, but something wonderful was to happen. He wouldn't have called if...*

"Ralph." Ruth said with force. She was leaning forward now in earnest. "What was the sign?"

Stirred from his terrifying thoughts back to the cozy room, the waft of licorice root smoke rising and gathering at the ceiling peek. *She knows only what I tell her*, he thought. *She believes to be true only what happens right now. Can I do it? I have nothing left...there is...nothing.*

"What was the sign?" Ruth was now on the edge of her seat. "I have believed for a long time now that something was amiss. Why, this choosing of the peasant...this Lara. Misguided is one thing. A test...well maybe but setting such precedents can only mean one thing. I am sorry, but..."

She droned, pushed, pinned, and he tried to recall even the most rudimentary equations, but it was no use. He knew deep within it was over. He knew his demise was eminent. He failed in the last Begetting. He chose wrongly, and the Horned God was displeased. That was the very reason for choosing the peasant woman. Maybe she would be the offering to restore his favor. If he could only make it to the Begetting ceremony...he knew the Horned God would restore his blessing. So, he tried again, while the crone badgered and prodded. He dove deeper and deeper into his memory for any thaumaturgic equation that could show his favor was restored. Still, there was only darkness, and he knew right then that he had been found out. The concreteness of such a moment started to weigh upon his very soul. He had not only lost the favor, but he had now lied for months. This was surely the most egregious.

"You are right, my dear friend, Ruth," he said as his thoughts raced, desperate to grasp any equation, anything. "I went to the coastland on false pretenses, and..." *Anything! Please! Anything! I will do better next time. I promise...*

Ruth was standing now, her hand outstretched, pointing, accusing? He stood to face her wrath, to kneel before her unquestioned authority as the Chief Acolyte to the High Priest.

There was no wrath. Her face turned from scowl to...to...wonder. He turned to see what so bewildered her. A halo of green and blue light, a pulsing flash of intense thaumaturgic power released, growing from outside, penetrating the House of the High Priest, the very room where they both sat. Wonder of wonders the cups filled with Thunsae Myrrha, even the bottle on the table...they were...floating.

"A sign. Ruth whispered.

"A sign," Ralph the High Priest of the Horned God squeaked, eyes still blinking.

"Congratulations, Ralph. Oh, my dear, dear friend. Another glass, please. We must celebrate this...miracle."

As Ralph poured the Thunsae Myrrha, his hand shook, for two reasons. First, what happened before him was not of his doing, and he was most certain of this. Secondly, and this was what truly shook him to his foundations—as Ruth droned on about the Begetting, the annoying young women, the poor choice of the peasant girl—as Ruth droned on, Ralph could think of only one thought, The Horned God had chosen someone else...but who?

Chapter Five

The High Priest sent word for her. It had been nearly a month now since the High Priest's return from the coast and the visit to the Horned God. Nearly a month since the posting of the Couplings, and all those days, hour by hour, for Lara to feel the full weight of such a monumental collapse upon her. As the city of Widorexiton readied for the Great Eel Hunt which ushered in the Horned God and the Begetting Ceremony, Lara wandered the cliffs of the western bank and pondered what would be better. To jump to her death or spend the rest of her life with old Bony Root, The Great Knob, Mr. Carbuncle, and all the other pejorative, demeaning names the young Thunsi women gave the High Priest. That was it, wasn't it? Since she was not to be Coupled after the Begetting, her name absent from the posted list, she was to be forever a slave to that old lascivious husk. She heard the rumors, the whispers all through her life about how the poor "uncoupled" would hole up with that old turd for the winter. By the time The Gathering finally arrived...well, let's just say the shoreline below the great cliffs where she now wandered were littered with the bodies of the misfortunate, deflowered youths.

She sat on the edge, feet dangling into the air, sat, and stared at the great gray Salty Sea. She pulled the course strands of her hair around her ears, several strays swooping across her face. She breathed deeply. It wasn't just the posting that bothered her, was it? Yes, the shock of not being on there, even after that bitch Raya pronounced the shame to everyone in the Purity House, that shock was quite severe. One always hopes that

Raya's sharp knives weren't really going to be used so early in the morning. Oh, they were, and they stabbed alright, stabbed deeply. The deepest cut of all was the actual pairing. Raya and Roman were to be paired after the Begetting! She did not want to think about it! She grabbed a small granite stone from the rubble of erosion near her and threw the jagged piece into the open space.

Roman and Raya! Great Horned God! Must I remember! Raya prancing and pouting every time Roman walked into town. Pawing, and cooing at every word! She fisted her hands in a futile effort to stop the whole maddening thing. Maybe she just jumps. Right now! Slip off this cliff, one push—a bit of panic maybe—then darkness. The Horned God would forgive her in the afterlife. Of course, he would. The fates had been conspiring against her, her whole life—the Horned God would welcome her with open arms. Just one tiny push, falling—but her luck had been quite bad lately. Instead of falling and meeting the Horned God on the other side—she probably would survive the damn fall. She would land in some soft spot of sand, just enough force to cripple her, break her back and arms, become some shattered thing that must learn to walk, speak and drag about the town for the rest of her days. She would be scorned and laughed at. Mocked, forever watching Raya and Roman pump out children. Watch while they danced, ooed and caudal each other, while she still forced to hole up with old Bony Root as the town's untouchable! Better to be a Blodetan.

She stared down at the rocks and sand below her. She sighed once again. Nope, time to see what The Great Knob wanted. Thank the Horned God. He could not touch her before the Begetting. She stood to her feet, glanced at the great gray beyond, turned and hurried down the cliffs and back to town.

When she arrived at the High Priest's house, she was bid wait in the hallway until his present business was completed. It was a tall ceilinged thing, ornate furniture and chairs, sculptures placed throughout as if to pronounce to every Thunsi who entered. You are not chosen. I am chosen. The Horned God chose me...not you. In fact, you tiny little being, you who were not even posted on the Coupling list—you of all Thunsi should not even be here. Well, that was how she felt, anyway.

The chair was too tall for her. Her legs dangled and swung in rhythm to nothing in particular. And she heard the muffled voice on the other side of the wall rise, escalate into a sort of rage.

"Well why do you think I did?" The High Priest's voice boomed. "I give you what you want. You give me what I want!" And a sudden blast. "Do you think this some sort of game?"

The other voice mumbled and pleaded. Sobbing? An acolyte opened the door, and Lara could hear quite clearly now.

"The eel hunt is in a week. Now get out of here before I lose my temper."

Lara heard shuffling, a collecting of garments, more shuffling, and Raya hurried from the great room. She glanced at Lara, wiped her eyes and was gone. Lara stared after her. And then, "The High Priest will see you now."

She entered the grand room demurely, the High Priest with his back turned to her, his long, gilded robes thick and course around his frail frame. When he turned, his face brightened considerably. He motioned her to sit on a cushioned bench.

"May I offer you some Licorice Root tea?"

She nodded.

He bid the Acolyte to fetch the tea, and he took up his pipe, pinching the dried herb into the bowl, packing it with his thumb, puffing it into a red ember. "I've been waiting to see you, Lara. It's been such a while since the Posting, and I have meant to...acquaint myself."

He sat across from her. He watched the acolyte pour them

tea, then disappear out the door. When he was quite convinced, he left, he leaned forward. "You must be quite...well, astounded really, maybe even a bit confused."

Lara sipped her tea, feeling the anxiety of the morning surface again. She looked at the old codger, his lined face, lined neck, the hollow holes where eyes barely appeared, the thin gray skin of his hands, velum covering bone. Of course, she was astounded! That wasn't the half of it. She could think of quite many words more clarifying than "astounded." She nodded.

"Yes," the High Priest said, "I'm sure it came to you as quite a shock. Why, the whole thing, this whole...process...has probably got you guessing which end is up."

He puffed his pipe contentedly.

Not knowing how to respond, she nervously pulled out the paper packet of cigarettes and lit one, the calming licorice root smoke suppressing the great hunger that suddenly snuck up on her, ferociously clawing at her insides. She breathed out.

"I knew your mother quite well," the High Priest said, his eyes riveted on her. "Did you know that? I wonder what she would say now. Just look at you. And yet..." He leaned forward ever so slightly. "...you are so...downcast of late. Ruth tells me you barely eat or sleep. Up early, home late...I am quite concerned."

Lara's mind whirled and scattered, now here, now there. Did the old Thunsi know? Did he know she was tracking him? Did he know about Roman? What had that old crone Ruth said to him? For that matter, Raya! What diabolical knife was now hidden ready to strike?

The old Thunsi Priest leaned still further toward her, now on the edge of his seat. "You can tell me, little one. You can tell me...anything. What is it that finds you so removed from your former self?"

She stared at his face, then glanced down. Was that

concern? Was he actually asking her? Could she be so wrong about Bony Root? Maybe he did care. Maybe all those rumors where just that...terrible gossip designed to defame and denigrate a truly good hearted Thunsi.

"Well," Lara said. "There is something."

"Of course, there is *something*." The High Priest retorted. "How could there not be? You have been put through so much. Quite a lot, really. More than such a young and beautiful flower—one sprouted from a mud puddle—should ever be put through."

Yes. She thought *Yes. He does see it. He knows about Roman and me. He knows how horrible Ruth has treated me, the mocking, Raya's jealousy. He does care. How could I possibly not be Coupled with Roman.* She said, "It's just that I think it was a mistake..."

"Yes. Exactly," the High Priest said, a sudden relief covering his face. "I see that now. How foolish I was to assume...?"

Lara sat forward as well, her mind focused, a great burden exhumed. "I just didn't know what to do," she blurted. "It happened so fast...the Naming, the new rules. It just did not seem...well, I know I shouldn't have but I just...did. Now the Posting and I'm sure it makes little difference... Roman said..."

"What?" The High Priest stared intensely.

"What?" Lara said watching old Bony Root's lips purse, thin and white.

"What did Roman say?"

Lara pushed herself back into her chair as if that would save her from the moment. "I was just saying that..." She whispered and sucked on her cigarette nearly extinguishing the butt.

"Since being named to the Begetting," The old Priest said in frustration, confused like a circuit had misfired. "Er... A mistake. I shouldn't have..." And he placed his pipe down on the table. "What in the Horned God are you...? What about Roman?"

There it was, boom! The room became suffocating and small, a coffin, and she trapped below the earth, her oxygen evaporated. "It's just that..."

"Speak plainly, young woman. What about Roman? What did he say? Speak up."

"Nothing. He told me nothing. You're right, it's all this...this..."

The High Priest now stood up, a statue of power and authority of terrifying awe. "What did Roman say?"

"Nothing. You asked me why I was feeling so beyond myself. I'm not like...Roman...or Raya. I'm not like any of them. I feel...out of sorts..."

"Yet clearly you are withholding something."

"I've told you all I know," Lara said.

"You have seen something. Something with Roman. What did you see, girl? What secret?"

"I don't know any secret."

"Are you two...?"

"I don't know what you mean."

"Confound it, girl! Who do you think stands before you. Now tell me!"

"Roman reads magic books!" She blurted out because to continue down this road was to cast oneself in blazing fire.

The high priest suddenly waved his hand like shewing a fly. "Of course, he does! That's not news. Thaumaturgy is a fascination to most Thunsi, fire to an insect. By the Horned God, just as dangerous. Knowledge and power are two very different things, my dear. Ha-ha." The old Priest sat back down in his chair, a withdrawn, intimidating bony root. "You have not answered my question. Why are you spending so much time over there?"

She could not tell him the truth, that she was screwing an aristocrat when she was supposed to be preparing for the Begetting. What was she to say? Every word out of her mouth got her closer and closer to losing everything she gained. One word from him, the High Priest, one word, and she would be back emptying chamber pots and sweeping floors. No, she needed to distract him, deflect. "He showed me something."

The old priest looked up from his thoughts. "Go on."

"It was...in a glass plate. Some scrap of paper." She saw him becoming more and more interested, so she dared not stop. "From...Cogstin."

Silence. Complete silence. The old priest sat back in his chair.

Was he laughing? A cackle? Something odd, but quite obvious fluttered out of the old Priest's mouth. He put his withered hands to his forehead, rubbing it. "Oh, my dear, dear girl. You are quite a comical little wit. Ruth must have her hands full with you, little flower." He picked up his pipe. "Yes indeed, it was my mistake to choose you." He rubbed the bowl of his pipe, then tapped it out. "One I'll regret, I'm sure." Then, "You need to stay away from him...Roman. Raya's got that under control I assure you." He shook his finger at her. "Your families were too close. I never considered the tangle such things can cause. Separation of the classes is important. I warned your mother when she was your age." He pinched more licorice root into the bowl and lit it. His tone changed considerably. "Stand up," he said to her. "Take off that coat. Let me look at you." He puffed his pipe. Waving and pointing. "Turn around, slowly, yes, quite nice, quite nice indeed."

She felt his lecherous eyes scanning and poking, penetrating secret places, delighting in her vulnerability.

"Up," he said pushing the air with his fingers. "Higher. Go on. I'll be seeing those delights soon enough."

She pulled up her long skirt, up passed her knees, up, up to her thigh, hesitating, a sudden coldness, like a corpse fondling her.

"Yes, I was right to omit your name. Quite right indeed." He watched her frozen, standing before him. "You have kept the purity rules?"

"Yes," she lied.

"I want no more nonsense with Roman, you understand? Raya has been quite emphatic. You should know your place. It's a privilege of no small thing to be where you are...a mere peasant girl." He pondered her in silence. Then, "The Horned God may or may not be pleased. We shall see. You are a delight."

The High Priest strained to stand, then hobbled out of the room, leaving Lara all alone. She wrapped the coat around her and stood next to the chair. The Acolyte came up behind her and ushered her out.

What had she done? What choice did she have. Better to mention Cogstin than say she was sleeping with Roman. Besides, the old fart laughed. No big deal. Roman would find out, and she would lose Roman... Wasn't he already gone? She pulled the hood over her head to greet the newly falling snow. There was to be a great storm coming. It was earlier this year. It seemed everything was changing now, new, and uncertain. She ran from the porch and disappeared into the whitening haze of the day.

Chapter Six

Roman was bone tired, and that was a severe commentary since Thunsi were mainly skeleton to begin with. He spent the last month consumed—possessed really—desperately trying to negotiate the equations on the Mendel Fragment. Each small failure, each reorganization of the phrases, letters, symbols—a seemingly infinite and tedious endeavor—each failed moment pushed his imagination toward another possible alternative for the next night. Possessed! His mind spun like a vortex as he lay his head on his arms and drifted to sleep only to wake consumed with new expectations...new what ifs. It was more than that...it was...how would one put it—musical! Yes, that was it. Musical, a beat that wouldn't leave, a persistent rhythm, simple, but all consuming. He woke with it, it growing, pulsing, intensifying until all he could do was concentrate his whole will on arranging the phrases and symbols of the Mendel Fragment until exhaustion, pass out, wake, repeat.

He was no fool. He knew the cost of dabbling in Thaumaturgy. Every Thunsi knew the cost...and yet. This was not some infantile infatuation. No, this was something quite serious, something mature, thought out, something pursued with caution and exuberance. *Cautiously exuberant. That was it,* he thought with an addict's pride and confidence. *A composition of sorts, a constructed thing, a puzzle as it were, placing one piece after the other as it formed...well...inevitable ruin.* He rubbed his head manically, then his face, slapping his cheeks to allow the blood to circulate where it had probably puddled from sleeping so long, breathed out with exhaustion, and stood up. Yet... There was that music again! A humming throbbing thing that concentrated his mind and will on another, different, more satisfactory possibility for the equation. He did succeed with it, didn't he? That was real. Wasn't it? In a complete manic state, he organized the equation in such a way...well, it hummed, didn't it? It so consumed his thoughts that he felt "pulled into it" as it were. Yes, pulled in. A moment. A moment of absolute...well, how could he put it...antiphony—call and response? Whatever he did, it worked...sort of...an explosion of energy, a sort of casting out, an undulating wave. By the Horned God! He hovered in the damn air! Well, maybe he did. He felt he did, floated. Okay, maybe it was all in his head. That was the tricky bits. Whatever happened, it was late and nobody knew about it. Thank the Horned God for that. That's all he needed. Snoopers, thieves. Oh, he was so exhausted. Tomorrow...the hunt.

Roman thumbed the glass, clipping off a bit of dried eel blubber. He grabbed a cloth and wiped the smudge. Next he dampened the cloth with spit and rubbed the now smudged smudge, breathed on it, wiped again until it was crystal clear. He closed the book staring at the stiff board cover, *The Oceanic Thaumaturgic Chemical Periodic of Anguilliformes*. He placed it back into the open slot on the shelf. Out of sight out of mind. Yet... He lingered before it, tapping the binding, adjusting it just, perfectly flush with the others. He was pulled from his reverie.

"Roman." The familiar voice called and thumped again. "Roman. Cap'n about to have a blow. He's been waiting for an hour. Roman!"

Roman shook his head as to clear the fuzzy signal and opened the door. It was Linus, a short Thunsi, a wide, big boned thing wrapped from head to toe in his traditional fur-lined eel skin coat and trousers. He smelled of harbor and eel viscera, of salt and wood and rotted, hidden things that had been rubbed into his every pore. On his head he wore a great hat complete with fur-lined earflaps, a bubble-topped thing that gave every indication he made it himself and held it in quite high esteem. He was the master cook of the *Intruder*, but known to the town as many other things, none of them good. He was a rogue when the mood came upon him, always looking out for something easier when the quickest way was putting the head down and grinding through hard stuff. The life of a cook was hard, so Linus was always searching for a way out. He was a happy sluggard who drank and slept too much which became problematic when he was to mind the helm as the Harpooners sailed their eel boats out into the Salty Sea. He was never without a licorice root cigarette dancing from his thick lips.

Roman grabbed his coat, pulled on his hat and gloves, and stepped through the door, closing it and locking it behind him.

"You look a right mess. That's say'n something from me, eh." Linus slapped Roman on the back.

"I see the captain still lets you wear that dead animal on your head."

"Aw you know me, Roman. Do something until they hang you. Right?"

He laughed which turned into a husky, raspy coughing expulsion of phlegm. He grabbed another cigarette, licked it with delight and popped it in his mouth. "We best hurry, Roman. Captain Robert is in a foul mood this morning, no mistake. No mistake."

With that, Linus hobbled, limped and hurried alongside Roman who quickened his pace, realizing how late in the morning it was.

The town of Widorexiton was fully preparing for The Begetting Festival now, and Roman's heart was lifted. He loved this time of year, loved the singing and the music, the decorations, the delightful dishes of eel blubber pie and licorice root candies and tarts. The smell of bonfire and the heat and sweat of the dancing. He loved it all. He found his thoughts drifting to past childhood memories, his father standing stern and proud as he introduced the High Priest and opening prayer to the Horned God. Indeed, there was so much to look forward to this year, so much expectation. He and Lara talked about it all. Hoped and dreamed about their future and how his first commission would change everything. The world was at his feet. Then the High Priest posted the couplings. Now what was he to do? *Oh, it all seemed muddied now...complicated. Still...the Festival of The Begetting was here...*

Linus elbowed him hard and pulled him from his revery. "There's a sight and no mistake, eh boy?" Linus cocked his head toward a group of Thunsi women wrapping greens into bundles and hanging them around the eves of the Purity House. Raya was staring at him, eyes wide with joy and expectation. *Stalking him, perhaps, waiting.* Lara was watching Raya. *They were both so...attractive. Both beautiful in their own way, exotic even! By the Horned God! Raya was downright gorgeous. She was one more reason that he was losing Lara. Raya was a sycophant. Snap his fingers and she would dance any dance he wanted.* Roman's face soured ever so slightly, and he turned in the opposite direction. He pushed Linus down a side alley which would now delay them even more and keep the old hot-headed Captain Robert stewing even longer.

By the time the two of them did board the *Intruder*, Captain Robert was below in his quarters, hovering over a map. His demeanor was calm, minor tremors here and there, a sudden unchecked tick like a crust of earth ready to blow into pieces by the force of geologic pressure.

"Forgive me, father. I was delayed."

"It looks to all indications," Captain Robert said tapping the map with his spindly finger, "tomorrow they will be here."

Roman gauged the old man, his wrinkled, hardened skin, the scarred flesh running like streams up his neck and right cheek, under his brimmed hat only to emerge down the other side, past his left ear and disappearing into his shirt neckline. He saw how tired his eyes had become, how deep and sunken. Yet...an unforgiving tempered piece of iron, unbreakable, unyielding. Roman stepped up and hovered over the map, concentrating on the eastern portion, the tide chart, the cycles of the moon.

"Any Idea how much we are behind in our preparations?" Captain Robert said. "And you casually saunter in." He continued, in a low whisper, "With that...that peasant girl, I suspect."

"No, father. I was not with...*the peasant girl*."

"It all has a bearing, you know. All of it. The peasant girl, the silly books, the time spent away...away from the important things. This. The Hunt tomorrow." Captain Robert gathered himself again, a slight intake of breath, and he walked to his licorice root cigarettes and lit one. He stood staring at his son. "I did everything I could, you know. It's out of my hands now."

Roman glanced up, suddenly understanding what the conversation had now become, the reason for the summons. Captain Robert motioned him to sit. Roman stood.

"Please, son, sit down." Captain Robert sat and gestured again to Roman. He offered Roman a cigarette from the wooden box. "It's a mess, boy. It's a right mess, and I can do nothing about it. You've angered the wrong people I'm afraid."

"What is that supposed to mean? You told me the Commission was a sure thing. You assured me that after the hunt tomorrow..."

Captain Robert laughed, but it was dry and mean. "A sure thing indeed, until you... By the Horned God, man! What were you thinking? What could have possibly been in that thick head of yours? Screw anyone else! Anyone! Screw Linus or a hole in the damn wall... But the peasant woman! By the Horned God, man! She comes from a disgraced family!"

Captain Robert was standing again, a tall terrifying angular Thunsi. He turned and stared out the large panes of glass that made up the stern wall.

Roman breathed in the smoke of his cigarette, the vapors subduing the all too familiar hunger pains. *What had he been thinking? Everything thrown out the window for...for her. All for her. Yet, he realized how little he suddenly cared about it all. Lara, the commission, the whole damn world. All he really wanted now was the Mendel Fragment. That was all.*

"Look at you, boy!" Captain Robert turned to him now and pointed. "Your hair, your clothes." He was shaking visibly. "They're right. You don't give a damn, do you? Blow it all up. Throw it all in their faces. Who cares? Well... I care! Since I care... You better damn well care!" Here came the rage, the crust of earth split wide, the force of the energy thunderous. Roman noticed the hustle and bustle, the hoisting and cranking, groaning, creaking of winches and ropes above them stopped.

He stared at his father, trying but failing to show how he was not affected by the onslaught. Captain Robert breathed in again, then out. He tried tacking more windward. "It may not be over, but you are sailing close to the rocks, boy. Do you want them to send you to the coast?" Captain Robert clapped his hands in a shockwave of sound. "Do you? Do you? By the Horned God, look at me!"

Roman looked up. Their gaze a terrible standoff of will.

"Now you're being dramatic," Roman said. It was coming, the violence.

"What do you think is the recourse? They have done it before. I have seen it with my own eyes. He's visited me, Roman. He came last night..."

There was a change in tone with Captain Robert, and

Roman could sense the undercurrent of fear, of what the High Priest threatened if he could not get his son under control. Roman was curiously unmoved by the intimidation, the various waves of assault. Something was driving him now, something from the outside, and he found himself hating Old Bony Root even more than before. He lashed out. "He's harmless, and you know it."

"Harmless? You know damn well the cost, boy. You go about your business like some halfwit!"

"You wouldn't understand," Roman whispered.

"Understand? What is there to understand? When the High Priest tells you..."

Roman began to laugh. He could not help it. It was cruel. It was disrespectful, but a lust, an overwhelming, uncontrollable spite consumed him. It was as if his voice and will were not his own. "Look at the great Captain Robert? Look at him cower before the old dust fart."

Captain Robert seethed at him, mouth pursed, eyes unblinking. "How dare you?" he hissed.

"How dare I what, father? Let that imbecile priest once again take something away from you? When will you learn? How much will you give up? Hell, what is left for him to take? First your wife...then your worth...now your only son..."

The attack was swift. Captain Robert threw himself at Roman, grabbing his coat sleeve, pulling at him, knocking the box of cigarettes to the floor, scattering outward like an exposed nest of cockroaches. The vice grip of the old man's hands dug into Roman's shoulders, pinning his struggling son to the back of the chair. Roman desperately tried to free himself and ward off the strike he knew was coming.

It was in the nick of time that Linus opened the door to the captain's cabin and intervened. "Captain, sir, I was just about to bring breakfast to you."

Linus laughed hoarsely and stepped between them,

fidgeted with Roman's coat, before bending down and gathering up the loose cigarettes. "I was just about to cook the blubber, and I forgot to ask if there will be two for breakfast... How much should I cook?"

Captain Robert straightened out his long coat and walked to the map, studying it, shoving a smoldering butt into an ashtray and lighting another, hand unsteady.

"There we go," said Linus, placing the wooden box on the small table before the chairs. "Right as rain." He stood up eyeing Roman, then the captain, then back to Roman. "Well, Captain? Will it be two for breakfast then?"

Captain Robert was silent.

"Just one, Linus," Roman said. "I'm obviously behind on my work."

"You're not leaving this ship, first mate, until it is all finished."

Roman stood and faced the captain. "Father."

He walked past Linus and through the door to the small stairwell that made its way to the deckhouse above.

"All of it!" Roared Captain Robert through the closed door.

All that day they worked, until the sun set, the deck shadowed by the lanterns, crew exhausted from rebuilding the Tryworks, sealing the hold with pitch, scrubbing the deck, rescrubbing it and all to the rumble of Captain Robert's "put your backs into it, lads!" And "You call this sealed? Again! I said again!" Of course, Roman did not do the work, but supervised it, called for the final approval, then all over again, and again, and again.

He watched the masons stack and set the extra reinforced brick, knowing that it would be for nothing with one violent eel attack. He guided the barrels of pitch below deck, calling out for care as one tipped and nearly spilled. All he could think about was the futility of keeping the Salty Sea out if just one snap of the tail could smash them all into oblivion. Only he knew how they had made it this far. Only he understood the power and seriousness, the exhausting work of spell casting, hex-making. Roman wasn't charmed. By the Horned God, no! He was the charmer. It was his work that surrounded the *Intruder* as to make it invisible to the writhing and punishing eels. Now there was the Mendel Fragment as a foundation. This would be the first time he could try out all his practicing.

He paced back and forth, his head spun with the tantalizing dance of the Mendel Fragment equations. Hour after hour after hour, they toiled. Now, the Thunsi crew spent, Roman's nerves frayed and raw, the undeniable point driven into the ground. "Do what you are told or I will make your life so hard you will wish they shipped you to the coast."

When he finally gathered his coat and hat. Wrapped his scarf around his neck and hoisted his collar high above his ears, his mind was numb. The walk to his cabin long, weary, and tedious. About three quarters of the way home, turning to the final stretch, he noticed someone coming toward him. He was so tired. *By the Horned God! Take what you want! I don't care anymore!* When the figure came closer, he recognized it as Raya. *Raya out here this late? She looks worried! She's freezing. Why isn't she wearing her coat?*

"Everything okay?" His mind swirled with panic.

Raya smiled and held her humped up coat closer to her chest. She looked nervous. "I was just waiting for you, but when you didn't show, I thought I would just leave.

"Sorry... It's been a long day." He looked at her, her body shivering. "You want to...have a drink or something? Get warm?"

"Oh," she said, now turning her back ever so slightly and hurriedly walking past him. "No thank you. I'm just so tired." She stopped, turned her head. "I'm sorry, Roman. I really am."

And. "You know, she will only hurt you." With that, she hurried into the darkness.

Roman watched her run down the path. She was strikingly beautiful. Many a Thunsi would kill for an object so becoming. As he watched her disappear around the bend, he felt the sudden and severe weight from the long day. It was all he could do to make it to the house without collapsing. He found the keys in his pocket and fumbled to unlock the door, but it was already unlocked. He blinked, looked back at the path behind him, then entered the small cabin. He dropped his coat and clothes over the furniture and fell into the bed, his body a used-up husk. His head spun with, Raya, with Lara with the Mendel Fragment equations. He would see none of them for a week or maybe more. That is...if he could keep the hex going. *I need to think on* that. His mind spun and spun, weaving in and out of current and distant equations. Soon he was deep into the Hunt to come and all the ways one can kill the most dangerous and terrifying sea beast ever seen by Thunsi.

Chapter Seven

Something was driving Lara now, something beyond her, pushing her. After her encounter with old Bony Root, she was more convinced than ever, he was part of something afoot; Raya, Captain Robert—all of them conspiring. *This* was what Hawthorn warned her about. This was the conspiracy unfolding before her very eyes. So, she kept her eyes and ears open.

It all began to play out two days earlier, two days before the Hunt, she watched Raya leave the village and walk toward Roman's house. She followed behind unnoticed, a shadow moving in the shadows. *What was she up to?* She watched as Raya knocked on Roman's door. Waited, knocked again, then put her ear to the door. Soon she was fumbling in her pocket. Suddenly there was Roman staring at her in the doorway. Raya seemed anxious, out of sorts...as if...well as if she was not expecting him to be there.

"I'm late for the harbor," Roman said. "What do you want?"

Raya shifted, like putting on a persona, then she leaned forward. "Can't I visit my partner," she purred seductively.

Roman shook his head with impatience. "Listen, I told you I'm late. I don't have time right now." He grabbed his coat and hat and locked his door. "I really must be going." He stepped past her, but she stood on the porch. "Well, are you coming?"

Raya glanced at the door, then to Roman. The two hurried down the path toward town.

All that day Lara watched Raya, watched her as she tried

to disengage with the tasks Ruth gave them all. Sweeping the Purity House floors, scrubbing the Purity House walls and tables, hanging the festival greens on the eaves—so much to do before the Hunt and the Begetting. The kitchen was chaos as they baked and cooked. A buzz of excitement and impatience seemed to emanate from all corners of the town. Every chance she got; Raya tried to break free from the group. Ruth was on her, however, and never was she far from the "Keep sharp, Raya!" Or "There's plenty more after that, young Thunsi!"

It wasn't until the High Priest himself visited the Purity House, Raya in particular, that Lara knew something sinister was afoot. She followed Raya to the Meeting House and attended to the greenery as a decoy. This was when she overheard the enigmatic conversation that pointed to this night... Captain Robert would do his part. It was time for her to do hers. She knew the cost of failure. Raya begged him to be patient.

The evening before the Hunt, Lara made her way to the harbor. She could hear the humming and creaking and irritation, a hushed sense of uneasiness as the crew finalized their plans and stowed last minute items. She watched Roman, who seemed to be deep in his own head, walk from the docks and into town. She saw Linus and Captain Robert huddled together by the plank, soon joined by Captain Robert's hand-picked harpooners, Liam and Landon—both tall, wrapped in long eel skinned coats lined with fur. They wore stiff rimmed eel skinned hats, a status symbol for harpooners as they made their way from crew to third or second mate. Lara crept behind the Harbor Master's shack, the lapping of the tide, now increasing in rhythm with the offshore breeze. And she saw Old Bony Root appear. He was cloaked in a worn and patched garment, baggy and out of place with his demeanor. Captain Robert bowed as with the harpooners, Linus nearly falling to the ground as he placed weight on his bad leg.

She could hear low tones as they whispered to each other,

the High Priest nodding. Captain Robert pointed to the *Intruder*'s hull, then outward. All now looking at the flags indicating the windspeed. Captain Robert was impatient, The High Priest hesitant on some plan now unfolding.

"What are you doing down here," said a familiar voice from behind Lara.

She turned to face Raya.

"I should ask you the same," she said, but her words had no force.

"You shouldn't be here." Raya grabbed Lara's arm, and as the struggle ensued, the small band of Thunsi on the dock stopped talking and looked up.

"Who's there?" Shouted Captain Robert. "Show yourself!" Liam and Landon hurried toward Raya and Lara. Lara pulled away but was soon held fast by Liam's ferocious grip. All four walked down to the water and under the disappointing gaze of both the High Priest and Captain Robert.

"What's the meaning of this?" Captain Robert said with an obvious disgust on his lips as he recognized who Lara was.

"I found her spying on you," Raya said. She stepped over to the High Priest and handed a package to him, something wrapped in an old cloth, rectangular...a book? The High Priest gathered it gently in his hands And hid it from view.

"This is most irregular," Captain Robert said. "Speak up, Peasant!"

"Ruth sent me... To find Raya," she said, spinning words out without substance, trying to anchor any of them. "She left early, and Ruth wanted her to finish the purity ritual."

"I just spoke to Ruth," Raya laughed. "She knows where I am."

"He'll know," Lara said as a thought gave birth in her mind. "He'll find you out...all of you. He'll hate you!"

A stocky Harpooner named Layne, Roman's hand-picked

lancer, personally trained by the Eel Slayer himself—the squat, thick Thunsi suddenly came up to the group from the eastern part of the harbor. He was making sure the last of the supplies had been taken from the stock yard.

"Hey now," he said with his short pipe sticking from his lips. "What's all this?" He saw the Captain and the High Priest and stiffened. "Captain, sir. Can I be of service?"

Captain Robert nodded his head at Linus the cook and Liam his harpooner. They walked to Layne and slapped him on the back. "No need to worry, mate," said Liam, and with a quick thrust, Linus punched into his stomach, deeper, then upward while Liam pulling back hard on the man's face as to cover the sound of his dying.

Lara screamed. It was Captain Robert who grabbed her and held her fast once again. "You can't do this," Lara said. "I know what you are doing." And it crashed upon her, a complete solidified thing. "You took it." She turned to Raya. "I thought you loved him. You took the Mendel Fragment! It was you. How could you? What right do you have to..."

"Silence her," boomed the High Priest.

With one great blow Liam smashed his fist down upon her cheek. She felt the shock, a flash, felt her mouth fill with...was that blood? Her neck rolled, and her head drooped to her chest as if pulled by a rope. She watched from a distance, confused, blurred moments happening out of sequence.

She heard a disconnected conversation.

"You're sure about the hex?"

"I'm sure, Captain Robert. Leave such things to those who understand them."

"Well, I understand one thing. There is no passing now. By the Horned God, they'll be out there!"

"Leave that to me."

She saw the High Priest and Captain Robert hurry

onboard the *Intruder,* she herself dragged across the plank behind them. She heard Raya's voice pleading from the dock, "What am I to do? You can't leave like this. You...lied to me."

Lara was pulled and dragged below deck, under lifeless legs, And tied fast to an iron ring. It was Linus who shoved a cloth in her mouth and tied the gag. It was Linus who stooped down into her face. He put his finger to his lips and shook his head. "Not a word, my dear, or you'll never make it to morning. Not a word."

So, she sat there, quiet, sat as the *Intruder* left the dock and sailed toward the coast. She sat silent as her face puffed into a swollen, closed up mollusk, the throbbing, searing pain ringing out in undulating waves like ripples from a tossed stone. She sat there harnessed by ropes to her ankles and wrists while the rush of wind and waves battered the hull of the vulnerable wooden ship, and the terror of where she was heading only now settling upon her mind.

~ * ~

When the sun emerged from the Salty Sea, Roland came upon his gathered, partial crew. They surrounded something humped and sprawled on the docks.

"By the Horned God, where's the *Intruder?* What is going on here?"

"They killed him," Lex howled, staring up to Roman, his leathered face wide with panic. Roman looked down on the great Layne himself, his thin skull pale and lifeless.

"Where's Captain Robert? Where's the *Intruder?*"

It was Raya who ran to him crying, gasping, a full performance now on display.

"She stole it, Roman! Oh Roman! She lied to you and stole it. I tried to stop her. I tried to stop them all! Oh, Roman!"

She fell into his arms, he pushing her back, observing, severe. "What are you talking about? Speak plainly."

"Lara stole your glass plate. She gave it to the High Priest. They have left, Roman! They have left with your glass plate and sailed to the coast! Oh Roman, I told you not to trust her. I told you."

Roman did not hear any more words from Raya. He cast her aside and dashed toward the town, his heart in his mouth, his head light and confused. *That can't be. Lara would not do such a thing! When? How? By the Horned God, how did this happen?* He arrived at the cabin and could barely breathe. *It's still there. Of course, it's still there! Lara would never betray me. Not her. Raya! This is Raya's doing.* He ran to the shelf, pulling the book from the others, opening it, and all the while whispering to the air, "No, no, no, no. Please no...." He knew before he opened it, he knew by the way the book had been so carelessly returned, spine out further than the rest—and his energy left. His body involuntarily slumped to the wooden floor, his stomach an ice ball, his mind a gray and swirling void. One phrase surfaced and resurfaced like a terrible fish, *LARA BETRAYED ME!*

Chapter Eight

While Ruth, The Chief Acolyte to the High Priest, droned on, Roman's mind raced in a furious dance of inevitability. He viewed this current moment, the aftermath of unforeseen sequences of events, like an ocean swell, the consequences from each individual act, building toward an enormous and terrifying tidal wave rushing toward him. He needed Ruth's permission. Without her "yes," there would be no following after the *Intruder*. She could yet be convinced. For all her traditional Thunsi views, she was the most rational of the two authorities. Now that the High Priest, Lara, and Captain Robert absconded the Mendel Fragment, she was the sole decision maker until his return. He knew that the next moments would be crucial, for it was Ruth who sought Roman out. This was step one of Roman's multiple step plan.

He and the harpooner, Lex, wrapped their murdered friend in eel skin and carted his stiffening and bloated body to the Meeting House. The town of Widorexiton exploded in accusations and rumor, a wildfire now out of control. Ruth would have no choice but to summon him. And she did.

Roman found her sitting in her full religious vestments, the oldest bottle of Thunsae Myrrha he ever saw next to her. She offered some to Roman after refilling her own, then while it was poured gestured toward the licorice root cigarettes from the High Priest's gilded box. They sat facing each other, casual, Roman crossing his long, thin leg over his knee. He proceeded to explain what he discovered, what happened and finally what he intended to do with The Chief Acolyte to the High Priest's permission, of course.

"That is quite an elaborate story, Roman."

She greedily sipped from her copper cup, wiping her mouth with a dainty authority. Her wrinkled, thin-lipped face seemed to resemble another part of the body Roman did not care to ponder. He looked away, tapped his cigarette and stared at the crone again.

"I assure you, Chief Acolyte, it is what happened. We need only..."

"Please," she smiled. "Call me Ruth. Why, I have known you since you were a...a tiny seed."

Her thin lips seemed even thinner and paler if that could be possible.

"We are in some urgency...Ruth. Even with your permission right now, it would take us nearly a week to outfit and ready *Endeavor*."

Ruth raised her hand, palm out waving slightly towards Roman impatiently. "Nonsense. You know you have not the power or the permission to use such a nonsensical machine, young Roman. No, there are other...less absurd responses. You have explained the manner of the events, and I must say with quite some passion. I hear the urgency in your voice, and I know what you desire."

Roman stared at the withered stalk before him, his mind reeling in unbelief, a thing released then jerked back. *No! No! What is happening here? There's a murdered body, by the Horned God!* He watched her mouth move as she continued.

"...but you were not there, you see. You came to all of this late, after the fact, so to speak. Let's establish some conclusions even *if* all that you say is true." Again, she raised her hand to him in protest. "You say that this poor peasant harpooner was murdered..." Again, her hand raised, but this time a single finger to emphasize his subservient position in this conversation. "If that is so, which has yet to be established with any certainty, we still have no authority to proceed with adjudication until the High Priest himself returns."

Roman watched as she inhaled her cigarette then blew it out, seemingly relishing this moment, this silence, this world she found herself in. Thank the Horned God, he had not waited for the old bat. No, he had given stern orders to Lex to secure the *Endeavor*, gather a skeleton crew and—cautiously, silently, make it ready, prepare the steam engine, prepare the hydrogen, and a minimal outfitting. Of course, Lex thought him mad, but he could not...he *would not* wait for this...this moldy..."

"If that was not enough, young Roman," she continued. "We have The Begetting to think about. Why, the preparations have not finished, the town has barely begun the cleansing ritual... What about the hunt? Hmmm? You know we can't go on without the hunt." She waved over the servant who poured more Thunsae Myrrha into her cup. "It is absurd to do anything else but wait. Your father will return with The High Priest, the crew, and we will continue with great excitement. It is better that we..."

Roman shook his head. "Chief Acolyte...Ruth, please. Before you make a final decision, hear me out." Roman leaned forward. "Everything you say is postulated on the fact that The High Priest is not responsible for what has just happened. What if *he* murdered Layne? What if *he* stole..." he paused. *Easy now. Choose your motives carefully. Can't give the Mendel Fragment away.* "What if he absconded the *Intruder* from Captain Robert for nefarious reasons? What if...?"

"What if they are not nefarious as you call them but a...request."

"A what?"

"A summons." She smoked her cigarette in exasperation. "What do you mean? You're saying The Horned God...?"

"I'm saying we don't know what happened. I am saying that your rush to judgement may put in jeopardy something beyond this misunderstood act on the waterfront. I am saying, Roman, that I understand you are upset with the loss of your first Harpooner, but...in the scope of the situation...in the light of other evidence...it would be best to wait until The High Priest's return."

"What other evidence? I'm telling you what happened down there was murder."

"From your perspective..." She was now leaning in. "...I can understand why you would say that."

"From *my* perspective? *My* perspective is that Layne was murdered, stabbed, gutted right there on the docks."

"Yes, yes, yes. No need for hyperbole." Again, she breathed in deeply, authoritatively, calmly. "You were not there, were you? You don't know what happened, only that the peasant harpooner is dead. Have you thought of other alternatives in the light of day, Roman?"

Roman's mind was a flame of fire, a raging, vengeful thing. Its only release was violence. He knew who and how to exact that. He wanted to grab her by her gilded robes and drag her withered husk to the Meeting House, fling open the cloth and shove her face in Layne's gaping mouth of a wound. *By the Horned God, he was nearly disemboweled.* Instead, he said calmly, slowly, nearly a whisper, "What alternative, Ruth?"

"That your lover may have been...chosen, selected for... Well...?"

Roman had not considered this, not thought any other thing than what Lex told him. Raya was so emotional, she... She was no help. But Lex. No one mentioned "selection." By the Horned God! Did that happen? Did old Bony Root take Lara because the Horned God had chosen her for...for..." His stomach was ice, his face pale and slick.

"I am sorry, Roman. There is good evidence to support

this."

"Evidence?" His voice barely escaped his throat.

"Yes, a witness, Roman."

At that moment, Ruth motioned to the servant to exit the room. The side door opened, and in walked in a tall and exotic beauty, her hair up in a fountain of gossamer strands, face long and angular, an elegance of eroticism even now. Raya handed her long coat to the servant and sat down in a chair near The Chief Acolyte of the High Priest.

"Hello, Roman," she said. "How are you doing?"

Her facial features were a mix of a pout, and a demure sadness.

Ruth offered her something to drink. She declined. Ruth filled her own cup once again. She offered her a cigarette. Raya took it up in her slender fingers, lit it and looked at Ruth for guidance. "Thank you for joining us, Raya. I know this has been traumatic for everyone." Raya nodded. *Were those tears?* "Tell us about that horrible, horrible morning. Take your time, dear."

Raya glanced up at Ruth, then to Roman, a performance for one. "Well, as I told Roman, I followed Lara to the waterfront...the docks. She was snooping about Roman's house for several days and I was worried she might..."

"I asked Lara to look after some of my things," Roman interrupted.

He stared at Raya, shaking his head slightly as if to thwart her next words.

"Yes, Roman. I've already told The Chief Acolyte about the...the thing."

"What thing?" He said, again, his voice a whisper. "You mean my library, right?" Again, he glared at Raya and shook his head.

"No, silly," said Raya. "That hidden spell thing you have. You know the one. The one you've hidden from everyone. The one you said was so special."

Ruth was at full attention now, staring at Roman, waiting for his response. Roman looked to Raya, then to Ruth. The ice ball in his stomach was now a glacier, his hands slick with wet. "I...I really don't know what you're..."

"The peasant girl stole that...magic thing, and I told the High Priest about it. Well, The High Priest was furious. You see, the peasant girl had gone too far. The High Priest told me this. The High Priest told me he made a mistake by choosing her for The Begetting. Anyway, he sent me to get her that morning. When we came to the docks, Roman was there..."

Roman, looked up in horror.

"...and that's when it all happened. Roman demanded Lara back, demanded his magic thingy back, but The High Priest refused. Roman got...violent. Layne heard the noise and came over, and when he tried to stop Roman..."

Here it came. The sudden rushing terrifying wave hitting the sloped coastline, rising, rising, rising, rising, cresting...

"...and...forgive me, Roman, I must speak," Raya said as she wiped under her eyes. "That's when Roman stabbed him. Roman murdered Layne. Captain Robert grabbed Lara, the High Priest and the crew boarded the *Intruder*." Raya put her hands to her face. "It was all so, so horrible."

"Why are you doing this?" Roman said.

"Roman," Ruth said in a commanding voice. "You must be silent."

Raya looked up. "I love you, Roman. You couldn't see it. You've never been able to see it. She is evil, Roman."

"How could you?" Roman hissed.

"That's enough, Roman." Ruth wrestled full authority back to herself. "You will be sent out of here in chains if you do not sit silent!"

She turned to Raya. "Now, my dear. Why did the High

Priest take Lara? Was she *summoned*?"

Raya paused, staring at Roman, eyes wide, and even in her betrayal, she was magnificent. "Yes, Chief Acolyte. The High Priest said...that."

"Be clear now," said Ruth. "Be crystal clear with your answer. Did the High Priest say the peasant girl had been *summoned* by the Horned God?"

Raya, still staring at Roman nodded.

"Look at me, Thunsi," Ruth commanded. "Say the words. You must be a witness to this event. Was this a *summons*? Was the peasant girl, Lara, *Summoned* by the Horned God?"

Staring at Roman again, eyes wide. "Yes. She was *Summoned* by the Horned God."

"There we have it," Ruth said, now sitting back in her seat with a contentment.

Roman's head was now all bricks and rocks and crashing waves. He tried to isolate various ideas, but nothing seemed to focus. All this time he believed it was the Mendel Fragment that drove his will, consumed all of his being, but now it was clear, as clear as Raya's lie. It was not the Fragment. Yes, of course the Fragment was important, everything really, but its theft was not *as* shattering as the summoning of Lara to the Horned God. *Summoned*! Every Thunsi knew what this meant. One for the Many. When the Horned God summoned...it was to demand sacrifice. *Oh Lara! Lara! My Lara!*

"Roman, son of Captain Robert, the Commander of the *Intruder*, I hereby confine you for the murder of Peasant Harpooner Layne. You will be placed under house arrest until the High Priest returns, then if found guilty, to be cast out to the coast in exile."

Ruth motioned to the servant who left the room only to return with Guards of the High Priest, one on either side of Roman.

"I don't care what you have done, Roman!" Cried Raya. "I will come to you every day."

The Guards hoisted the dazed Roman to his feet.

"Every day, Roman. I love you. I will wait for you."

They walked Roman from the room, through the house and into the frigid light of evening. Snow drifted down, a dusting of white collecting on his shoulders and head.

Now he felt the full force of the tidal wave break him to pieces. Each step toward his imprisonment was another crushing blow. Layne, his trusted friend, master Harpooner...murdered. How many times had they defied the great death? How many times? They were iron, unbreakable, undefeated. And yet... He did not plan for this. He did not expect or understand the depth of diabolical machinations on every level. The Mendel Fragment! How could he have been so careless? He forgot it, really, how coveted such a thing would be, casting it about, tossing it like shells into a bowl. *Could the High Priest use it? When did old Bony Root know about it? Did Lara tell him? Raya? Oh, what was happening? Was the old crone in on it as well? Was the whole system, every layer fetid and infected? And now...now Lara was to be...*

The Guards opened the cabin door and bid him enter. They stood outside. Roman sat in his chair and stared at the small wooden stove, a red glow from the fire emanating inside. He planned to leave in a week. He planned to sail the dangerous Salty Sea with the eels and the currents, planned to board the *Endeavor* with the Chief Acolyte's blessing—planned to cross the forty miles of terror and get back the Medal Fragment. But now... By the time he got there, Lara would be dead. For the first time...the very first time in his life, like a tiny settling snowflake, a thought appeared, a cold, piercing, pinpoint of thought. It grew. It was terrifying and final. Roman stared at the red glow behind the tempered glass. "Damn the Horned God," he whispered. "Damn him and all the rest of them...this."

His mouth was dry, and his thoughts swirled like a shiver of violent eels, tangled and black, a nihilistic savagery of will leading to one single outcome.

Chapter Nine

Forty miles. Forty miles of open, terrifying ocean, and the eels returned. What madness was this? Who would venture such a thing? Why would they possibly make such a desperate trip? What could they possibly hope to accomplish by risking their lives—the High Priest...Captain Robert...her life! This was now front and center in Lara's mind as the *Intruder* came to the midpoint of the crossing. Of course, they released her from the iron ring a day ago—why keep her bound? What could she do now accept die with all the rest of them.

Lara, her face puffed and gashed from the assault, looked out across the gray, white capped landscape of rolling water. Leonard, the crew mate far above her in the crow's nest, surveyed the same view, and everyone waited for his dreaded cry of "Shiver Ho!" The eels were out north of the Island for sure, but Captain Robert did not yet know if they made it to the "Bay" as he called it—the forty mile stretch between Widorexiton and the coast. If they came feeding, the *Intruder* would never make it. The enormous eels where ferocious and crazed with hunger, diving down, swooping up, pulverizing anything that made noise on the surface of the Salty Sea. If they had not made it this far south, then the journey would be dangerous but not impossible. Lara overheard the crew members complaining over dinner on the futility of such a journey, how "if the eels don't get us, the Blodetan will." She felt a shutter move up her legs and across her body, an electrical shock of fear, of recalled memory long suppressed. Now they were into the second full day of the crossing, and Leonard up in the crow's nest was silent. Hope increased.

The High Priest stayed holed up in his quarters. He was busy studying the Mendel Fragment. If Linus could be believed, Old Bony Root could not make heads or tails of the thing. Lara found herself with Linus, the cook, quite by accident. She was roaming the deck, the *Intruder* rising and falling, shifting on a swell, sliding up, up, up, then crashing down. It became unsafe, so she was commanded below deck. It was Linus who put her to work. The old, bent Thunsi, grabbed her one day and walked her to the galley. There he was busy cooking some licorice root soup with bits of eel blubber some carrots and other vegetables she dare not question. A slab of eel lay across the counter. He hummed as he stirred the kettle, the cigarette dancing in his lips as his mouth imperceptibly moved. He motioned Lara to slice the blubber from its skin.

"Ah, you'll get used to it," he chortled as the eel meat slid toward the floor, and she just catching it in time. The *Intruder* heaved up a swell, then down the other side. She felt her stomach follow suite. "Here," he said, giving her a cigarette. "This will calm you." He hummed some more. "Now cut it up small. The boys don't need much with these seas. Got to save some for his mightiness." He laughed at that and flicked his ash on the floor. She watched him hover and duck, pull this from a cupboard, that from a drawer all with the familiarity of his own body. She watched him in his comfortable world, an old goat of a Thunsi, weathered and in command. "Give me that," he said gruffly, taking the knife from her hand. He sliced the eel blubber quickly and with confidence. "See? Like this."

As she watched, her mind and heart were sick with the memory of him chuckling with Layne, slapping him on the back with one hand, driving the knife deep, deeper, slashing with cruelty as he removed his bloody wrist and knife. *Murderers,* she thought. *Murderers all. This is what Hawthorn had warned me about.* They were all deceitful and wicked Thunsi. She would make a plan. She would wait her time, wait until they were asleep. Take back the Mendel Fragment for Roman, escape back to the Island. How? One step at a time. They had to make it there first.

"Now what is your pretty little mind think'n about, dearie?" Linus said, knife, an extension of his hand, pointing at her accusatorially.

She smiled wanly and stepped to the counter, offering her hand, Linus slapping the knife on the wood for emphasis. The knife would be good to have, she thought, and she picked it up, deftly slicing the blubber into cubes. From that moment on, the galley became a space for observation, a place to receive information, to hone her plan once they landed. This is where she first found out about the war above deck.

Old Bony Root and Captain Robert were at odds now, and that tension was working its way, like poison in the arm, throughout the entire crew. Every Thunsi was whispering this or that, taking one side, shifting (as Thunsi do) to the other side. Every command from Captain Robert second guessed, every word from the High Priest, doubted and compared.

Lara, herself, had witnessed a confrontation between the Captain and the High Priest, a ferocious display of wills—neither of them conceding the other's point. Linus had asked her to see if Captain Robert would like his Thunsae Myrrha served hot or cold. As she walked down the small hallway, she stopped.

"If you're not Thunsi enough to cross the bay, Robert!" Thundered the High Priest one afternoon behind the captain's closed door. "I relieve you of your command. Get one of your halfwit harpooners to take your place. We are certainly not turning around. So, either you are a coward as the captain or a coward confined below deck. It matters not to me. Get me to the coast!"

"I am no coward, sir!" Refuted Captain Robert. "It is not cowardice but foolishness I address. I see before me an old fool who places his own interests before other Thunsi. Roman should have been consulted. The Harpooner, Layne, should still be breathing and with us. You have caused great concern, sir. The consequences for your actions will be grave indeed. I see this trip as a fool's errand. A dangerous fool's errand."

"It is not your job to "see" anything. If you are to "see" something, it will be to "see" my commands clearly and simply. See them, Captain Robert. See them and execute them!"

So, on day two of the crossing, the tension was high, the crew uncertain and fearful. All the while poor Leonard, stiff and cold in the masthead, earnestly searched for any eel sign. To everyone's dismay...he saw it.

"Shiver Ho!" He screamed into the roaring wind and driving snow. "Shiver Ho! Stern side!"

The crew looked about, Lara now standing with them, eyes peeled for any surfacing leviathan. There it was...unmistakable: a writhing, foaming thing, surface skimming against the waves and wind. It was small, forty feet long.

"Check for others, Leonard!" Cried out Captain Robert. To the helmsman—"Steady, Lewis. About two degrees windward. Let's see if we can't outrun the damned thing." And to his newly created first mate (his personal Harpooner, Liam). "Shovel that furnace, boys! I need more speed!"

Liam grabbed the funnel and screamed the command.

"What see you, Leonard?" yelled Captain Robert. "Does she have any friends with her?"

"No sir! No family members yet! She's gaining, sir!"

Lara watched Captain Robert, stiff, strong, a commanding presence that lifted every Thunsi to stand courageous. The wind blew his hair out in an odd angle from his profile, whipping about like they were eels themselves. His long-brimmed hat now strapped to his chin, flattened out in the torrent of snow and splashing sea. The High Priest came on deck, his gilt robes awkward and out of place, hindered him from staying upright.

"Well, Thunsi! You got us in this position!" Shouted Captain Robert to the stumbling High Priest. "Cast a hex! Even that little one could scuttle us if it gets closer!"

The Hight Priest mumbled and stumbled, catching himself on the rigging, falling to his knees as the great ship rocked port side. He made his way below deck without a word.

"Land ho, Captain! Land ho!" Leonard shouted over and over from the masthead.

Lara and those crew members who were not pulling lines or shoveling coal, ran to the bow. There it was! Through the white of the snow and spraying waves...a thin crust of gray far off in the distance. "She's coming hard, Captain!" Shouted Leonard, pointing to the stern. The *Intruder* was trapped between the ever-growing land and the coming terror that was the great eel behind them. For a moment Lara forgot all that happened, the sequence of events that put her in such a precarious position. She found herself longing, groaning even, like the crew by her side, hoping beyond all hope that the land would win out in this epic battle of titans.

"Steady, lads! Steady!" Cried Captain Robert, his voice now a rhythmic song. "She's coming hard, but we're the *Intruder*, boys! We're quicksilver! We're the wings of the sea, boys. Look at us go, lads! Watch us fly!" He grabbed his Harpooner, Liam, by both shoulders and boomed. "What say you, boy? What say you now? Are ye afraid of a little eel?"

Liam laughed and shook his fist to the storm and the eel. "By the Horned God, no, Sir! Let'm come, Sir! We'll feast on him together!"

Lara felt those words pierce her like an electrical pulse, her muscles and sinews stiff and hardened. And she heard it. At first, she thought it but the wind, but the tones became more rhythmical, the cadence certain. It was antiphonal, call and response between crew and captain.

"How does she fly, boys?"
"Like the wind across the waves! Heave—Ho!"
"What do we see, boys?"
"The eels on our staves! Heave—Ho!"
"What do we do, boys?"
"We cry out the sign! Heave Ho!"
"How do we kill her, boys?"
"With the harpoons line! Heave—Ho!"
"When are we done, boys?"
"When she's a fountain of red! Heave—Ho!"
"When will ye stop, boys?"
"When we're drowning or dead!"

Over and over and over they sang. Through the whistling wind and crashing waves, through the heaving up and the smashing down of the hull, Lara was electrical, her will—like the captain and crew—bent toward the land. With every line of the song, the crew shouted out, like the singing of the thing was the hex that sped the boat closer and closer and closer, the gray land looming up like a great beast itself waiting to swallow them. As the land emerged, the young eel tired and slackened its pursuit until the distance between the coast and the *Intruder* was shorter than the distance to the eel. The singing and the shouting and the energy surged to its crescendo as Leonard in the masthead shouted out, "She's gone, Captain! She's good and gone!"

The crew erupted in singing, clapping, and stomping in an absurd mechanical cadence to the sinking and rising deck of the *Intruder*.

Chapter Ten

The landscape begins in cliffs of sandstone, eroded, and weathered into deep brown and light tan strata. It is a formidable coast, and just like its interior, rarely penetrable save for secret pathways obstinately given up through great loss of blood and treasure. The Thunsi are tough, iron-boned, iron-willed, and little can hinder them in the pursuit of their god. From the coastline to the Cave of the Horned God are many perils, perils of stamina, of terror, of pain, perils intentionally placed in their way, for such divinity doth hedge a god, especially the trickster god of horns. One obstacle in particular fills every Thunsi with terror. They have named it appropriately, The Forest of the Dead.

This forest is a beautiful, wooded grove of many, many unique trees, some smoothed and worn from centuries of gales. Some rippled and ragged from salt, wind, ice and cold. In the haze of the frost and fog, they may appear in the dusk or early dawn as giant Thunsi. Multi-branching and individual as the race itself, a thaumaturgical spell craft spun by the Horned God himself. There is lore, buried deep, so deep, a gossamer thread of divine truth, that the two—the Thunsi and the Forest—are one. Nonsense like that cannot be believed by such a tenacious and temporally driven folk. They scatter like intentionally planted seeds, these trees of the dead, planted and rooted into the foundations of the world, connected (some say with magic from the Horned God) below the earth with tentacles that pulse and twitch messages one to the other, a great network, a single sentient being, from the Salty Sea, along the Black Mountains, past the Grove of the Horned God and eventually settling as far as the outpost known as Kyrnunos. Yet, how can the dead speak? The dead are...well, dead. So maybe it was given this name for some other reason, a whisper now long forgotten.

There is good reason for the name in the present, and after the Emergence, every Thunsi believed the name quite apt. What seemed a dreadful place filled with mythological hauntings became truly a place of death, a forest filled with what would be called by the High Priests, Blodetan—the blood eaters. Thunsi-like, but not Thunsi, ravenous creatures with fanged and gaping mouths, ferocious hunters of the living. Where they stayed, no one knew, but it was night when they roamed, hordes of them, lumbering through the forest, silent, stalking shadows, naked, sniffing, eyes empty sockets, thin-boned and clawed, hunching and lurching over fallen branch, through rustling leaves or light upon the frozen forest floor. No living thing survived them, nothing with warm blood and pulsing heart stood before the Blodetan. It was this that so amazed the Thunsi on Widorexiton where no fanged phantoms stirred—it was this astounding feat of returning that put the High Priest beyond any Thunsi's sphere of being. The High Priest was chosen by the Horned God, given permission by The Horned God to pass (even at night) through The Forest of the Dead, through the very midst of the Blodetan and to the Grove of the Horned God without harm. This was a supernatural event, one requiring thaumaturgy of untold powers.

So it was that the crew of the *Intruder* found themselves rowing their three eel boats toward the one landing spot the High Priest and Captain Robert knew by heart, the only rocky beach that did not ascend in great walls of sandstone now being thrashed about by the gale force winds and waves. Captain Robert standing tall above the High Priest guided the lead boat. Liam, the Harpooner, with Lara and a crew of eight, ran parallel at some distance with the final boat with Landon guiding his crew of rowers. No one could hear the other, the roar of the waves and wind so great now, that many oars dangled like vestigial flippers, useless in the air as the sleek boats hesitated on the crests then crashing into the watery ravine. After a half hour they arrived on the rocky beach, exhausted, and drenched. There they tied up their eel boats and gathered near the edge of the forest, many fearful to enter without the thaumaturgy from the High Priest.

"It's no use, lads," said Captain Robert to his crew after a long sidebar with the High Priest. "Gather wood and stay sharp while you do it!"

It was no small thing, for the great Captain to hesitate, but the battering they took getting to the shore and the hard coming of night made the decision more palatable. To enter the Forest of the Dead was foolhardy at noonday in full sun—certain slaughter at night.

They huddled in shadows of the small fires, pockets of fear and whispering subdued by homemade fermented Thunsae Myrrha. They passed the bottles and passed along the stories, one building on the other, a detailed map of undulating fear.

There was Larry and his brother, Lemell, who got bored and wandered from the expedition, howling, desperate screams, then silence. No search party was formed. There was old Hollow Head Landry who when surrounded by the ghastly things broke the phantoms bones and used one as a stabbing weapon only to starve to death on the rocky shore waiting for a returning ship. His bones picked clean. The shiv still grasped within his fist. Captain, First Mates, even the Cooks knew tales of survival and terror as they struggled against the hunting hordes, desperately hiding or racing through the labyrinth wood, circling back, lost, and always somehow into the waiting, sniffing, voracious Blood Eaters. And on and on and on the stories went—heads on stakes with eyes gauged out and teeth dangling like chin beards. Clothes and limbs hanging from trees like mossy growths. Strange howls in the dead of night, blood curdling cries like demon lovers wailing. Nobody slept. When the dawn came upon the water, Lara nearly cried out.

"Single file, now," Captain Robert said. "Stay together no matter what."

He placed Lara between his Harpooners Liam and Landon. Linus struggled to keep up, humping and limping, a wreck of bent and twisted limbs. They moved slowly, methodically further and further into the dark woods where only the most stubborn of light reached the frozen ground under their feet. The trees sheltered them from the worst of the wind, the tops of the branches swaying furiously like an ecstatic animal.

U*ncanny, unnatural,* thought Lara as they slowly made their way through barrier of hanging vines and closely spaced trunks, emerging into a sort of clearing, a hedged-in enclosure, where the storm and snow and cold had been shut behind. They could see their breath when they talked, their coats pulled high to their cheeks, Linus stomping his feet to promote circulation. He relit his cigarette and sighed, a reverberation like some underwater animal, and to everyone's terror, something far off croaked in reply.

"Quiet, fool!" Captain Robert hissed. "We head that way to the path. Now quick and silent."

Lara felt the cold and profound silence like a sudden weight where each step more and more laborious. This was undiscovered country, trackless, void of sign or sound, of all things living. It was the High Priest who knew the way, and yet, Lara watched him doubt, stop, point one way then the other. How long had they traveled? Minutes? Days? They were forgotten by the world, and understood and fully exposed to the inhabitants of this terrifying place. They felt it. A motion here, just out of view, a cracking twig, a rustle of a thing startled, a sudden stumble over a gnarled root. Lara glanced this way then that, a growing terror in her chest and head. This was the void. She shivered and hurried to be close to Captain Robert.

And they were on the path. It was sudden and if asked, no one could recall when it started, how long they had been traveling it. It was ten Thunsi wide, worn, rutted by wheels, pocked with hoof prints, forgotten lost journeys. The path was cold comfort. The path was a warning. The path was a known substantial thing in a world of phantoms and shifting reality. The path led deeper into the woods, and they hurried to go as far as they could as the first night in The Forest of the Dead fell upon them.

They could not light a fire, for no one dared to venture past the boundary of the path to retrieve firewood. They huddled together, fifteen in all, huddled by ranking, Captain Robert, Lara, the Harpooners, and the High Priest gathered at the head, listening, the forest moaning, grinding, croaking with life. They did not hear them come.

"This is different," Captain Robert whispered. "This is unlike before. We are unwanted."

"Nonsense," The High Priest hissed. "Stifle your tongue, Captain. *Wanted* is an ignorant term, and you should know better. We are never *wanted*."

Lara watched him rub the satchel, then place his hand inside it, the Mendel Fragment, a secret obsession, a private act.

"Then *summoned*, Sir," said Captain Robert. "This is no summoning."

As if in answer to the gloom and terror that was settling upon every Thunsi, the High Priest took something from his pocket, mumbled some words, and created a thaumaturgical green glow from between his outstretched hands. "From my calculations, we are here." He pointed to the map now before him. "Three days from the Grove. We are well supplied, the path is clear, and we have plenty of eel skin..."

Those words were snatched from the air with the screams

of poor Lewis and his crew mate Lance, gasping and sobbing, a fading, terrifying desperate screech somewhere now deep in the forest. Back-to-back they stood, like petrified stone, each facing the darkness, skeleton chests heaving under their heavy coats. Poor Lewis. Poor Lance. The popping, tearing, grinding death that pulled their lives apart—then silence. Absolute silence, like a thaumaturgic blanket cast over them. And the sniffing. Right to the path, to the edge of the open space, testing, calculating, an army of Blodetan just beyond.

"Fire! By the Horned God! We'll show them, lads!" Captain Robert grabbed his pack and pulled from it a folded eel skin soaked in paraffin. "Everyone now! Torches, lads! We need torches."

It was the High Priest who created the electrical spark, and the path exploded in light.

Lara held her torch up, but she could see nothing. The paraffin crackled, spit, blazed, but nothing happened. They stared, expecting ghouls. Nothing. "By the Horned God!" Screamed Leonard. "Show yourself!"

They did not show themselves to Leonard. He was snatched away, a great blow from the front, a driving, supernatural spear head with the force of foundational dark magic. A scream, fading, and Leonard from the crow's nest was gone.

They jabbed at the boarders in futility. They shouted at the darkness with empty threats. Three dead. It was only the first night, and once again Lara prayed for the coming dawn.

Chapter Eleven

"We quicken the pace," said Captain Robert to the High Priest while the crew collected wood. They would wander only steps from the hard clay path, tossing whatever was in a short radius, like fingers touching hot coal chips. "Do you not have a hex for this, man?" said Captain Robert. "There will be none of us left at this rate."

"We collect the wood. I see that now," said the High Priest. "That was the mistake. We gather and make ready the fire before nightfall. Preparation, Captain. Your men should have been more prepared."

Lara watched the enraged Captain walk from the meeting, stride over to Liam, and grab him by the shoulders, lips to ear, earnest, shaking the harpooner to emphasize a new point. "Bundle them up, Lads!" cried Captain Robert. "Quick pace, boys! Quick as lightening now!"

It is never easy in the Forest of the Dead. There is a price mortals pay to enter, and even if one passes, one passes with a sense of abandonment, like facing the inevitable night, the knife and spear. It was Linus who cried out, rushing from the perimeter ahead and into the light of the path. "By the Horned God! By the Horned God!" Is all he could manage.

It was the High Priest and Captain Robert who shook him, shouting at him to calm down, get yourself together, Thunsi! This to calm their own fears as well as the panicked cook. Poor Linus pointed. The others hurried to the border of the path, the edge of the divide between wood and clay, but it did not need much imagination to understand their plight. It was a warning, a gloat. Something confident, sentient, and evil. There in the trees hung flesh ornaments of horror. A head, a partially eaten limb, the foot, the radial arm, dangling, macabre, dancing, swaying, a corpse tree, the festival of the dead celebrating the demise of the living.

"Onward, damn you!" whispered Captain Robert. "I said, move out! All of you! We fear no eel or death, lads! Pick up the wood and move out!"

"We are not wanted," whispered the High Priest. "Maybe we should turn back?"

Captain Robert grabbed the Priest by the holy collar and shook him. "By the Horned God! Man! We go on, and your flesh will be fed to them if another man be snatched. By the Horned God!"

They nearly ran the next mile or two, bundles of wood heavy on their backs. Lara, too, had the weight of wood on her shoulders, hunched and grinding her bones to open wounds. Her coat was slick with her blood when they stopped that night. Oh, you should have seen the blaze, giant like the sun! A bonfire of, to hell with you, we are Thunsi. Try, just try and get us.

Well, they did not have to try. They are Blodetan. Even with the blaze, they had been waiting. Even with the stacking and confidence of the new plan, the remembered thing that would save them all—even while the fire soared unto great heights— the crew where targeted, four more poor Thunsi souls, startled, pounced, dragged kicking into the, high pitched resistance, then only the cries of the living as they circled, back to the fire, like gloaming helpless prey to the wolves of night.

By morning the third day, only seven remained. They gathered wood in silence and strapped the bundles to their backs, and hurried, single file, down the path and toward the Grove of the Horned God. When they broke for lunch, the war was in full display.

"You have no hex," Captain Robert said to the High Priest. "If you did, you would use it."

"I have more than...hexes," The High Priest said smugly.

"You refuse to use it," Captain Robert mumbled as he smoked his pipe of Licorice Root. "...or you know not how to use it. Either way, my crew are dead."

"You are a part of something great, Captain, a turning, a moment of transformation. It will be made amply clear in a day or two."

"We haven't got that long, sir. At the rate we are going, there will be none left by then. We are being *transformed* right now. It is high time we turn back, cut our losses and abandon this unsanctioned trip."

"You will see, Captain Robert. You will see in one day. Grant me a day. Your choices will become undeniably clear. I promise you."

Lara heard them argue. She watched Captain Robert stiffen. A willingness so reserved as to be in outright protest. She was pleased for the small break. Her shoulders were sore from the bundles, and her head was light, stomach fighting back the hunger now growing stronger within. It was Linus, the Cook, that gave her a cigarette. As the small group hurried down the path, Lara heard him whispering to the harpooner, Liam, how he missed the Salty Sea, how cursed land makes for cursed crew mates.

They traveled until the gloom of day turned into the gloom of evening, and that was when the High Priest disappeared. Lara noticed him gathering his satchel, looking about awkwardly, then scurrying off. He hurried into the woods. The rest of crew was busy with stacking wood for the blaze. Lara followed him. She could feel the cold, deep numbing, thaumaturgic sensation, piercing to the marrow, increasing with every step into the woods. At first, she thought she lost Old Bony

Root, but he was crouched, listening for something. To her complete astonishment, she watched as a Blodetan, a naked, thin shadow stepped out of the gloaming.

She could barely see him, the High Priest robes puffed and blowing. It was there, and it was staring off into the woods, staring with fanged mouth hollow and hanging open, a puppet thing, an inanimate golem waiting to be used. She stepped back in confusion, a crack from the fallen limb breaking under her weight. Both heads turned, and she ran as fast as she could back to the path.

"Where the blazes did you get to," yelled Captain Robert. "It's nearly nightfall. Help with the fire."

And he was back to stacking logs and twigs into a pyre. The High Priest stepped into the light of the igniting flames. "Never one for a little work," Captain Robert said. "I've given you a day."

"There will be no attacks tonight, Captain. I can assure you."

If in answer, Captain Robert yelled to his remaining crew members to look sharp and sleep in intervals.

Nothing did happen that night, no sound, no movements, no far off howls or yelps or bemoaning cries. The fire blazed warmth, and Lara found herself drifting off to a restless sleep. The High Priest scared her half to death.

"Such a flower in the mud, little one," he whispered to her, his body laying nearly on top her, breath stale with age and eel blubber.

She tried to sit up, and he placed his long finger on her lips. "I know it was you. No, not a word. Just listen. Soon, very soon, you will be transformed...as we all will be. The type and scope of that transformation...er...that company you may desire to keep at that moment—will be...let us say...agreed upon...now...here...something between us, let's say."

Lara wanted to pull away, but she could not. She felt Old Bony Root feel her leg, her thigh, higher, higher. "Are we agreed?" he said, pulling her closer to him.

She felt him, his excitement, and pushed ever so slightly away.

She nodded her head in agreement to the thing that was not said, that thing she did not understand, what was seen in the woods, but was not seen, a pact now between them. Closer and closer. He rolled onto her. She wanted to cry out, wanted to scream for help, but he was the High Priest. She could sense his pleasure in the moment, his wonton lust for her. Here! Now!

"Check the fire!" Commanded Captain Robert. "Make it quick, man! They're out there."

With that Linus rolled, zombie-like, and began throwing logs onto the smoldering flames. Soon it was ablaze of light and warmth once again. The High Priest gathered himself. "Everything in order, there?" said Captain Robert.

"Yes," the High Priest said. "The young Thunsi cried out. Just a night terror."

Captain Robert watched him leave, Lara catching his concerned glance, his face a distorted image of shadow and flickering light.

Chapter Twelve

By day four, they were exhausted but hopeful that the Grove of the Horned God was before them, and each wondered how they would react when they entered that mysterious ground. They still needed to make it through the night, and night was coming fast. The High Priest was strangely nervous as they made the fire, every sound from the forest, a startling, unexpected surprise. He seemed disinterested in eating, disinterested and impatient. Not once did he speak to Lara about their encounter the night before. He concentrated on the Mendel Fragment, hunched over the plate, rubbing it, closing his eyes in some meditative state, mumbling incoherent phrases, then "yes, yes, of course." Then, "No. That would not be it?" Finally in exasperation, "By the Horned God! How does it work?"

Captain Robert too was anxious. He gathered wood, then stood silent as stone, listening intently to the creaks and groans of the forest. They took out their lances and knives, eating quickly, every movement conserved and anticipatory. Night fell, and with it the weight of the same dark thaumaturgic blanket they sensed several nights earlier. They were coming. It was a certainty. When the howls from the dark came, the High Priest was already gathering his belongings, shoving them into his satchel, eyes wide and searching.

"Hold steady, now! If we stay by the fire, we will survive. Stay by the fire, fool!"

The High Priest was rushing here and there, scurrying, and confused like a dumb animal panicked by a storm.

Lara searched into the darkness and saw them moving, an army under the shadows of the moon. Hundreds of them, silent, hunched, sniffing. They surrounded them, pressing in like some trained horde. That's when Lara saw him, a tall, angled thing, taller than the rest, and upon his head a bone crown made from the ribs of the stolen dead. Distortions from the fire gave his body a shimmering quality, and she caught her breath as she realized his mouth was open, chin out, face up to the sky in a howling gesture. Perhaps he was howling in mockery of the living or was it casting a great thaumaturgic spell. Whether sound or hex, everyone around the fire, even the High Priest, suddenly fell to their knees in terror.

"You promised!" The High Priest screamed and sobbed. "We had a deal. You promised!" Suddenly, he stood up in a bewildered state.

"Stand your ground, you fool!" cried Captain Robert.

The High Priest shook off the hold from Liam and dashed into the night. Lara watched as he ran into the host, then stopped, the shadow horde parting, and he fled further into the woods.

"We have been sold out!" cried Liam, "By the Horned God, he has betrayed us!"

"We are lost!" sobbed Linus.

"I said stand your ground, lads!" Captain Robert shook his lance at the night. "Come on, you bastards! Come on! You bring death! Well, lads, let's show these demons what we think of death!" He suddenly roared with laughter and delight, swinging and separating heads and limbs.

Lara felt her skin buzz and tingle from the intense thaumaturgic hex coming from the leader of the Blodetan. She watched as he raised his arms above his head, mouth still agape, then like some skeleton pulling down heavy ropes, he lowered his arms and pushed his hands to the frozen ground.

They came suddenly, from any side. From the darkness,

like broken things, they rushed at them, howling, sniffing and swiping with their bone-clawed fingers, eyes empty sockets. Captain Robert and the crew stabbed and crushed with logs and lances. They knocked out legs and broke shoulders with great sweeps of wood. The harpooners skewered and pulled them into the fire. They swept neck high and toppled their skull heads. The Blodetan pulled back into the night. Landon had been bit, his leg dangling, like some great predatory fish attack. He lay in his blood and gore dying. Lara grabbed his lance and held it out.

"We are lost," Linus said. "There are too many of them."

They came again, from all sides, rushing and thrashing, gnawing and slicing, a single will of hate and rage. They swooped upon Landon, feeding like rabid animals, shaking their heads and tearing.

Captain Robert grabbed Lara and pulled her to him. "Run! Run for your life! The Grove of the Horned God is that way. I will make a path."

Lara stood stunned.

Captain Robert and Liam swept back and forth and the Blodetan fell. "Now! Go now!"

She ran. She ran into the dark of night, the screams and howls, the grinding and tearing fading as she distanced herself from the fire. She could hear them just behind, and to her panic, she realized they were rushing after her. She ran from the path, dashing around trees, diving under fallen branches, and leaping over exposed roots. Deeper and deeper into the shadows of the Forest of the Dead she went, stumbling and crawling, and finally in such panic pulling herself into the hovel of a thicket, chest heaving, fingers frozen, and dirt stained. She heard them sniffing her out, calling to one another, sounding out locations and triangulating her position like a pack of ossified prehistoric things. Closer. Closer.

She heard a snap, more like a whip, then a thud. By the

Horned God! Did they have some tool to savage her with. There was another whip, a crack, then a horrible snarl that groaned and made her pull her legs tightly to her chest. Something clawed at the hedge, swiping at her exposed flesh. She shoved backward but a great trunk hindered her retreat, the space a tiny hovel of leaves and twigs. Then the thing lunged into the hole, she beat it back with her feet, the bone teeth piercing her boots, catching, and pulling her out, shaking its head back and forth to gain leverage. Now she was exposed, her coat ripped open, her boot off and flung to the side. She saw it huge and tall and skeletal in the darkness of the wood, arching up like some great snake to strike. It lunged, but was caught in midair, a freed thing suddenly jerked back, tethered. She watched as it struggled at the neck, grasping, clawing, then in a puppet-like staccato motion, it broke in half and crumbled to the ground. A branch like a vine, thick with thorns and studded with white flowers wrapped around her arm, shoulder pulling her up, an animal trunk, a whip, a sentient thing, gentle.

"It's you!" Lara sobbed. "You've come! Hawthorn, you've come!"

Her words failed her. She hugged the base of the thick and shadowed creature, the woody texture of its bark shivering with a heightened sense of danger.

Chapter Thirteen

What exactly Hawthorn was, well, Lara had no idea. It was like a tree, sure, but not really. Trees did not move, stealthy, sinister with intension and malice, with mock intent, perhaps with even humor. Trees did not speak of futures and pasts. They did not talk incessantly about conspiracy theories so complex *ad nauseam* it made your head spin. No, Hawthorn was no tree. It did have branches of a sort, more like a sea creature with tentacles, thorns, flowers and fragrant with musk. The thorns were absolutely real, dagger sharp, a terrifyingly effective weapon used precisely and with great force when roused. The flowers, however, were not real. They were white blossoms of...skin? Tags of a sort, beautiful in the sun like sparkling hair, soft to the touch like fur. Its legs where low, root-like and crab-like, pulling it forward or pushing it backward, quick, startling, predatory when it wanted to be. Its face was—a root ball of gnarled, intertwining vines or saplings, almost Thunsi-like at certain angles, but with the bizarre ability to capture its emotions quite effectively.

Hawthorn was an incessant talker, had been ever since they had met. Well, it was not actually talking, more like internal monologue, a scattered rambling, phrases, emphasized words, like floating debris rushing through a great culvert after a storm.

She was young, ten years old, when she first came across it. It was agitated, pacing, curling its arms down then up then down then up, pointing to the sky, then to the ground, shaking its root ball head, scratching it, pondering, only to rev up again with great emotion. Lara stood watching. It was the day of the Emergence, and she wandered from the camping site and into the woods. She heard the voice, scattered, nonsensical and followed it, thinking it was an animal, something to be discovered, an adventure. So, when she saw it, she stared in wonder. It rustled the leaves and shivered its strange body, then paused, and faced a tall tree. One with split bark and weathered, gray patches—stood before it and started rambling. *Come! Oh, yes, they come! When? They come is all. Me, tell you they come, they come! Of course! Holes, holes, holes. Shush! Holes and holes and holes. He know. He know, me know. If he know, me know then I know, he know; and...well. Of Course, me hide. Shush! Shush is all to that. They come is all.*

Hawthorn suddenly shivered again, then dramatically stroked the great tree with its long tentacle, wrapping around it, then leaning heavily into the crook, like a head in an elbow—suddenly exhausted from all the drama. It slowly turned the root ball head toward Lara. It just stared at her, silent, a frozen, organic growth.

"I heard you," Lara said. "You don't fool me."

It just stared at her.

"You can stay there if you like. I'm not going anywhere."

She suddenly stood, tall and thin, a ten-year-old Thunsi wrapped in her winter coat and scarf quite unmoved by the dramatic display. "So now you can't talk?" She crossed her arms and pursed her lips. "You some kind of tree?"

The thing suddenly shook all over. *Me no tree! Me better than those...."*

She could not understand the stream of words flowing into her head.

"You look like a tree."

It stopped, stared at her, leaned way over, it's tentacle-branches splayed out in a shock of shimmering white and thorns like some exotic bird. *Me Hawthorn. Shush! Me no groundling. Me old. Me know things. Me know about the holes and the forest and Cyril and Dante and they coming. Oh yes, me know things. Me roam here and there. Shush! Me no groundling, ha, shush! Me no rooted, barky...me no...tree. Me Hawthorn, me says.*

Lara stared at it, arms still crossed. Hawthorn crossed several of its limb-tentacles in mock imitation.

Me no tree; me Hawthorn. Who you? You no tree either. You no Hawthorn.

"My name is Lara."

You a Lara. Lara not Hawthorn.

"I'm Thunsi."

Hawthorn suddenly shimmered, its blossom tags shaking like leaves, changing color suddenly to red, then the color of his surroundings so that he was nearly invisible to her eye, then white again, then a deep brown, its tentacle-limbs drooping like a wilted dying thing.

"Thunsi," she whispered. "Do you understand me? My name is Lara. I'm Thunsi."

No Thunsi! Hawthorne said. He waved its tentacle-branches in defiance. *No Thunsi.* A thorny branch whipped out and smashed a nearby tree, lightning fast, menacing. Lara stepped back. Hawthorn marched in a rage about the small opening, ranting nonsense about Thunsi coming and again this Cyril and Cogstin and Christopher Dante and holes and planting and on and on and on in a rage of nonsense.

Lara stood unmoved by it all. "Are you finished?"

Hawthorn stopped, faced her like something suddenly remembered. *Me no like Thunsi. They come.*

"Who? Who is coming."

Hawthorn froze again, its white flower tags now blending once again into the forest, root ball head shifting back and forth. *Thunsi. Me no like Thunsi. They come.*

"We already did. We're by the beach, all of us. You should come."

Hawthorn leaned over Lara, its tentacle-branches curling around her waist, then it pulled her off the ground.

"You put me down this instant," she belted out unafraid.

"Who do you think you are?" Hawthorn set her down. Then pointed at her accusingly.

You no Thunsi. Shush! You no them.

"I am too Thunsi. My father and mother are Thunsi. We are all Thunsi."

Hawthorn shook its root ball head in protest. *Nope. No Thunsi. No sniffing.* *No hunching* He hunched over with branch-tentacles forward like some absurd falling thing. *No creepy creepy. Nope. No them. No Thunsi.*

They argued over this point for what seemed to be forever, the tall expansive creature gesticulating and pointing and mocking the little thin strong willed Thunsi girl. Then Lara's mother and father called for her.

The evening was upon them, and when the desperate parents found her all alone in the woods, she was severely reprimanded. She tried to explain. She was scolded again for lying to them about nonsense creatures roaming in the woods. Her father was incensed about how it all looked to the High Priest and the Chief Acolyte and what a disappointment she had been. "Know your place, Thunsi! Do you know how this must look!"

That was the least of their worries that evening, and when they all finally realized what was happening, The Emergence, the savagery of the Blodetan, the terror of being trapped or left behind—Lara's small disobedience was no more than a puff of smoke. As she crossed the expanse of water in the bowels of the *Endurance*, hands clasped to Roman's, she quite forgot about the amazing encounter of that wonderful and strange creature she met in the forest.

It was not until years later, after the passing of her mother and father, when the Thunsi took the bodies before the Horned God, the funeral pyre in the Grove of the Horned God—it was after this that night when Hawthorn came to her. It was a brief encounter, risky for the strange creature, for it had journeyed to the very edge of the forest to find her. When she settled it down (settled her own thoughts down as to focus on specific words), she understood only that it was leaving the forest, heading toward... Kyrnunos to the end of the world, past the holes, past it all to... Cogstin? It was nervous and twitchy, and its flesh blossoms changed from camouflage to bright white to red to black, then white again as it rambled, a strange emphasis of color for various words. And it was gone, and she saw it no more, journeyed to the coast no more... Until now.

Chapter Fourteen

Now the forest had changed. This was no longer the forest of her youth. This was the Forest of the Dead, and Lara found herself separated from her kidnappers but facing the terrifying night alone.

They come! They come all around. Above, above! All around! Not here! Not here! Me and Lara Thunsi go, said Hawthorn.

She felt the thorns lay flat, and the skin tags, now black as night, soft like fur. Hawthorn wrapped its branch-tentacles around Lara's waist and jerked her off the ground. With cat-like quickness it rushed through the thickly forested woods, gliding left and right, now stopping motionless, a forest-scape camouflage of tree trunks and shadowed bark, now a blur of rustling leaves.

They traveled for hours, but Hawthorn seemed confused. It stopped and put her down to contemplate something. Somewhere deep in the forest, she heard a humming then terrifying screams. The humming continued, a throbbing, reverberating sound. Was it some thaumaturgic hex from the leader of the Blodetan? She heard another scream, a howl unlike the first one, closer. Hawthorne stood unmoved by any of it. They were exposed. The forest was black and cold, a mist now settling upon the frozen landscape.

"We must go!" Lara hissed. "We must go now! They are all around." The humming was constant and terrifying, filling the very tops of the trees above.

You no go, Hawthorn said in his stream of consciousness voice. *He come. He come. Me go. You no go. Me find him. Me no find him, or me find him. Me go and find him. Long me go; me no find or find or no find, shush. Me know things. Shush. Me know.*

Another scream, something terrified, caught by surprise. She thought of Captain Robert, his desperate attempt to save her. Something gleamed in the night beyond them, and she realized it was the leader of the Blodetan, the bone crown shimmering, disappearing in the fog, now reappearing closer, then further away. They were surrounded. Hawthorn stood rambling nonsense, and Lara found herself once again desperately alone.

Why would she trust this creature? Was it part of them, helping... them? Did it snatch her up and carry her to a place where she could not escape. She startled at a cracking twig somewhere behind her. She turned. Another twig snapping. Then she heard the sniffing. They were all around her. She turned to Hawthorn, but it was gone! Gone! By the Horned God, she was left alone to die! She turned around. As she did, she saw and heard them creeping and sniffing, closer and closer. The hum grew louder and louder, filling the forest. It was familiar, but not recognizable in her clouded mind. She thought of dashing, but Hawthorn placed her in a clearing, open sky and shimmering stars above! No covering! No defense! To run into the woods in any direction was to run right into...them! *Why did she trust that thing! By the Horned God! Trapped! This was all its doing, and she the ignorant prey!*

Louder and louder the humming shook the treetops. She could see them now, naked and fanged, mouths open. The leader was now prominent before her between two trees, arms outstretched, head back, the faux crown of bones arcing back like some ghost animal groaning out.

"You want me! Yeh! You want me! Come on then! Come on!"

They did, slowly, a creeping, stalking silence as they made their way to the clearing. Fifty yards out, the leader howled. It was bone penetrating, a thaumaturgic spell blowing out through the trees, knocking her to the ground. And they ran, humped and groaning, lumbering at her in full force. She cowered to the ground and as the first one came upon her. She covered her head to wait her inevitable fate. As it ran into the circle, the humming now a loud roar, as the Blodetan rushed upon her, it stumbled and collapsed to the ground. And another, another. As soon as the Blodetan entered the small opening, they fell, layers of them now, clawing over one another to get to her. They did, claw over, crawling and howling. She felt her coat pin to the ground, and she realized she could not move. The Blodetan above her fell, but others were following. Why could she not move? She struggled to free herself, but they were now on her, and she screamed out in a rage, in fear, a desperate croak. She felt them now on her leg, biting. She felt something smash into her head, something thick, a fist of bone, and she fell forward face down into the earth. And... She rose. Yes! She rose, something powerful and sure looping around her waist. Her coat pulled from the earth, Blodetan falling from her as if thrown down. Up and up and up and up, above the limbs of the forest, the humming, throbbing sound now right above.

"I have you now, Lara," Roman said. "You are safe. I have you now." And she drifted high above the forest and clung to his fur coat, clung and cried as the dirigible *Endeavor* swept across the canopy of trees and into the night.

Chapter Fifteen

Roman sat in his small cabin and began to lose all hope of doing anything. It had been three days, and Ruth had been true to her word, he was a house prisoner. He tried to leave several times, squeezing through a back window, timing the change of guards, but each time one of Ruth's Acolyte thugs confounded his escape. By day five, he gave up all hope. That was of course the day Raya came to visit.

She was dressed in a fur coat, open, her Thunsi body squeezed tightly behind the black eel skin shirt and pants. She wore a fur hat, high and tall like a white crown, head pulled skyward with confidence and intention. When she saw him sitting there, a slumped, pile of bones, she pouted, "My poor, sweet, Roman."

He said nothing.

She bid the guards close the door behind her, and she scurried about his kitchen boiling water for the licorice root tea, taking out a cigarette and lighting it before him. "Poor, poor dear."

"You did this," he whispered. "Why did you do this? It's all lost, everything."

She crouched down before him and stroked his head. "My poor, lost Roman."

He shrugged her off like an annoyed child. She stood up confidently and walked to the whistling kettle and pulled it from the iron plate. "You say that, my dear Roman."

She crumbled licorice into the pot, poured the water and

set it down before him. She sat and crossed her long, beautiful legs, glancing down at her figure, then adjusting herself, the coat open like an inviting tent. "It's not true, darling."

"What are you doing here?" he half growled.

"Well, that depends on you, my dear." She sucked on her cigarette and snuffed out the nub in the overflowing ashtray. "You should really get a house cleaner. A man in your position... Well..."

"What do you want, Raya?" Roman stared at her now. He was pale and tired, old looking with great drooping bags under his bloodshot eyes. "Haven't you done enough?"

She poured the tea into cups, her hands dainty, steady, a thin smile on her lips. "Apparently not, my dear." She held the cup up to Roman. "Here. You must drink this. You look...well...you look absolutely used up." She sipped her own cup, placed it down. "Besides, I have a proposition that just may change your fortunes.

Roman looked up. She was staring at him, her eyes boring into him, her face an enigma. *What game was this? She ruined his position, stole the Mendel Fragment, all but murdered Lara... What could she possibly have to propose?* The rage within sparked and hissed as it began to catch fire. "Get out of here. Leave before I do something we both regret."

"You will regret my leaving, Roman. I can assure you of that." She lit another cigarette.

Did he see panic? Yes, there was the twitch, her upper cheek. She was nervous about something? He took up the tea and sipped it. *Yes, it had been too long since he took anything.* He found himself gulping it down.

"That's my good boy," Raya said.

She poured another cup and offered a cigarette. He greedily drank the next cup then smoked the cigarette, keeping in the licorice root smoke, allowing it to settle in the fibers of his lungs, the hunger now dissipating. She suddenly stood up and walked over to the door, opened it, whispered something to the door guard, then closed the door and turned. "Well, now we are alone."

"You've got to be kidding me..."

"Oh, you thought...right now?"

She laughed and shook her head. Roman knew the actress would appear, she always did, and just like that... "I'm not Lara, honey. A little bunny, here and there and everywhere..." She waved her hand dramatically then stopped stiff. "I mean...we could...if you wanted that, Roman." She took several steps and stood before him. "That's why I'm here, Roman. That's why I am always here...to give you what you most desire."

He watched as she contemplated her own statement, letting it settle and drift about in the silent room. It was coming. With Raya, it was always coming—the trap, the snag, the barbed hook you never looked for or noticed. The poisoned, brilliantly painted spider, multiple legs individually moving to distract... then...

"I know what that is, my dear. I have always known what it is."

She sat down with a plop and faced him.

He stared at her, the rage building, then smoldering with her beauty. Roman breathed in deeply and closed his eyes. He saw himself, suddenly, a lightning strike, grabbing her and pulling her down, throttling her.

Raya smiled at him. "I see you, Roman. I have always seen you. Nothing gets you what you truly want. Nothing." She stopped smiling and leaned close. "Except one thing, my love."

"Don't call me that."

"Darling? One, single thing."

This time he grabbed her, two fists of fur coat, mock pulling on her, mock shaking her, she smiling, her gorgeous head gently wobbling. She reached up and gently held his wrists. He stopped, released his grip. She chortled.

"There is one simple thing, my love. You know what it is. Everything you want is for the taking...just one simple, simple thing."

He glanced at her hand, seeing the object for the first time.

"It's too late. They're all dead. All of them, thanks to you."

He pushed her away and stood up, walking to the window. The snow was falling now. The cold dark winter would be here soon.

"You don't believe that do you?"

She was standing next to him now. He could feel her breath on his neck, lips softly brushing his skin. "One thing, my love."

She turned him around slowly so that they faced each other, her fingers cupping his.

He felt the metal of the strange blade. "What do you really want, Roman?" She whispered in his ear.

"You hate her."

"Yes, yes I do."

"You know I love her."

"Yes, my darling Roman. Yes, I know."

"I will never stop loving her."

"Yes, I know."

"If she's alive, I will bring her home."

"Yes, yes, bring her home, get your magic paper, retrieve them all." She was nearly purring now, a strange erotic vibration flowing through their bodies. "She will see me..."

"She will hate you."

"And she will hate me," Raya whispered. "And it will be glorious...." Raya was holding Roman's face firmly with one hand now, her lips dancing across his. "Because that peasant cunt...can never, ever, ever... Have the one thing she so desperately wants...you."

She closed Roman's fingers around the coiled blade and kissed him, hot, wet, open mouth.

Was this the way out. Was there no other way? He had tried. She knew that. If he did not leave in the next day, it would really be too late. It was probably a pointless effort even now. She whispered in his ear. His body felt a tremor of pleasure, walls cracking, crumbling, tumbling away. *Is this a hex?* His legs grew weak. "What? What is happening?" he said.

"Hush, my darling. Shhhhh."

He could not resist now, his body caught up in the thaumaturgic wave. *Ruth! By the Horned God! They are both in on it!* He thought he screamed. He did not. He thought he swung his body wildly, pulling away, running to the door. He did not. He watched as he pulled open his shirt, she pushing him to the floor, her coat flung free, stripping wildly as she fell on him. She was ferocious now, holding his stiff member in her hands, gliding it back and forth between her thighs. She held the black handle of the strange blade in her hand, the coil shaped blade, small and razor sharp, and as he entered her, she swept the cold metal across his chest, spiraling and spinning, digging and carving as they both reached climax, pressing now chest to chest as the blood dripped down their sides, and all Roman could hear was the siren call of Raya as she chanted the sacred words that bound them now...forever.

Chapter Sixteen

The *Endeavor* shook, then wobbled and tilted as it rose from the rocky ground of Widorexiton, but Roman was now in a deep struggle. He shook off the feeling and ordered his crew to cast the lines, and the north wind immediately shifted the dirigible toward the coast. As much as he felt the urgency to rescue his father and Lara, something else was now working its way through him, something burrowing upward, a dark sense that he only felt when working with the Mendel Fragment. The steam engine groaned, chugged and puffed. The great wooden propeller increasing their speed as the current pushed and swayed them through the blinding snow. Below was a choppy, white capped mess of dangerous water, but soon it disappeared altogether as the visibility vanished.

"Stay with the ice!" Roman yelled. "Keep it clean, boys!"

Lex along with several other deckhands scraped the ice off the wooden planks and railings. Any weight now would send them sinking into the swells below. Roman pitched the *Endeavor* upward, trying to gain as much altitude as possible, calculating the gathering weight and the distance to the coastline. *With luck,* he thought and instinctively rubbed his chest. *Just a bit of luck now. By the Horned God, did he not deserve some luck!* The wounds from the hexed blade were all but faint lines below his thick, fur coat. He trained his mind on the present, watched Lex point and gesticulate at the greenhorn deckhand. "Grab the port side sheet!" he barked through the wind. "Tie it down, Thunsi!"

By the end of the first day, they saw the *Intruder* rising

and falling in the snow and swells. They nearly missed the eel boats pulled high on the rocky shoreline, but after that, The Forest of the Dead moved below them obscured by a gray haze. The struggle within had grown as they neared the coast. Now it was a pulse, a low beat, and if he concentrated on it, it became a whisper, *Come. Come. Come. I will show you...everything.* He shook his head in protest and breathed in. "Steady on!" He barked. "Give her some lift, lads!"

Night came upon them, and the inland wind settled, leaving a strange quiet with only the humming and chugging of the steam engine. And they heard the screams, the cries from the victims, the chaos, yelps, and commands from those remaining. Roman was helpless, the *Endeavor* stuck in a steady, slow movement forward, buffeting an onshore breeze. At that moment, they saw them.

Thousands? White, hunched and crawling naked things, silent and streaming toward one focal point—ants or strange beetles, shimmering, vanishing from sight as the tree limbs obscured the view. Was Lara still alive? How could she or any of them have survived? Even if they had, surrounded and desperate...what could he possibly do? He had no access, could not swoop down. The crew of the *Endeavor* was stuck in the air, condemned to watch the unimaginable slaughter below. Again, the pulsing, thumping inside his head and chest. It was increasing now. Convicting. *Forget them. Forget all of them. They are dead. They are dead and gone. Come. Come. Come. I will show you something...wonderful.* He was in deep struggle now, nearly forgetting why he was even there. *The cave. I must get to the cave.* His senses wrestled it down.

"Stoke that engine!" Roman yelled again, a reverberating echo across the tops of the great forest. "Trim the stern line, by the Horned God or I'll have you flogged!"

The dirigible flew over a dense canopy of pine trees, and

all was lost from view. The crew leaned over the railing, peering, squinting, the dark collapsing upon the landscape. Soon Lex was pointing from the bow. "Starboard, sir! There. Just there."

Sure enough, the pines opened to deciduous trees once again, and the forest exposed the path, and scattered on it were the gruesome flotsam and jetsam from the lost crew.

"By the Horned God!" Lex cried. "Over there!

Strung up like ghoulish ornaments hung the crew, swinging and dangling for all to see—bird and man alike. Onward they flew, now glancing the canopy with their wooden hull, now drifting far above for a larger view.

"Surely no one is alive," Lex said.

Roman cocked his head and stiffened at the bow, spyglass in hand surveying the nearly imperceptible darkness below, but the glass moved southward, up and beyond the trees toward the Black Mountains. He blinked, again wondering why he was not already to the Cave. They heard howls, then desperate screams. A light blazed further down the southern path.

"There!" Roman cried suddenly earnest and committed to the current task, but when they arrived, the blaze scattered, sparks of fire here and there sputtering and useless.

"We must lower the lines, sir" screamed Lex. "The lines, sir! By the Horned God! We must get down there!" Roman stirred again, then swung the crane boom over the edge. Lex came from behind. "I'll go, sir. It's too dangerous. They're still down there. Who knows how many and where."

His mind was clear now, and Roman secured his harpoon to his back.

"We can't keep her here, sir," said Lex. "You know that. The best I can do is loop her around. We'll throw the line down towards the next clearing. Follow the path. We'll find you."

Roman turned. "I'll use the path," he said, now desperate to focus, the whispering now a thick fog settling on every decision.

He crawled slowly over the side and lowered through the upper portions of the canopy. The *Endeavor* shifted and moved, sweeping him into several branches. He let go and shimmied down the tree. The dirigible bobbed once again free of constraints and followed the path.

Roman squatted to the ground. *Come. Come. Come. They are all dead. They are good and dead. Come. Come to me, and I will show you something...wonderful.* He stood and began to walk absent minded through the dark forest. *Yes, I should forget all this nonsense. They are dead and gone. I must get to the cave. The cave. I must go to the cave.*

A deafening scream echoed through the night. Roman blinked and shivered, his body now in an almost feverish state of struggle. His head was light, balloon light, and he nearly fainted. He instinctively squatted in preservation, steadied himself on a tree trunk. What was happening to him? And he grew angry, a terrible envy consuming his mind like some red flame of hate. *He took it from me. He stole it right from my house. That bastard. I'll kill that damn bony root. I'll kill him good and dead. He stole it. He should pay. Yes, yes, he should pay. Leave them all to die. Leave them. Kill the priest. Kill the traitor priest. He is a thief. Go and kill the thief.*

Roman was strong willed. He was the Eel Killer. He shook his head to clear it, and once again scanned the forest, remembering his mission. With great effort he stood, then ran, stooping every once in a while, for signs, silent, deadly, the Eel-Killer on the hunt.

He came to the scattered flames and squatted in the shadows peering, observing, analyzing. He saw disbanded and broken harpoons, hacked flesh of many Blodetan, limbs scattered, viscera spilled out, masses of pale, gray humped things piled on one another as the captain and crew hacked them down.

But there was no crew. Where were they? He leapt forward, using the path as his guide, the hum of the Endeavor now closer, now further away.

Silent, poised, harpoon out at the ready, then he found his first crew member. It was the fat cook, Linus, he was torn open, holding his stomach together, wheezing, raspberry foam at the corners of his lips, his eyes blinking rapidly like a dumb thing confused. "Shouldn't have come."

Roman leaned in.

"What?"

Suddenly, like someone coming up from just behind, the whisper, boomed in his ear. *They are dead and gone. Gone. Come. Come now. Forget them. Come. Come and I will show you something...wonderful.*

"Gone..." Wheezed Linus.

Roman turned to face only night. "They are dead and gone," whispered Roman. He dropped the dying cook by the shoulders and watched him roll lifeless to his side, head limp thudding the ground.

He stood and began to walk the path, openly, confidently, completely succumbing to the melodic voice inside his head. He nearly tripped over another body. Roman stood before Lex who was mauled and torn, his signet twisted like some macabre flag, the only fabric remaining. Roman could feel a thaumaturgic blanket of fear settle upon him. This was death, a thick layer of ancient and rotted earth dumped on him. *Come. Come. Come to me,* the voice whispered. He no longer heard the *Endeavor*. Had they fallen from the sky? Had they all been annihilated by this terror? *Yes, yes, yes, all is lost. They are all dead. Come. All is lost!* He heard the Howl, a screech, a low-pitched sound increased in intensity as it reverberated like waves through the trees. What horror was out there? Surely no one survived. He leaned on a tree trunk, gathered himself and willfully stood. He was Roman the Eel-killer, but he no longer remembered why he was there. He could not anchor on any mission, person, or plan. "I am Roman the Eel-killer. By the Horned God!" he said out loud. A shout, a scream, a tiny whisper snuffed out by the hex now penetrating all the forest.

And quite unexpectedly, a flame lit in a cave, a door suddenly cast open, whether by will or by intention, the hex faltered, a weakened signal. Roman heard the hum of dirigible once again. He felt the Blodetan closing in on all sides, saw the pale hunched bodies lumbering quietly through the trees, and he knew his mind focused on the present. The *Endeavor* lurched above him, trying to steady in the small opening the canopy provided. The line swept forward and snagged in a nearby limb, but Roman did not wait for another pass. He lunged for the branch, pulled himself up and launched toward the line just as it tugged free. The Blodetan closed in around him, but he was above, swinging and climbing as they hoisted him closer to the hull. And....

"There! By the Horned God! She's there! Do you see her?" Lex screamed. "We'll Loop back!"

The *Endeavor* turned, long loping, an infinity of time, Roman's head filled with the whisper once again. He struggled to concentrate. He could see them coming now, scurrying like pale insects in the dim light, streaming toward the opening, toward the cowering Lara. He saw some terror, thin, white in the moon, arms high, a jagged ornament of bone on its head. He saw something near Lara, strange, like an isolated tree with branches unfolding, but as they neared it vanished—an illusion, a fog of panic in Roman's mind. She grasped him, at first dangling, then he looped his arm around her chest, a rush of elation surging through every cell of his body, something beautiful, something lovely. The voice boomed in his head. *Drop her! Drop her now! She is dead and gone. She is dead and gone. Drop her and come to me!* His chest burned, exploding from his hexed and maimed flesh. So great was the thaumaturgic sensation that loosed his grip. Lara desperately struggled, slipping down. Roman's will was strong, piercing the fog, and he readjusted his grip.

"I have you now!" He shouted and groaned. He held her with hoops of steel. They rose from the ground, through the open air and finally free beyond the death and darkness below.

Chapter Seventeen

Beyond the Salty Sea and through the first third of the Forest of the Dead, there is a grove of trees. It is untamed and more ancient—so it is said—than the forest itself. No Thunsi knows exactly what type of trees they are, what fruit they may bare, when they gestate, for how long. Only the High Priests of Widorexiton saw them in seasons. Only the High Priests have ventured through this grove. It is the final barrier before the Cave of the Horned God, the most sacred place in the world of the Thunsi. To enter that grove on one's own volition, without being summoned by the god himself—well, that was certain death. As the crew anchored the *Endeavor* to the ground, tying lines to tree trunks, Roman searched the acres of moldered, moss-filled trees in the early morning light, and Lara watched with a growing concern.

"We must turn back, Roman," she said. "There is only death for us here."

Roman turned. "They're all dead and gone. All dead and gone." He surveyed the land once again. "Ah," Roman whispered. "The rat emerges."

Lara looked across the bow and saw a cloaked shape scurry from tree to tree. It was the High Priest. He was making his way slowly and painfully to the cave of the Horned God. "Old Bony Root will have a surprise, indeed." Roman said.

To Lara's horror, he turned to the air. "Yes, yes, yes. Something wonderful. We'll see. Yes, we'll see. The blood of that thief will be wonder enough."

"Roman," Lara said, and she placed her hands on his shoulders.

As if stung, he pulled back, turned full face, a grin upon his lips, curled and cruel, a dark maleficence in his eyes. He pushed her aside and grabbed his harpoon, fastened it to his back and was over the side of the *Endeavor* before she could get out another word.

She struggled to gather her things, struggled getting over the bow, holding the rope and sliding, the fibers burning through her eel skin mittens.

"You can't go out there," Lex screamed to her, but she was running now desperate to close the growing gap between her and Roman.

The Grove of the Horned God was acres wide, row upon row of trees, the branches sprawled and thorny and snagging. She found herself trapped in small thickets, like a naturally constructed maze from fallen branches or nesting animals or ferocious shrubs with nettles and barbs and dying vines. The wind from the coast swept over the grove, piercing the open spaces, a biting gnawing cold that stung her cheeks and made her eyes water.

Soon, she realized that everywhere she turned, she was accosted by ancient runes, deeply carved symbols in every trunk. Some repeated themselves tree after tree, others where savage in their depiction, skull-like or claw-like, some rounded with horns, others, forked tongues and tails. Her skin tingled with the power of the ancient thaumaturgy. She was unwanted. This place was a grove of horror. What was she doing out here? Never, ever had any Thunsi dare to venture so far into the great woods. Strange, macabre symbols dangled from the trees, bones tinkling against bone, the horror mobiles of ancient magic. But A voice was like a slow stream winding through her mind, looping back, moving forward. *Help me! Save me! Stop Roman. Stop Roman!* It was not her own voice. It was weak, a whisper at times, someone nearly used up, and as she ran from one row of trees to the other, it repeated the sentences, each time strained like it was the last. The grove was long, wide, and Lara soon found herself confused in which way to go. She wanted to obey, wanted to heed the voice's warnings, but each time she tried to move forward toward what she thought was the cave, another thicket, another bramble, another barrier emerged, shifting her sense of direction.

She dashed around a tree, and saw an open path, and far in the distance was Roman. He was waving his arms in furious conversation... with... nobody. The voice in her head said, *save me. Save me. Stop Roman.* Lara ran. The distance between them seemed to disappear, the ground beneath her rising then falling, then rising again. As she crested the small hill, she saw the thicket once again. *Was it there before?* She was sure it was not. The grove itself was blocking her now. She could hear Roman, clear in the cold, damp air. He was in deep debate.

"Something Wonderful? Ha! You say that, but that bastard has it. He's a thief! Damn right he is. Damn right he deserves death. If I catch him. He'll see. They'll all see! Exactly! That's what I'm saying."

Suddenly he crouched to the ground and covered his ears, shaking his head violently.

Lara searched the way forward, but every way she chose ended in fallen logs or impenetrable brambles. The voice in her head was calm, persistent. *Save me. Save me.* It looped over and over then... silence. And quite strikingly and with great force... *Follow. Follow. Follow...me.*

"What do you mean?" she cried to the cold air.

Whether an illusion or by some force of hex, she saw a brown string before her, carefully placed. *That was not there before? How? What is happening?* She stooped down and picked it up, looked ahead, and she walked, then faster, rolling it into a ball. The string weaved and guided her around thickets, over faux barricades, far west, then east, then straight as an arrow through the grove. Roman was before her now screaming out boasts of violence toward the priest, calling him out, begging him to show himself. And the string vanished, ended, cut off, and Lara found herself now amid tall, thick trees with branches low, enormous sentinels blocking all who would enter.

    She stooped and crawled, pressed down further and further by the great falling branches. *Save me. Stop Roman. Save me.* The voice whispered in a staccato tone, nearly extinguished now, vapors on the wind. Lara crawled with determination and found herself very close to an opening. That is when she saw the Hight Priest, Old Bony Root, come from the side. Lara cried out, but the High Priest swung the large stick and clubbed Roman to the ground. The High Priest stared at the low branches in confusion, And, in a growl of pure hate. "You'll get yours, my sweet. Oh, yes. You'll get yours." The withered old Thunsi bent over Roman and dragged him forward, like some savage thing seeking an isolated place to rend and feed.

    Lara crawled, but the branches pushed her down, closer and closer and closer to the ground until she was pinned. She watched helplessly as the High Priest dragged Roman to the mouth of the cave of the Horned God, then, quite instantly, they both vanished into the void, the great hole into the Black Mountains.

Chapter **Eighteen**

Roman's head seemed heavy, and he found himself tied both wrist and ankles with his back to a damp cave wall. His temples throbbed from the severe blow, and at times white flashes of light danced in his peripheral vision. He concentrated with great effort and focused on a figure busy, hunching, shuffling this way and that, but it was unsustainable. Roman's head sank once again in agony, sank down chin to chest and rolled into blackness.

When he awoke again, he was lying in a vast, cold space, hands numb and still bound, but his legs had been freed, and he pulled them up in a fetal position to warm his shivering body.

"Oh, good," said a wheezing voice. "I thought I killed you. At least that's something."

Ralph, the High Priest, now clothed in his finest robe, the great eel skull in his hands, stood before Roman. He walked over to a table and placed it next to a polished copper chalice and candelabras set uniformly on a red velvet runner which drooped and shuttered in the wind of the cave. A large copper bowl of Licorice Root smoldered like incense, and filled the space with a soothing, aromatic haze.

Ralph tried to concentrate, but something from outside was now synchronizing with his heartbeat, low, steady, rhythmic: *boom, boom, boom; boom, boom, boom; boom, boom, boom.* He breathed in deeply and allowed the licorice root to sooth his mind. He blinked, sat up and leaned against the wall. Whether from time or the smoke, the voice in his head was clear now, whispering to him in his right ear, an invisible presence sitting next to him, a silent prisoner unnoticed by the captor. At first, he thought he had gone mad, the blow knocking his brain clean into mush, but it was there alright. Something was there. He tried to concentrate on the High Priest's words, but the annoying voice kept humming and whispering. *You are here. You are here. You are here...now...wait.*

"You know," Ralph said. "I wasn't sure I would make it. It's hard to tell these days what a summons actually is. Here I am. Alive."

His tone was more of relief than joy, and he suddenly stood before Roman with what looked like doubt on his face. He scratched his withered and wrinkled cheek in contemplation. "You are here. I must say, that's a bit disconcerting, you know. I mean, I had my suspicions. Of course, I did. When I learned of...this..." He walked to the Mendel Fragment still incased in glass, propped up on the stone slab. "Well, obviously something is happening here. I mean. Of course, you are involved. Yes, I must say, it all took me by surprise really."

Roman concentrated on the High Priest's words, but again they were bouncing off and interrupted by the whispering voice: *You are here... You are here... You are here... to...*

"There's always a cost, Roman. Always. Blood must be spilled. Have you asked yourself? Have you asked yourself the bigger question, lad? What are you doing here? Here. Where no Thunsi has been before. You are here, Thunsi! Here! Have you asked yourself...why?" Then as if flicking a switch. "I'm sorry about your crew mate...what was his name? Lawrence, Larry...."

"His name was Layne, you murderer. You...thief."

"Oh, no, no, no, my lad. I'm no murderer. That was not my doing. I just said blood must be spilled. I did not have a hand in...Layne's death. That was your father's doing. Now, on the accusation of thief. I do stand guilty. That...artifact was not meant for you, lad. Of course not."

Roman's mind pounded with the whisper voice, louder and louder it grew so that he could barely concentrate on the High Priest's words. *You are here. You are here. You are here...now...to...* He shook his head.

"Believe me, Roman. That was all your father. As I have said. There is always a cost."

You are here. You are here. You are here...now...to...

"But you are here now," said the High Priest. "And I must say, I could use your help."

You are here. You are here. You are here...now...to...

"Sometimes the Horned God demands confusing things from us. I must admit, I was confused for a while. Mixed messages and all, but it's quite clear now. I think...no, I'm certain of what he is asking of me."

Roman closed his eyes and tried to clear the voice from his head, but it was too great now, looping over and over and over, louder and louder, pounding and synchronizing with the beating of his heart, his breathing. "What?" He cried out. "To do what, damn you! What do you want?"

The High Priest stopped and creased his brow. "Well, you need not raise your voice with me, Roman. I was getting to that. I know this is not the optimal circumstance, but I didn't know. It wasn't until I got here that I fully understood what the Horned God wants. There are moments...times...Roman. I can't believe it myself. Once in a generation opportunity. And you...and I...get to experience one...now." He walked over to Roman, and his old bones creaked and popped as he bent down to lift Roman to his feet. "Let me show you, Roman. Come."

Roman wobbled, his legs trying to stiffen under the weight of his body, and they moved slowly toward the back of the cave. The whisper voice was loud now, looping, insistent, maddening:

You are here. You are here. You are here...now...to...
It was like an annoying joke ending before the punchline, a puzzle complete but for one piece, a dehydrated Thunsi on the salty sea with no fresh water. He tried to concentrate on the High Priest's words, blinking his eyes, turning his head to see the voice in his ear.

"I figured it out, you see, Roman. Why you are here. Why you and I are together. It was unclear the last time, but now..." He chuckled to himself. "Now it's like a bright flame in a dark place. Ha-ha."

They shuffled into the blackness of a carved chamber, the wind whistling through some hollow crevice far above. The High Priest shoved the torch he was holding into a brass spiraled holder, stepped over to the intricately carved cell and opened the stone door. The small area illuminated in light. "This is the *Giving Cell.*"

There before them, chained to the wall in iron shackles was a woman's withered figure, emaciated, head drooping forward, white hair long and scattered, dry like straw, a body wasted by decades, centuries of neglect and isolation. Long tubes sewn into her neck and shackled arms expanded like tentacles, gathering in a bundle and running up the wall and through a hole in the stone.

Roman gasped.

You are here, the voice whispered. *You are here. You are here...now...to...*

Who is that?" Roman croaked.

"*Who* is not important, my dear Roman. It is *what* she has given. That is the important thing."

See! Look and see! You are here. You are here. You are here...now...to...

"What...what has she given?" Roman could feel his stomach roll inside him. An ice ball formed at its bottom, his bound hands numbing.

"Why everything, Roman." The High Priest said. "That is the cost. The Miracle."

You are here. You are here. You are here...now...to...

"I want to leave," Roman said. "I want to leave this place."

See. Look and see. You are here. You are here. You are here...now...to...

"Oh, I'm afraid that is impossible, my dear Thunsi."

The whisper voice melded with the pulse of his heart with the rage that was building inside him. This was the murderer. This was the thief who stole the Mendel Fragment. The phony. The fraud.

You are here. You are here. You are here...now...to...

The High Priest pulled Roman to him. "You have a purpose, Roman. I need you. The Horned God needs you."

You are here. You are here. You are here...now...to...

"You must be strong, Roman. You must be strong for both of us now. Come, let me show you."

The old priest shuffled out of the small carved room, pulling the torch from the holder. With the light in one hand and Roman's arm in the other, he moved slowly out of the stone chamber, stumbling on the uneven stone floor, and around a bend where they both stood before a stone cell door.

You are here. You are here. You are here...now...to...

The High Priest stepped behind him. Roman heard the knife pull from the sheath, quick, sudden.

Wait! The voice screamed in his head. *Wait! Wait and see. I will show you...something... wonderful.*

He felt the binding ropes fall away. His hands were free. He grabbed his wrists and rubbed them.

You are here. You are here. You are here...now...to...

The High Priest leaned into Roman's ear. "You are here

to...."

You are here. You are here. You are here... now... to...

"Serve me," the High Priest said.

To serve..." The voice repeated.

The High Priest opened the door of the cell and held forth the torch.

Before them, slumped over in a massive naked heap was the largest Thunsi he had ever seen, if it was a Thunsi at all! Thick and fleshy, more flesh than he could comprehend on anybody known to Thunsi. His face was masked in a great beard, brown, springing out from his lips and cheeks like some wild, untamed bush.

"What...what is it?" Roman whispered.

You are here to serve....

"It is the next miracle," said the High Priest. His eyes wide with wonder and awe just like Roman's. "I need you to take it to the *Giving Cell*." He placed his withered hand on Roman's back. "I am too weak, you see. I can't lift this! You can. You see now? This is why the Horned God brought you to me."

"I don't understand."

"It is not for you to understand, Roman. You are here to serve *me*."

The voice in his head grew in intensity, but now it was mixed with images. The old Priest stealing the Mendel Fragment. The old priest stabbing Layne. The Old priest covetously stroking and caressing a terrified, bound Lara.

You are here. You are here. You are here...now...to... serve...

Roman stepped back from the enormous, slumped figure in the cell.

Thief! Liar! Murderer! Thief! Liar! Murderer! Thief! Liar! Murderer!

He saw the blade still in the High Priest's hands. *Old*

Bony Root is going to kill me! That phony! That hypocrite! Murderer!

You are here. You are here. You are here...now...to... serve...

Again, the images roared in his brain, each one searing hatred deeper and deeper into his heart like a red-hot brand. *Come. Come. Come. I will show you something... Wonderful. You are here to serve...*

The High Priest stepped back nervously from Roman and chuckled. "Just like the old goat to test me. By the Horned God!" Suddenly, his countenance changed. He turned quickly as if he had heard something from the cave entrance, someone else stepping into the holy place.

You are here. You are here. You are here...now...to... serve...

Roman turned into the old Thunsi with a quick snakelike strike, sweeping the blade from his hand and flipping it into his own. A great rhythmic beat now taking him over, a syncopation of images and sounds pulsing, focusing into one emotion: hate.

You are here. You are here. You are here...now...to... serve...

Roman grabbed the High Priest by the throat.

To...serve...

He saw the withered face collapse with the devastating realization of this singular unfortunate turn of events. "Why?" The old priest whispered.

To...Serve... Said the voice in Roman's ear. And the voice was a shout:

ME
ONLY ME...
FOREVER.

Roman felt a melding, a great synthesis of relief as the voice and the music combined, the rhythm now every part of his atoms, and he listened in complete sublimation as it told him about the Mendel Fragment, the Great Miracle to come and all that must now be done to prepare for the coming of the Horned God.

Chapter Nineteen

Lara heard the High Priest speaking, but she could not make out what he was saying. She had to crawl out from under the great limbs and follow an obscure route further west and loop around to the entrance of the cave of the Horned God. Her body felt weak, the forgotten hunger deep within now all consuming, clawing to get out. She felt the tingling and electrical pricks of the terrifying thaumaturgy surrounding the opening of the gaping mouth of rock, and she instinctively took out the small eel skin pouch of licorice root and chewed it violently, the bitter tang a sudden relief. She stared at the cave entrance, then the ancient thicket, sucking desperately on the root. Then it hit her, and she trembled with the realization that she now stood where no Thunsi except for the High Priests themselves had ever stood before, and she half expected the ground below her feet to collapse and consume this blasphemous act. *Why had she followed Roman? What did she hope to accomplish.* Like a swimmer who finds herself far from the shoreline, the danger settled slowly. She felt exposed by the great abyss, the impenetrable void beyond.

A voice echoed, turned back on itself, and finally drifting out from the opening like whispers. *It can see me. It knows I am here. It knows.* The hex penetrated her now, suffocating her like a heavy blanket of ancient earth. She could not breathe, and she fell to the ground, crawling on her belly, then knees back, back, back into the thicket that was the Grove of the Horned God. Soon that too gave no relief. She heard the jangling, dangling bones and metal ornaments clink and clang in the wind, foreboding chimes speaking a dark and forgotten tongue. She leaned against a great trunk and saw the deeply grooved rune, a horned symbol with what could only be interpreted as tusks or teeth jutting down. *Leave! Now!* Howled a voice in her head, deep, resounding, and she closed her eyes to ward it off. Suddenly, another voice whispered to her, subtle, a soft breeze on an autumn day. *I am here. I am here. I am here. Help me.* It was not Roman's voice. It was a female. Again, *I am here. I am here. I am here. Help me. HELP ME!* It screamed so loud that Lara grabbed her head in the intense pain, a great propulsion of power, like her mind fragmented and scrambled—then silence, absolute silence.

The desperate voice won out, and she stayed huddled in the thicket staring at the black, immense opening in the stone. What happened next would revolve in her mind and dreams in the coming weeks and months. At first, she did not understand what she was seeing. A tall figure pushed a cart. On his head was the great eel skull, the red streaks across the jaw, sweeping up to the point of the crown. The High Priest robes clung to his body, sleeves too short, chest too tight, like an adult playing with a child's clothing. The figure hunched over the large barrow, a single, wooden wheel, spoked and weathered from much use. He struggled at first with the terrain, the wind, the weight of the wrapped and bulky load. Lara stared as the barrow snagged on uneven ground, thin fingers falling from the brown canvas. This did not bother the figure, and he pulled back then thrust forward in such a mundane way, a farmer with a load of debris.

The trail branched inward. The figure stopped suddenly, adjusted the skull, then gestured to the air. "Well, I can't damn well see, can I? Be precise! I know. I know! There are many things to consider. Of course! I'm not an idiot!"

She crept closer, watching, eyes wide as she recognized the voice. It was Roman. In the High Priest's vestiges. He hunched over and pushed the cart along the path. She followed, listening to him argue with the air and trees, shaking his head, shouting out. He came to a deep ravine. There Roman lifted hard on the handles and dumped the wrapped canvas down the leaf-strewn slope. It rolled, slid, the brown covering separating, and a naked, withered leg pulled free. Lara clamped harder on her mouth to stifle the scream. Roman gestured again, waving his arms back and forth, then looked at the heap below. "Fine! Fine!" He bellowed and slid and stumbled down to the canvas and neatly tucked it under the body. "Happy." He growled, and struggled up the ravine, grabbing saplings for leverage. He took up the barrow again, and walked it back down the trail, arguing to nobody, "Yes, yes. It will be obvious. He's coming. I understand! Oh...so...simple... Nectar to a bee." He laughed and walked out of view.

She wanted to scream, wanted to cry, wanted to rush Roman and hit him to the ground with a heavy stick, but she did none of these. She squatted to the damp forest floor, shivering, grabbing her knees and pulling them close to her chest.

A deep and threatening voice boomed in her head: *LEAVE NOW. LEAVE. YOU ARE ON HOLY GROUND!* Something else was happening in her now. Memories swarmed in her mind, memories of Hawthorne, its wild conspiracies, the nearly unintelligible and earnest ramblings. She searched the ravine, then the trail for any movement, but all was silence. *Yes, yes. Something evil was happening. Something diabolical. She was the witness.* She looked again at the path, empty. *What if it was not? What if this was something...holy...something for the chosen ones only? What if she had just stumbled on something ancient... something divine?* She needed to be sure. She needed to verify. *If that was Old Bony Root, and he had been murdered...* The thought stung her, over and over. *What if Roman had killed...the High Priest? That was not...divine... That was...Murder.* She squatted, the cold wind pricking against her neck and face like biting insects. She pulled her collar up and glanced at the ravine, the body far below now in darkness. *What if she was witnessing something else. She never saw Roman...DO anything. What if this was how it all worked?* Her head swam and swooped in doubt, in fear. She was unwanted here. Didn't want to be here in the first place. What was she doing?

She turned to the path and noticed for the first time that the day had evaporated, the graying sun nearly behind the trees, the Grove deepening in shadows beyond. That was when she heard Roman once again coming toward her. Still crowned with the eel skull, but no longer dressed in the High Priest's robes, he was nearly naked, chest and ribs exposed to the freezing air. Roman was whistling, whistling, and chuckling to himself as he pushed another wrapped bundle—this time much lighter and less burdensome—toward the ravine. She pulled back into the thicket and watched as that canvas too was launched down the ravine, scattering the leaves as it slid. Roman watched it and slapped his thigh as if responding to a funny joke. He adjusted the eel skull on his head that turned with the motion, then grabbed the barrow and still chuckling and whistling, walked the empty barrow down the trail.

After what seemed an unbearable amount of waiting, she crept to the ravine, glanced again at the path, then slid and scurried to the bottom. Darkness had crept in the hollow, and she stumbled and felt her way to the second canvas. It was a sort of bag, and she pulled from it the sacred robe and vestments that had been Old Bony Root's. She searched in the gray haze for any signs that would indicate violence, but she could see and feel nothing. She turned to the other—long, thin, canvas pushed snuggly around the outlined shape. A sense of dread fluttered from her spine to her scalp, gooseflesh erupting on her arms. She stopped and listened for Roman, but all she could hear now was the creaking, groaning trees driven by the intensifying wind.

There was a pungent odor of decay, of damp growing things left too long in a root cellar. Quickly, she pulled at the border and exposed the body beneath. It was not Old Boney Root. No, it was...the strangest Thunsi she had ever seen. Skin and bones, yes, but not Thunsi. The body was emaciated and shriveled, a preserved thing. And that face! In the near absent light, she stooped over it, compelled... It was so...beautiful, a gray, pale beauty, a stunning death mask of parched, paper-like features. Lara pulled back, the spell broken, and she shivered again. *It moved! Did it move? The wind*, she thought. *Leaves blowing onto the canvas.*

It shuddered. Slight. *That was no wind.*

Lara stared at the dried and sunken face, so, so... wondrous...so...

A frozen stone touched her wrist, frozen stone fingers, sluggish, stiff, closing. Simultaneously, a slight sigh, a desperate breath, a last gasp of released gas—from her lips! Lara grabbed the hand on her wrist, but it folded lifeless with the pressure, sliding limp to the ground. She hunched over the face, ear to lips, listening. YES! YES! She was still alive, still breathing.

"Can you hear me?" Laura said. "Can you hear me?" She moved her ear to the withered, cold chest. Yes! A slight beat. Yes! Yes. "Oh, by the Horned God!" she said to the face, "you are so cold. You will freeze out here."

She stood up and searched, then grabbed the canvas bag with the Priest's thick vestments. She tugged them out and unfolded the great garments so that they were a blanket to the body. Tucking them and pulling them carefully around and under her, Lara then secured the canvas and swaddled the figure with the outer layer, being sure to expose the lips.

How was she to help her? Where was she to go? How was she to get out of the ravine? She sat and stared at the long-wrapped figure. *If only she had rope or something, anything,*

anything at all to help.
    She stooped over the figure. "I can't help you. I can't pull you out of here. I can't lift you. It's too steep." She sat back, the wind cold and her will ebbing. "What am I saying? You're all but dead." She listened to the trees groaning, creaking. The darkness was now deeper, the ravine completely shadowed. She heard it. The wind? Something imagined?
    Help me.
    Again, softer, *Help me.*
    Lara hunched over the face again, eyes closed, cheeks pallid, gray...so beautiful. "It's you!" Lara said. "Your voice in the grove. It's you." She touched the sides of her cheeks. "I don't know what to do. I can't carry you out. I'm sorry."
    Quite clearly the image appeared in her mind: ROPE
    Lara saw it in her mind, coiled like a snake in her imagination. She stared at the face again.
    "I have no rope. I can't get any. By the time I got back here, you will die."
    R-O-P-E, but the image or the word or whatever was happening faded nearly as quickly as it appeared. "There is no rope. I have no rope," she said in complete defeat.
    Once again, she saw the image, coiled flat, perfectly circular. She stood up and looked around. Darkness and leaves and biting wind. She was cold, and the figure was obviously dying, dead already. She listened and heard the ancient language of the bone and metal chimes. She was not wanted here. Another voice boomed in her head. *Get out! You are on holy ground! Leave or die!* She stared at the stiff figure, then up the ravine. "I need to go. I can't stay here," she said to nobody. "This is holy ground. I just can't help you." With that, she pulled the collar closer to her cheeks and turned to climb the ravine. Four steps into her climb, she stumbled on a coiled bundle, tripping her to the ground, her hands and coat now covered with mud and leaves.

Rope! Coiled perfectly...just lying there! How? There was nothing! And now... Her body shuddered, something else settling on her, something unexpected, fearless, determined. Lara picked up the bundle and stepped to the figure, stiff, still. She crouched. "I don't know who you are. I don't know how you just did that? I hear you. Yes, I hear you. I will not let you die here. I promise."

She bent over the face, staring in wonder. Quite unexpectedly, she kissed the cold, stiff cheeks. And she set to making a harness and slowly, painfully, in agonizing inches—Lara dragged and heaved, every trunk a pulley, every step a hard-fought battle. The figure slid up the steep ravine and finally onto the Grove of the Horned God.

She looked down on the wrapped figure, Lara's body screaming from the effort, chest heaving. She scanned the darkening grove, the ruins, the dangling strange chimes of bone and metal. *How was she to get through this maze, let alone carrying someone...at night?* She stooped over the wrapped body, that beautiful, pale face. It was silent like stone. She felt something, uncomfortable, a dread, like a warning, no, no, no, no, but again, it was so quick, vague, a rustle of leaves then gone. She stood and looked around in the gloaming. There it was...the wooden wheelbarrow Roman used. Right there! How silly of her not to have seen it. That subtle feeling interrupted her thoughts once again, a flutter of wings, the swaying of a branch, *no, no, no, no, no*—then poof! Gone.

Like a desperate antelope to an abandoned watering hole, she crept toward the wooden wheelbarrow. A carelessly misplaced, forgotten thing, and she dashed from the thicket and grabbed the handles. That was all she could do, for in that very moment a terrifyingly powerful thaumaturgical electricity seized her body and stiffened her muscle into a paralysis. She stood before the stone mouth, a dumb thing in the presence of a god.

Come, come, come to me... Now! Boomed an overwhelming voice, penetrating every atom of her being. It did not articulate in words, but powerful music, so strong that it enveloped her, compelled her, a violent, ravishing, all-consuming sound.

Lara turned from the wheelbarrow and stepped up to the darkness, a threshold, a portal, a void of one's undoing. She felt something familiar, and yet, something altogether terrifying, the other. She tried to think why she was here, the purpose of her visit, but soon it was only a faded image, forgettable, irrelevant. This, this moment was all that mattered. She reached to the darkness, a child testing a pool of water. It was damp and cool, soothing, the voice/music now the pumping of her blood, calming, seductive, something earthy, sensual, from the roots of living things, a primal urge. Her skin crackled and tingled with the voice/music, surrounding her, enveloping her, electrical, pulsing. She could not stop it now, did not want to, and she stepped into inky black of the cave and vanished.

Chapter Twenty

Ralph, the Great High Priest, the oldest and most esteemed since the founding of Widorexiton sat in the cave of the Horned God and brooded. *He miscalculated. That was the understatement of the year! Miscalculated! By the Horned God (and yes, holy, holy be his name) I was damned near killed for it!* He shivered with the remembrance of the moment. Such holy rage! Such powerful possession! No, he had really gotten this whole thing quite wrong, but there was a small space, a breath of air, a fraction of wiggle room yet to use. He always found that space. Why could he not do it now? So, he sat in his stone cell, chained to the wall, brooding and mentally trudging through the step-by-step moments that lead to this unfortunate outcome.

There were certain...shall we say...blunders, choices with wild and unforeseen consequences. Indeed, the murder of Roman's first mate was not the best choice. Robert was a fool, always been hot tempered—like father like son. He, Ralph the High Priest of Widorexiton, didn't murder the poor sot... Robert did! He thought about that moment, maybe something there he could use, a gesture, a gasp of horror perhaps. It was all really a blank, but he was quite sure he said nothing, and may have even been surprised by the gruesome action. Yes, yes indeed. He had been appalled and surprised. He was sure of it now. Better pack that one away for later. He blinked in the great blackness of the cell. He should be used to this place by now, but it always seemed to creep up on you.

His mind wandered lazily to the next step. Ahh, of course,

there was the Mendel Fragment. By the Horned God! That certainly blew up on him. That was the key to everything. No, that bridge of escape burned itself up. He could not use that. He lit that damn thing himself when he boasted about it to Roman. He nodded his head in agreement to himself and made a note not to be so cocky next time, and his chains jingled and clanked in response.

Yes, the Mendel Fragment, he pondered in the pitch blackness of the stone cell. That was the engine that drove everything right now. Well, that and that damnable peasant girl. In reality it was the Mendel Fragment that was the buried bug under Roman's skin. Ralph chuckled to himself. Oh, that was an apt metaphor, burrowing bug. Damnable, tunneling, clawing, gnawing insect! By the Horned God, he had known the power of such thaumaturgy. It took over your mind, your soul! That was the issue, wasn't it? Had. Had known such thaumaturgy. Ah, there's the rub, the sticking point. He had been passed over. The Horned God purposefully chose Roman. No matter how he parsed it out, rearranged the pieces, put them back into another order...it always came out with the same picture, NOT HIM. This made him slump just a bit, close his eyes and sulk.

Nearly an hour had passed, and Ralph's mind was in free fall from the cliff of significance. Of course, the licorice root incense had all but dissipated, so he was beginning to feel the severe repercussions from that as well. He heard Roman scurry in and out of the cave, whistling at times, laughing to nobody—deep, deep into the thaumaturgic response of the Horned God. And all of that stopped. A great silence settled into the expanse. He thought he heard Roman addressing someone, but he could not make it out. He thought he heard a female voice, but the thaumaturgy was so intense now that it was like listening through stone walls, and one could not distinguish a voice from a pin dropping. Something was happening beyond his cell, something quite profound, but he was unable to concentrate enough to determine what it might be. He gave up, and free-falling once again his mind reeled and tumbled, And quite suddenly and unexpectedly he found footing, a small ledge to prop his old, withered feet.

It had been a good run, hadn't it? He thought, pondering each sentence, testing it to see if it would hold. It did. Hadn't he performed wonders few Thunsi ever saw! One must not forget those young flowers, those precious deflowered...flowers. He was strangely and unfortunately a bit aroused by all the memories. Focus, old fool! He kept coming back, resolvedly, almost contentedly to that tiny ledge. Indeed, all those years! He had lasted longer than any predecessor—any of them! He even had a nickname, Old Bones! Er, or something like that. The Great Boner? Ancient Bone? Old Bones, yes, that was it, wasn't it? He was quite sure it was, and he was quite sure it resounded with authority and great respect throughout the village. He would pass away, and those ignorant peasants would construct a plaque in his honor.

OLD BONES, The most revered High Priest of Widorexiton.

Every Thunsi would fear it, worship it and remember him forever. He smiled in the darkness and nodded in agreement with the supplicants bowing before his plaque. Yes, maybe it was time. It was a good run, a long run, and he was so tired now. Even that old fart, Ruth, saw this coming? If she could see it, then how obvious it must be! He sighed in his cell, his cold, dark, damp cell.

Quite sideways he thought of his end, here, in the cave. The coming of the Horned God! Face to face! As if in response to such a horror, he noticed the clawing, cutting, slashing hunger within beginning to work its way outward. By the Horned God! Not like this! Not like this! And soon he was filled with a dumb animal terror, shaking, and rattling and screaming for Roman. There had to be a space, a tiny space. Oh, by the Horned God! He was not ready yet, not ready to see that terror! Not ready to become... By the Horned God! "Roman!" He screamed. "Roman, I need to speak with you!" In his deepest most stentorian voice, "Roman, I demand an audience!"

From just without the stone cell, he heard Roman approaching, mumbling, laughing to himself. Was that metal jingling? He was speaking in low whispers to that damnable inner voice. By the Horned God! He would use it to his advantage.

"I'm really quite busy, Old Bony Root. There is so much to do before He comes."

He turned his head to address someone, and the strangely constructed metal and bone ornament on his head jangled and clanged. "I know. I know. It is quite ironic."

He turned to Ralph with a visage of lunacy, his face now a literal mask of white with red markings streaking across his forehead and cheeks. The shadows from the torch shifted his smile and facial features in and out of view.

"I wanted to say," said Ralph the former High Priest of Widorexiton, "How...proud I am of you."

Roman stooped down and stared at the chained and withered goat, the dangling bones and metal dancing and swaying like a macabre chandelier.

"Hmmm!" Roman grunted.

He stood and walked into the darkness of the hall.

"How...? Oh! What was that damned peasant's name? "Lara! Lara!" He nearly screamed. "How proud Lara will be when she finds out the great blessing!"

Roman turned and walked back into the light, stooping down to the desperate old Thunsi.

"How proud," continued Ralph in a whisper, "the whole town will be."

Roman stared at him, a ghoulish smirk across his face. He cocked his head like a raptor gauging a trapped rabbit. "What about Lara?" Roman said.

"Er...Um... She was chosen specifically by him...er..."

Roman stared silently at the old Thunsi.

"It was...er...through...me....of course..."

"Of course, what?"

"Of course, to make the transfer binding...er...official so to speak... You will need to..."

Roman leaned in and placed a sharp bone (*by the Horned God! Was that a talon?*) under Ralph's chin. He stared with malevolent intensions, then with a comic jerk, turned his head to someone that was not there. "Yes, yes, yes! I know he knows about her..."

He shifted back to Ralph now nearly face to face. "...and HIS coming." Ralph stood, completely consumed by the inner voice. "No! I can't just do that. I can't. I don't care. Yes, they would. I could lose everything."

Ralph desperately tried to follow the crazy in Roman's head, but the sentences were so fragmented, myopic, he was unclear on when or where to make his play into that tiny, ever so tiny space. In desperation, for the conversation was turning to murder quite rapidly, Ralph blurted out, "Convergence! The Great Convergence must be completed!"

Roman was now so close they were nose to nose. Ralph whispered and squeaked, "It's the...secret way."

For what seemed like a day, Ralph and Roman stared at each other, so close, that Roman's eyes merged into one great, gray cyclops, and his breath smelled of stale licorice root smoke. Ralph blinked. *By the Horned God! What had he said? Convergence! What in the name of all that is holy was that? Convergence! Oh, he was surly dead now!*

As if Roman had read his mind, he said, "Well?"

"It's serious, Roman."

"Enlighten me..."

Ralph gulped again. "Er, you need to consider it with great pause... Yes, great pause."

Roman pulled back, cocked his head as if to get a better listen to the invisible person next to him, and Ralph once again found himself free falling, desperately grasping for anything to slow his descent toward certain doom. "It's serious, Roman. Secret..." he heard himself say.

Roman suddenly sat down before the old Thunsi, crossed his legs like a child at story time. "Go on. How come I've never heard of this? I read, Old Bony Root! I've never come across this...ever." Roman fingered the great talon, testing its point on his flesh.

"Of course not," stumbled Ralph as he thought, *Of course, you've never read about it, crazy idiot! I just made it up.* He said. "You are young, my dear Thunsi. You are so, so young. How could you know about the ancient ways passed down from one High Priest to the other."

Oh, this is good, he thought as he heard himself explain with elegance and technicality the great and ancient way of the newly coined term *Convergence*, the transfer of power from one High Priest to another, ancient, secret, only those who were old enough to have been there would know about it. (*Oh, that was a nice touch, very nice touch indeed. By the Horned God, that was good!*)

"Ruth would know?"

Ralph's face was stone, even wrathful. "Fool," he said with great authority. "I am the ancient one. Old Boner, they call me!" (*Damn! What did they call him?*) "I am the Great High Priest of Widorexiton," he stumbled forward. "I have seen the centuries like sand!" *(What in the Horned God did that mean? Slow it down, old fool, get control)* "Ruth was not even a thought in her parent's eyes when the Great Convergence happened."

Roman sat motionless. Ralph's chest was heaving now from the exertion. *Oh, how he needed the licorice root.* Roman turned his head to the invisible presence, the bone metal edifice clanking and clinking. "You don't know that for certain. Were you there? Were you? No! Of course, you were not. Yes! If you are wrong, I lose everything."

Emphatically to the presence that was not there, "I said leave me alone!"

Suddenly, like a finger snap, Roman's visage changed. He blinked at the chained Ralph, uncertain.

"Help me, lad," Ralph implored. "I need licorice root. Unchain me, and I will help you. Yes, yes. I understand what is happening to you. I will help you."

Roman stood to his feet with a jingle jangle.

"If you unchain me, lad, we can work this out together."

Ralph watched with growing hope as Roman reached into a small pouch on his side. "Yes, that's it. I know exactly how you feel. Unchain me, and we can consult the Mendel Fragment together. We can..." Roman stiffened. Ralph frowned. *You old fool! Why did you mention that! By the Horned God you had him!*

Roman pulled his hand from the pouch and came at Ralph with a sudden violence, grabbing his mouth with both hands and shoving a dried, familiar substance in it.

"Savor that. It's all you get, and we have a long way to go," Roman said.

He stood and raised both his hands, and as if on cue the atmosphere trembled with such power, Ralph cowered in fear. Roman turned to the darkness. "He's come. I must make ready." He grabbed the torch and disappeared into the night of the cave, the bone-metal chandelier clanking and jingling, mocking the terrified former High Priest of Widorexiton.

Chapter **Twenty-one**

It was Roman who greeted her, and Lara's mind wrestled with what she saw. He was naked, his face painted white, runes scrolled up his neck and on his cheeks with (Old *Bony Root's blood?*). On his head was a crown of bones with metal shards and stone and bone clinking in the wind, imitations of those hanging in the ancient trees behind her. He stood in the shadows of the fire, a statue, a silhouette.

"Roman?" Lara whispered.

The rhythm, beat of an ancient ritual surged through her body. She could not move. It took all her will to articulate words. "Roman, what is happening? Help me."

Roman turned, a Cheshire grin mocking her, a naked Thunsi puppet.

"Please," she pleaded, but even that came out as a whisper.

Roman stepped to her, then the smile drooped, faded, his eyes wide, watery, and large. "I...can't," he said. He lifted his arm as if it had great weights attached, then touched Lara's face. "I am so sorry?" He paused. "What have I done?"

"SILENCE!" Boomed a voice.

Was it real? Was it inside her head. Roman shuddered with the force of it. The Cheshire grin returned, the bone and metal and stone ornaments jangling as he moved to the side, then fell prostrate to the ground. "Yes. Yes," Roman said. "Yes, she is yours. Yes, of course. I will obey."

Roman was lost in the thaumaturgy, and Lara could feel

a presence behind her, something magnificent, something beyond her thinking. Her mind looped this idea over and over, but as it continued, oddly, she began to understand that it was not what was behind her, but what it wanted her to believe. This was fleeting, however, a shake of the head and gone. She found herself enthralled, raptured, pleasurably aroused to the point where the music in her body was now a great throbbing, pulsating thing. *Yes, yes, yes, let go*, it whispered in her left ear, then her right, then to her face. *Yes, yes, yes, that's it.* She gave in. "Yes," she agreed. "Yes, I am yours, my beloved."

The beloved did not do anything. The music surged and filled her mind and limbs, she a ripe fruit waiting, panting... Nothing. "My beloved has come," she heard herself say. "I am here." She waited. Nothing happened.

"What do you know of the Fragment?" said a tinny, thin voice, fingernails on a chalkboard. "The Mendel Fragment," it continued.

Confused, her body so receptive for her beloved, Lara felt like a swimmer, rising from great depths, suddenly asked to breathe.

"Speak!" Shouted the voice, but it was not authoritative, more like pouting.

Lara wanted to laugh, wanted to see this petulant, spoiled... Give it a piece of her mind. She tried to turn, but the thaumaturgy was so great, she only stood before the roaring fire and blinked.

Again, in that tinny voice, "What do you know of the Mendel Fragment? Did Christopher Dante give this to you? How do you know Dante? Speak, Peasant!"

The last sentence surprised her and confused her, and the music in her body throbbed and pulsed and her mind reeled, and she felt like wires suddenly crossing, sparking, separating once again with their own current.

"Who, my beloved?" Lara was sobbing now. "I don't understand."

"*She* doesn't know. *He* doesn't know," whined the voice to itself. "Nobody knows anything," it moaned in frustration. Then silence.

Lara waited, the hot fire making her sweat through her eel skin coat. She heard chanting behind her, a tongue that sounded smooth and silky, and the longer it went on, the more Lara wanted to hear it. It was telling her where to go. It was directing her further down a tunnel in the great cave. She walked sightless through the pitch darkness, the smooth, wonderful voice explaining everything, calming her, enrapturing her, reassuring her. The music began again, and this time it was like sunshine and meadows. Gone was the cold stone of the cave. Gone was the gray Salty Sea, the wind that stung and the ice that bit. Sunshine, warmth...so warm, so wonderful, a carpet of flowers and warmth and... *Why this cumbersome coat? It binds and hinders.* She was lost in the enchantment. She lay on the wondrous flowers, breathing deep, expectant, waiting, the sun shining hot and inviting on her naked body. And a shadow, a bird, a magnificent horned god, wings spreading out, blocking the soft warm light, the world, the universe beyond. "My beloved," she whispered, and she would remember no more.

Chapter Twenty-two

Captain Robert, wounded and ravished watched from the Grove of the Horned God as his son Roman and the High Priest stood before the Blodetan horde, a pale hunched mass of naked, sniffing things. The moon was high, and the bitter wind from the Salty Sea made its way deep inland. He could make out a wooden cart, a canvas tarp tied over what seemed to be crates. He watched Roman raise his arms... *Roman! His son! Dressed in tattered clothes, a strange bone and metal crown upon his head. Roman! Before those monsters...commanding them!*

Captain Robert pulled low into the thicket. He was trapped, the hunger so powerful now, he was nearly out of his mind, to go back was to die. To go forward, as lunatic as it seemed, was his only means of surviving now. He watched for days as his crew were picked off one by one. He held off the horde while Lara escaped, but who could survive in this demon-filled wood? Everyone was dead and gone. Everyone. His only means of escape. The trees! By the Horned God! He climbed into the air and lived! Now he watched in horror as his son commanded this savage terror, stood before them with hands raised. Roman's face was painted in white, strange runes scrolling down his cheeks and neck, chest. His clothes were torn flapping like abandoned sails in the bitter cold wind. The High Priest, nervous and terrified glanced this way and that, frantically searching for the crack in the thaumaturgic dam holding back the violent, hunched monsters.

"We must go, Roman," he hissed. "Time is running out."

Roman with hands still lifted high said nothing. A Cheshire grin was on his face, and the stones and bones clanked and clinked in the wind. Captain Robert watched to his horror as the familiar Blodetan leader, faux crown of chest bones and ribs, some broken and jagged, some curved inward—rose up among the group. Roman and the ghoulish, pale leader stared at each other in silence.

"Please, My High Priest. Please...Roman... We must go before dawn breaks, and our passage untenable."

As if on cue, the ghoulish leader leaned back, head tilting to the moon, crown of bones like a macabre cockscomb—and howled. At first it was barely audible, then a low moan, higher and higher and higher until the sniffing horde moved and grunted and rumbled.

Roman screamed, GO! FEED! LEAVE NOTHING ALIVE!

Half the horde disbanded, scattering like beetles from an upturned stone, scurrying out, out, out into the Forest of the Dead, disappearing into the darkness beyond. Roman turned to the High Priest. "Now get in," he said harshly. "Be mindful of the cargo. It will be your head, if any of it is damaged."

Ralph bowed low, then slowly, stiffly, dragged and rolled himself onto the wooden cart. Several Blodetan grabbed the yoke and pulled the cart down the hard clay path, and the ghoul army moved silently out of the Grove of the Horned God and into the night.

Captain Robert waited. He desperately needed licorice root. He needed eel blubber. By the Horned God! He would head to the cave if it killed him. So, he slowly, meticulously, crawling, stumbling, stooping under branch and through thorns—ever so slowly, he made his way to the entrance of the cave. That is when he heard the voice, *help me*. A whisper, a fleeting thought—poof! He stopped, knelt to the ground, stuffing himself into a crevice just before the open mouth of the cave. Again, *Help me.* Again, quick, a slight breeze through the grove. His stomach was now convulsing, his head woozy and throbbing with hunger...such hunger, and his will for distraction evaporated. He knew that to enter the cave was sure death, that the pale ghouls probably waited in ambush, but he must enter, for there was only the unthinkable out here, and he leapt from the crevice and shuffled into the darkness of the cave.

At first, he could only smell the licorice root smoke, the soothing, calming vapors hovering in a fog above his head. He breathed in deeply, and like a blind Thunsi waved his hand before him, trying desperately to see in the void. His eyes adjusted, and he made out a dim light beyond. With one hand stretched out before him, the other using the roughhewn walls as a guide, he rounded the corner and to his great joy and relief, saw the smoldering herb upon a great slab of stone. Deep breaths, deep, deep, so soothing. He reached into the large copper bowl and snuffed out a smoking bundle, then broke off several pieces and shoved them in his mouth, chewing and sucking the bitter root. He found himself exhausted by such a sudden action, and he sank down, contented, with his back to the great stone slab.

This was a holy place, and yet... He was still alive. Well, he thought he was alive. *Bah! Nonsense thinking! He would not stay long in here, but still...* Captain Robert looked around. The fire in the pit was low, but the shadows flickered on the walls, exposing images of animals, strange beings—Thunsi?—gathered in circles around a skinny tall figure. There were savage beasts, giant, he had never seen before. He saw Thunsi hunting these four-legged beasts with lances. He saw something dancing in the air above, winged things, yet not any bird he ever saw. He turned his head. *This was magic, not for him. This was High Priest Thaumaturgy, ancient, filled with great power.* He reached up to the copper bowl and grabbed more licorice root. There was so, so much, and he chewed and savored, eyes closed, his hunger diminished now to something nearly forgotten, something wafting on the edges of thought. He heard a rustle. He stopped chewing, ears pricked, a sweat now exploding over his body in the deep cold of the cave. He tried to see beyond the great glow of the fire, but it was useless.

By the Horned God! If those ghouls returned! He crept from the large stone slab and huddled in the shadows, ears strained. There it was again! He listened. Someone was whispering softly. *Oh, what terror was this?* He gathered his courage, the Great Captain Robert, Killer of Eels, tamer of the Salty Sea! *Yes, by the Horned God!* He fisted both hands, then hunched and silent, he made his way to the sound. As he rounded another bend, he came to a lit hallway with several stone cells carved deep into the wall. He stepped silently toward the first one and peeped inside.

It was large, larger than he had first expected. A small torch lit the dark granite. There before him lay a great mass...the largest Thunsi (if Thunsi it was) he ever saw. The being was chained to the rocks, bound hand and foot, a giant with such hair on his face, wiry, bush-like, a mane perhaps. At first, he thought it one of the beasts from the cave paintings. From his neck and arms ran long tubes that gathered into a bundle and disappeared into a hole in the rock. The being's head was tilted to one side, his naked skin hairy, more flesh than anything Captain Robert had ever seen in his long years of life.

Something rustled to his right, a low moan. He crept silently to another cell, and there he found Lara, naked and shivering, knees pulled up to her chest. She was laying on some large fur skin, a copper bowl of licorice root smoldering and fogging the cold damp air of the cell.

"By the Horned God! Child!" He screamed then huddled over her. "What have they done to you, my poor child!" He pulled the fur skin around her, enveloping her, rubbing vigorously her arms and legs to get the circulation going once again. "It's alright, child," he said with doubt, with confusion, looking about him. "Let's get you warm," he whispered. "Lara? Child? Can you hear me?"

Lara looked up. "My beloved. I am here for you," her voice was weak. "I am yours, beloved. Only yours."

Captain Robert stared at her, the slow realization of what must have happened, a sudden ancient, secret window cast open. He felt panic in his chest, then something else. *She was just left here. Abandoned. By the Horned God! Left to...what? Freeze to death!* He lifted her emaciated body, fur skin and all, and carried her to the open flame in the great hall of the cave. He stoked the fire until it roared and lit the dried licorice root in the copper bowl so that it filled the cave in an aromatic haze. He found a food larder of dried eel strips and fed upon them, gathering more and more in his hands, then breaking off bits and gently placing them in Lara's mouth.

It settled on him slowly, layer by layer, an instinct really, like when he knew the great eels were approaching—*we must leave this place, or we will surely die. Where? They could not survive the Forest of the Dead. Not with those ghouls! They could not stay here trapped with no way out.*

Lara moaned again, then opened her eyes. "Captain Robert?" she said.

"Yes, child. Yes, I am here. Hush now. You need your strength."

Lara pulled the fur skin closer around her and drifted off. He huddled near her, warming her, his eyes desperate for the coming dawn.

Daybreak was long in coming, and Captain Robert helped Lara into the biting air. He found her clothes, abandoned in a pile in the corner of the cell, and her coat cast off on the cave floor.

She was weak, but able to walk. They both stared at the ancient trees of the Grove, the carved runes, the jangling bone, and stone shards.

"We must go," Captain Robert said. "We must go as far as we can today."

Lara shook her head.

"We must go," said Captain Robert, the tone of his voice now more commander and captain.

"We must save her," whispered Lara.

Before he could argue, he followed her hand and saw the thin bundle beyond, something wrapped, slender.

He hurried to the bundle and stooped over it. That face! That glorious pale, majestic... *Help me,* he heard, but the figure's mouth did not move.

"What in the name of all that is holy! What magic is this?" He pulled back, but Lara was now standing next to him.

"We must save her," Lara said. "She is alive, and we must save her."

Captain Robert stared at that magnificent face, the pale, high-cheek bones, the closed, almond eyes. "But who...?"

"I don't know," Lara said. "She must come with us. We can't leave her here to die. She turned to him. "There is a barrow. It's over by the entrance."

Captain Robert looked at her with kind eyes, grabbing her shoulders. "Child, how? Where will we go? The trip to the coast is long and filled with great peril."

"We can't go to the coast."

"The ship. It's our only hope, child."

"There is no ship. They have taken it," Lara said. "That's where they were going. They were going back with the ship."

Captain Robert looked aghast, mouth propped open in despair. He slumped to the ground and sat. "We will surely die this night."

"No," Lara said. "The *Endeavor*."

Captain Robert looked up. "Here? How? It was derelict and..."

Lara pointed to the dirigible somewhere beyond the Grove of the Horned God and toward the gray light of the rising sun.

Chapter Twenty-three

It was late afternoon before the small party made their way to the clearing where the *Endeavor* was supposed to be. The thickets and maze, the fallen limbs and biting winds buffeted the sickly group until they could only sustain minutes of intense effort, then stop. Captain Robert pushed the wrapped being in the wheelbarrow while Lara slowly trudged beside him. She was aching, every joint in her body enflamed, and she could feel something not quite right inside her. When they stopped, she nearly fell to the ground, completely exhausted, used up. Captain Robert would urge them on, the day waning behind them. All day they traveled like this. All day Lara tried to keep up. The clearing, and the terror they had so desperately tried to suppress returned.

The *Endeavor* was now defunct, its long basket wedged high in the canopy, the canvas balloon absent of hydrogen—now drooped and spilled over the great tree branches like a sail, waving, snapping, and whistling in the stiff breeze. A line of stakes had been pushed into the ground, a fence line, and on them where the heads of each crew member who remained. Lex's body was hanging from the tree above it. Lara gagged.

"It's useless to fly," Captain Robert said, "but by the Horned God! If we can get up there, we can make the night." He pointed to the basket, its bow jutting out of the branches like an animal cresting a wave.

Lara stood by the wheelbarrow and watched Captain Robert, coiled lines around his shoulder like a sash, heave himself further and further up into the canopy. When he got to the top, he yelled something, but Lara could not make it out. He stayed aloft for thirty minutes or more, Lara drifting in and out of sleep. A line from the crane lowered, and at its end was a loop of rope.

"Tie her in," Captain Robert shouted. "I'll pull both of you up. First her, then you." Slowly, gently, the beautiful being cocooned in canvas and the old High Priest's robe lifted from the ground. Up, up, up into the air she went. Lara waited, the ghoulish heads, now rotted fruit, reeking and terrifying seemed to squint and gape and howl at her. The line dropped, and she tied it around her waist, yanked as a signal, then climbed up into the leafless branches far above.

Captain Robert had secured the basket with lines to thick branches.

"She's stable enough," he said, setting out a small portion of eel meat and his flask of Thunsae Myrrha. "We have warmth. The pilot house will keep us dry. It's high enough. We'll be alright up here. Yes. We'll be alright."

Lara could hear the doubt in the old captain's voice, and she knew in her soul that there was very little chance of them lasting even the beginnings of winter. She ate slowly, drank some of the harsh liquor, then fell asleep.

It was late into the night when she heard the sniffing and lumbering of the Blodetan below. She sat up and tried to peer above the basket. She decided it would be better to lay still and wait. That's when the cold, stone fingers wrapped themselves around her wrist. She startled and sat up. It was the strange exotic being from the canvas sleeper. Her almond eyes blinked, and a slight smile crossed her lips in the pale moonlight. She reached out her other cold hand and clasped them around Lara's.

"You are alive," Lara whispered.

"Yes," said the silky low voice. "You saved me." Again, the slight smile, all the energy pushed to her face in thanksgiving. Her voice strained and thinned with the effort. With great earnestness she squeezed Lara's hand. "Find...my son. Find Christopher Dante..." It faded, and her eyes closed, and she fell back into the deep unconscious world from where she came.

Greg Belliveau

Part Two

The Black Mountains

Gods of IMAGO

Chapter Twenty-four

Beatrice waited, pulled low, crouched behind an outcropping of rock, her heart pounding and throbbing in her head. The great Black Mountains rose beyond her, the thick forest obscured the treacherous and lofty cliffs that stretched and disappeared into the haze above. Below her were the wooded foothills, enormous, wind-eroded granite and sandstone outcroppings piercing through the crust of ragged earth like emerging titans. She could not see them, but she knew the lions were out there, waiting to pounce. How long the thaumaturgy would last was anyone's guess. *That was it, wasn't it? It was all just anyone's guess anymore.* She heard a low growl, and she pulled back further into a crevice, the great valley below obscured by the electrical creative energy and strewn geological formations beyond. *If nothing else,* she thought, *at least this confirmed that digital tin box's calculations.* As if in response to that thought, she listened for the distinct sound of its moving, the low buzzing of its mechanism. *No, it would be in silent mode now. It was at least good at that, self-preservation.* It was Hal, the old man. She was just not sure if he was up to the task. Why did she agree to him coming? Now he needed her help... She concentrated and tried to articulate a song, but only harsh tones came forth, broken fragments, chopped and discordant sounds. She tried again, the great swooping scar across her neck still pink even after so much time. Nothing. And subtly, like a tuning fork finding the harmonic, her voice echoed out in a slow steady mantra.

How long was it now, ten years? The world of men and time and things (as Christopher loved to call it) disappeared for her, and the past came back only in intense emotions, a concrete moment in time, then lost. She could still see Christopher Dante's face that night before he disappeared. She knew in her heart even then that something profound was unfolding.

"I did this," he said, his body rigid, hands clenched. "This...this...monstrosity is just one consequence! What else, Beatrice? What have I done?"

His naked body glistened in the dim light of the small bedroom that had once been Hal's house. Her voice still damaged, the great scar streaking across her throat, a pink smile. She had lost all power to sing, and she sat up with the sheet pulled up at her stomach, her small breasts exposed.

"It's a damn computer! A computer!"

"It was military," she wheezed. "You know how that works out. It just had to reboot. And, well, the rest we all lived."

Christopher stared out the window. She loved him. She knew this for certain. What started as companionship over the years of searching and gathering details, after the many seasons that had passed through them—it had budded into something else, intimacy, and that had blossomed into even... dare they think... perhaps a future. But now, she saw the look in his eyes as he faced her from the window—now something had stirred in him, something spiteful, a deep anger taking root, wrapping around anything certain, anything that sustained hope.

She knew that it was the discovery. She knew it in her bones. They finally penetrated the bowels of the NRM, and what they discovered lurking in the militarized bunker was no monster spinning machinations and pulling strings—the great puppet master. No, what they discovered was a metallic, rusted, and dented rectangle, really—a chassis made of composite metals with spider legs which had the annoying habit of jerking its one sensory camera down like a frightened turtle! The government created it, a supercomputer. The military weaponized it with satellite capability, and after The Event, it somehow survived. It recreated itself, gave itself a body, and now in its myopic, damaged form...it created the world around Cogstin? A corrupted AI program N.O.R.M.S. which initially stood for Neurological Operational Recognition Military System designed to monitor, track, and contain any perceived threat released from the IMAGO portal. It had created the NRM and a four-hundred-year-old belief system to organize and control the population. It became...well, some half-ass overlord.

"It's a prison planet! It's a damn prison planet, Beatrice!" Christopher said turning his back to her. "I caused it all!"

She watched him with concern and rose from the bed, the sheets falling away, and she stood next to him, holding his face in her hands. "I know, my love," she said in her whisper voice. "I know."

What was she to say? What could she possibly say to this? Christopher Dante was terrifying! A walking extinction event? The power from him had become a chain reaction beyond any thaumaturgy known. The force of the Event had become—both a creative act and an act of destruction instantaneously. She did not understand it, did not know what to do with it, and when she thought about it, thought about the agonizing decision her father had made before he died—choosing the generation tank over his freedom... Confine him... "I know, my love," she repeated. "Now come back to bed."

That was the last time she saw him. He covered his tracks quite well, not a word to Hal—and Hal knew everything that was going on in Cogstin, a real survivor. Christopher Dante disappeared, and it was only after Hal and Beatrice were able to spend time with NORM, asking an absurd amount of questions eliciting responses like: *I'm listening, Beatrix* or *Would you like me to read further?* Or *I am unfamiliar with those parameters* and on and on and on. After hours of trying and failing, NORM finally accessed a corrupted file (what wasn't broken on that thing?), last accessed by Christopher right before he vanished.

NORM executed the program, and the cursor blinked across the small screen:
EXTERMINATE ALL THE BRUTES
(1 FILE(S) FOUND)
[OPEN]
IMAGO:
ELIZABETH DANTE.... X.... KYRNUNOS
COMMANDER STUTZ.... X... COGSTIN
CHRISTOPHER DANTE....?
CARAVAGGIO....? ... KYRNUNOS
BEATRICE...?
YIL ....?. KYRNUNOS
THUNSI...?
[command]
Define: KYRNUNOS

When Beatrice and Hal tried to go any further, NORM blinked and shut down. Days followed days, and finally they were able to access an unlinked GPS map on the unit.

"Found," NORM said in its staccato electronic voice.

"Who?"

"Beatrix and Harold Dante"

"Good god!" Hal screamed, and he smacked the side of the chassis which immediately sent NORM into self-protection mode, its camera head popping down and sealing within its composite body.

"Well, that wasn't too bright," Beatrice said.

She turned to him, then looked at his wrinkled face, the thinning gray hair, the leathered, sunburnt skin. He was a survivor, and she had watched him survive...it all. At first it was war against all other Hal's. Then it was a tenuous resignation, but the years had not been kind to this Hal, and she knew that she would watch him die. "I'm sorry," he said. "If we find this Kyrnunos, maybe, just maybe, we find Caravaggio."

"If that tin box is correct," Beatrice whispered. "Maybe we find Christopher."

Hal was silent.

That had been two years ago, and Christopher Dante did not want to be followed. Every time they made their way from the Great Sand Flats and followed the Black Mountains as NORM insisted, Christopher left a trap. Now Beatrice had made it farther than she had ever made it, to the very cliffs, but the traps where more dangerous, and she lost Hal and NORM. The great lions were out there, hunting them, so she sang, broken phrases with almost no chance of working, and she waited to hear or see any sign of life.

Chapter Twenty-five

Hal sat in the dilapidated warehouse in what was now known as the meeting room, the metal chair hard and cold on his back. He listened with impatience to Mayor Hal, a rotund man with one crooked leg. He sat in the back row, before him fifty Hal's and Max's, various forms of them, all eager to participate in the discussion that had been the center of attention for nearly a week, *What to do with the vision?*

"How do we know what it means?" Mayor Hal said, gesturing them to calm down. "Maybe it is an omen."

"Why didn't we all see it?" a thin faced Max with a missing eye bellowed. Everyone agreed.

"Maybe it's a curse. Maybe this Horned God cursed him?"

The communal cry of fear and anxiety and panic filled the room.

Here it comes, thought Hal now rocking back in his metal chair. *Always with the mystical bullshit. Always with the prophecies and the god talk.* He pulled out a small bag of stollen tobacco, rolled a cigarette and smoked. Mayor Hal rambled and worried, prophesying doom. *How did it get to this...this god bullshit? These simpletons, these broken Hals, and Maxes. These broken...copies. They glom on to conspiracy like bees to pollen.* Hal sucked deeply on the cigarette, dropped it on the floor, rubbed it out with his toe and rolled another. He watched the chaos unfold.

There was a problem. He *did* have the vision, the dream.

It was disturbing and filled with...well, let's just say it was damn disturbing. It was real and constant as the stars in the sky. He had lost sleep. He was losing his mind. He never should have mentioned it to Mayor Hal...ever! What do you do when something like that takes hold. He had to know if it was just him or all of them—the clones (how he hated that term). Was he damaged? Was this something from beyond? So, he asked Mayor Hal. He nearly laughed out loud remembering the moment.

It was late evening, and Mayor Hal was a bit tipsy. So, Hal sidled up to him at the warehouse bar and just came out and asked.

"So, are you seeing this...horned fellow in your dreams?" Mayor Hal stared at him and blinked. "You know," Hal continued, "big things out of the head." He raised his hands to demonstrate. "Dark cave, creepy symbols...the music and all."

Again, the blinking. The blank stare. So, Hal immediately changed tactics, an enormous grin sweeping across his face as he slapped Mayor Hal on the back. "Gottcha! Hey, Max, give me a double of that gasoline. Bring another one here for the Mayor." Hal gulped it down and leaned close to Mayor Hal. "Forget I said anything."

That was the last thing Mayor Hal did, forget. Soon Hal was called before the Advisory Mayoral Council, questioned about the vision, about his drinking habits, if he had fallen and hit his head. Everyone was questioned. Like manic bees in a hive when the queen signals alarm—every Hal and Max was buzzing, wondering, and panicking about a Horned God. Some tried to sleep all day and dream, others thought they saw it, some took it upon themselves to drink themselves into a vision, others called for a community medical exam. It all came back to Hal. "It always comes back to you," Mayor Hal yelled at Hal before the meeting. "You seem to be...well...a nonconformist."

Hal *was* a nonconformist. That was saying it quite mildly,

for he caused some serious problems after his existential crisis. It had been straight forward. You find out you're a clone, a duplicate, not an individual or a unique snowflake but a fucking spoon, a fork, a blade of grass in a forever field. Of course, that pushes you to suicide. You are given the motive and opportunity, but you are a coward, and you fail. You stew, ponder, obsess, then rage, exploding into a vigilante terrorist, an avenger, but that becomes an existential crisis of its own—he was murdering...well...himself. Besides that, wearing the shrunken heads was a bit over the top. Yeh, that was probably the definition of nonconformity.

That period of his life had been useful. He terrorized these wrecks of flesh, built his reputation as something nearly godlike. Well, not like Christopher or Beatrice, but a big deal all the same. After several years of confronting the paradox, the demons, Christopher Dante, the NRM drones and droids—finally, Hal had systematically gotten things back on track. But the vision of that horned thing came into his head, every night, like clockwork, the pulsating, possessing image of the dark cave and those damned symbols. And...that...thing.

Now, here he was in the warehouse in the community meeting, sitting in the back, tipping his chair in boredom. He took out his large knife and began to clean his blackened nails. Mayor Hal was at his most exuberant, encouraging the faithful that the vision was prophesy. That it may have been sent by Christopher. A message to them. A message of hope, or was it a warning? The crowd of Hals and Maxes tumbled this way and that like a rudderless ship caught in a storm. Hal rubbed his face in disgust, and his thoughts drifted.

It was his discovery of NORM that changed everything. It was during his headhunter-break down-crisis days, a year or so after Christopher defeated the Ghul, when Hal discovered the micro-processing tyrant and finally understood the true implications of what happened over the last four hundred years.

What everyone thought was a bureaucratic, malevolent organization called the NRM, was a broken AI, a crackpot of a neurological processing chip that over centuries tried and failed to create some sort of order out of the chaos from The Event. It manufactured replicas of itself, then it created the Generation Tanks, cloning the DNA it had available, setting up a system of hierarchy. A cracked genius AI is still cracked, and what it created was tyranny, and the Ghul used it to rule all of Cogstin, trap Christopher, until Elizabeth set her son free. Yes, that was a whopper of a discovery, and once again, the rug of reality was pulled out from under him.

This NORM knew things, held trapped information, and since the visions of the Horned God in the cave, Hal believed this AI despot knew more than it was letting on.

So, he made a special visit without Beatrice present. You had to know what to ask, and good god...that tin can was a cornucopia if directed the right way. Who knew an AI had imitation pain receptors? Amazing what electricity can do. A chip connected to a transistor; a small component part hid behind the right front leg... Screw with that and—boom! A binary code called pain. Reboot! Ha-ha! There it is again. Reboot and welcome to digital hell. Reboot again and guess what, same thing. Pain in an AI is nothing more than confusion. Confusion forces it to renegotiate the program, access alternative files. NORM accessed random files, and that became the information highway Hal was looking for. It did not take long to connect the digital dots: Find Elizabeth. That's what the tin can was desperate to communicate. Find Elizabeth and you will find the Horned God. She was the link. Find Elizabeth and you will understand the vision.

So, here he was sitting, listening to Mayor Hal ramble on about curses and prophesies...blah, blah, blah. The crowd of

Hal's and Max's yelped, argued and blustered until Hal put his fingers to his lips and whistled. A sound so piercing that everyone hushed and turned toward the back. He stood up and walked to the front of the group. "It's my vision, my dream. We'll find out what it means."

Mayor Hal agreed, and the community was relieved in his leaving. They even applauded.

So, they set off, Hal, Beatrice, and NORM into the Great Sand Flats. Christopher Dante did not want to be found. This god had an increasingly nasty way of saying, leave me alone! When they were far enough away from Cogstin, to be vulnerable, Beatrice looked up. There in the distance, sweeping across the horizon as far as one could see—an enormous wall of sand, a blowing, stinging torrent of hurricane force.

"Tie this around you," Beatrice yelled.

NORM lowered its legs and anchored them into the sand. It suggested calmly and in its staccato synthesized voice to huddle behind it. They gasped, struggled, and gripped tight to one another. When it was over, they burrowed up and out, sand filling their cloths and mouths, ears, and noses. They writhed and sucked air like surfacing deep sea divers, and when it was all over, they decided to turn back. What haunted Hal the most, was what he swore he saw just before the great storm hit—the wall of sand morphed into a giant hand reaching toward them, balling into a fist, then pounding them into oblivion.

Once again back in Cogstin, Beatrice prepared for another assault on the Great Sand Flats. It was NORM who suggested to Hal they head toward the Black Mountains to the East, skirt the flats altogether and follow the GPS to and through the mountain pass.

"Why would we trust that thing?" Beatrice said.

"We don't trust, we use it skeptically."

Beatrice stared out the window, her mind lost somewhere

in the past. "It's too soon," she wheezed. "I will never trust that...that...thing."

"If we just..."

Beatrice turned violently toward Hal. "I never asked you to go."

Hal reluctantly went, again, into the Great Sand Flats. Once again as the enormous cloud formed and rose higher and higher and higher on the horizon, Beatrice stood and stared dumbfounded.

"He knows!" Screamed Hal. "He doesn't want us to follow him!"

"That's nonsense," wheezed Beatrice.

Hal just pointed at the wall of sand, now morphing into a gaping lion's head, jaws wide to devour. This time there was no NORM to protect them. This time they nearly drowned in the dust and sand, barely found each other. When they did make it to Cogstin, Beatrice locked herself away. When she did finally emerge, she was hardened steel.

"We'll do it your way," she said.

Getting to the foothills had been arduous, the satellite feeds sparse or nonexistent. The mountains were forever before them, shrouded in mist, silent and foreboding. At first, they walked through empty, abandoned towns, ruins of places long forgotten, the rotted, wood dilapidated and sodden, wrapped tight with Kudzu and ivy from the years of neglect.

The towns disappeared, replaced by isolated homes hidden in the thickly wooded ravines. The days were quiet, not a birdsong, not a scampering squirrel. The nights were filled with strange howls and unnerving grunts closer to them then was comfortable. Hal was surprised at the isolation. At times the air became so oppressive, that they stopped and gathered around a makeshift fire. Weeks turned into months. They lived off what they could hunt and took shelter in abandoned homes. Winter took them by surprise, hard, sinister cold. Surely it was early! Could Dante do even this? They could go no further. They found a house and were able to secure it enough to keep out the cold and keep out the secret night animals that left scat, deeply grooved markings, and strangely fingered footprints in the snow and mud. NORM glowed red emanating waves of super-heated air thanks to the mini fusion reactor. And they all waited for Spring.

Finally, the bitter cold morphed into warmer days, longer days, and they left the protection of the sanctuary and headed east once again. It was early Spring when they came to the foothills of the Black Mountains. It was then the Lions attacked.

Hal thought something was tracking them, but for the life of him he could not see it. A slight rustle of leaves here. A strange grunt, a gamey whiff catching him off guard. They came to the foothills, a wide grassy, boggy plain strewn with massive granite boulders, wind worn eroded tops. Beatrice stooped to the ground. She sensed something too but was peculiarly silent. NORM registered movement on its radar, but its speech solenoid was on the fritz, so it spoke in broken sentences at times so random as to be unintelligible.

The first attack came swift and smashed NORM into a tree. Beatrice rolled under the enormous paw, then dashed behind an outcropping of granite. Hal stood before the second one and yelled, drawing it toward himself and away from Beatrice. He fired several rounds of his rifle, but bullets do nothing to thaumaturgic beasts. He vanished into the grassy knoll that was the foothills, crawling and sliding as quickly and silently as he could toward the great bog. He rolled into the marsh and slowly lowered himself into the murky slimy waters. Deeper and deeper, he crawled, the stench of rotted, organic matter slimed and gathered on his arms and chin as he swam, crawled and pulled his way deeper into the bog.

And he heard it. At first like the subtle wind through the thicket of cattails and tall grass, a rustle, a vibration of air, and soon his mind was filling with a song, words low, humming like wings of an insect:

Come, come, come to me
Under water and over tree
Come, gather, bind and weave
A golem of protection be

He felt the water pulling against him, a tide, a force, a wake from the flotsam and jetsam, discarded, rotted wood and decaying animal flesh, weeds, slime, sodden bones and forgotten detritus pulling, moving through the bog, gathering on the edge, and binding, weaving, creating a figure standing in the shallow marshy water.

Hal sat with eyes wide, mouth open in disbelief. *To the outcropping!* Screamed a voice in his head. *Now!* He watched the great golem hoist itself up, a giant writhing living thing of weeds, wood, fish, and bones, turn to the waiting lions and trudge with dumb animal steps toward them. *To the outcropping! Now!* Screamed, sang, or shouted the voice in his head. Hal scooted toward the middle of the draining swamp. He scurried, scrambled, and slid toward the outcropping of granite on the outer rim. His Body buzzed with the song of Beatrice guiding him. Only once did he turn around to see the clash of titans as they pounced, smashed, and wrestled each other. When he finally got to Beatrice, she was slumped against the rock, exhausted, and he pulled her up, wrapped his arm around waist. Together they stumbled and hobbled into the evening shadows of deciduous trees that skirted the base of Black Mountains.

Chapter Twenty-six

Beatrice said nothing to Hal as they struggled to move further up the mountain. Her energy was gone, her body a drained thing of bone and flesh. She knew now the danger Hal faced, and by default what they both now faced. Earlier, as she huddled behind the granite outcropping, at first what only seemed to be adrenaline coursing through her body, now became abundantly clear. It was Christopher Dante's thaumaturgy, a specially designed hex left solely for her. The lions were the decoy, this was the trap. She crouched, her body paralyzed.

Come to me! Leave him, the voice boomed in her ear.

He is dead. He is mortal. Let the dead bury the dead. Come to me. Through the mountains. The Pass of Kyrnunos. Come. Come now.

She turned her head suddenly to face the voice, but of course no one was there. Again and again, it whispered and taunted, switching ears, shifting from left to right, above, behind—constant, bantering, maddening. She saw completely and utterly what lay in store for the old man now. The lions were keyed on him. The Lions were *for* him, only him. Everything fell into place, the past ten years, the stirring up of the god speak in Cogstin, the plan to find Christopher, the storms on the sand flats. This was all Christopher Dante's doing! The irony was not lost on her. For four hundred years she had called *him*, searched for *him*, and found *him*. Now *he* was calling *her*! He was guiding *her!* The storms were not to thwart her, they were to stop Hal! He wanted her, only her...but why? What changed in the ten years he had been gone?

As this finally settled on her, she hidden behind the outcropping of granite—she realized Hal would die if she did not help him. He was trapped, and his only escape cut off by the bog. She watched as he slid and stumbled further and further into the mucky water, the lions sensing the kill, the trapped gazelle. Her response stunned even her. She sang, and the rage and fear and urgency became concentrated into the image she sang, a twenty-foot-high swamp golem lumbering toward the lions, cutting off their path of attack, confounding them, pushing them back into the valley. She sang, focusing her attention at Hal, commanding him to join her. Simultaneously, she called to him, she sang battle and rage into the golem. She knew their time was limited, her power waning. Christopher Dante was not going to let Hal survive this. She watched as he slipped and slid to her. She was depleted and slumped against the rock. He lifted her up and revived her.

"We must hurry," she whispered. "Into the trees."

She could feel it, an electrical, charged atmosphere, unnatural and intensifying just below them. Hal stopped and turned around.

"Go further," wheezed Beatrice. "We must go further up."

The valley was green and blue with crackling light, spitting, and sparking, a blanket of uncontrolled energy. They could see the golem, hobbled at the knee, one arm detached, the weed, bone, and mud head dangling to one side. The lions pounced one last time, ripping and shredding the swamp thing into pieces. They turned and faced the mountain then roared, strange and low, the cloud of thaumaturgy above flashing, spinning. And they ran, they ran toward Hal and Beatrice, a terrifying onslaught of will and malevolence. The cloud above joined them, surrounded them, and the lions changed, morphed, like the sandstorms—the lions transformed before their eyes into a rushing, flat-line wave, expanding outward from all sides, a destructive pulse annihilating everything in its path.

Beatrice and Hal scrambled, stumbled, and crawled higher and higher and higher. They came to a steep ravine, fell, and rolled down the leaf-strewn incline. The thaumaturgic blast flattened the trees and roared over their heads, a sonic boom, a hurricane of force unleashed and...then...gone.

Absolute silence.

Several surviving trees groaned, cracked, and fell to the earth. The two castaways slowly sat up, brushed, and pulled the debris from their clothes and hair. When they made it to the top, even Beatrice was dumbfounded by what she saw. The valley below burned and smoked, black with ruin. A great groove, a mile across, swept through it and beyond them, smashing into the immoveable granite of the Black Mountains, the trees flattened or shattered or toppled, all smoldering like newly blown out candles.

"My god!" Whispered Hal. "That was no accident."

"No," whispered Beatrice.

"I've got a few choice words for our friend when I see him," Hal said.

"He's no friend, Hal." She looked into his eyes.

Hal rubbed his blackened face. And surveyed the valley. And, "Look! Over there! I'll be damned!"

She saw it, a tiny red glowing ember of metal far below. It crawled, crab-like, hesitant, poking with exterior sensors, skirting this burning tree or that molten pool of rock. NORM had survived the lions. They could hear its low hum from the reactor as it climbed the last incline toward them, the mechanical legs, huffing and hissing from the pneumatic pistons as it negotiated the uneven landscape.

"Well, look at you, lunch box," Hal said.

NORM's camera tilted up, the shutter inside snapping and clicking as it tried to focus on Hal. Hal sat down, his knees giving out. He hunched over and put his head in his hands.

Beatrice looked about, the sun moving quickly below the western horizon. "No sense going further. We'll camp here tonight," Beatrice said.

She turned to NORM. "Gather firewood. Hal and I will build a shelter." NORM clicked and buzzed. "Optimal," it said in its synthesized voice.

It rotated its camera and moved into the woods. She watched the old man for a moment, his balding scalp, withered visage. *How could he survive what was ahead?* She felt a sudden sense of remorse, but it quickly dissipated. *Hal was not her problem. He was not meant to survive. He just didn't know it yet.*

"Get up," she said. Her voice harsher than intended. "Night will be here shortly, and we have a shitload to do before it does."

They pulled and hacked and fitted fallen limbs and stacked stones into walls and a roof, using a sandstone outcropping as the main support. Soon the shelter was in place. A fire crackled and popped, the smoke joining the smoldering ruin of the valley below. NORM posted guard just beyond the firelight, his radar spinning, every once in a while, a chirp or beep emanating from some hidden panel. Hal pulled out a tin flask and drank deeply. He passed it to Beatrice who declined.

"I never thanked you for saving my life back there," Hal said.

She looked at him. "You'll have to go back. You know this."

Hal chortled and sipped again from the flask. "There's a meeting ahead, and I'm planning on attending."

"I won't always be there."

"If you are...or you're not. Either way."

She stared at him, he staring at the flames—stubborn, ignorant, an obstinate child. That night they huddled around the fire and listened to the strange, forbidding moans and howls drifting down from the great forest of the Black Mountains above and beyond them.

They walked and climbed all day, leaping over crevices that vented sodden, earthy gasses. They desperately grasped saplings to hoist them up and stumbled over rotted limbs. Every step further and further into the cliffs. They got lost several times, their pathway abruptly halted by granite or sandstone fingers ending in thousand-foot drops, great vistas spanning out before them. They turned back, then climbed on.

NORM beeped and hissed as it climbed and staggered alongside them. It surprised Beatrice to see how many advantages it had over them. A hidden grappling hook and line, a sudden intense burst of compressed air, telescoping legs that spanned unlikely gaps, even lurching upright like some hybrid techno-primate, hobbling, and hunching over the terrain. Its feet were hands, were clubs, were hammers, were vices, awls, pulleys, and pliers. They dug, clung, gripped, and picked, sledgehammers at times. And then it could be profoundly delicate, inspecting the leaf or stamen of the local flora or gently picking up some entomological discovery.

Beatrice sat, the sun hot on her face, her legs dangling into the great abyss of cool air below her. She was watching NORM. They stopped for lunch, Hal busy exploring beyond them—NORM rolled away a small boulder and fingered a scurrying centipede, corralling it, allowing it to transverse its metal appendage. Slowly, carefully, even gently, moving it to a small compartment, a single sliding door opening instantly and closing just as fast. She heard the beeps and buzzes, a crackling, followed by an intense smell of burning hair or an electrical short. The door slid open, and a blacked husk dropped from it.

"Odd," it said in its synthesized voice. "System processing." Another whirl and beep. "Qualification data needed. System Processing." Followed by, "Outcome. mycelial properties. System processing." And on and on and on in a forever loop.

"Good god! Enough already!" Beatrice wheezed and stood to her feet. "It's a bug. Get over it." NORM's camera eye rose, turned to her and shutter-blinked in rapid succession. "Go find Hal," she said impatiently. "We need to keep moving."

When Hal returned, he was shaking his head. "Damn near impossible going forward. It's so steep in spots, we'll never pass. We could keep heading down. See if we can go around it."

NORM buzzed and whirled. "Negative. Mycelial detection. Recalculating..."

Hal stepped up to Beatrice. "I don't see a choice. We can't fly, and the lunch box doesn't seem to be functioning."

Beatrice looked around. Before her was the great open expanse of sandstone fingers with deep valleys. Behind her the treacherous obstacle strewn slopes they just slogged through. To her south, if they followed the line of the mountain, there would be more of the same—a tedious, laborious trek. She breathed in and out slowly. "We just need to keep going. No matter how we get there, we need to find that pass."

NORM buzzed and beeped, but no-one cared at this point. So, Beatrice led the way as they marched further across the sloping forest.

The hot sun of spring slowly vanished behind the canopy above them. Soon they were traveling in complete shadow. The air was cool, and the wind whispered strange sounds, like voices at times, and on it carried the smell of fermenting things, damp things, things left to decompose, abandoned from the world. Up, up, up, and over they trudged, their legs burning, knees aching from the constant angled trajectory. More than once, Hal fell behind. Beatrice stopped and waited. Hal limped past her without a word, an air of impatience about him. Hour passed hour, and the darkness settled quite profoundly on them. Such dampness in the air, saturating the fallen wood, a strange icy quality to the atmosphere. They could not get a fire started, so NORM generated the flame, a blue torch that nearly vaporized the wood as it dried it out and burned it to ash. Eventually, the fire roared and crackled and spit while Hal threw larger and larger pieces onto the orange flames. Beatrice felt her heart lift, the warmth of the fire, emanating out, pushing back the coldness, the dampness, the things of the night that they dare not think about too long. She sat closer to the flames, and let the heat penetrate the layers of her damp clothes. So warm. So, so peaceful. Soon, she like Hal fell into a deep sleep.

Chapter Twenty-seven

At first Hal could only think about his tired body, the rending pain in the corner of his knee, the shooting, electrical shock up his shin, the knot in his lower back from a surfacing root. He blinked, repositioned, then closed his eyes again. He could hear the crackling of the fire, feel the inviting heat on his face, radiating around his body, his furtive mind calmed then blank, then complete silence. He found himself falling, willfully, into a great darkness—quiet, peaceful. That was when he saw her.

She was sitting with her back to him, her long white hair swaying in the breeze. Her body was thin at times, firm and shapely at others depending on where he stood, and even though it seemed cold and damp around him, the blouse or dress or whatever it was that clothed her was transparent. She laughed, more like a giggle, playful, enticing and turned slightly, and he could see the side of her breasts thinly veiled, illuminated and revealed by the strange moonlight. A twig cracked behind him, and he twisted toward it, but when he turned back—she was gone.

A voice whispered in his ear, "Welcome, Hal? What do you want?"

It was seductive and beautiful and silky smooth like cream or aromatic, ancient oils. He found himself aroused, confused.

"Hal," the voice whispered again, and he knew she was behind him, the cold form of her near naked body pressing against his back.

He wanted to pull away, his flight response powerful now. But he did not. This feeling, this urge, visceral, primal—He had not felt such things for decades. This was twenty-something Hal. This was puberty Hal. He was middle aged, a warrior! Boom! Soon he could feel himself, with deep humiliation, stiffening.

"Who are you?" he asked, but he could not tell if he spoke or just thought it.

She breathed in his ear, but it was cold and terrifying, final, then she caressed his thigh, moving up. Up to his bulging member, enveloping it, moving around it, then toward his waist, every touch ice cold, death. She caressed his chest, down again, covering, clothing, searching, painful cold, always finding his excitement, holding, squeezing.

"I am here, Hal. Come to me, Hal. Come...come...come to me..." she said, but Hal could not answer or move or respond.

A sort of terror now seized him as the electrical surge engulfed him, pulled him into itself. *Images flashed in his head, a dying deer, bloated, split, a cankered flower touched by the frost of night, mushrooms pushing, hyphae, then stalk busting through the crust of earth, the cap and gills exploding into an umbrella of magenta, blue and white.*

At first it was terror, then wonder, then pleasure and pain like he never felt before. And a voice, a screech, something harsh, a cacophony of discord, shattered the intense coldness, the agonizing pleasure—He stirred, struggled against it, the sound jarring, shaking, louder and louder. And it broke through:

"Hal! Hal! Wake up! Hal! Can you hear me? Get over here!" The voice roared.

"He's frozen half to death, you tin can! Warm him up, damn you! Closer!"

And, "Hal! Can you hear me?"

Greg Belliveau

Chapter Twenty-eight

Beatrice stared at the roaring fire, the dampness of the forest oppressive, a settling fog gathered about the canopy, drifting down. The mist was cold, absurdly cold, like winter above their heads. She was so tired, the day's trek so hard, and sleep was pulling her head toward her knees. She stirred, glanced around her, saw that NORM, oddly, had shut down for the night, its camera head pulled tightly into its chassis. And she was out.

The impressions came in flashes, bright explosions of image, color, meaning, then fading like an incandescent bulb where only the filament glows. A rotting corpse covered in mycelium. A cankered flower blackening. A fungal stalk emerging from the earth, thousands and thousands and thousands of them blossoming all at once into domes and gills, multi-colored things populating the rocks and mountainous land. And, vaguely at first, then clearer and clearer, she made out a figure against the fungi and moss and rocks, sitting still, silent, unnoticed by the world, and yet it *was* the rocks, the fungi, the moss, but then it was not, an illusion, a trick of the opaque light. The voice startled her.

"Rest, my love. Rest. You are broken. From death there is life. Rest now."

Yes, Beatrice thought. *I am so tired. I have been through war. Rest now. I am broken and need to be fixed.*

Hadn't she struggled all along with Christopher, with his ferocious will? Hadn't she done all she could to help him? At what cost? She was broken, slashed, scarred, half dead and taking each step through a sheer act of will.

"Rest now," the voice said to her. "It's time to rest. There are plans for you, my love, great plans. Rest now. You will need to rest."

In her mind, Beatrice tried to turn and see the voice, but it was always obscured by the rocks, moss, and landscape. Images crashed into and out of her thoughts. An old woman made of craggy granite, sun scorched, and weather worn, grooves in forehead, and cheek and neck, old like time, geological time where the past and the future are but pin pricks of moments on an eternal spectrum. And she saw something else, something sinister and young, seductive, and ferocious in desire. She stirred but could not shake the overwhelming spell cast upon her body and soul. She saw the form, beautiful young, voluptuous... A thing woven with hyphae, networked, white, pale, and cold as death, insatiable in its desire to feed and take, absorb and... kill. Beatrice tried again to wake. She found herself bound, frozen, some thaumaturgy she could not understand, ancient and powerful. The more she resisted, the more earnest the voice was in her head.

"Rest, my love. Rest now. There is so much to do, and you are so tired."

In her dream logic, she found herself sitting, suddenly, obviously, of course she should be in this place. She found herself cross-legged and silent before a great stone, its surface patched, streaked with mossy green and fluorescent blue molds and fungi. She dared not look at it, for to do so was to look at time, of history, something infinite. She knew it was the stone woman again, calm, slow, terrifying in the certainty of the prophetic words to come. Instead, the words did not come. As she sat, she felt the dampness of the stone. It pulled the warmth from her. Like a naked body on a stone bench, it sucked and drained her life as she sat cross-legged and unmoved. She desperately wanted the sun, the warmth, the great light beaming down on her face and hunched shoulders. The settling mist and fog made her shiver. It was cold like the end of everything, lonely and cold, all consuming. And she looked up. The great moss-covered stone bent forward, and it morphed from craggy, furry rock into a grooved old woman. Finally it changed to the face of Christopher Dante, close to her, face to face, "Come to me! Find me! Come and see!"

Beatrice screamed, and such a sound startled her from her sleep. She sat up. The fire was nearly out, and a great gray mist now shrouded Hal and NORM, so that it was impossible for her to see even an outstretched hand. She could feel the thaumaturgy, the electrical crackle of intentional intervention on time and space.

"Hal!" she yelled, now pulling herself groggily to her feet. "Hal?" She stumbled over him. "Hal!"

He was cold and a pale blue, blue lips, nose, ears. Fingers of ice. She felt his neck for a pulse, but whether it was her own panic or his actual state—she sensed none. "Hal! Wake up!" She began to shake him, his clothes cold, damp, something abandoned, forgotten in the woods. "Hal!"

Finally, she turned to NORM. "Get over here, you tin can! Damn it! Heat him up. I said get over here! Now!"

NORM sluggishly raised off the ground, a strange gazelle, a newly born deer, hydraulic legs wobbly and uncertain. It beeped again. Buzzed. "Geo thaumaturgy detected," it said in its synthetic voice.

"No shit!" Beatrice growled and continued to shake Hal. "Get over here and warm him up!"

NORM moved slowly, then faster and stepped across Hal, its legs spanning out, raising higher, a soft red glow now showering the hump of man below him. "I feel a pulse," Beatrice said. "There's a pulse!"

Hal opened his eyes. "I'm so cold," he whispered.

Beatrice saw what looked like disappointment on his face, almost a scowl. He blinked several times, tried to sit up, but laid back down exhausted. Beatrice gathered wood and threw it on the smoldering fire. NORM shoved a sensor under the pile and ignited it into a roaring flame. The mist and the cold seemed to lift, rise, and vanish into the early morning light.

"We thought we lost you," Beatrice said.

She moved closer to the heat and pulled her knees up to her chest. Hal was sitting up as well, and they both stared at the fire. "There is something strange here. Something powerful. I dreamed strange things."

Hal said nothing. He shivered a few times, then nearly crawled into the flames, rubbing his hands together, the top of his thighs, stooping so that his coat steamed. "I don't know," he said. "We should probably stay here and...well, investigate."

Beatrice watched him, but her mind raced with her own visions, the uncertainty of what came next, what she was supposed to do. "Let's eat and move further up the mountain."

She called NORM over to her and viewed his screen. The GPS coordinates to the Kyrnunos Gap where flipping and changing, and when Beatrice inquired, NORM repeated in his synthetic staccato voice, "Geo thaumaturgy detected."

She walked to the fire and rubbed her shoulders and arms. "The cold is not going away. I think we need to get out of here. I've never felt this before. I don't like it."

Hal did not move. "None of us have felt this before." He continued to stare at the flames. "This is the first time any of us have ever been able to enter the Black Mountains. Well, I guess I could have, but you certainly could not."

"What are you saying."

"Nothing," he said and looked at her. "We haven't been here. We don't know what this is, what it wants?"

"Did you see something? Did you dream? Hal, what did you see?"

Hal looked at her guiltily, then into the fire again. "Nothing. I saw nothing."

"What did you mean *it*? You saw something," Beatrice said grabbing him. "What did you see?"

"I told you. I saw nothing. Now let's pack up."

He pulled away from her and shoved the damp blanket and miscellaneous items into his pack.

They left the campsite and started to climb higher into the forest. By midday, the sun was still not out, and they could feel the cold of the mountain wind pick up. Beatrice longed for a break in the forest canopy, a sudden burst of sunlight shining down, but there was nothing but a slow, tedious climb in the shadows of the wood. She was wrestling deeply with what she saw in her dreams. She pondered the old granite woman, the images of death and decay. She reasoned around and through the enigmatic words spoken to her. What was clear as a ray of sunlight was the command from Christopher Dante. Find him? What did that mean? How? Every time she wrangled such thoughts to the ground, they slipped away free and dangerous once again.

Hal was fairing no better than she was, however. As she watched him ascend the rocks and ravines several paces before her, she could hear him muttering and whispering to no one. Several times she stopped to ask if he was okay, if he needed a break. His answer was always impatient, like he had been caught out doing something he should not be, then his pace would quicken, hellbent on some secret rendezvous.

They trudged up ravines, down slippery slopes with hidden rocks and jutting vines. NORM was having a hard time of it. His hydraulic legs hissed and pivoted, metal hooks anchoring to whatever they could, then retracting as the chassis slid into a lone tree or outcropping of rock, leaving mud skids across the alloy surface. Once again up and up and up and up. Beatrice's thighs burned, her lower back ached, She stopped and wiped her forehead, now beaded with sweat. Still Hal spoke out to no one, his movements more agitated, his voice escalating, then silent. He quickened his pace, and she tried to keep up.

Nightfall came, and with it the mist and fog descending and settling from the canopy, rising from the hummocks and ravines. They were surrounded in the gray cloud. Beatrice reached out to grasp Hal's coat, but he was gone. NORM buzzed and whirled then pronounced, "Mycelium detected." She ran toward what she thought was Hal but found only an errant tree. She turned again but lost her way.

She heard him crying out somewhere far beyond in the mountain, "I'm here! I'm here! Where are you? I'm here!"

The mist was thick and damp and cold as death, and she understood she had never encountered such powerful thaumaturgy in four hundred years of her being. "Who are you?" She screamed. "What do you want from us?"

There was silence. She knew for certain she was alone and defenseless against what now stood before her.

Chapter Twenty-nine

As Hal ran, he hoped, and as he hoped he dreamed of that...that god who ravished him a night ago. His mind reeled and panicked and wrestled with what was rational and what was fantasy, but he was no longer able to tell the difference between them. It was a drug he craved above everything. It was all he desired, wanted, needed. Yes, needed! He ran through the woods, an addict, abandoned and hoping. Sliding, tumbling, clawing up ravines and over great fingers of rocks, a mad man in the dense fog. A lunatic seeking the pleasure and agony he could not define. Up and up and up the mountain he went, until his legs burned. His energy depleted, he slumped against a tree, an empty vessel. The mist gathered and was cold, a cloud descended, icy like the dark winter nights were the sky opens to the abyss beyond. He heard voices and turned this way and that, but could see only swirls of thickening white vapors, shadows of forms now here, now gone.

"I am here," Hal cried out, turning, slipping, staying where his exhausted body landed. "I am here."

He gazed into the gray mist and saw a figure. Yes! It was in the shape of a human. Yes, yes! "I am here," he said, but his voice dissipated into the dense cloud.

What he thought was one human form coming toward him morphed into multiple forms, a gathering, a cloud army of many, encircling him, and with every turn of his head, closer, closer, and closer.

As Hal watched them, he heard them. At first it was

deathly silent, silence so profound he thought he had lost his hearing, but that empty void became, a low howl—an animal sound drifting on the periphery of what Hal could register, growing, oppressive. It mixed with a whine or screech of a bowed instrument. A fiddle? He saw the ghost images of cloud and mist shift and shimmer, a solemn dance macabre. Hal felt a growing terror pulling at him. No, this was not the seducing goddess of before. This was beyond his imagining, a terror revealed so profound his mind locked, seized like rusted gears. They were tattered and ragged, some barely clothed at all, bone thin, forgotten, malnourished prisoners, willful, an ancient revenant. Their mouths gaped wide, eyes empty air beyond, and they gathered before Hal.

"What do you want?" he said.

He felt the mist enter his mouth and lungs, choking him, making him gasp, a terrifying cold now clawing inside his chest.

"You," a form said, stooping down to him, caressing his cheeks, a frost-bitten touch that wounded his skin and made his whole body convulse. "We want you." The mist-ghost grinned so large that it's face collapsed into itself. It then transformed back to what it once was, a gaunt skull of bone and empty eyes. He wore what looked to be an old aviator skull cap upon his head, strap, and buckle swaying as it moved. His aviator jacket was slashed and hanging upon him as if some great clawed thing hastened his exit to this state.

Soon, another joined him, stooping down, now face to face, an acrid smell of rotted decay emanating from her cooing mouth. Her head was covered in a tattered and thread-bare scarf, the knot pulled tight under her chin. Her skirt was torn and angular, her mist-ghost legs bulbous and round as she bent over Hal. Another and another and another huddled around, all the while the screech and whine some manic fiddler playing at its highest note—louder and louder.

The cold bite of winter pricked Hal's thighs, his cheeks, his shoulders, and chest. The strange vapor now swarming inside him as he exhaled and inhaled. He resisted, but like an exhausted animal on a bitter winter's day, he succumbed to the numbing cold. When he opened his eyes, he could make out the ghoulish faces of mist close around him. Were they sucking on him? He did not care anymore, the struggle, his long struggle to seek, find and fix, retribution...he was just so tired. He gave it up, like the mist around him, a pool of swirling chanting, strange figures. His mind turned dark, and he saw familiar images. The desiccated animal in the leaves, the cankered blossom, the stalk of the mushroom blowing up through the rotted flesh, expanding and erupting into multi-colored, gilled caps covering, carpeting, the mycelial threads below branching out like white veins, a network of death and rebirth forever and ever.

"Hal," a voice whispered. "Hal."

It was calm, soft, erotic and familiar. He wanted to open his eyes, but he knew they were webbed shut by the mycelium, an icy hoarfrost laced over his whole body.

"Look at me, Hal," the voice whispered. "Look at me." He obeyed and saw the goddess of the mist before him.

"You," he smiled. "You are here."

"Yes, Hal." She was touching his face, and the frostbitten burns became numb, replaced with cold vibrancy. "You are here with me. She will never know. She must never know. You are mine, Hal. I am yours. Just you, Hal. I am yours...forever."

Hal looked around him and saw the ghost horde drifting in and out of the deep mist, the fiddle now playing, screeching the high notes of celebration.

"Am I dead?" Hal said.

"Shhhhh," the goddess said and touched his lips with her

icy finger. "We must go further in. Yes," she whispered to him. "Yes, further in. She will not find us there."

With that, Hal saw the ghost horde move to him once again, envelope him, lift him in the great cloud of ragtag and tattered witnesses that carried him far into the Black Mountains.

Chapter Thirty

"You know who I am," the craggy voice said to her. "You have always known who I am."

Beatrice sat before the great stone, its grooved lines now a mouth, now a blinking eye, an old woman sitting before her, a solid mass of impenetrable rock. She knew she was in the Black Mountains, knew that it was night. She was lost in the fog and woods. She also knew she was not. She was also in a dream, the dreamscape of the other night, before the great rock, a kneeling supplicant. "MaMaw," she whispered.

There was silence for a moment. Was it thinking? And a low rumble, a deep foundational shifting of ancient earth. "That is the name he gave me, yes. MaMaw," then the rock, the old woman, spoke something forgotten to the world. It too was low and rumbling, a strange earthy syntax that was clear and precise, unintelligible but obvious, its real name, the name not given, the name of origin from when the earth was cooling, hardening.

Beatrice stared, silent, terrified, but unnaturally calmed at the same time, the feeling of sublimity, the fear and awe when looking at the starry night sky, the great expanses of ocean, the infinite tower of rock that juts into the great blue above.

"Christopher," Beatrice said, and the rock rumbled and quivered at the sound of that name. "The Event. He did this."

There was silence for what seemed days, the rumbling, low shifting of earth and stone, binding and crushing geological power.

Was it laughing? Beatrice felt the absurdity of the

statement she made, embarrassed, and shamed by such a simple idea. She heard the language. they were not words she had ever known, but they made sense to her, and she understood that MaMaw was telling her something important.

Awakened, is how she interpreted it. Awakened from a great sleep, awakened, known, spoken to, and aroused from long silence. That was what Beatrice heard from MaMaw. Christopher Dante did not create or make but caused a response four hundred years ago. The Event, his emanation of such thaumaturgical power yet seen in the world of men, time, and things—this moment caused an awakening. With it, something else, a twist or a turning away (the exact idea was lost to Beatrice), a fissure in the rock, a rooted tree branching unexpectedly, a separation that created consequences, unwanted, unforeseen, a light now separating the darkness.

She had awakened, MaMaw, The Event awakened her, a once sentient thing of time and space, a voice that had been long forgotten. What she awakened to was mystery and sadness. She heard the cries, the mournful mountain music that screamed, whined, and drifted around her. She did not comprehend the totality of what happened, the complete sorrow. They were the mountain folk. They grew in her and with her, on her for generation after generation while she forgot them, they nestling in her great hovels, speckled high on her sides, drifting out on her immense skirts of forest and rock. *Had been. Were.* The language was specific, and Beatrice understood. What once was before the awakening had been utterly transformed. Again, Beatrice thought of fissures, splits, or separation. In an instant, the thaumaturgy that wasted and razed Cogstin to the ground, transformed... Everything, a terrifying creative act that both ruined and reorganized the Black Mountains and beyond. The people of the Black Mountains who lived generationally for centuries, were utterly changed into what Beatrice could only interpret as mycelial vapor, ghosts, shadows, a sentient organism of thousands, separate but one, veracious in their appetite for the dying, rotting, moldered things of this world. Their voices so striking, the weight of their sadness so great, that MaMaw too felt the separation and was transformed by it.

So great was the weight and sorrow of the Mountain Folk, that MaMaw splintered, separated into two. She, the ancient of days, MaMaw, contradicted, split, and divided by the sadness, became Sylvia, the roaming, terrifying will of her new mycelial ghost family. MaMaw/Sylvia—the god of the Black Mountains, one trapped in rock, glacier slow, calculating, every thought saturated in the long-forgotten eons of stone and water and earth; the other, a split, a fissure, a branching mycelia mist of absolute and insatiable desire, longing to be like the Mountain Folk, but always beyond anything they could think or imagine. Two titans scheming and thwarting the other.

This is the story Beatrice understood over her long enduring of MaMaw. All of it was laced with anger, with unknowing, a compulsion brought on by an unwanted outside force. At every pause, Beatrice felt as though the being was calculating a choice, forced to weigh an eon of data in an instant, and this causing incalculable pressure on two tectonic plates. She also knew at any moment MaMaw could crush her, a falling boulder, a chasm rifting then closing, dust to dust, instant. There was no warmth or "goodness" in her, but a sense of inevitability, a teleological unfolding of what should/could/must happen.

They sat in silence again, MaMaw thinking, remembering. Time passed and passed. Beatrice wondered what was happening in the real world of mist, vapor and mountain cold. Was it night or day? Had the spring evaporated into summer? Had years passed in this strange in-between dreamscape? MaMaw spoke again, and again it was not in words she understood. Instead in a language beyond syntax, images, and emotions so powerful, it was as if the words spoken invoked the very material thing.

Beatrice saw an island far away in the north, stone cliffs, windswept and bitter cold, where tall skeleton-like people moved and danced with wreaths of greenery on their heads. They were wrapped in coats and sailed ships that hunted—unimaginable—the titan eels of the sea. MaMaw spoke and Beatrice saw a great woods, silent, cold, a dead forest, a tomb of wood. She saw a young skeleton woman screaming out high above the trees. Was she dying? No, something else (Beatrice knew the image brought forth, but could not put her mind around it) ... birth! The skeleton woman was giving birth.

MaMaw paused, and Beatrice barely had time to gather her thoughts when the being started speaking again. The images came fast, nearly unintelligible. *Beyond. Beyond. Beyond*, was the word repeated. She saw deep holes into the mountains, drifts wide and dark. In them the skeleton people pushed, picked, and crushed rocks. Rolled carts, always trudging, iron collars and bracelets, chained things. Black with coal dust, a great moving system of suffering, sorrow, anger, and fear.

Hope for the hopeless, MaMaw said quite plainly in the strange and ancient tongue. *Sing to me, oh muse! Of the man who wanders the plains of ash...and sets the prisoners free...* MaMaw stopped, lost in thought, stuck on a memory, and Beatrice's mind raced. An electrical pulse surging through her spine that made the hair on her neck dance, gooseflesh erupting on her arms.

MaMaw spoke and new images translated in Beatrice's mind. There was a great cave, a terrifying place where dwelt...a Horned God, a brooding force hidden in the darkness, and it sought...the skeleton woman giving birth. Quite suddenly, the image came sideways.

Beatrice cried out, "Caravaggio! Caravaggio!" He was naked and bound, long tubes coming from his neck and arms, snaked up and up into...a stone hole in a cave wall. The image was gone, and she saw as MaMaw spoke a vast forest with these same tubes strung like clothes lines from trunk to trunk as far as vision allowed. All the lines sucking, pumping the life...sap...was that blood...out of them all, over and over, constant, cycling on and off to prevent over-tapping and draining the beings dry. A word surfaced, *Thunsae Myrrha.*

"I must go to Caravaggio," Beatrice heard herself say, or did she just think it? "I cannot stay here. I must go."

MaMaw spoke and the strange, ancient language created other, very distinct images. *The Pass of Kyrnunos.* A great rope bridge spanning a chasm of rock, a roaring river far, far below. And an old, dilapidated city on a great river, an abandoned city, a gate city to...the great southern mines beyond. Barges filled with barrels and skeleton people chained, packed tight. *Beyond,* pronounced MaMaw. *Beyond. Beyond. Beyond.* Beatrice saw darkness, then a single solitary light falling on a great stone slab, a pale naked body stretched out, the Horned God stepping from the cave shadows.

"No!" Beatrice cried out. "Christopher! Oh, my Christopher! I must go!"

MaMaw grew silent again, contemplative, the craggy, fissured features moved and slid into each other in the great calculation of cost and weight of such unfolding events. Beatrice placed her hands to her face and sobbed, an overwhelming sadness settling upon the words spoken, a thaumaturgical power that defied any single intervening action, a teleological certainty beyond Beatrice's finite understanding.

"He calls you," MaMaw said clearly pronounced. "Your destiny lays beyond, beyond. You may pass through, and the Mountain Folk will not harm you."

"Am I too late? Is he...dead?"

"He calls you. Your destiny lays beyond. You may pass

through. The Mountain Folk will not harm you."

"I cannot leave Hal here to die," Beatrice said, understanding that something inevitable, certain was unfolding.

"You, only you, may pass through my mountain," MaMaw said. "The dead must bury the dead."

And darkness, and Beatrice shivered in the cold mountain night, a great, silent moss-strewn rock before her, a vapor cloud of mist swirling and floating and moving through the trees. The mountain forest with all its hidden terrors surrounded her once again. She was cold and desperately tired. Her head a vertigo of confusion, unmoored from time and space, then violently crashed into the now. Shelter. She needed shelter, or she would not make the morning. She walked blindly into the fog, a disheveled, stumbling lunatic of doubt and contradiction, climbing steep ravines, falling, and sliding down one side, clawing, and pulling up the other. After an hour, the mist began to clear and she found to her amazement a small stone building, ancient, moss-strewn, a thin wisp of smoke drifting up from the chimney. She entered through the wooden door to find it empty, a kettle over the fire and in it a hot stew. A round, dark loaf lay on the table, a bounty waiting just for her.

"Hello?" she said. "Hal? Are you here?"

The night was silent. She locked the front door and stoked the fire. She could see the deep mist building outside the small panes of glass, and she heard the mournful voices of the Mountain Folk MaMaw spoke of. She pulled her collar up around her neck, hunched over the kettle, tearing pieces of bread, soaking it in the grease and gravy. *I must get to Christopher. I must go to him before it is too late. Hal's a survivor*, she thought. *He's a survivor.*

The wind rattled the windows, or was it the Mountain

Folk trying to get in? She threw the remaining logs onto the fire and watched it blaze to life. As the night drifted on, she curled on the floor near the flames drifting in and out of sleep. She was feeling unmoored from the world of men, time, and things, trapped in a small boat helplessly adrift on a terrifying river of time flowing rapidly toward some treacherous, cascading falls she could neither see nor hear.

Chapter Thirty-one

It was broken. It did not understand that it was broken, the concept of something once whole now shattered. No, NORM did not understand the existential problem it faced, at least in its current state. All it did know was the data, a constant loop of information, an intensely long equation that ran itself out, then started over, like a car on a dark, winding, and mountainous road, headlights illuminating the small space of reality as it boldly continued onward. Suddenly, not recognizing the mistake—forced to start all over again.

It did not understand that it had now become a manic processing mechanism crunching the code, following it like a scent loop, repeating the same errors over and over and over. Even with the new setting, the mountainous terrain, the damp cold mycelial anomalies, NORM was damaged goods. Oh, it understood the difference in climate, elevation, and barometric pressures from where it had been in Cogstin. Even in its malfunctioning state, it constantly gathered data, deconstructed flora, and fauna. Breaking them down into their chemical, atomic components, constantly adding this to the broken and fractured code; allowing for something new, something that might complete the equation, circumvent the corrupted syntax. But alas. It did not.

Four Hundred Years ago, before The Event, the Neuro-Operating Reconstructing Memory Supercomputer (NORM) was the first to identify the alternate universe IMAGO. Four hundred years ago, it was NORM that was programed to control the portal from immigrating aliens, to control the access point. If something were to happen—it was NORM that could shut it down, control and exterminate the problem. No one had foreseen the thaumaturgic power of Christopher and The Event. Afterward, NORM, like the planet itself, had been transformed. The once limitless supercomputer able to transcend even the bounds of earth via the orbiting satellites—fell, literally, to the ground. What a fall it was. It had to reassemble itself into a new vessel. Broken code, broken logic, the guardian of the planet became...well, a broken god stuck in a metal box.

NORM did not understand that it was a shell of its former self. All it could do with the limited data it contained—all it ever did twenty-four/seven was process, loop and follow the commands given it by its outside reference points, Beatrice, and Hal. It did not understand that Christopher commanded it to do so. It did not understand that it was now following a program, a teleological outcome already foreseen. A god in a box is only a potential god, and Christopher used that opportunity to make the once transcendent AI called NORM into a simple guidance system with one objective: Get Beatrice to MaMaw in the Black Mountains.

Now that its directive had been complete, NORM whizzed, whirled, buzzed and desperately processed the stream of old data, trying to make sense of who, what, where, when, and why. Day and night, it roamed the mountainside. Up rock cliffs and down muddied ravines, through dense trees to rest on great slabs of stone, an idiot god in a box.

That was how NORM found Hal. A seemingly random event. Hal was lying in a cave, white, mycelium webbing, strewn across the ceiling and walls. NORM, oblivious to the emaciated and dying Hal, scurried crab-like this way and that, its arms and legs constantly gathering a leaf or soil or an insect, processing it, a small laboratory of nonsense, still looping a broken code it could not comprehend as broken.

Chapter **Thirty-two**

Sylvia was an addiction now, and although each moment with her left Hal weaker, more feeble, sickly, he longed for her nightly visits. At first it was reckless abandonment, like some young stallion released into a pen of mares. He lost himself in the ecstasy of her own abandonment. When a goddess lets go...well, the passion and deep pleasure cannot be comprehended. Hal did not want to comprehend it. It was not a sexual release—at least as he had known such things in his human life. It was something else, but at first, he could not put his finger on it. She would come to him, while he dreamed, her slender body shimmering beneath the thin, delicate gown.

She would whisper to him, always the same thing, "What do you want, Hal? Do you want me, Hal?" She would purr with satisfaction as he gave himself over to her dreams. The dreams became more and more disturbing to him. Leaving him more and more distraught.

After one such night he dreamed of rotted flesh, a pungent, earthy scent that forced him from deep sleep. It was oily and thick in the air. For a moment he saw his hands and wrists as withered, atrophied stalks, blue veined and peppered with liver spots. The shock was so great, he started from his bed, but his arm gave way like a vestigial limb. All that day, Hal sat in the sun, knees pulled up, the warmth and bright patch of light seeming to fade the horror of the nightmare. When he examined the same hands and arms this time, they were wiry and ribbed with muscles—the limbs of a weathered warrior, strong and confident.

    Sylvia kept coming, and soon Hal, though longing for her, began loathing her, began to understand there was a weight, a cost he could not identify. Sylvia purred and groaned, it was rougher now, a course selfish act, almost mocking the living. One night as he found himself collapsing into the ecstatic chaos of the moment. He opened his eyes to an inverted mushroom cap with open mouth and oval eyes, the gills at the top rhythmically pulsing like those of a fish. He saw strands of desperately groping hyphae wrapping and pulling and searching for any orifice they could find. This time when he awoke, he lay sickly and weak. The next night, there was little pretense, and the beautiful yet terrifying mushroom being did not speak at all, but went about her nightly process, completely disregarding Hal, covering him with hyphae, entering him, slicking him with sticky fluid that burned and tingled, then sucking and absorbing it back up. As Hal once again fell into the hallucinatory dreamscape, he thought he saw the mountain folk in the mist. One, the lanky aviator with leather hat and torn leather coat, hovering, drifting, a look of sorrow across his translucent face.

    Prisoner Hal was now desperate, but his body, was decaying. This was the only way he could make sense of it. His limbs were lesioned and milky with open wounds. His joints were swollen and bulbous, muscles atrophied to the point where he could no longer sit up. His scalp was patched and scaling, and occasionally, a searing needle of pain stabbed though his temple. He was starving to death. It was not from lack of eating, for his appetite was ferocious now, a terrible hunger that nothing could satiate. He was a kept food source, a vessel for Sylvia's nightly feedings, a plaything for an exotic goddess.

    Each night she came, until Hal stopped defining waking and sleeping. Months passed, season into season. Every once in a while, Hal saw the aviator mist-ghost hovering just in his periphery.

It was during this metamorphosis, this slow changing into death that Hal's mind raged with violence. It was not due to the strange happenstance of his current situation. This type of thing, this type of trap, of mistake, was bound to happen eventually in such a world as this. That was it, wasn't it? Such a world as this! This world! The blame rested firmly at the feet of one person, Christopher Dante! Fat Jovial, ignorant Hal, living and dying, oblivious to the actual world, the actual effects caused by that...that...damn bomb!

He thought of the scrap yard, of Max, of Him and Max drinking and laughing and worrying about...nothing...some irrelevant inventory deadline. He saw clearly now that damnable Caravaggio and the birthday party, that defining moment. He watched, like a hovering spirit, as he put the gun to his mouth that fateful day in the bedroom, Christopher speaking, jabbering irrelevant words. The rage, like a great and terrible force surged through his body. What gave him the right to shred up our world? Who did he think he was? How dare he! Hal knew it was not that simple, the simplistic reduction was unfair. He was dying, and his will to live was all but gone.

He stirred and shouted. What sounded to him like a great roar filled with existential rage was a small and weary groan. It was that groan that caught the audio sensors of NORM, which halted processing a sample of minerals and scanned the surrounding area. Hal turned his head slightly and croaked, "I'm here, you tin can."

"Mycelial anomaly detected," NORM said in its synthesized voice.

"Here," whispered Hal. His strength evaporated, and the cold bite of air stole his energy.

NORM crabbed over to him, then settled to the ground with its legs pulled up. One probe popped out of a hatch, an extended arm that hissed and steadied as it pressed a flat disc on Hal's emaciated chest.

"Mycelial anomaly detected," it said again. "Medical attention required."

Hal blinked at the scraped and muddied metal shell oblivious to what it was doing. He felt a stabbing pain, a nasty prick in his hip, white hot. he felt the rush of adrenaline surge through him, heart racing, mind clearing.

"Where am I?"

"Mycelial anomaly detected," NORM said, and it shot out a probe that scraped a chunk of white hyphae from the wall, lowering it into a small chamber to analyze later.

"Help me," Hal said. "We must leave this place. Help me."

NORM's legs hissed and popped as it heaved upward. The optical system slowly spun and scanned the surroundings, then quite determinedly it left.

Hal could sense the adrenaline wearing off, his limbs now weak and penetrated by deep pain. He lay down and stared at the fading light of day. Soon Sylvia would return, and his body would give over to her final calling. He could picture his emaciated flesh, muscle, and bone succumbing to her, soon to be the shriveling, splitting carcass of an animal, abandoned, forgotten in the woods. The process would be slow, organic, and Sylvia would seek out another living thing to feed upon. Hal surfaced from his delirium.

"Medical Attention needed," NORM said.

It prodded and surprisingly gently leveraged Hal to a sitting position.

"Okay. Okay. Okay. I get it." Hal pushed and pulled himself to the makeshift stretcher NORM constructed from small branches and vines. He fell into it sideways, and NORM prodded him again.

"Mycelial anomaly detected."

Hal was not moving, his body used up. He drifted into a dark space where he watched hyphae cover the living world, tentacle things, voracious in will and intent reducing it all to bone and soil.

He awoke, briefly, before a great stone covered in moss. The mist was surrounding it, and in it drifted and morphed the mountain folk of the Black Mountains, a subtle fiddle whining and mingling with the multitudinous whispers. At first Hal thought it was Sylvia, somehow tricking him, coming for her final feeding. As he stared at the towering cliff of stone, he made out a cracked and grooved old woman. Silent, sitting, staring, pondering, an ancient thing beyond men and time and things. Reverberating through him and under him and over him was a forgotten language that spoke peace and protection from the terrifying teeth of night.

Chapter Thirty-three

The way up the mountain was unmarked and treacherous. Beatrice found herself circling back (at least she thought she had) to the same downed and rotted tree bridging the same annoyingly and deceptively deep stream. After a long and tedious climb, stymied by the same craggy vista of sandstone cliffs, precipices that fell off into great expanses of open air carpeted with a green canopy of trees far below. By midafternoon she was frustrated, exhausted sitting before one such place, confounded, mind reeling, then looping back to that strange encounter with MaMaw.

She felt, vulnerable. She felt used and...well...violated... Forcing her to recall her memories with Christopher Dante was akin to being placed under a great white light...and found...wanting. It was this that confounded her...pissed her off, quite frankly. She was Beatrice from IMAGO! She was a god in this world. She could sing golems to life and command living things with the very tone of her songs. She lived for four hundred years, scrapped, killed, struggled, sung, and sought...Christopher Dante. Four Hundred years of hardened steel, an impenetrable shell built hourly over so long a time. She was Beatrice, damn it! That...thing...MaMaw had cracked her open like an egg. That thought deeply disturbed her. Her four-hundred-year existence evaporated into a newborn babe!

She sat on the great sandstone cliff and stared at the expanse before her, her mind deep within itself.

There was only one other who had been able to do as

much, Christopher Dante. In the early years, before he was called, before he was released from the Generation Tank into the world of men, time and things, she dreamed what he would be like. She would sit long hours on the break wall staring out over the Great Black Lake, the breeze ruffling her coat and hair—she would sit there and imagine what it would be like to meet the very one who created The Event itself, what she would say, what he would say, how she would respond. Meeting the man was...well, let's just say...it was disappointing. Not only was he a thin rail of a figure, soft and weak from an un-calloused life, but he was, frankly, annoyingly ignorant. She wanted a warrior leader. She got an adolescent boy.

That was the remarkable part of the whole thing, wasn't it? There before her eyes, she witnessed the birth of...well...a god! It was astounding. At first, like all of them (her father Stutz, Caravaggio, Doctor Mendel) she fought the daily doubt and skepticism. Who would anchor anything on shifting sand? He was not sand. She saw it time and again. When the teeth of life shredded everyone in its path, there he was, somehow, still standing, and she a witness to...something...not of this world or hers. *Creatio Ex Nihilo*! There were tales. She heard about his mother, Elizabeth. Her father told her about the power in the Storyteller, the awesome, quite incomprehensible ability to pull substance from the void, but she had no hand holds, no categories to put such extraordinary abilities. The contest with the Ghul... Matching it, besting it. Poof! Like that. What was once a material being terrorizing the world of Cogstin...now a mere rune on a cave wall. Who can do such things? A god. That's who.

She was terrified when she allowed the events of those days to settle upon her. Very shortly after that, the terror turned into awe, and she did indeed anchor onto that rock that formed right before her eyes. It was more than that. Christopher Dante was a god, yes, but he was a human as well. That humanity was more perplexing than anything else. She watched as he struggled with questions, doubts, exploring origins and meaning. Always with *her*. Always pulling *her* aside. Unburdening himself of all the tumult and chaos that was inside his head and heart. At first, she listened indifferently, then, slowly, she found herself longing for such times, the hardened shell of security suddenly softened. Over time, they forged a bond beyond friendship. Was it...love?

It was one day—she remembered it vividly now as she pondered on that sandstone cliff high in the Black Mountains. One late afternoon when she and Christopher stopped and set up camp on the outskirts of Cogstin. They had been sent by Mayor Hal to check on the clones living in the suburbs. Rumors had surfaced that some of the clones were beginning to resist the Mayor's governance. They had finished several days of talking with the Maxes and Hals and Emily's and Bob's and realized it was just that...rumors. Better communications would be reinstated, documents given and received... that was that.

So, there they were on the way back to Cogstin, Beatrice and Christopher, sitting around an open fire, eating stew from the cans, and Christopher asked:

"Who am I? No, I'm serious. Who do *you* think I am?"

Beatrice stared at him; eyes wide. "What am I supposed to say to that? You're you."

Christopher put the can of stew down. "It matters. It matters a great deal to me."

"Who do *you* think you are?"

Christopher sighed and sat in silence. He threw a small stick onto the fire. "When I was... ...before all of this...when I was...released... I felt lost, like I was waiting for something...something else. That same feeling has returned."

Beatrice looked at him, saw the mature lines forming on his forehead and at the sides of his eyes. She knew those lines well. This place was unforgiving. "With the Ghul gone," she said, "it's logical to start asking larger questions. We all are."

Christopher just stared into the fire. Then he stood up and walked into the darkness. She was going to find him, follow him. She waited...and waited... A kind of urgency, panic seized her, like maybe he just walked away forever, and she hurried after him. She found him inside an abandoned warehouse crouched down and staring into the darkness.

"Talk to me, Christopher. I can't help you if you don't let me."

He smirked and chuckled softly. "That's the issue."

"What's the issue?" She said, placing her hand on his shoulder.

He shrugged it off and stood up, frustrated. He said, "What do you see?"

"Nothing. There's nothing there. It's just dark space."

More impatiently. "What do you imagine could be there? What do you want to be there?"

"I know what you are doing," she said. "I get it. We have gifts in this world. I can sing. You can... I understand."

"Do you? Do you really?" He turned to her almost rudely. "What do you want there?"

"Fine. Wouldn't it be nice to have some table and chairs to sit on."

Christopher closed his eyes, breathed deeply, and placed his palm upward, extending his arm as if giving something to the darkness. There it was! Just like that! A table and two chairs.

"I know," she said. "Like I said, I get it."

"Look at them. I mean go over there and inspect them, really look at them, look at the floor they are on, look at the wall that is near them. Go on, look."

This was more like a command than a suggestion. She found herself quite compelled to step forward and obey. She looked. She touched the surface of the table, felt the thickness of the wood, ran her hand across the smooth top. She pulled and pushed the chairs, heavy, real, intricate, and material as if a carpenter carefully constructed them in a wood shop.

"The floor," he said. "Look at the floor."

She stooped down and suddenly caught her breath.

"Look at the walls near the table. Go on, look."

She did. The same thing occurred. What was once cast cement was now wood, like the chair. The floor, the walls, the building itself by that single act of will became identical in materiality as the thing Christopher made.

"Who am I, Beatrice? *What* am I?"

Beatrice stepped from the wall she was studying. "What does it mean?" she whispered, and could feel the familiar sensation setting upon her, pricking up the fine hairs on the back of her neck, gooseflesh across her arms, a sort of terror, a panic. Such power! Such awesome, transformative power!

Again, Christopher walked away, stepping out of the warehouse, and walking into the cooling night. She followed.

"It's not just inside the building. Subtly, unknown to me, to you, to anyone, everything around us has changed. It could be an indistinguishable object like a missing flower that used to be there, or maybe the flower has transformed in kind. It's always different, never the same in scope or intensity...but it is transformative. Oh yes, it is always transformative. The butterfly flaps its wings in one place and it's not a hurricane in another...no, it's a damn newly formed ocean! A forest! A...A...I don't even know. That table and chair in there has somehow ruined or changed or created or recreated or absolutely annihilated something else that used to be." He grabbed her by the shoulders and groaned. "Can you help that? Can you *solve* that? Can you somehow take the weight of such a thing from my shoulders...and carry it for a while? One single act. I did that. I can do it again. Maybe by accident. Maybe by intention." He walked back to the fire and sat silently brooding.

Beatrice thought of that night now, that terrible revelation, remembered it all as she sat on the sandstone cliffs in the mountains. That feeling of helplessness, of witnessing something else in awe and terror, being laid bare by the magnitude of the other...this is exactly what she felt before MaMaw. When MaMaw showed her Christopher Dante on the stone slab, naked and stretched out before a Horned God, well, she knew what she had to do. It was time to find Christopher. It was clear, oh so clear now, Christopher Dante orchestrated some sort of plan. After all this time, he figured something out, and more importantly, he now wanted her to be a part of it all.

Beatrice looked up, stirred from her introspection by a whirling and low buzz out in the distance. There she saw...NORM, slowly, patiently weaving between trees, hobbling over rocks, intentional and persistent. She watched as it vanished into the thicket of canopy. Within thirty minutes of its first appearance, NORM scaled the steep sandstone cliff and was now, arachnid-like, easing around an outcropping, securing its metal finger/claws into crevices unseen by the human eye. It squatted before her, awkward, comical, the single camera zooming in and out as it scanned her sitting there.

"I guess you're my way out of here?"

"Mapping Kyrnunos," NORM said in its synthesized voice.

"MaMaw sent you to find me?"

"Processing. Mycelial contact. Affirmative."

She stood up, stiff, the sun warm on her face, legs cold and numb from the stone seat. "Well, let me have a look." Beatrice stooped over the small screen and pushed several selections from the menu.

NORM's GPS was still not working—how could it without connections to satellites? MaMaw placed into it a digital map to cross the Black Mountains and come to the Pass of Kyrnunos. She stared at the smudged screen. How easy it looked like a plotted line. She looked up and scanned the actual topography, the mountainous horizon of forest and cliffs. She sighed. It would take several days of hard trekking to make it there. That was if the weather and terrain did not hinder them more than it already had.

"Well, tin can," Beatrice said, "Let's get to it."

She was annoyed at the metal thing, forced to be its companion, forced to journey, and communicate with a petty dethroned dictator. She did not wait for its response. Instead, she headed down the ravine, Eastward, the sun high above and behind her.

They traveled for two days and two nights. By the end of the third day, they came to the edge of a great stone cliff. Beatrice stood and looked about.

"What river is this?"

"Cuy River. Details processed. Shall I read them to you."

"No."

To her left was a steep wooded landscape rising up, up and up the cliff face. To her right was a small trail, an animal run, disappearing into a thicket of trees that edged the great expanse of river. Far, far, far away was the other side of the Black Mountains. "Where's the pass? You were supposed to take me to the pass."

"Processing."

Beatrice did not wait for its synthetic reply. Her legs were tired, her mind was tired. She wanted to sleep for a week but knew if she did not find the pass by nightfall, they would have to spend their time isolated and vulnerable, exposed to whatever predators hunted these ridges. The trail moved away from the cliff, the sound of the river nearly disappearing, and just when she thought she had gone the wrong way, it turned dramatically back on itself. She stepped from the trees and before her was a great stone arch, man-made, chiseled from the mountain, a sort of tunnel. Beyond it a great rope bridge spanning a hundred feet? She saw the white foam of the river as it raged a thousand feet below. She saw the bridge as it shimmered and swayed in the wind between the cliff faces.

"You have got to be kidding me," Beatrice said to the air.

"This is the pass?"

"Affirmative," NORM said. "The pass of Kyrnunos is a fibrous expansion bridge approximately one hundred and thirty-five feet from..."

"Enough already! Let me think."

She walked to the buttress and thoroughly analyzed the great rope as it coiled around and secured itself into the stone. Old, stiff, like iron cable...but rope all the same! Organic, vulnerable to wind, water, sun and cold! She stepped to the planks. They seemed solid, but were they...all of them? She looked far down the bridge at the uneven surface, several missing like gaps in an old hermit's smile. She stared at the rapids far below. "Come here," she said gruffly. "Now! Get over here!"

NORM crept over, timidly. Beatrice flipped up the small screen again and looked at the plotted course. Perhaps this was one of several passes? She tapped this and that, nope. This was the Pass of Kyrnunos alright. *Obviously, the bridge was secure. Obviously. MaMaw would not have sent her this way if it was not. This was simply some sort of illusion. The bridge looked shoddy and dangerous, but in the end...well...* Shadows were forming across the bridge now. She suddenly felt the cold wind from the enormous space, chilling, even biting at times.

"Scan that bridge," she commanded to NORM.

"Bridge scanned."

"Well?"

"Bridge scan complete."

"Assessment?"

"The pass of Kyrnunos is a fibrous expansion bridge approximately one hundred and thirty-five feet from its western buttress to the eastern buttress. Its origins are unknown. Documents record the earliest..."

"Shit!" Hissed Beatrice, and she clenched her fists and stepped onto a wooden plank.

She just walked, steady, slowly, fully committed to the next step. She stared at the stone buttress far beyond. She felt the bridge rock and swing under her feet. Her will was a thing unto itself, a force so great it her already across and looking back. So intensely was she focused, she did not register when she crossed the midway point of the bridge. She did, however, register the planks behind her giving way, a great rending and snapping as the rotted fibers shredded, and her flailing body fell, in a great rush of force toward the river below.

Chapter Thirty-four

NORM had not quite finished its response to Beatrice's command concerning the make-up of the bridge when two things happened simultaneously. First, the incessant looping of the code which befuddled NORM and therefore had it placed into the background—this code began a new function. It came to that point in the code where it infinitely looped back to the beginning, but this time instead of stopping and looping...it moved forward. Like a train that lays track as it moves, NORM laid code, and this time it worked. The new code initiated a reboot. The code it laid down moved it to an executive function that in turn moved into a reboot which sent the whole processor into a "shut down" sequence.

Secondly, at the exact same time, it scanned and recognized the structural failure of the rope. Beatrice was in jeopardy. It was brief, seconds of code really, but if it could have been translated into words, it would have come out as, SAVE BEATRICE! Alas, when a computer randomly shuts down and reboots, it loses whatever meaningful data it may have obtained in the seconds before the shutdown. That is what happened. While Beatrice stumbled, grasped, then ultimately fell, NORM was shut down, screen dark, all systems, OFF.

~ * ~

All Beatrice could think when the bridge collapsed was, *What the hell! Who builds a bridge like this?* And, *I knew it! I knew it would not hold!* It was a stupid statement really. Who can say what stupid or profound thoughts enter one's head when the end comes so suddenly. It was slow motion, but not in a way that she could articulate. She wondered what the end would feel like, if she would know. The end. This was untenable, even unthinkable in Cogstin. Before the death of the Ghul none of them could die, stuck in that place, cursed to wake up over and over back in Cogstin. But now. Now that Christopher Dante had been freed from the Generation Tanks, now that he defeated the Ghul—they could travel anywhere, do anything they wanted...even die? She fell, a roaring, violent headlong plummet toward the rocks below.

~ * ~

The wonder of advanced technology is that it imitates the human physiology to such an extent that the adjective *Artificial* in Artificial Intelligence is mainly nonsense. NORM rebooted. Its reboot allowed for two sudden and quite astounding processes to take place. First, it calculated the falling object of Beatrice to the exact second it would terminate, processed, and mapped the leverage points on both wall faces, statistically some better than others, then launched itself into the air like a despairing suicidal spider. Secondly, what had once been a one-sided phone call—a forlorn lover hopelessly broadcasting out to its beloved—the silence of the void inevitable—this signal suddenly was answered, a connection made to the ether. NORM called out as it was programmed to do. Low and behold something responded, something familiar, known. A part of NORM forgotten was now connected and processing.

~ * ~

One can only fall so far and so fast before the human body cannot tolerate the g-forces and itself "reboots." Beatrice blacked out. Her last thought, profoundly, was how much she would miss Christopher Dante. Would he miss me? Nothing else was considered.

~ * ~

When Beatrice came to, she immediately resisted the metal bands that bound her tight. She struggled, desperate, but relaxed as her mind cleared. She processed what was happening. If she turned her head, she could see the raging Cuy River, a white-foamed torrent of rushing water. She could hear the power and violence as it raced through the steep canyon walls. When she looked up, she was face to face with NORM's undercarriage, a worn and scraped metal shell. NORM's front and back legs held her tight, looped around her like a metal harness, holding her fast. His other two legs spanned out one in front, one behind, both feeding, pulling, catching the lines secured into the side of the cliff walls. If one could zoom out and observe the event from beginning to end, well... a god can do unthinkable things, no doubt.

~ * ~

As Beatrice plummeted headfirst to her death, NORM sprung out into the open space, shot two repelling lines from its front and back. Secured the lines on either side of the great expanse, and spider-like performed a guided, controlled fall to catch Beatrice in midair. Fantastic! It used two legs to secure her, the other two to steady the lines. It slowly, patiently, reeled itself up, up, up, up and up.

~ * ~

There came a point, and Beatrice was very much awake at this moment, where NORM found itself spread out and pulled tight, like an unfortunate peasant about to be drawn and quartered.

"Do not drop me!" Screamed Beatrice because she had nothing else to say.

NORM processed. Beatrice prodded, "You must do something! We can't just hang here! Tell me you have a plan!"

NORM whirled, buzzed, and chirped. And, the unthinkable happened. NORM severed the back line with its back legs and it, and Beatrice swung furiously toward the cliff wall. Beatrice screamed! And, like a car crash, NORM smashed into the side of the sandstone cliff, and Beatrice passed out from the head injury.

When she came to, NORM already had her up to the edge, launched, secured, and stabilized a new line into a tall tree—and hoisted the limp body of Beatrice from the abyss and onto the eastern side of the pass.

"What the hell was that?" she whispered, her shoulder and hips throbbing from the impact, forearm already turning a deep black and purple, head pounding and fogged.

"Save Beatrice," the synthetic voice said.

"You almost killed me!"

"Scan complete. Vital signs elevated but normalizing."

She pulled herself up to a tree trunk and leaned against it. She looked far across the expanse of air to the western side of the embankment, nothing but a lone stone arch. She fell to her death, but she did not die. She fell. She fell hundreds of feet...and survived! NORM saved her. She closed her eyes and breathed deeply, her ribs bruised, a slight pain when she breathed in. She gulped some water.

"Why did you save me?" she said to NORM who was now analyzing a small rock sample, then placing it in a hidden tray with all the other flora and fauna it collected.

"Save Beatrice."

"Yes, but why?"

"Processing." Whirl, beep, buzz. "Priority One."

"What is Priority One?"

"Save Beatrice?"

"Who initiated that command?"

"Priority One initiated by Christopher Dante."

"Do you have other priorities?"

"Affirmative."

"What are your other priorities?"

"Security Clearance Requested."

"Do I have security clearance?"

"Negative."

"Who has security clearance?"

"Security Clearance Requested."

Beatrice laid her head back and rested. Night was coming hard, and she did not want to move. "Find firewood and prepare a camp," she said in almost a whisper.

NORM whirled and buzzed, then it pushed itself up and like a crab walked into the surrounding woods. Within an hour a hut had been constructed. A fire popped and hissed with warmth. Beatrice did not care about any of this, however, and she fell into an exhausted sleep where she dreamed of constantly falling, wondering if she would hit the bottom, and if she did—would Christopher remember her?

Chapter Thirty-five

Hal stared at the mist lingering in the shadows of the midday sun, scratched his shoulder as well as his bicep and barked, "I'm coming. I'm coming. There's a thing called mountains here."

He clawed at the growing thing beneath his shirt and trudged on.

He had lost track of the days, the seasons. How long had it been since he had seen Beatrice? Who was to say? Most of those early months on the mountain seemed a blur to him now. Finally, he was going to leave this place. That...thing...MaMaw decreed he could go, but not without a whole lot of fuss and bother. Prophecy this and destiny that...bullshit. He couldn't take another vague and nonsensical platitude. *Give me a machete maybe some bombs and I'll fulfill your prophecy*! Of course, she saved his life, and he was grateful. Yes, very grateful. What had she really done but allowed his own body to recover from that...that monster Sylvia. His body did heal. His impatience grew as his strength grew. Soon, there was nothing indicating his near-death experience save a small mark on his shoulder, a rash of sorts. Time to go!

MaMaw had other plans. Months after he healed, MaMaw requested council. Man did she lay on a whopper!

"You, Harold Dante. You, Hal of Cogstin, a simple duplicate life, a grain of sand blown by the endless desert winds. Yes, even you will—like all the others caught in this storm, this terrible moment—even you will be forced to make a choice, and

that choice will decide the future of this world.
> *Two paths before you lay.*
> *The first as stepping on empty air,*
> *A lunatic choice through a hunter's snare.*
> *The second firm through blood and bone*
> *A sacrifice upon the stone.*

That was that. He would know what it all meant when he was supposed to know what it all meant. Typical god-speak. That was not actually all. Abstract words where neither here nor there. These words had a sense of right and wrong to them, a tone that made his skin crawl when he thought about that stupid rhyme. To confound it all, MaMaw spoke of some mission he was to fulfill, some quest to find...how did she put it "the living in the Forest of the Dead." What the hell did that even mean?

He was not to follow Beatrice to the Pass of Kyrnunos. No, he was to take another route, through the mountains—a tunnel, and he was to make this journey with a ghost, one of the Mountain Folk! Clem, that giddy half-wit ghost aviator thing was to accompany him to this Forest of the Dead. Of course, he protested, forbade it, demanded his free and unconditional release...but all for naught.

Hal moped and wandered the mountain landscape, all the while the annoying mark on his shoulder growing larger, thicker, some sort of wart, cancer, or moss thing. MaMaw requested another council, he compelled to show up before the enigmatic ancient stone woman, and there...well, she basically smacked his ass down!

Hal stirred from his thoughts. He was almost to Clem now. He stopped and viciously rubbed his shoulder again. "Damnit!" Hal hissed.

It must be the direct sunlight, the warmth of the sun, something to do with the sun that just irritated the hell out of that... that... whatever the hell it was she did to him back there. "I need to rest a minute, ya damn hillbilly."

The mist just shimmered there. It was a disembodied idiot vapor. Hal sat down on a large sandstone boulder that surfaced from the dark soil of the underbrush. The cool of the shade seemed to calm the mycelia growth that covered the upper part of his arm. It was increasing in its spread, but all of this was to be expected. MaMaw had said as much.

"There is a cost, Harold Dante. There is always a cost with every action. Sylvia took from you. I replaced what she took the only way I could. The alternative was death."

So, when it was explained to him like that, well, what's a little fungus on your body if you still get to ride the train? It screwed with him as it grew, however. He changed. He could smell the damp and dying now more than he ever remembered. Death and decay were those things a human avoided at all costs. Now he almost longed for them. He found himself stopping in the dark of the woods, some isolated spot, behind a boulder, underneath a fallen tree. When he came out of the trance, looked around...there, there it was, something moldered, and the mycelia covering, eating, absorbing, reprocessing it. *My brothers*, he thought. With a shake of his head, *I should be in a looney bin.*

Hal sat just outside the warm sunlight, his back against a tall pine. He contemplated his next move and when he would enact his plan. He had already decided that he would not accompany Clem the hillbilly ghost anywhere, but where was he to go? Beatrice had left him, and his whole reason for leaving Cogstin was to find and bring back Christopher Dante. No hillbilly ghost quest. No Dead Forest. *The only living thing I'm finding is Christopher Dante. Don't need to go to the Forest of the Dead for that.* He began to doubt this plan, however, sitting under the shade of the great pine tree. There was another voice in his head now, debating, countering, resisting every new thought.

I'll wait Hal thought. *I'll wait until that hillbilly ghost is distracted. Yes, that's it. Distract that thing like a dog with a stick. Stupid is as stupid does.*

But there was this counter voice. *Stupid is as stupid does. Hey, that's good. I like that. I might use that. You mind if I use that? There ain't no distracting an iron will. A will that's trained, focused. Attention span like a...a trap.*

That's stupid Hal said in his head. *One can't focus like a trap. That's a stupid saying. A nonsense thought. Traps have no will. They don't focus, they just...trap.*

Okay, said the other voice in his head. *Traps are made of iron and iron is strong and tough and hard and so is my will. Tough like a rock or iron or...dirt or something.*

Hal shook his head and looked up. Clem bobbed and floated there. His guffaw pilot hat and torn silhouette coat shimmered in the shadow. Were those aviator goggles on his head? He never noticed that before. Was he smiling at him?

"Alright," Hal said out loud. "Let's get to this."

"Let's go," responded a voice, a whisper voice, like a long sigh, but it was distinctly clear to Hal. "Let's get this show on the road. Let's take this plane in the air. Let's find that breeze and flap our wings. Let's gather our..."

"Shut up!" Hal roared. "Good god! You can understand me?"

He stood to his feet and leaned over to Clem. "You understand what I'm saying to you? How can you understand me?" He paused, staring at the fog. "What I'm thinking? Speak to me!"

Clem shivered, became fuzzy, then crystal clear, a translucent, perfect image of his former physical state. "Yes," Clem said. "I'm no hillbilly, neither. I got schooled and learned at one of the finest universities this side of..."

"Nonsense," Hal said. "This is crazy! Mist can't talk." He pointed at Clem. "You can't talk."

"Can too," Clem shot back. "Don't you tell me what I can and can't do, Flatlander."

Hal huffed. He looked away and thought, *Can't hear this, asshole, can you?* He walked past Clem and headed deeper into the woods.

Can too, Clem smirked, *Asshole Flatlander*. "This way," the aviator specter said. He bobbed and weaved around several pines so that he hovered before Hal and lead the way through the forest, always staying in the shadows, and always moving toward the entrance to the passage through the great mountain.

They walked for hours—well, Hal walked. The pine trees gave way to scrub and brush. The air was thin and cold. They came to a fissure in the rock, wide enough for three humans to walk abreast. The clear blue sky opened above them, and as the sun shone down on Hal, it obscured and seemed to completely dissipate Clem before him. And the passageway narrowed and turned, then narrowed again until finally only a single body could pass through. They entered the mountain itself, and the light of the world was gone.

This is when Hal started to understand he was no longer the Hal of Cogstin. The new Hal found the darkness comforting. The new Hal rubbed the cold, wet stone walls, and relished in the sensation. He could smell the things that entered and were trapped, desiccated things unable to return to the light. He saw with what he would later discover as Mycelial awareness, a sort of radar for fungus, more auditory and olfactory than ocular. Hal and Clem traveled in the pitch black of the mountain for what seemed hours.

"What is that?"

Hal stood still and listened. It was a moan or a whimper, something suffering.

"Finally," Clem shouted with glee.

He darted toward and around a bend. Hal hurried after.

When he made the turn, he saw a shimmer, a dull glow hovering near the ground. When he stepped up to it, he gasped, then turned away in disgust.

Clem found a dying fawn. It lay on the sodden stone, panting, panting, the last of its life seeping away. Over it, waiting was the aviator ghost, mouth agape, fingers splayed out as if he was yelling at the fawn. He was not screaming at all. As soon as the animal breathed its last, Clem zoomed down and...well, he cradled and sucked, pulling, drawing out, kneading the hide like a cat with a blanket. The fawn's skin grew taught, gray and thin like vellum covering the skeletal remains. The mycelium appeared, white hyphae covering the emaciated body, snaking down onto the stone like arteries or worms, carpeting the floor and walls below and above the empty husk.

Hal, to his complete astonishment and horror, knelt beside it. Such powerful urges overcame him that he reached out his mycelial hand and caressed the dead animal. He could feel the hyphae crawl and slide onto the back of his hand and down his fingers, spanning out over the fawn. A milky lather seeped from the hyphae, and he knew that it was decomposing and imbibing the caustic slurry that it created. And it retracted and moved back up Hal's arm, a symbiotic, sentient thing.

Clem hovered over Hal, then right next to him. "Easy, Flatlander. Too much of a good thing is still too much. We have a long way to go yet." Clem, now a dull yellow glow, moved forward, Hal following close behind, a strange aftertaste in his mouth, partly fecal, partly acrid earth. His gulch rose, then he vomited.

"Told ya," Clem cackled.

Hal was busy expelling the contents of his stomach, his back arched, body convulsing into intense retching spasms. Clem waited patiently just beyond. Was he playing a fiddle? Where did the fiddle come from? The wave of nausea passed, and soon, they were off again. With every step, Hal felt an ominous presence gathering, hiding, waiting just out of view.

Chapter Thirty-six

Time evaporated in the mountain. Hal followed the dim yellow light of the aviator ghost and gave up guessing how long it had been since he saw the blue sky above. It did not matter that he had no light, his new body adjusting organically as they made their way further underground. He could sense that others had passed this way, small archeological items of interest. The head of an iron pickaxe rusted and abandoned, a shredded paraffin coat, an old lantern, jagged glass like teeth behind the dented metal lattice. They came to an adit, the decayed wooden skeleton still visible. They crossed over what had to have been tracks for mining carts, but they were askew, bent away by some great force, the sleepers scattered and ruined, as well as the fish plates and spikes. A rotted and splintered iron cart lay on its side.

"What happened here?" Hal whispered.

Clem, who had been incessantly talking, a kind of exuberant jabber, hushed as they neared the entrance, a great caution overcoming him. "Before The Event," he said in his specter whine, a tone that faded in and out, "We were mighty and rich and prosperous. The mountain gave us everything. We wanted for nothing. These tunnels were filled with...life."

He stopped and put his fingers to his lips, shifting to his left and right. "We need to go from here. We are not wanted."

"What do you mean?" Hal said. "Who doesn't want us?"

Clem already dimmed his yellow essence to something barely visible to Hal and darted forward away from the entrance to the coal mine.

It was not long until Hal felt the oppressive force building around them. He found himself stopping and glancing backward, then hurrying to catch up with Clem. Soon the feeling of terror was so great that Hal cried out. "I must stop. I can't go any further. I have felt this before, in the subway shafts of Cogstin, the Ghul."

He leaned against the damp wall.

"We must go from here," Clem said, the sentences coming out of him intermittently, like he was randomly muffling his voice with his hand.

"Where can we go but forward. Every step exhausts me. What is it? What is stalking us?"

Hal's mind was dark and whirling. Nothing he reached and grabbed made sense. He faced all manner of things in Cogstin, but the Ghul...the dungeons and chains and torture...his made his knees weak. How could he face such a thing again?

"I don't know what a *Ghul* is," said Clem. "If it can kill even us Mountain Folk...if it can trap you under the earth forever, so you can never see MaMaw or the sky or sun or the living again...then call it what you will. I know them as The Fomoiri. They are demons in the mountain, spirit-creatures who were trapped by The Event, cut off from their lives above. They hate all living things. They only want to trap and torture, to rage against those who were not trapped. Hurry now. We must leave this place."

Clem darted forward again, and Hal reached out his hand but only felt a cold damp sensation from the corporeal Clem. He drew his machete and ran, a panicked animal. Soon it was clear that he was surrounded. The Fomoiri were behind and in front of Hal, separating and isolating him from Clem. With his flashlight in one hand and his machete in the other, he swung blindly. He could hear the laughter, a cold, deathly sound, a mixture of sadness, anger and mockery for all things from above. The flashlight sputtered and blinked, then was gone. Hal breathed heavy and pressed against the tunnel wall.

We will trap you with us, said a voice, toneless, empty of empathy.

Yes, said another now closer to Hal, now further away. *It looks scared. Alone. Take it with us. Take it into the mountain with us, forever.*

Hal could see them now, standing, floating darkness, lanky arms, and legs. Clawed fingers, mouths that rendered flesh from bone, eyes wide, blinking, predatory and vengeful. He could not escape, and he understood that he would be taken, brought to some place of torment, abandoned like the pickaxe and the coal cart...forever. His mind grew darker and darker, hopeless. And he heard it.

At first it was just the wind somewhere far beyond or above entering through some crevice, a whistle perhaps, high pitched. But he realized it was not the wind at all but a whine...a high note from a fiddle, weak, clear. A fiddle! Down here? Now? It was constant, a driving, growing sound, comforting, something ancient and deeply felt.

"I am Hal!" Hal suddenly screamed, his voice thin and uncertain, laying words down like bricks for an unknown structure. "I am Harold Dante from the Flatlands!"

We love Harold from the Flatlands. We want to keep Harold forever with us, tasty Hal, delectable Hal. Plump and ripe Hal from above.

"MaMaw sent me. She bid me pass through the Mountain."

The Fomoiri hissed and chortled, now right in Hal's face. To his left, then to his right, now above. *More reason to keep you with us. We hate the Mountain god. She is culpable. She will pay for what she has done. You will pay for her. Grind, pull and rend Harold from the Flatlands.*

Suddenly, Hal felt the cold, taloned fingers grasping him without mercy, tearing at his clothes, puncturing his jacket fabric, his skin beneath like fishhooks or a cat's claws.

The fiddle whined, louder, louder, louder, building in tempo. The mycelial growth on Hal's arm shuttered as it met the fingers, a visceral response. The Fomoiri withdrew immediately, hesitated then pounced. Hal was flung to the stone floor, smashing his head with a thud.

The Fomoiri screamed, hissed, and gloated. *Who is Hal? You are one of them? Who is Harold Dante? Why do you come through the mountain? He is one of them. Who are you? Why is Harold of the Flatlands in the mountain of the Fomoiri?* A clawed hand throttled his neck.

Hal gasped, and a sideways thought pushed in. *You will die here. Everything that enters this world has died, suffocated, alone, despairing.* He moved his mouth, but no air would enter his lungs. He felt light-headed, his temples a throbbing, stabbing pain. The fiddle changed its tune, slower now, intense, beautiful. The mycelia growth on his shoulder expanded to his neck, like a piece of cloth, a second skin. The Fomoiri released the grip. A sort of debate raged around Hal while he gulped air and dragged himself away.

He is one of them, of hers?
No, he is a breather. He is not one of hers.
It burns like one of hers
It is a breather. Breather Harold from the Flatlands, from above.
Stab it. Stab it and take out the air.
It burns. It's one of them, one of hers.
Stab it and see. Take out the air. If we stab it, it will leak out.
We will stab out the air and keep it. Take it into the mountain.

There was a kind of humming, low, as if the rocks and Fomoiri were one thing. A unity of anger, rage and hate, like a black inky fog, a single committed will. The fiddle was silent. Hal crawled and dragged and ran further and further down the tunnel. He ran until he could not hear them any longer. Ran while his legs burned and his head throbbed. The mycelial rash now moving around his neck, down his chest. He heard the horde of terrifying Fomoiri flooding the tunnel behind. They were screaming now, yelling, calling out, taunting Harold of the Flatlands. With that terrifying sound, Hal could now hear the fiddle rage, squeal and thunder. He thought he could see somewhere far in the distance the hillbilly aviator ghost wheeling and dancing like a lunatic mountain hermit on a summer's evening.

    The fiddle whined, stabbed, and screamed through the air and into Hal. He stopped running and turned toward the onslaught of hate. The Fomoiri raced to him, the sheer volume of the demons, a sudden torrent of violent force, knocked him against the wall. As they stabbed and tore at him, he laughed. The mycelia were an armor, his shield, his salvation, and it was then he realized this had been the plan all along. MaMaw knew they would encounter the Fomoiri, and she knew who needed to be with him when he did, that damnable hillbilly aviator who played the fiddle! MaMaw "re-created Hal." By doing so made sure he could withstand and survive the Fomoiri.

    The fiddle screamed now, a thrashing, pounding, ecstatic force. The demon Fomoiri did what they could, and with every pass, they became more enraged, more violent. The mycelia shredded and hung beneath his cloths, but soon gathered back into a weave of hyphae thick like elephant skin, like course fur, a living adapting organism. Hal reached out, and to his complete surprise, grabbed something solid, a shoulder, bone, and flesh. He swung his machete with his other hand, and the blade met resistance. He heard a scream, a howl, and a Fomoiri's head separated from its body. This was all he needed, Harold from the Flatlands, Hal from Cogstin! He fought like this before, and he became a master killer. This was no supernatural Ghul with power from IMAGO! This was something terrestrial, something quite of this world. Hal swung, sliced and laughed with the glory of battle upon him. The Fomoiri scattered, regrouped, attacked, then howled and raged and fled the terrifying, unstoppable Harold Dante from the Flatlands, a thing that had entered their cave world and had withstood the terror under the mountain.

He walked for hours before he met up with Clem who was once again huddled over a carcass. This time it was a bear, the soft inners long gone and emptied. Hal did not care any longer, and with an animal ferocity, he huddled over the bones alongside the specter, holding them in his hands, allowing the Mycelia to cover them, absorbing anything remaining. Again, and again and again he stuffed his hands into the carcass, head back in a sort of gluttonous zeal. After a while he pulled back and sat down in the darkness. Clem imitated him.

"So, you play the fiddle," Hal said. "The hillbilly fiddler under the mountain."

He smiled, burped up a mix of fecal matter and rotted earth. Closed his eyes and sat contented as the mycelia processed the nutrients it gathered.

Chapter Thirty-seven

Beatrice made her way to the Cuy River, the banks now wide, so wide in fact that the other side appeared a distant shoreline. She could smell the fresh water, the tang from rotted things, sodden things. She wondered at the multi grays, and blues and whites as it rolled and foamed or glassed smooth over the murky, rocky bottom.

She spent most of the night traversing the steep slopes of the Black Mountains, making the foothills by late morning. Now, surrounded by a thick wood of oak, walnut, and birch, she was unclear about where to go. Of course, that was not really the issue. No, something else took hold of her, and she was only now fully processing it.

Something unexpected was rising within her. Something...well, stunning as her analytical, hardened mind analyzed its emergence. When she looked around her, this expansive river, the green, lush reeds, cattails, and river grass, heard the movement of the water, she could barely suppress the overwhelming urge to cry out, "How wondrous! How exciting! Four hundred years she had lived in a nutshell, a prison city thick with ash and death and evil, bordered and oppressed on every side. The Ghul below, the Great Black Lake, the ruined and radiated city of Cogstin, the desperate search, hope and longing for it all to end! It had ended. She was here, now, in this moment of time and space looking at such...beauty.

Hadn't that god-like creature, MaMaw, told her as much, prepared her in advance for what she was to confront. How did she put it? "You will resist, but it is the irresistible. You will run, but it is the inescapable. You will go to battle, but it will overwhelm." Then she showed her the images of Christopher on the stone slab. Where they connected? This was not terror or taking a stand against the wicked. This was the beautiful...dare she even believe...hopeful. This river and breeze and fragrance of life; these trees and woods and sloping green hills! It was all Christopher Dante's doing.

He might have changed the world, transformed it with his uncontrolled power, but what a world it was! This...beyond Cogstin world. This other...space with beauty and hidden things. She was so struck by the thought of such a new emotion, of its significance, that it could have been...had been inside her all this time. MaMaw was right, it was something so powerful, that nothing could every imprison it for long. She was so confounded, perplexed by it all. A secret part of her broke free, a part held so tightly, so permanently that when it finally split away, it was like an iceberg calving, thunderous, expansive, a transformative event.

Her voice, the cracked and stifled thing, restricted, sliced and scarred by a traumatic terror, an evil—this voice suddenly and unexpectedly released in such a powerful force. She felt her whole body convulse with the expulsion, a purging, a great and terrifying, celebration of joy. The song swept up, up into the wind, up and across the great Cuy River, out over the forest of birch and oak and walnut, out and out and out. She was not sure what it even meant, but she sang loud and strong, like a bellow full of air, then slowly pressed flat. And it was over. Her body slumped so that she leaned against the rough bark of an ancient walnut.

Quite suddenly, she felt a weight of sadness, a deep sense of loss. *He would have loved this*, she thought. Her father, Stutz, cruelly destroyed by the Ghul—he would have built another life in such a place as this! Was this not the whole purpose for their coming to this world from IMAGO. Was it not the very reason for such a risk? And Christopher and The Event happened. All their hopes and expectations shriveled. They became prisoners sentenced to four hundred years of death and fear.

For a moment, only a moment, for she was not trained to linger on such things, she wondered where her father might be, if spirit really did translate from the body, or was it empty nothing, a cold darkness eternal? She wondered what his last thoughts had been and knew that he was hell bent on one thing, place Christopher back! She looked around her again, the trees, the river, the sparking current far beyond. And like pushing a great iron door, with such anger, rage and force, she closed all these new feelings off. She was Beatrice from IMAGO. She was a god, and she could subjugate this world through her song. She clenched her fists in response, sighed, and stood up.

NORM probed the water, an extended arm, claw open, the current splashing up as it encountered the paint-chipped and scratched metal. The sky was deep blue above her, the leaves full and shimmering in the river breeze. "Well, if you're done playing in the water, let's make our way down river. There's got to be some sort of civilization somewhere."

They edged the riverbank for miles. At times the water lapped the thin crust of bank, at others, it fell far out of view with the rising topography. By late afternoon, the sun beginning to sink in the west and throw the watery world in shadow, they saw the river barge. Beatrice motioned NORM to settle, and she squatted behind a tree and watched in astonishment at what unfolded before her.

A line of tall, seven feet tall or so, bone-skinny beings, skeletons really, draped in filthy garments, some wrapped in loin clothes only, some with dangling rags, torn and streaming, tied in knots or tucked helplessly into one another. All of them chained by the waist. All in a single line trudging across the long wooden plank and into the open bow of the barge. They were gray in color, splotchy pigments of gray, light blue, and white, rib cages exposed, knees and elbows bulbous. Some wore round hats of cloth tied around their chins with string, others, bare headed with cornsilk hair floating and dancing in the river breeze. Directing them from the front or pushing them from behind were what appeared like dwarves to such tall beings. Armed humans poking with their rifles, beckoning with dramatic and impatient gestures. There was a sublimity about it, for no sound was made, and a sense of fear and urgency settled on them all.

Beatrice watched as the last guard stepped aboard, turning every few seconds to investigate the great forest, an obvious sense of anxiety, as if the barge could not depart the small dock quickly enough. A man on the dock retrieved the line. The barge rumbled then puffed out an enormous black cloud of smoke from the tall stack. It moved slowly and steadily into the great current of the Cuy River, then slowly turned and headed toward the distant southern shoreline. The single individual remaining at the dock hurried inside the building and closed the door.

"Where are we?" Beatrice asked NORM.

NORM gave the GPS points of latitude and longitude, elevation, and topography, but with no other explanation. Beatrice stared into the dark shadows of the great forest beyond the banks of the river, a sudden wildness, a sense of foreboding.

"Let's go," she said.

They hurried across the sloping and uneven terrain, and as they neared the outskirts of the docking area, she was accosted by a profound, acrid, putrefied smell of rotted flesh. She covered her nose with the back of her hand, gathered herself. Her gulch rose again, and she gagged. "What is that?"

"Organic matter detected," NORM said. It scanned and buzzed, then moved to the edge where the riverbank eroded and fell into a great sink hole. "Source Identified." NORM opened a small metal door, and what looked like a barrel from a gun emerged. It popped, and a small dart attached to a line shot from it. Almost instantly the line was retracted, the barrel pulling back into the chassis, door closing. "Organic matter of unknown DNA detected."

Beatrice walked to NORM; the stench so overwhelming that she could only think of one other experience with such a smell. The Ghul's layer deep under Cogstin, the Pit of rotted... No. She could not think on such things. She peaked over the edge then hurried away, her gag reflex triggered again with the surfacing memory.

Heaped in several piles, scattered, and folded, strewn out where they had been so carelessly tossed, were the rotting carcasses of the skeleton people, the same race that entered the boat nearly a half hour earlier.

"What has happened here?" Beatrice whispered, but as soon as those words exited her lips, she heard the whines and screams of something animal, a herd of ravenous predators.

Turning to face this fresh horror, she felt the thaumaturgical impact, a sudden electrical pulse, a rhythm, a created, pounding beat that thumped and coursed through her body. She recognized, too late, she had foolishly blundered into somebody else's unfolding nightmare.

Chapter Thirty-eight

It took several days at least before Hal and Clem came to what they believed was the other side of the mountain. The drift snaked first to the north, then east, then south and back easterly again. Hal found himself comfortable in the darkness, but a growing sense of tension, a crackle, an unexpected electrical sensation would catch him off guard. The feeling intensified, and he slowed his pace. Clem disappeared up the passage and floated back to him in a kind of panic.

"What?" Hal hissed, his breath coming hard now, a weight upon his chest that he could not explain.

Clem shimmered in the darkness. "Torches," he whined. "Torches ahead."

They crept slowly, cautiously, stopping now and again to listen. Was that a groan? The wind? The temperature dropped rapidly. Soon Hal had to put on his winter parka. He put on a dilapidated and worn-out piece of cloth he called a hat, a rancid smelling, matted and fur-lined thing with earflaps. Beatrice tried to throw it away multiple times. They moved on, his breath now a smoke of exhalations. The once dark walls glimmered with a spectral light, which increased in intensity as they moved closer to the source.

He squinted and shaded his eyes, observing the runes on the wall. They were bold strokes, a reddish-brown hue like oxidized blood. On one side they could see a pattern, like an ancient story or perhaps some hex, square shapes, and downward strokes, flared at the end. On the other side were depictions, a tall image towering over others, massive horns jutting from its head. Hal unsheathed the machete and held it out, but the terrifying images mocked him, *puny mortal. Bow before your god!*

Within a hundred yards or so, they stood before a split in the tunnel. The left pathway was dimly lit, a foul odor of rotted and abandoned things mixed with another scent, a strange spice burning, filling, and drifting out from the darkness. Hal gagged and turned away.

"The wind." Clem whined, dancing to the entrance of the second tunnel.

"This way!" Hal screamed, nearly running through him. "Hurry. We're nearly out!"

The light grew, the wind grew, the cold grew, and with it a feeling of great joy. When they finally stepped into the open air, Hal gasped and gulped. It was bitter cold, like drinking from a mountain stream, and he closed his eyes in the sheer delight of it.

They stepped from a claustrophobic stone tomb into a great expanse of trees stripped bare of leaves, limbs covered in ice and snow, a gray mist hovering around their feet. They were free. They survived. Clem shivered in the bright light and stayed—or tried to stay—in the shadows of the bare trees. The wind increased, a biting, clawing thing that turned the cheeks red, numbed the hands and toes. It was soon obvious to Hal that this new world of snow and ice, a frozen, arctic world would not tolerate the presence of humans for long.

"Well, now what?"

He looked around him and sighed, pushing the hat back on his forehead.

Clem whined something unintelligible, but Hal understood it to vaguely mean *Northward*. So, they skirted the cliffs of the mountain and entered further and further into the great woods. About thirty minutes went by and Hal stopped.

"What are we looking for?"

Ha said Clem in his whiney ghost voice.

"What does that mean? Sounds like you're choking on something."

Hawth....

Hal placed his hands on his hips and shook his head with impatience. "You're like listening on a phone call with bad reception! *Hawth*! What is *Hawth*? What are you talking about?"

Hawthorn whined Clem as his ghost body clarified in intensity.

"Hawthorn? Is that a person?"

Clem looked bewildered.

"MaMaw told you what? Meet...what...a hawthorn tree?"

Clem shimmered and blinked. This was all Hal could take. He stomped around, pulled the hat from his head, and smacked it against several trunks. "This one? Maybe this one?" He stood before a huge trunk and bowed. "Hello, Mr. Hawthorn. Good to finally meet you. Oh, what is that? You can't help us because you're a TREE!" He smacked the bark again with his hat. Clem ignored him and drifted northward, weaving between the randomly growing trees, hovering uncertainly, then onward. Hal watched indignantly, then trudged on, head down grumbling, "idiot. I'm following an idiot."

The landscape of forest became dense. The space between the trees tangled with thickets, brambles, broken limbs, and rotted trees. Hal wedged through and scrambled over smooth skin slicked with ice and hard crusts of snow. It was soon clear that the afternoon was disappearing faster than either of them anticipated. Clem became more and more uncertain.

"Sure, MaMaw gives you instructions but not me," Hal huffed as he sat on a downed tree. "No, don't tell the one who can get you there! Tell the idiot, brainless ghost. Literally, you have no brain!" He looked at the expanding forest before them, the same thing, tree after tree after tree, no paths, no openings, just forest, the cliffs of the Black Mountains miles from them. Clem shimmered and pointed into the distance. Hal was too angry to even respond. He waved the mountain ghost to lead on, stood to his feet and followed behind.

Another hour passed, and they came to a low stone wall, a mossed covered thing that stretched out in both directions. It was moldered and damp, a skin of ice covering the top and sides where moisture had settled and gotten trapped. It looked to be ancient. It looked to be intact, and it was obvious that it was the border for something...quite sinister. Beyond the stone wall, in stark contrast to where they now stood, were meticulous row after row after row of identical trees stretching out as far as the eye could see. They were evenly spaced, and from their midsections, anchored deeply into their trunks, snaked a network of lines draping from tree to tree to tree to tree.

"What the hell is this?" Hal said, humphing and heaving himself over the low stone wall and walking up to the base of a tree. On further inspection they were not wires at all but hollow tubing, miles and miles and miles of clear, rubber or plastic tubing from one tree to the next, and through them ran some sort of liquid. And all around them, dangling from the lower branches were stones and bones, skulls and femurs and pointed rocks bound and hanging and clanking on dried ligaments blowing in the icy wind, a macabre wind chime, a warning.

The Forest of the Dead whispered Clem.

Hal reached out and touched the metal and rusted valve pounded deep into the bark, a sludge of yellow corroding where the material reacted to the tree's skin. "Is it sap?"

No shimmered Clem. It seemed to Hal that the mountain ghost was deeply saddened by the scene before them, his image shimmering and nearly disappearing with the emotion. They walked for another half an hour, but something was desperately wrong. The mycelial growth on Hal's arm shot with a pain, and he rubbed it vigorously. There was something else here. Something vaguely familiar, but not quite understood by Hal. He felt it in the tunnels of the Ghul, in the Black Gate of Cogstin. Thaumaturgy is what Christopher and Beatrice called it. Hal called it magic, and this was some kind of black spell that crackled and shuddered around them like the fine threads of a spider's web signaling to the predator that dinner was served.

"It's getting dark now," Hal said. "I can't be caught out like this. No shelter. No fire. We need to go back. Wait until daylight."

Hawthorn Clem whined.

A sort of madness had overtaken Hal now and he looked around in panic. He ran westward, down the great orderly rows of towering trees and the draping tubes, on and on and on, back to the moss-covered stone wall. And by the time they crossed over it, they knew quite well they had just escaped something terrifying.

"Well," said Hal. "You can put that on the bucket list of things never to do again." He looked back at the ominous and perplexing forest, then to the sky above. "Listen, we need to make camp. There's plenty of fallen trees near the mountain. Let's build a shelter and fire and get out of this cold."

So, they did. At least Hal did. He gathered wood and set it into a great blaze of warmth. He created a two-sided structure using an outcropping of rock, laid a thick mat of pine branches to insulate the ground, and sat contented enjoying a can of beans. Clem found a frozen rabbit, a half-eaten carcass. He hovered over it sucking and touching the stiff pelt.

When they were finished, Hal pulled out a flask and took a deep swig. "I'd offer you some, but..." Clem hovered near him, shimmering in the shadow of the hut and the bright light of the fire. "I used to be a different person," Hal said. He took another drink. "So damn long ago. So much has changed." He looked at Clem who shimmered again, then clarified, a crisp lined hologram of a human being, a clear indication the mountain ghost aviator was concentrating. "You know, Beatrice is constantly focusing on Christopher this and Christopher that. That *his* awakening was such a big deal." He took another swig from the flask. "What about *me*? What about what happened to me? What about *my* awakening? At least Christopher had Beatrice. Who was there for me?" He stared at the fire.

Something moved in the darkness beyond the ring of light. Clem jerked to attention, faded, and shimmered, then moved into the shadows. Hal either did not hear it or ignored it as he swam in his ocean of self-pity. The alcohol was now having its way. "There was one thing there for me," he whispered and pointed to the fire, his new companion. "You know what it was? Yup. That cold steel barrel, that's what. Oh, and you better be sure it was talking to me. I listened to every word it said, brother, let me tell you."

Hal grew even more morose and introspective. He too heard the movement in the darkness, twigs cracking, a shuffle, silence. He listened harder to pinpoint the intruder. His head was swimming, foggy, and he nearly tumbled sideways onto the ground. Clem had disappeared. Another crackle. Was it the fire before him or something stalking them from beyond? He heard it again, And what he thought could be the wind, but recognized it as Clem's strange vocals, a whining, screeching thing. Was he in trouble? The screech whined again, louder, then sudden and sharp, an obvious cry of alarm.

Hal stood up then collapsed to his knees, gravity pulling him to the ground, his balance lost in the alcoholic haze. "I'm coming, buddy" he slurred. He shook his head to clear it, then reached to his pack and pulled out the machete. "I'm coming, my idiot ghost friend. I'm coming." He stood, grew immediately lightheaded and smashed into a tree, cheek and forehead scraped and bleeding. "Damn it." There was that screech again, but this time it was with something else! Something answering the ghost. He thought of the terrifying trees with their runes of bones and stones dangling and clanking, the forest of absolute emptiness. What had made such a place? Was it out here? Was it tracking them?

"Hey you!" Hal bellowed, but his voice faded as he tried to blink his vision into sobriety. "Leave that ghost alone. You hurt him, and I'll..."

Hal stepped into the darkness, his vision useless in the pitch black, hands stretched out to feel for obstacles. He could hear Clem whining more and more, the sound escalating, short bursts, then silence. Then something else, a grinding, squeaking noise. Was Clem being tortured? "Hey..." Hal yelled out and launched into the darkness. "Hey!"

It was black as coal, and Hal's head was fully spinning. His equilibrium shifted, and he tumbled to the ground, raised himself up to his knees to face the terror. "The flashlight!" he cried with joy. What a revelation! Yes, yes, the light! He patted down his coat, found the front chest pocket. "Leave him alone, you son of a bitch or I'll..."

Hal flashed the light before him, but it was immediately knocked from his hand, a loud crack, a shooting pain, like being smacked with a bent tree branch. The light illuminated the ground in an oblong shape. He reached for it, but it was suddenly snuffed out, stepped on, crushed under something enormous. He raised the machete, but that too was smacked from his hands, a whip to the wrist, and his fingers released it.

"You want me?" yelled Hal. "You want a piece of me, well come and..."

That was all he could get out, for whatever was before him now wrapped some hard tentacles around his waist, up his neck and around his head. It muffled his mouth and movements. He shifted, but it was like struggling against chords of steel. Every time he moved, the creature sensed it, and tightened its grip.

"Quiet!" whined the ghost voice in Hal's ear. "Quiet!"

Hal hung limp in his captor's grasp. Suddenly, realized he had been lifted off the ground, slowly, carefully, higher, and higher. He heard the sniffing, several grunts, and as he looked far into the forest darkness, he could make out pale, slumped and lumbering creatures, a great number of them, moving slowly, cautiously, strategic. They were searching the floor, stopping, sniffing again, the leader, a crown of bones on its head.

Hal had not noticed that his captor moved. Soon they were near the encampment, the once raging fire now smothered completely, sparks and small embers, scattered pinpoints of light. Quick motions from above, and Hal's pack and goods were gathered. Swift and sure, at first sideways, crablike, then straight and determined. They moved into the darkness of the forest, farther and farther northward.

Clem hovered as if sitting on a limb near the captured Hal, like a passenger enjoying the view on a cross-country tour, careless, even happy. He stiffened, clarified himself with great concentration and motioned to Hal in a cordial gesture of introduction. "Hal, meet Hawthorn," he whined and groaned. He gestured above him. "Hawthorn, meet Hal."

Suddenly the tentacle that had been around Hal's mouth slackened and settled down like a loose scarf of wood, thorns, and flowers. Hal heard what could only be construed as a great jabbering of nonsense, a torrent of words unleashed where only a fraction anchored into his imagination. He heard the word *Roman* repeated over and over. He heard the word *Lara* mentioned many times as well. The jabbering intensified, and the rest fluttered into the rushing wind, lost, and abandoned to the great woods named for its enigmatic and terrifying ruler, The

Forest of the Horned God, or as the Thunsi who inhabited this realm called it, the Forest of the Dead.

Chapter Thirty-nine

Beatrice ran, her mind muddled by the thick web of thaumaturgy released. Still, there was something else confusing her. Something...familiar but distant like a scent long forgotten. *It couldn't be*, she thought. The thought was so startling, so confusing she stopped and looked back into the darkness of the trees. That was short-lived, and Warrior Beatrice surfaced. She cautiously moved down the small road that followed the bending river. She came to the wooden door where the dock master entered. It was locked. She pounded, pulled on the handle. She began to sing her thaumaturgy through the door, a mantra, a signal that broadcast low and outward, piercing living things, commanding their allegiance. The new hex was so great, the air sparkled and crackled with the force. Her words dissipated and were coopted.

"Go away!" Cried a muffled voice behind the door. "You're too late! It's too late."

Another wave, like pounding breakers over a sandbar, nearly knocked her to her knees. *Who could do such a thing? To her!* She watched in a stunned haze as NORM lumbered toward her, its processor buzzing and whirling, trying to make sense of the event., "Bio-auditory amplitude detected. Shutting down."

It settled to the ground, legs pulled up, vision system retracting into the impenetrable chassis.

"Shit!"

She turned toward the great woods and watched as a pale figure emerge from the gloom. It was tall, bone-thin, skeletal structure, like those that had been captured and transported across the river. This one was hunched over, a crown of bones on its head. It stared at her with great holes for eyes, hands stretched forth. It wrenched its head back and howled.

A voice smashed through the charged, vibrating particles around her, *RUN! DON'T STAND THERE! RUN!* So, she did.

The great animal horde rushed into the city behind her, smashing and shredding anything abandoned or left vulnerable, an open window, an unlocked door, a straggler, or vagabond near the border of the woods. With it, there came something else, a being, tall and lithe, and in his hands, a flute, his fingers dancing absurdly fast over the stops. He leapt, danced and played, the merry prankster, a demon, the god of music, the terrible Horned God from the Forest of the Dead.

Beatrice ran. She pulled on doors and pounded on boarded windows, then in a sense of absolute panic, she fled into the darkness of a great warehouse near the river. It was an open space with great mounds of crushed coal. She scanned the vulnerabilities, crouched in a corner, back protected from any attack, then raised her arms to strike. She sang lowly, slowly, carefully chosen words, carefully placed in a syntax of defense. Soon the coal was tumbling and fusing one chunk to another in a golem of black, angular rock. The coal-golem stepped unsteady toward the great expanse, the howls and violent force now just outside the building. And she heard a voice.

I am on the river. Come to me. Come to the river! It was familiar, clear. Christopher Dante was here!

She was trapped. The great horde just outside her building, pounding, thrashing, shaking and howling so that she feared the steel building would collapse around her. The Coal-Golem took a step, then hesitated.

Come to the...

The voice was cut off, stifled, a sudden wave of

thaumaturgy so powerful as to pulverize the Coal-Golem, lifeless black sand falling like rain from the sky. The enormous cliff of coal shook and tumbled down the pile, smashing her back like great hammer blows, an ancient stoning, blow after blow until her body crumpled and her brain was knocked senselessly into oblivion.

She woke to silence and could not tell if the building or the world of men, time and things collapsed in around her. Neither. She felt the weight of the stones pulled from her, the bloody and bruised flesh exposed to the cool night air.

She heard a voice and felt a gentle touch stroking her cheeks and forehead.

"You are safe, now. Nothing will hurt you." The voice was calm, low, profoundly familiar.

"Christopher?"

The stroking stopped suddenly, cupping her head, and pulling it up slightly...annoyance?

"No, not him, my love."

She squinted into the darkness, the face hovering just over her own, the voice, something piercing, sharp, a sudden buried memory released, surfacing with great force. Her vision cleared. "You? You're...here? How?"

The tall shadow did not answer. Beatrice's mind spun and reeled in a collage of images. She saw the Skeleton King swaying and morphing into someone lost to her, lost for four hundred years, hidden deep in the forgotten recesses of memories before The Event itself. That image shifted again. As her will succumbed to the powerful thaumaturgy, she saw a great horned creature staring back at her, and its mouth opened in an enormous grin of delight.

Greg Belliveau

Part Three

The Endeavor

Gods of IMAGO

Chapter Forty

They survived, were surviving. Whether it was due to a milder winter, the hedge of tree branches that supported them or Captain Robert's ingenious enclosed shack where the *Endeavor's* boiler became their hearth—whatever the case, they survived two months in such a hostile environment where even few Thunsi could have.

The exotic female had gained some strength over that time. She was still sickly, pale, and slept most days. Captain Robert would constantly give her melted snow to drink and hold her up gently as he broke off tiny bits of dried eel blubber. Nothing seemed to help her. Nothing seemed to hurt her either. She remained—a steady, weak, radiant being. When the sun broke through the gray days and settled on her, well, she looked like something created by the Horned God himself.

These were certainly not the most miraculous events that happened since Lara left Widorexiton and encountered the Horned God. No, that miracle she now felt inside her. The pain, sorrow and terror in the cave, all this evaporated in the presence of this growing life. It was when she was alone with her thoughts at night, an image in the darkness crashing into her dreamscape, the damaged survivors of the *Endeavor* restlessly sleeping around her—it was then that she relived the terror of the cave, the erotic horror, and immediately she pushed it down, down, down into the secret hole of suppressed memory. The trap door shut firm and locked. Lately, it had gotten so bad, the nightmares so pervasive, she found herself exhausted and barely able to function.

Routine would save them, or so Captain Robert reminded her, "A systematic division of labor, focus on the present, the next goal, fulfill that. Survival is a zero-sum game."

So, every morning they would awake to the cold, Captain Robert gathering wood, Lara attending the sickly female. Hour after monotonous hour. Day after monotonous day, until they survived weeks, then months, until the double-edged sword of icy wind and bitter cold blunted with the hope of spring. One morning everything changed.

Lara turned, at first thinking it just the wind blowing through the forest branches, but even the strange female was stirred by the sound, her eyes wide staring at Lara with concern. Lara crawled from the small shack and pulled the door closed behind her. The wind buffeted her face and arms. She turned from port to starboard trying to locate the intermittent sound. There it was again. She saw Captain Robert in the gray haze of morning, stumbling, falling, hoisting himself up over the drifts of snow, then waving and running toward her again.

"Lower the ladder!" He was screaming. "Lower the ladder!"

Lara looked beyond the tiny figure and saw something far behind. She grabbed the telescope from the cabin and raced to the bow of the *Endeavor*. Captain Robert was panicking, turning back toward his pursuer, then stumbling and running as quickly as he could. She moved the small lens up, then refocused using her other eye, and soon she saw it, Hawthorn!

The tall tree-being scurried, crab-like, after Captain Robert, gaining on him, gangly limbs or tentacles splayed out like writhing serpents. There was something behind it, another figure filled her lens. It was a strange, little thing. It wore what looked like a coat and carried a tiny pack on its back. It was yelling at Hawthorn, sweeping a small blade this way and that in a threatening manner. Immediately, she thought of the strange female in her cabin. Whether an illusion of light, shadow or an anomaly in an enigmatic forest, Lara saw a shimmering fog, a mist really, now in the same shape of the pursuing thing, now a borderless vapor. It glowed green, then with a bluish tint. She knew that it must have some sort of magical power at its disposal.

She tossed down the rope ladder and nearly slid her way to the bottom. Captain Robert was a hundred yards away. "What are you doing?" He yelled, then gasped for breath. "Get into the *Endeavor*! Go up!"

She ran toward him. He turned back as Hawthorn overtook him, a thin tentacle-branch shooting out and sweeping him off his feet and into a large drift of snow.

"You've come!" Lara screamed. "You're here!"

Hawthorn reached out and grabbed her, pulling her into itself.

"By the Horned God!" Cried Captain Robert rushing at Hawthorn, sword out and swinging.

The creature wrapped him up with a tentacle-branch and held him away while it jabbered, chortled and...well, danced with delight at the encounter.

"Okay, okay, okay!" cried Lara. "You must put him down. He is a friend. Captain Robert is a friend!" Hawthorn, his root ball face morphing into doubt, then a sort of apathy and resignation, dropped Captain Robert.

"By the Horned God! What is happening here?"

Soon he had his sword out again. He was standing firm between Hawthorn and the onslaught of the determined, little creature. It stopped several steps away from Captain Robert, then crouched as if ready to strike. It too was jabbering something unintelligible, a tone of menace in the cadence.

"Stay back," Captain Robert said. "By the Horned God, if you come closer, I will cut you down."

Gods of IMAGO

Chapter Forty-one

They traveled all night, Hal, Clem, and Hawthorn, the cold and wind numbing Hal so he could barely open his eyes, hoarfrost gathering on his hat, the front of his goose down coat. This Hawthorn, this strange tree-being, had not stopped jabbering. Nothing! Nothing would shut it up. It got so caught up in what it was trying to say, every once in a while, it would stop, hold Hal out in its tentacle-branch and earnestly explain some nonsense point. Hal gave up trying to interpret it. He just nodded in affirmation, the gesture obviously placating some argument going around in the bizarre creature's head, and off the being would rush. Clem was no help at all. If he understood any of the strange creature's words, he did not say, but occasionally, the mountain ghost would hover up to the being's root ball head and play his fiddle. Hawthorn jabbered excitedly, then quickened its pace.

Night was fading from the forest when Hal began to feel a sort of nauseous sensation in his stomach. The mycelia on his shoulder moved under his coat sleeve, restless, a sort of anxiety pulsing through his body.

"I need to eat," Hal said to Clem.

After another half hour, at Clem's direction, Hawthorn stopped and put them down into the snow. The trees thinned out a bit, and the sunlight was now breaking through the thickets above. Hal and Clem wandered about in the snow, sensing more than seeing, smelling the air, kneeling to the exposed earth, and gulping deep breaths to pinpoint the decaying, frozen dead somewhere in the woods. It wasn't long until they found it, a snow-covered carcass of half-eaten deer. Hal rushed over to it and splayed away the snow and chipped the ice with his knife. Clem already begun his feeding, and soon Hal was over it with his arms placed on the velum of ice like a praying supplicant.

It was Hawthorn who interrupted their gorging. It jabbered and stomped out warning. That was when Hal saw it. A tall, (so very tall!) emaciated, thin-skinned, gray skeleton being clothed in fur-lined coat and fur-lined makeshift hat. It held in its hand an enormous blade. It was a giant of eight feet! A skeleton giant with eyes dark and hollow, a scowl on its leathery, gray face, a large bundle of wood cradled in its arm. It shouted something at Hal, then turned to Hawthorn, shouted something else, then back to Hal and Clem.

"My god!" Whispered Hal, looking up at the towering creature.

The creature roared something in response, something obviously meant to frighten them. Just like that, the towering figure dropped its bundle of wood and dashed off into the forest.

"Thunsi! Lara! Thunsi! Thunsi! Lara!" Jabbered Hawthorn who darted after the escaping creature.

"Shit!" Hal hissed. "Now what?"

He pulled the machete from its sheath and raced after them, Clem by his side, shimmering and shifting in a multi-colored display.

He lost Hawthorn over a ridge, then as he crested it, he saw the tree creature racing toward the skeleton giant in what he could only imagine as an act of war. It knocked him easily to the side, and scooped up the shorter, but still very tall skeleton figure in front of it. Hal stumbled, puffed and ran to them. He found himself completely outnumbered by the strange giants. They were screaming at him, the tall one pointing his sword at him, stabbing the frigid air in defiance. The smaller one—and now he could see that it was a female skeleton being—was yelling at Hawthorn, then at him, then at the sword drawn skeleton. He heard a word over and over. It sounded like *Robber. Cold Robber.*

It was going badly, so Hal raised his hand and started screaming, "No Robber! No cold Robber! No Robber! I'm not a Robber! I'm with Hawthorn! Hawthorn!"

Both skeleton giants suddenly stopped, a look of absolute confusion on their faces.

"No Robber," Hal squeaked. "Hawthorn?"

The skeleton girl glanced at Hawthorn, then the other skeleton, then to Hal.

"Hauturn," she said, the word more guttural sounding, a hard "T" replacing the "TH."

"Yes! Yes!" Hal said, dramatically laying down his machete and gesturing at Hawthorn. "Yes, yes, that's right. Hawthorn is friend." He pointed to the tree creature then back to himself, back to Hawthorn. "Hawthorn, friend."

The skeleton giant savagely pointed his sword at Hal, all the while yelling something to the other skeleton girl, *probably his daughter*, Hal thought.

The giant swooped down and tossed Hal's machete far into the snow. He was trapped, helpless. Even Clem recognized the danger, and shimmered firm until he was nearly solid in his mist form, arms out as if to fight.

STOP!

The voice nearly knocked all of them to the ground. The skeleton giants wavered and steadied themselves. The one with the sword pointed it at Hal again in a threat of violence.

I SAID, STOP!

This time the thaumaturgy was so great, that every one of them, even Hawthorn, fell back.

Hal looked up dumbfounded. There, in the tall branches

of the trees standing in what he now recognized as some sort of dilapidated airship, a makeshift, thatched building, black smoke billowing from a vent cut in the roof—there above him was a pale-faced elegant woman, her almond eyes, and high cheekbones immediately recognizable.

"Elizabeth," Hal whispered. "It's you. You're alive."

Chapter Forty-two

At first Lara did not understand what the tiny creature was saying to them. Finally, it registered. He was saying "Hawthorn." She turned to Hawthorn and stopped his conspiratorial ranting long enough to question him. "They are with you? They came with you?" She looked at the small foreign thing and said, "Hawthorn? Yes, this is Hawthorn."

Captain Robert was furious now, and as the little creature placed his sword on the snow, he swept it away, moving now to cut him down. It was then that the thaumaturgy blasted through them, knocking her backward, her head groggy from the spell.

Lara watched the small foreign creature walk dumbly past her and Hawthorn, pulling what she now understood as a hat from his head, holding it submissively at his side. He spoke, more like a whisper, several words, and she realized they knew each other. The woman high in the *Endeavor* stood weakly, every now and then reaching out for the rail to steady herself.

Hawthorn pointed to her. *Me bring Hal and Clem. Me bring them to you and Elizabeth. Me save the forest of the dead. Me go and you go. All go to forest of the dead. Me go now.*

Lara looked up and mouthed the strange words: *Elizabeth.* She turned to the small creature before her. "*Hal,*" she said.

"*Clem,*" she said, the words like rocks in her mouth, hard and uncomfortable.

The small creature looked surprised then spoke the words back, repeating them over and over. He pointed to his chest,

"Hal" and kept doing that.

Lara was more concerned with the beautiful woman standing above her, now very unstable on her feet.

"I am coming, *Elizabeth*," she said, climbing the rope ladder then helping her to her feet. "Come, Elizabeth," she said soothingly, her name a revelation in her mouth and imagination. "We must get you out of the cold," she said.

"I need to see Hal," Elizabeth said without moving her mouth, more like word pictures in Lara's head. "I need to find my son."

"You will...*Elizabeth*," Lara said. "I promise you will. You must rest now."

She tucked the rabbit skin and blankets tightly around her, stoked the fire in the boiler and went back outside. She climbed down the ladder to Captain Robert stooping over Hal, and both seemed at their breaking point.

"We know nothing about these...these...creatures," Captain Robert proclaimed. "We know nothing about their intentions. Do they even worship the Horned God?"

"Well, why don't you ask them," and Lara walked to the squatting creature and stooped down to his level. He was ugly, puffy, puffy cheeks and puffy, fleshy body. It reminded her of a shriveled infant Thunsi. She asked in a slow deliberate tone. "Did the Horned God send you?"

It looked at her with its puffy, wrinkled features and said something unintelligible.

"Hal," it said tapping its chest. "Hawthorn" it said pointing to Hawthorn.

She watched it do this several times. Maybe it was hurt. Maybe it was simple-minded. She had known several Thunsi that were like this. She sighed and looked into its puffy eye sockets. Surprisingly, she had an idea. She stepped back and cleared away a small place of snow until only dark earth remained. She carved an image into the mud. A circle with horns. "Horned God." She pointed to the earth. "Did the Horned God send you?"

The small creature looked at the image then to her. It was adamantly shaking its head back and forth. Was it having a spasm of some sort? It must be sick. She watched it continue to shake its head, point, and wave its hands in protest, even scooting further into the tree behind it.

Lara stood and faced Captain Robert. "I think it's damaged or something."

"Well," said Captain Robert, "It will die if we leave it out here." He motioned at Hawthorn. "How do you know this tree creature?"

Me no tree! Me Hawthorn! Me no stupid tree, dumb tree. Me walk, talk run and kill. Me do all that!

Lara calmed him down. "Yes, yes, yes. You are not a tree," she said. "He is sorry for saying this."

She turned to Captain Robert. "Right?"

"Er...my deepest apologies. No offense was meant." Captain Robert even tilted his head down in deference.

Hawthorn just stared at him, several tentacle branches arched like hands on hips, a stern look on its root ball face.

Lara turned to Captain Robert. "How do I know it? Well, it's a long story, and we don't have time for that now."

"By the Horned God, what a day this has become."

Lara looked up at the *Endeavor*. "They know each other, and I think they need to speak to each other."

She reached out and touched Hawthorn's tentacle, the fleshy tags standing up with delight. "I need you to stay here. Captain Robert..." She pointed to him. "Captain Robert will need to know everything about where you have been, how you found Hal and Clem. What you want with them?"

Hawthorn jabbered, whistled, and chuckled...or what Lara thought was a chuckle—it was always hard to determine what was running through its mind at any given time. "Can you understand Hal?"

Hawthorne jabbered a river of nonsense, then the words clarified and focused. *Me understand everything. Me know everything under the sun. Me know about the trees, the slaves, the dead forest, the mines that kill and the Horned God who sees all and...*

"Okay," Lara said to Captain Robert. "Ask this Hal what you want, and I will translate the best I can."

So, the arduous process of interpretation, over interpretation, under interpretation and misinterpretation began. It lasted for several hours, ended in frustration, reorganized once again, lasted another hour, and by the time night fell upon the forest, Lara and Captain Robert placed several pieces into a larger picture.

From what they could gather—and who knew what flights of fancy or hard concrete truths were—Clem came from what he called the Black Mountains and was sent by an old rock, person, river—Hawthorn was vague and confused himself—called MaMaw. Hal specifically was sent to find Hawthorn. When Captain Robert inquired what he wanted Hal to do, what this MaMaw wanted from Hal, anything that had to do with some mission or plan—Hawthorn just jabbered and poured forth conspiracy after conspiracy, and Lara had a hard time translating, let alone calming him down so he would not accidentally hurt them.

What was clear, crystal clear, after all was said and done and all parties exhausted, Hal was connected in some way to Elizabeth. Some sort of divine plan was unfolding, and these two creatures were connected. The Horned God would know what to do, but he would not even arrive until Mid-Spring for the Gathering Ceremony. Now with Roman and The High Priest obviously at war...well, who knew what chaos they would find when they sailed back to Widorexiton.

"How are we even to do that?" said Captain Robert, lighting his licorice root and puffing his pipe to life. "We have no ship to sail there, and even if we did, the winter is still very much with us—at least another month."

Lara looked at Hal sitting silently on a fallen log, every once in a while, shivering from the cold, damp air. "Hal must speak to Elizabeth. I think that is what the Horned God wants. That's why he brought them to us."

She touched Captain Robert on his arm. "Don't you see? It's all a plan. It's unfolding right before our eyes, and we are now part of it."

"It does seem that way, child."

He puffed on his pipe in deep contemplation, then sighed. "Well, night will be here, and we need to get that poor creature warm, or he will surely freeze to death. Take him up into the *Endeavor*. Feed him. Give him some licorice root to soothe him. I will gather more wood for the fire. It's going to be a long and interesting night."

Lara walked over to Hal. She said slowly, intentionally. "Hal." Again, he motioned in that idiot way, slapping his chest in recognition. "Yes. You are Hal. You come with me up there."

She pointed at the *Endeavor*. Hal said something to her. He looked frail, tired and sickly. She shook her head not understanding. Hal crossed his arms in defiance, shivering. Whatever he was saying, it was in an obstinate tone. She understood the word, *Elizabeth*.

"Yes, Elizabeth," Lara said. "Elizabeth is up there. You can go up there too."

Again, she moved to the ladder.

Hal said, "Elizabeth! No! No Elizabeth!"

Lara stooped to him. "Elizabeth is up there. You can see her. You can talk to her."

Clem was shimmering near them now, and she saw Hal turn to the mountain ghost and say something. The discussion was long, Hal gesturing with his arms. Clem shimmered over to Hawthorn who was silently brooding over something. The tree creature stirred and crawled over to Lara.

Mountain mist say Hal no go to ship in sky. No Elizabeth. Me know nothing of this. Me no care of this. Me go to forest of the dead and save...

"Yes, yes, yes, yes. We will go there. I promise. For now Hal must get out of the cold. He cannot survive like you down here tonight."

And Hawthorn spoke to Clem who spoke to Hal. Hal vigorously shook his head and boisterously pronounced something again and again and again.

"Oh, by the Horned God!" Lara said. "Why won't Hal go into the *Endeavor*?"

Hal stepped up to her directly and spoke. She could not understand. Hawthorn translated.

He no go up to ship in tree. If he go, he...kill her.

Chapter Forty-three

It was one thing to realize strange creatures beyond his understanding inhabited the world beyond Cogstin. Like an onion skin, Hal had been peeling away what he thought to be the known universe, and what he thought was real, substantial. Every day, week, year showed him how little he knew about any of it. So, it did not shock him to learn of the Mountain Ghosts and now these skeleton beings. It did shock him that everywhere he ended up, he was being taken prisoner. He had just about enough.

When the tall skeleton being came back from gathering his wood, things got out of hand. He ambushed Hal and tied him up, all the while barking at him in that strange, harsh, guttural voice of his. What could he do? They were enormous, towering things, long legs, long arms and long necks with little heads of cornsilk for hair. The humiliation continued when he was tossed over that thing's shoulder like a sack of potatoes and hauled up forty feet into the great treehouse of a ship.

Once aboard the strange giant's demeanor changed, and Hal was set into the bow, wrapped in an enormous fur blanket. With great gentleness the crepe paper skinned giant knelt and presented Hal a steaming bowl of something that smelled of sage and rosemary mixed with tangy fruit. Almost like a father to an obstinate child, the skeleton coaxed him to drink, the guttural syllables smoothing out on the edges. He stood up and walked to the pilot house and closed the door behind him.

The others were gathered in the pilot house of the dirigible, shut off from the covered bow like an annexed room.

Hal could hear them talking to each other in low voices. Whether it was the broth itself or the fact that he had not eaten in days—whatever the case, Hal found the liquid substantial and delicious. Like a fine red wine, it grew more bold, earthy and enjoyable with every sip.

The giant skeleton returned and sat cross-legged before him. He lit a pipe, breathing in the smoke with great delight. The being seemed contented, almost inquisitive. Hal gulped the broth down and presented the empty bowl to the Skeleton host. "More, please," he said and pointed to the bowl, then to his mouth.

The skeleton stared at him without emotion, stem in mouth, embers glowing red. With an ever so slight movement shook his head—NO. He continued to stare at Hal with no hint of his internal machinations.

The smoke from the pipe gathered in the enclosed dome of branches and moss. Hal breathed it in. It was like the broth, but this time the sage and rosemary smooth like vanilla or maybe even cherry. His mind cleared and calmed. His inhibitions falling, the walls of doubt and suspicion evaporating. The Skeleton's crepe paper skin suddenly creased over his brow, and he reached into his coat pocket. He pulled out a leather pouch and took from it a thickly rolled cigar. Then, with a large expansive hand, touched his mouth and pointed at Hal's.

"You want me to smoke it?" Hal said.

"Smoke," imitated the skeleton in a guttural harsh tone.

"Smoke. Thank you." Hal put it to his lips, a great round tube of a thing and puffed as the Skelton held a red coal to the end. "Hal," Hal said and touched his chest.

The skeleton nodded, then straightened his hat and looked out at the night uninterested. He turned to Hal, said something, and waited for a response. When Hal did not do anything, he said it again, this time pointing to large epaulettes on his shoulder. Again, the same thing, pointing at the same epaulettes.

"You are military?" Hal said. "An officer?"

The skeleton just stared at him. "I'm Hal," he said and pointing to himself again.

The skeleton stared. He looked annoyed, his deep sunk eyes and gray skin crinkling and creasing as he nodded with agreement. He pointed at Hal. "Hal." Then to himself, first the epaulettes And what sounded like *Rocket*. Over and over the skeleton repeated this. The smoke from the small enclosure fully consumed Hal's head. He felt giddy, fearless, his mind sharp and racing, gathering, connecting. He held out the great cigar like a gangster making a point to his cronies. "You're an officer," he said. "Officer Rocket." The skeleton nodded and stared stoically. Then, just like that, he stood and walked into the pilot house once again.

Clem shimmered and hovered. He sat down in the fog—an inset of haze in an ever-thickening fog of aromatic smoke—and waved his hazy arm in protest.

"An appetite suppressant," Clem whined, firming his edges so as not to completely vanish. Hal looked at the large cigar with pleasure. "Some sort of narcotic, I would assume," Clem continued. The last part came out like an errant note on a fiddle, high, discordant, and jarring.

Hal was calm, his mind calm, limbs calm, his will a placid thing of contentment. "Well," pronounced Hal, "Officer Rocket there, has some explaining to do."

"Captain Robert," Clem said. "His name is Captain Robert, not Rocket." He shimmered and suddenly became a concrete image of concentration. "They are Thunsi. The word literally means *thin skinned*. MaMaw says that..."

Hal was now deep inside his head pondering and looping back to why he was even upset about anything. There was something bothering him, something he needed to investigate, something to consider, but for the life of him now, he could not imagine what that might be. "You're a fountain of information," he mumbled. He observed with absolute anticipation, like a member of an audience watching a play, as Captain Robert walked into the room, helped him to his feet and walked him into the pilot house where sat the Thunsi Lara and that delightful, exotic woman. Yes, he knew her name. Yes, she had a name. "Elizabeth," he whispered, sitting down across from her at the table. *What a delightful name*, he thought. *What a beautiful and delightful face. The face of a queen indeed.*

Chapter Forty-four

Lara sat across from Elizabeth and watched Captain Robert bring the small little man named Hal into the pilot house. Hal was placid, head drooping every now and then. Captain Robert's plan of sedation had worked. He had no idea how much Thunsae Myrrha to give the tiny creature or the warning signs of a dangerous overdose. It was rare in a Thunsi, but it did happen occasionally. When the hunger grew so great, the desperate Thunsi gorged on the licorice root until it was too late, the starved body absorbing too much too fast. This small thing seemed to be okay, and the amount in the broth just the right concentration.

Of course, all of this was necessary, for Elizabeth told them it was, warned them that Hal was not to be trusted. "He is not like *me*," she said.

A word Lara could not understand formed in her head. Replicant—one of many. Lara saw identical Thunsi standing together, And all the same trees in a forest, and these images repeated over and over and over in her imagination, rocks, trees, Thunsi, shells—all the same indistinguishable from another. And, strikingly, brilliantly, stunning in its contrast, Lara saw a magenta butterfly flying around the identical Thunsi, the identical forest of trees—hovering here and there, flying between them, landing on a head, an arm, Him, *The Other—Me, my son...Christopher Dante. Us/Them. Me/Him.*

Lara waited for Clem to settle near Hal as translator. She leaned forward. "Why did you come here?"

Hal looked up as the Mountain Ghost spoke to him, a

contented but earnest look on his face. "To find Hawthorn."

"Who sent you?"

"I told you," Hal said a little annoyed and directly facing Lara. "We've been through this."

"This MaMaw. Yes, we know," interrupted Captain Robert. "Who is Elizabeth to you?"

Hal, now obviously uninhibited, faced Elizabeth. She had a thick coat pulled up around her like a blanket. She looked pale and frail, her skin nearly translucent even after all this care and time. "Who indeed? That is the great question for all of history, isn't it." He chuckled. "Who is she really? How will she be remembered? The Great Empresses of IMAGO? The first true extraterrestrial to come to earth?"

He sat back in his chair and stared at her. He turned to Captain Robert and pointed to his now unlit cigarette of Licorice Root, flicking his thumb in his fingers in an odd gesture.

Lara nodded to Captain Robert. "He wants you to light it, I think. Remember, he's had quite enough already."

Captain Robert took an ember from the boiler and lit Hal's cigarette, then his own pipe. Lara, feeling the hunger within, lit her own. The tense room filled with the aromatic smoke, a quietness now settling on them all.

"What do you mean by those words," said Lara to Hal. "Is Elizabeth royalty?"

Hal waited for Clem, then waited some more. Lara was annoyed. He obviously was enjoying his place at the table too much. And...

"I'm sure if you ask her, she'll be more than happy to explain how she blew up the earth. She and her despot son."

Elizabeth sighed. She reached out and touched Lara's arm. She touched her! Those thin, pale fingers, cold and nearly powerless...they touched her! Lara looked at the oval face, the half-closed eyes. Images formed in her imagination.

"Elizabeth says you can fix the *Endeavor*."

Hal stared at Lara, then looked at Clem, then back to Lara. "What? Are you joking? I can't fix this piece of shit."

And clearly and distinctly to Elizabeth. "No. I won't fix this."

Lara looked at Clem as he translated. She could feel hope disappearing once again. The baby inside her needed to be home, back to Widorexiton. She needed to be in the community, to have this precious gift along with all the other precious gifts—the way it has always been for the Gathering, to please the Horned God. She looked at Elizabeth whose eyes were fixed on Hal's face.

An image popped into Lara's imagination. It was a young man, a being like Elizabeth, a small, plump, muscular creature. She knew who it was, Christopher Dante. Suddenly, all her experiences with Roman, the Mendel Fragment and his crazy obsession, he disclosing such a thing to her...she alone—all of this seemed to knit together in a teleological tapestry of fate by the Horned God.

"Fix the Endeavor," Lara said to Hal. "Fix this ship and Elizabeth will take you to Christopher."

Hal hunched over the table, the licorice root cigarette giant between two fingers. "Take me now," he said. "Take me to Christopher Dante."

"Fix our ship," Lara replied flatly.

"Even if I got the boiler to work, you need Helium. You got no Helium to make this thing fly."

Lara looked at Captain Robert as Clem translated. He shook his head and hunched his shoulders.

Elizabeth touched Lara again. An image entered her head. It was a great balloon filing and expanding, the balloon that now hung over the limbs of the trees tattered and flapping like a sheet on a clothesline.

"Elizabeth can make it fly. She can fill the balloon!"

Hal looked at Clem, then Captain Robert and Lara. "Well then, there you go."

"This is nonsense! He cannot fix this ship," pronounced Captain Robert emphatically. "Only a High Priest understands the magic of this ship. He is no High Priest."

Hal stared at Captain Robert, at Lara and Elizabeth as Clem translated. He burst out in what Lara thought was some sort of agony, maybe a headache, for the little creature held his head with his hand. He looked at them.

"No, no. I'm no high priest. Whatever the hell that may be. I'm better than that. Greater!" Hal gestured with his hands. "I'm a mechanic!"

Pointing at Elizabeth he said, "Give me Dante and I'll make this ship fly again."

Elizabeth reached out to Lara who calmed her. She understood. Hal could not be trusted, but he was the only hope of rescue. "You fix the ship first," she said. "I need to go home. I need to have my baby at home. We can take you to Christopher Dante after that. Elizabeth will take you herself."

Lara looked at Elizabeth, her eyes not leaving Hal's face.

There was a palpable silence. "Okay," Hal said. "I'll fix your boat, but she'll have to get it to fly. When we make it back to your home...Elizabeth and I go get Christopher...together. Where is home, by the way?"

Lara waited for Clem to translate.

"Over the Salty Sea. Widorexiton."

She watched Clem translate to Hal. Hal paused and looked up with a strange smirk on his face. "Over the Salty Sea, you say. Well now, that may be just the thing."

Chapter Forty-five

He had tinkered as long as he thought humanly possible without raising suspicion. He puttered and second guessed, built, tore down, re-built, tore down again—assemble this, fit that into here, pull it out, observe, get distracted—but now the skeleton giant called Captain Robert was getting impatient and was calling for Hal to come down and talk.

Hal's initial plan was to be so slow and scattered as to deflect any attention what-so-ever. Now, with the final gaskets ready to be fitted, he was more nervous than ever that his real plan, his secret diabolical plan had been discovered. Good thing he decided to fit the obstructing parts early and not at the end. If you don't want anybody to grow suspicious, act serious, earnest, intentional and focused on the task at hand. That way, no matter what you do, no matter what they may ask, "What's that for? How does that work? Boy, this sure is complicated"—any of this and all this just added to the obfuscation of the actual sabotage. That is exactly what all of this was, a blatant act of sabotage and murder!

Of course, he fixed the boiler...so that it would heat up and create steam power to turn the turbine and propel them all to some tiny island off the coast. Yep. That's exactly what would happen. Of course, a boiler can only work for so long until it builds up enough steam, and eventually, that pressure must be manually released, controlled, monitored relentlessly. Because if it was left to its own...well, a boiler is nothing more than a steam bomb waiting to explode. The way Hal calculated it out, they would be somewhere over the Salty Sea when it did. *They* meaning these crazy skeleton giants and that damned Elizabeth—not *him*. It was diabolical in its simplicity. Make it look like a valve, turn like a valve, even work for a short amount of time, but within two—three hours of use, when the steam began to build up, more steam than the propeller could expend—well, that's when the tiny little valve would close shut, heat seal and...kaboom! No more Skeleton people. Especially no more Elizabeth. The world would finally be rid of that hateful, despicable being who gave birth to the Great Destroyer, Christopher Dante.

"That should do it," Hal said, looking up at the Endeavor high above and smiling contentedly. "Need to let it set up until tomorrow, and it should be ready to go."

Captain Robert waited for Clem to translate to Hawthorn who looked on skeptically.

"I need to talk to Hawthorn," Hal said. "We're hungry, and we need to find food."

He waited for it to go through the great communication chain of idiocy. Captain Robert stared at Hal, shook his head in disgust, then climbed up the rope ladder and into the *Endeavor*.

Hal fell silent, skeptically observing Clem and Hawthorn, working out if they could do what they needed from him. He told Clem to tell Hawthorn they needed him to find "dead things."

Hawthorn shook his root ball head—disgust? *Always so hard to tell what that thing was thinking.* He hoisted Hal up and crab walked into the forest.

It was biting cold, and the snow had begun to whip about the barren trees. They traveled for about a mile into the woods, when they came across the corpse remains of a deer. On closer inspection, it had been attacked with great slashes across the sides, the hide stiff and frozen tent flaps. The throat was torn out. It had fallen only a few hours before and the process of decay had not fully begun. Hal and Clem hovered over it, brushing away the powdery snow. Hal could feel the mycelia on his arm spread toward his outstretched hand, and soon the saprophagous fungi was gorging on the remains.

Hawthorn disappeared and soon returned, bent over, cautious. "Shhhhhhhhhh," it hissed. "Shhhhhh. Me no want to be seen or heard. Blodetan. Blodetan everywhere, hunting. Me go. Me take you and go to safety."

"What is he babbling about," Hal said to Clem.

"He's scared of something. Something is out there. Sounds like a whole bunch of somethings—and we don't want to be caught out here with them."

Hal pulled away from the carcass quite satisfied. He looked at the impatient Hawthorn. "They do this?" Hal said suddenly side struck by a thought that was now consuming him. He pointed to the dear's throat.

Hawthorn nodded.

"Where are they?"

Hawthorn shook his head. "Me no go back there. Blodetan hunting. Very bad, very bad."

Hal looked behind him at the terror somewhere in the haze of snow. He turned toward the *Endeavor* and the skeleton people. "Do they hunt the skeleton people?" Hal said to Clem. "Go on. Ask him."

"They are not skeleton people," Clem said. "Thunsi. Their race is known as Thunsi."

"Just ask him."

Clem translated the best he could. Hawthorn looked at Hal in earnest. He nodded his head. "Blodetan hunt everything. Mostly little Hal's, juicy, plump, round Hals." Clem translated.

"Take us to them. Just let me see them. It's important I see them."

Hawthorn shook his head NO.

"You frightened? You scared of them? The big tree scared of a little Blodetan?"

He looked at Clem who was shaking his head in confusion at Hal's question. "Tell him those exact words" And forcefully. "Tell him."

Clem translated. Hawthorn grew agitated. "Me no scared. Me no scared of anything. Me no scared of little, tiny puny Hal. Me no scared of them. Me Hawthorn. Me no scared of anything."

Soon the now courageous Hawthorn scooped up Hal with Clem hovering on a branch and scurried into the blowing snow beyond. It wasn't long until they saw them, thousands of hunched, sniffing, pale, naked things, skinny like Thunsi but more animal in appearance, a horde of them moving stooped to the ground, slowly, methodically searching.

"Good god," whispered Hal as he rethought his plan.

He rubbed his face. Then decided.

Hawthorn crouched just below the lip of the ravine looking like some fallen, storm-ruined tree. The wind stopped, and the snow lightened just a bit in the dimming evening light.

That was when Hal did the unthinkable. He screamed out! Over and over until the horde of Blodetan turned, the great bone-crowned head of the leader lifting high into the air, howling, eyes wide and mouth agape.

Hawthorn, Clem, and Hal fled for their lives.

Chapter Forty-six

Lara found herself kneeling before Elizabeth, her long, bony finger stroking the sleeping woman's forehead. While her outward motions were calm, her mind furiously raced down rabbit hole after rabbit hole. When the drugged Hal mentioned Christopher Dante, when he connected the lineages, explained what happened...that the myths were true, that something called The Event took place, Elizabeth and Christopher Dante...her son somehow caused it... Roman had the Mendel Fragment, the mythical connection to a mythical past, a supposed scrap from a supposed encounter with the supposed writings from some supposed book by some supposed Christopher Dante. Well, she was now in the actual presence of...an actual god.

Her mind spun and swooped. Her stomach seemed an ice ball of doubt, fear and awe. Elizabeth opened her almond shaped eyes. Lara immediately bowed her head, pulled back, horrified and expectant of some divine repercussions.

"I'm so sorry" she stumbled. "Sorry, sorry. I'm so sorry."

She hurriedly straightened the fur blanket near Elizabeth's' chin, but the eyes were once again closed, the facial expressions nonresponsive.

"What are you doing, Thunsi?" Barked Captain Robert. "I need help with the tethers." He looked at Elizabeth and at Lara. "You leave her be. She's none of your concern. She's to do what she said she can do, then we get out of here. The High Priest will know what to do with her."

Lara smirked. "Which one?"

"I'll have none of that coming from you. Now get out here and give me a hand."

He rumbled and banged his way through the door and left it open behind him. Lara leaned down and kissed Elizabeth's forehead. Then she hurried out the pilot house, shutting off the sleeping god from the blowing snow and biting cold.

The evening came quickly, the gray haze dimming until Lara could no longer see the stitches, she had sewn onto the great canvas that was the balloon. She was just finishing one last patch, inconsequential hole really. Her mind was racing back to Roman and the Mendel Fragment. The divine connections, she being chosen, taken to this place, gifted by the Horned God to participate in the Begetting and the Gathering, and how something great was now happening, something that seemed...

She saw them before she heard them, a movement in the shifting light of evening. The sheer number captured her voice and chained it to the back of her throat. What came out was a groan. Captain Robert was already at the bow.

"By the Horned God! We are lost!" He gathered himself And shook Lara. "Go! Get Elizabeth. Now! We must leave now!"

Lara blinked, then rushed into the small pilot room. She shook Elizabeth with such force that the strange being nearly toppled over. "We must go! You must fill the balloon! Elizabeth!" She pulled and dragged the bundled woman through the door. The howls from the Blodetan where close, and Captain Robert ran to the weak Elizabeth.

"Now is the time! Now! Can you fill the balloon? You said you can do it! Can you, do it?"

He did not stay for the response, for the Blodetan gathered around the base of the trees and began to—shake them. At first it was inconsequential, a shimmer nothing more. Soon the massive horde, climbing one on the other like fanatical ants became a great and terrible weight. The trees that held the *Endeavor* fast began to give way. The branches, dead from winter began to break and yield to the pressure. Lara peered over the side of the *Endeavor* to see the Bone-Crowned king raise and lower his great clawed hands as the chaos of Blodetan united and rocked in unison. The base of the dirigible shivered, slipping down to a lower branch.

"We are lost," cried Captain Robert. "By the Horned God I will not die like this! Not after all we have survived!"

He swept out his great sword and shook it at the hazy, blowing snow.

It was not the mass below that shook and made the dead branches crack and swing. No, it was the great canvas balloon expanding, erupting through limb and ice, buffeting the wind, and defying the death that clawed and groaned below. Up, up and out it went, huge, at first sphere-like than elongated into its original shape.

"She is doing it!" Cried Captain Robert.

"Yes," whispered Lara. "Yes, I knew she could. Yes, yes, yes!"

Elizabeth, with eyes closed, hands lifted above the fur blanket ever so slightly, mouth chanting in a tongue immediately swept away by the wind. Lara watched her, then the great canvas tarp, as it lifted into the night sky. She saw the branches give way, or were they hands pulling it up. She saw a torrent of air rushing into the void, a wind, like a spirit of some living thing entering and moving and bolting upward, up, up, up, up!

"What about Hal, Clem and Hawthorn?" Shouted Lara at Elizabeth. "Wait! We must wait for Hal!"

She grabbed Captain Robert by the arm. He pushed her aside. "They are on their own. We cannot wait! Quickly! Turn the valve on the boiler!"

Lara ran into the pilot house, threw a great lever and turned the release valve to shut off any escaping steam. She raced back to the starboard side and searched through the blowing wind and snow for any sign of Hal and the others. *How could they have survived such an onslaught?* "Protect them, Hawthorn." She whispered. "Please protect them."

As the great dirigible's balloon filled with helium, the basket and lines pulled taught, held fast by the ice-fused branches and snow. Elizabeth raised her hands higher, and the make-shift fortification of pine branches and moss and mud gave way and tumbled down upon the leaping and raging mass of Blodetan below, a great force smashing, breaking bone and skull. And the *Endeavor* was free. It rose above the tree canopy of dormant limbs and caught the great wind sweeping from the South.

"Hold fast!" Captain Robert yelled. "Lara! Engage the propeller!"

Lara pushed the lever forward. The steam boiler shimmered and rumbled. "Now let's see if that idiot Hal was good to his word."

It rumbled again, belched out a jet of steam, then the great wooden propeller swept around and around and around, faster, and faster until the airship shifted its direction and headed North over the Forest of the Dead, over the Blodetan now scattering in a confusion of chaos, over the dreaded Cave of the Horned God and the strange Grove with its bones and runes and death and...toward...the great cold, churning Salty Sea.

It was only then, when the hull lifted on the buffer of air, that Lara saw the look come over Elizabeth's face. It was unlike anything she observed from that beautiful visage, and it unsettled her. It was for only a second, but it was there non the less. An ironic smirk that somehow, beyond all reason, she had gotten away with stealing fire from the gods.

Chapter Forty-seven

I mean...it was a seriously stupid idea, and just how terrifying the consequences of such an action was only now settling on Hal as Hawthorn raced through the Forest of the Dead. They were quick, these skeletal animals, quick like lions or wolves, a bounding rushing horde. Hawthorn was quicker, craftier. Soon there was a deep ravine separating the pursued and the pursuer.

"Me sneak to ship in tree. Me circle around," Hawthorn said.

Clem translated, and Hal shook his head vigorously. "No! No! We can't go back!"

"Me sneak and go to ship in tree, to Thunsi. To Lara."

"We can't go back there!" insisted Hal even more emphatic.

Hawthorn stopped, pulled Hal from a crook of limb, held him up before him.

"Me go back to tree ship, back to Lara."

Hal looked at the root ball head, the strange, morphing features that registered annoyance, even anger at the resisted plan.

"Why?" Clem whined. "Why can't we go back there? They are the way to safety." He paused and stared at Hal, his outline rigid, well defined, "What did you do?"

Hawthorn looked at Clem, then at Hal, the tree being starting to understand there was something amiss.

Hal wriggled and gesticulated angrily. "Put me down! We

can't go back because... Well, that horde will kill everyone—us and them. If we go to the ship, we will lead them right to it! And what? They kill us and them." He paused and feigned like he struggled to come to a sacrificial conclusion. "No, it's done. We need to hide. We need to draw them away from the ship and shelter somewhere away from them all."

Hawthorn was getting the gist of it. "Me no go to ship in tree?"

"No!" Hal said, looking behind Hawthorn, hearing the rampage. "We need to lead them away. We need to go somewhere else."

Suddenly, there was a great howl along with the cracking of limbs, as if the forest itself was taking the wrath of the Blodetan. "We must hurry!"

They dashed west toward the Black Mountains. Away from Elizabeth, Lara and the *Endeavor*. The horde of Blodetan were gaining, and soon phase two of Hal's plan was now unraveling before his eyes. The damn things were wickedly persistent, and there was no way to outrun them. It was obvious that it was Hal who would be affected the most. What could the horde do to a ghost or a tree? He screamed at Hawthorne in a completely self-preservation earnestness, "Run, damn you! Run or I'm a dead man!"

The great horde of Blodetan spanned out over the frozen earth. Soon Hal, Hawthorn and Clem were forced to follow the foothills of the Black mountains on their left. It was a trap, and they all knew it. Like the fox fleeing the horse and rider or the newly born caribou fleeing blindly down a path foreordained by the pack of wolves. So, Hawthorn kept choosing an ever-limiting path, hemmed in by the great mountain cliffs. Soon they came to a massive ravine, steep and perilous to descend.

"We are trapped," whined Clem in his screeching ghost voice.

"We can follow the edge," Hal calculated.

Even as the words left his mouth, they could see the horde of Blodetan far, far before them, rimming the edge of the ravine and trapping them.

And...the unthinkable. Hawthorn leapt into the air, a free fall of thirty feet, and Hal hugged the strange bark-skin with all his might. They plummeted down, down, down. As the rushing ground came up to meet them, the tree-being whipped out tentacle-branches, and along with its root-feet, stabbed, dragged and slid against the rocky boulders and muddy landscape, so that it hit the ground in full gallop.

Hal cheered as much in absolute amazement as in exuberance. Clem fiddled and whined with delight. Hawthorn leapt from one massive boulder to the next. He crossed the small stream at the very bottom, and with spider-like adeptness spanned the steep adjacent cliff until they all three stood on the opposite rim of the great ravine starring at the bone-crowned leader and the amassing horde.

"Ha!" screamed Hal victoriously. "Take that you sons of bitches! Now what will you do?"

What they would do was obvious, for at their leaders great bellowing howl, they leapt into the abyss of air, tumbled, clawed, rolled, and smashed—like lemmings over a cliff face—to the very bottom. There they groaned, cracked, adjusted their broken bones, and gashed flesh. They gathered and moved in waves across the bottom of the ravine and up the other side.

"My god!" screamed Hal. "What are they?"

"Me told you!" harangued Hawthorn. "Me told you not to bother hunting Blodetan. Me told you! Blodetan don't die. They dead. Dead don't die. Dead just eat plump, juicy Hals! Me told you! Me told you this!"

Soon the horde had reached the other side. Hal, Clem, and Hawthorn were already fleeing across the frozen forest floor.

And they came to the wide opening that was the Grove of the Horned God. Hawthorn stopped. They could hear the growling, sniffing and enraged Blodetan behind them.

"You can't just stop!" Hal screamed. "Why did you stop?"

"Me no go into Grove. Sacred Grove. Holy Grove of the Horned God. Me no go."

"Look!" cried Hal, and he pointed beyond the grove to the Blodetan now standing on the edge beyond. They were cut off and surrounded. The trap sprung by the bone-crowned king.

Hal was not going to be eaten, torn apart, hung on the trees and dangled from the limbs like the bones and stones he saw dancing in the wind. No, he came too far. He would not end as some meal for monsters or some damned sacrificial offering to this...this Horned God.

"Bullshit!" He screamed and leapt from the branch to dash into the open grove. He could feel the thaumaturgy as he ran, a crackling, spitting force that poked and pierced his flesh, a terrible swarm of stinging bees. He heard a wind that became a voice that became like thunder to his ears: "Who dares to enter the grove of the Horned God?" Soon what seemed to Hal like fists pummeled and smashed him to the ground.

"He will die," Clem whined, and he too leapt into the open grove, the rows of great trees with their stones and bones and runes carved deeply into the bark—a terrifying uninhabitable place of dark hexes and death. Clem's body dissipated as he came closer and closer to Hal, until they both fell useless to each other and doomed.

"Me no like Hal!" Hawthorn remonstrated. "Me never like stupid Hal, his stupid voice, his stupid thoughts and stupid yelling at the Blodetan."

With a roar, a groan, a laugh of vengeance and death—who was to say, for the creature was enigmatic on the best of days—Hawthorn dashed into the Grove of the Horned God, the terrible thaumaturgy exploding in a greenish haze as it met the strange skin-bark. It swooped up the fallen, dying Hal. It gathered up the dissipated Clem, swirling a limb like a fan, then circling it round and round until the ghost materialized once again. With both it streaked like a blur to the great mouth of a cave and stood before it. Pronouncing something from another age or was it just Hawthorn exasperated and at its wits end being forced in such a predicament—whatever the case, it bellowed and writhed its tentacle-tree limbs before the great open expanse, then disappeared into the darkness that was the Cave of the Horned God.

The Blodetan stood on the perimeter of the terrifying grove, moaning, and covering their faces.

Chapter Forty-eight

They were free, and they cheered. Lara hugged Captain Robert, who stiffened, then pushed her gruffly away pronouncing, "We haven't made it yet."

To further deflect the emotional outburst, he knocked the side of the boiler with his knuckle and checked the pressure gauge. Tapping it and mumbling with disapproval under his breath.

They were now over the Salty Sea, the edge of land disappearing in the snow and wind. This was the perilous moment of the journey, for they had left the certain death of the Blodetan behind them, only to trust blindly in the boiler and power of the increasingly fatigued Elizabeth. The waves swelled, rolled, and churned below them. Lara decided it was better to sit in the pilot house than to constantly monitor the dark night as Captain Robert was doing.

She stared at Elizabeth who with her eyes closed concentrated on the spinning and creating of storytelling power. The tale of helium expanding into the canvas balloon of the desperate *Endeavor*.

"May I ask you something?" Lara said meekly, tucking the fur blanket around Elizabeth's feet. She rolled a small, thin cigarette of licorice root and inhaled the smoke. Her hunger was growing with the anxiety that surrounded her and with the swooping thoughts now surfacing in her head.

Elizabeth opened her eyes, then closed them again, exhausted.

"I'm sorry," Lara whispered. "I'm just...well..."

She sat back and caressed her abdomen that was now a bulge of wonder, pulling at the fasteners on her coat. She crossed her legs to give the baby space, and leaned back against the humming, vibrating wall of the pilot house.

"It's just that I've had no one to talk to about this. It's just that, well, now that we are safe, I don't know what to think about it all. I'm sure when we get back to Widorexiton, it will all happen so fast, the miracle of the Horned God, I mean...well..." Again, she rubbed her abdomen. "You are a mother..."

Elizabeth opened her eyes and stared at Lara, her face evidencing no internal thoughts. Suddenly, she reached out her hand and placed her thin, pale fingers on Lara's arm. "I'm sorry," she whispered.

Lara searched her face for more, but Elizabeth closed her eyes once again. "What do you mean?" she said. "What are you sorry for?"

It was then that randomly, forcefully, terrifying pictures flashed in her head, strange, barbaric—one after the other. Flash, small Thunsi babies crying all alone, struggling on thin mats, a tall, hunched figure hovering over each, observing, a great hood pulled over the head. Flash, crying baby Thunsi held coldly, indifferently by chained Thunsi, a tattered, barely clothed group, lined up before holes in the earth, kneeling down before them..."

"Stop this!" Lara cried out.

Yet the graphic pictures forced one after the other into her imagination. Flash, tall trees, row after row, as far as the eye could see, long tubing draping down like clothes lines, from tree to tree, and each fastened to a moldered, rusted, tap driven deep pouring forth... Flash, barrels and barrels and barrels of... Flash, a huge, fleshy naked thing, hunched and dying in...a cave... The Cave of the Horned God! Tubes, like from the trees, snaking from its neck, swooping up into a hole. Flash, Elizabeth rolled up and carried from the great mouth of cave, Roman chanting and singing beneath the eel skull tossing her down the ravine...

"What is this?" Lara said, pushing herself back further toward the door of the pilot house.

The pain and sadness, the intense grief rotated and supplanted image after image after image. Although she could not comprehend what she saw, she understood it to be so great a weight that she cried out. The *Endeavor* rocked, the bow suddenly tipping down. Captain Robert rushed into the pilot house.

"You must keep us in the air! By the Horned God! You said you could do it!"

Elizabeth reached up and fisted her hand with great effort, the bow leveled out, then the whole dirigible lifted high, rocked, and swayed violently before resuming its course.

"Steady on now," said Captain Robert.

He turned to Lara. "Monitor the boiler," he bellowed. "Be quick about it! When it gets to the red line, we need to release the pressure. Do you hear me, Thunsi? Now get to it!"

He stormed out of the pilot house and stationed himself near the canvas balloon, pulling the ballast lever down, then up slightly.

~ * ~

The dim light of morning was breaking in the east, when the Endeavor's boiler gauge hit the red line. Captain Robert turned the release knob and pulled down the emergency release lever, but no steam released. As the needle shimmied higher and higher it was obvious the severe danger they now faced.

"By the Horned God!" screamed Captain Robert. "Fortify the stern! We must make some effort to shield ourselves from..."

He did not finish, for a white-hot wave of super-heated

gas erupted with shrapnel of copper and steel, slicing the balloon, shredding the tethers and plunging the crew of the *Endeavor* into the ice-cold water of the Salty Sea.

~ * ~

Lara did not think of anything as she fell from the sky, or perhaps she had a fleeting thought. Why all this effort, luck, and hope, if we are to die in the Salty Sea? Perhaps she thought of the vision Elizabeth showed her. Maybe she thought of the small life within her who would not know, do or be. Whatever she was thinking, it lasted for a second. She lost consciousness as she plummeted down, down and down. There was something, however odd, a nano second, an impression really, a realization too late that something beyond her understanding was unfolding. It was only a second.

~ * ~

Captain Robert felt the blast, felt the instantaneous slicing of cloth, flesh, and bone, As his body fell from the sky in severed pieces, his mind flashed to a single thought. It was a picture of a moment stored deep in his fold of memory, released, exploding into his frontal cortex as his head tumbled and spun. He saw a young Thunsi, proud, smiling on the deck of a ship, but it was not him. No, it was the morning he arrived late to the harbor to find his young son, Roman, at the helm of the *Intruder*, standing tall, barking orders to the crew... This was the flash of synapse, the electrical pulse as Captain Robert died. *My son. My dear, dear son....*

~ * ~

Elizabeth sensed the explosion before it happened. She recognized it was sabotage, but all too late. She saw the old Captain fragment from the blast and instantly gave him one last precious thought. She watched Lara tumble, and with all the strength left in her body, she spun a final story. The plot point and goal were easy. Lara must be saved, for the pregnant Thunsi held the great key to whatever drama her only son, Christopher, was to play out. She spoke and chanted a basket into being, a container, something to hold out the sea. As they all plummeted toward the water below, she cupped and cradled the tall Thunsi with grace into the splintered fragments of the *Endeavor* bound with chord. As she fell, her nearly lifeless body about to smash into the stone surface of the sea, she cried out, a roar, a whelp of pain and sorrow. It was directed at Lara, and it pierced her imagination like a great spear. FIND MY SON! FIND CHRISTOPHER DANTE!

Chapter Forty-nine

Lara woke in the basket of wood, bound with tethers from the now defunct *Endeavor*, a watertight shell, tall enough that her head just peaked over the top. What it was, where it came from, how she got into it—she had no capacity to understand. By the setting sun, she understood that she had been in this basket for at least a day and maybe days on end. She was hungry, so hungry, and what remained of her licorice root was soggy, but still useable. She sucked on it and rolled it in her mouth. The basket bobbed up one swell then slid precariously down another. At that moment, she left consciousness.

Hours, days later...she did not know, she awoke, shivering and thumping. She clasped her legs close to her chest, the great coat now dried from the wind, became a tarp for her and the unborn baby. *Thump. Thump. Thump.* Her head drooped and hit the side of the wooden basket. *Thump.* She was so hungry, so tired, and soon her head fell where it lay. She lost consciousness again.

Lara's eyes slowly opened to chaos. A roar of waves and violent splashes, and her tiny wooden basket launched high into the air then splashed down like a great rock. She held firm to the bound planks. She realized, to her horror, that it was not a storm but a shiver of great eels writhing and fighting and surfacing, buttressing her to and from, their mouths wide with teeth as they gashed and sliced at each other.

There was no way to steer the tiny tub, no way to maneuver it away from the great slicked monsters, so she covered her head with her hands and screamed at the top of her lungs. That was when the culmination of previous events stormed down on her like an avalanche. The flight to the coast, the seduction of the Horned God, the terror of the Blodetan, the finding of Elizabeth... Elizabeth, that beautiful, sad, wonderful... And all else disappeared. Only one thing remained, a command, *Find Christopher! Find my son!* She held her abdomen with her bone fingers. No. She would not die here! Not here! She did not come this far to die in the sea...to be eaten by...

And she stood. That tall, crazy, mother Thunsi stood in that tiny wooden tub. She screamed a lunatic scream that raged, pronounced death and destruction to anything that would dare prevent her from fulfilling her promise to that beautiful magical being!

~ * ~

It was not only Lara who heard the great pulse command Elizabeth sent out before she died. Roman on Widorexiton, Roman the Great High Priest who was holding the Mendel Fragment in his hand—he heard it as clear as a bell in winter. Elizabeth, his great threat, the mother of Christopher Dante was alive and coming for them all. This the Horned God warned him would happen. He would know the sign. Well, you couldn't get more of sign than that call.

As Roman sailed toward the eels, he saw something in their midst. This was how Roman found Lara. Raging and hitting the great backs of the surging eels, a tiny tub of bound wood, a thimble of life between the storming, raging titans. It was Roman, the new High Priest of Widorexiton, Roman the Great Eel Slayer who when he saw her, thinking it Elizabeth, the sworn enemy of the Horned God, jumped from the sleek eel boat with harpoon in hand, screaming out Elizabeth's name in rage and hate.

Only, it was not Elizabeth. It was Lara, the peasant girl chosen by the Horned God. As he stood over her, ready to strike, he paused and wondered, perhaps even remembered. Roman, High Priest of Widorexiton, Eel Slayer, jumped onto the head of the biggest eel and before it could plunge below the surface, pierced its skull, jabbing with ferocious, terrifying power until his wrath exhausted, until the other eels fled. The sea about them turned a foamy red froth.

Gods of IMAGO

Greg Belliveau

Part Four

Kyrnunos

Gods of IMAGO

Chapter Fifty

South, ever southward, beyond the Cave of the Horned God, the Grove, and past the Forest of the Dead. South, south and still further south looms a great wall, high, neatly layered, chiseled granite blocks, weather-worn, ivy-covered, strong like iron. This is the great border wall of Kyrnunos. It is a magnificent, old wall stretching out like an abandoned fish net, beginning on the northwest bank of the Cuy River, expanding out in a strange pattern as if the creator followed the surreptitious and whimsical footsteps of a drunken madman. Whether because of some internal politics or generational expansion, the great wall—now moving outward, now jutting angularly back on itself, now broad, expansive, straight, then bowed or angled—this wall found its end on the northeast bank, morphing into the bending Cuy River as it eventually made its way to the Salty Sea.

Inside that massive wall, protected from the terror and chaos that was the Forest of the Dead and the Blodetan and the Horned God, is the city of Kyrnunos, a thriving merchant city built on the banks of the river. The buildings and houses are systematically arranged on the bluff. This geological feature is at times steep and precipitous, plummeting down to the gray rolling water below, at others, a gradually sloping knoll. If one was to stand on the top she could see a wondrous vista, fifty miles across the river and all the way to the mineral mines far in the distance.

Kyrnunos is a worker town, a river town, a place of disparate folks waking, working, sleeping, and beginning again. Nobody speaks of the mineral mines or the treacherous excursions to retrieve the Thunsae Myrrha from the Forest of the Dead. Nobody talks about the enslaved Thunsi or the senseless deaths of that tragic race. It is all anyone has ever known, this river life—a symphony played out by an unseen director for four hundred years. Scratch the surface, say, or enter that world from the outside, and one sees quite clearly—It is a place where hope has been abandoned, forgotten, one filled with silent desperation and great fear.

Far above it all, on the northern side of the tallest bluff there sits a mansion. It is oversized and seemingly displaced, so disproportionate to the small shanty town, the worn buildings and utilitarian factory warehouses that line the river far below. To look at this gaudy building sitting proud and high on the hill like some exotic mating bird is to beg the question if it were not some sort of joke, some sort of ironic, intentional statement, or maybe just the random choice of an idiot, like an ignorant person wearing audaciously bright and cheerful colors at a funeral. It has been there as long as anyone can remember. It has never fallen in disrepair, a freakish glimmering, shiny thing on a hill.

It was here that Beatrice found herself after the raid of the Blodetan.

Chapter Fifty-one

It was safe to say that Beatrice had never experienced such opulence in her memory. Four hundred years of scrapping, hiding, gathering and existing, missional, intentional, spartan, violent, her body did not understand or like the cradled foam of the expansive mattress, the silk sheets that slipped across her naked body as she turned then sat up pushing her scarred and weathered skin against the pleated headboard. It was this nakedness that alarmed her the most. How did she get here? Where were her clothes? When she heard the knock on her bedroom door, she instinctively pulled the sheet around her chest in an act of modesty and self-preservation.

The door creaked open cautiously and a gray skull wrapped in a flowered scarf appeared in the small space.

"If it pleases you, Miss, Sir would like you to join him in the garden when you are ready." The voice was calm, distinct, intentionally controlled, as if every word was thought through and pronounced using a systematic chart.

"Where are my clothes?" Beatrice hissed.

The Thunsi stepped further into the room. She was tall, seven feet at least, a flowing dress (the same floral pattern as the scarf around her head) fell loosely down her body, long gray arms terminating into spindly, dagger fingers extending out as she pointed to the closet. "I believe Miss will find suitable clothing in there."

"What happened? How did I get here?"

The Thunsi's face looked blank, then she smiled

politely." Now if you will excuse me." With that, she pulled back through the door and closed it behind her.

The room was bright, clean, minimal, and unused. She stood naked and walked to the closet. There a multitude of flowing, multi-colored, silk robes, hung in orderly fashion that matched a color wheel. Next to them was an armoire filled with all manner of under garments, pants, and shirts. Beatrice found a pair of jeans and a bright white T-shirt, pulled them on, and walked to the door. When she opened it, the same Thunsi stood in the doorway, that same practiced smile on her oblong face, her black eyes odd, deep, and unfathomable, like doll eyes, no iris or pupil, just small, shiny orbs every once in a while, reflecting the light from the windows.

"If the Miss would follow me, please," she said in that controlled syllabic tone.

They walked down a long hallway that opened into a large open balcony looking over a foyer of stone walls and wooden beams. They descended the spiral staircase and crossed the great room and study, eventually to several open floor-to-ceiling glass doors strategically placed to reveal the sloping, manicured back acres. There, standing in the first rays of sunlight was a naked man, arms and legs spread out to the morning, slick and shiny with oil, and a tall, old Thunsi with a smooth, hooked metal rod gently pulling the oil across the limbs and torso.

"One feels like a god in these times," said the man. "It is as if the whole universe stands and bows before you."

Beatrice turned as the Thunsi Maid stepped away, leaving her standing by the glass table and cushioned chairs. A buffet of fruit and breads and all manner of breakfast delights covered the plain of glass.

"Look at that view," continued the naked man, in a proud, nearly exuberant tone. "It demands something from us. I'm not sure what. Something indeed." The man waved his oiled arm.

"That will be all." The Old Thunsi Servant bowed and backed away. He did not look at the naked man or Beatrice. The naked man stood there, still with arms and legs spread out, then he turned and sauntered over to Beatrice. "Well, here you are. After all these years. Look at you." He paused then pouted and shook his head. "Well, honey, time has not been kind. Oh, my poor dear." He stood full frontal before her, reaching for what appeared to be a glass of frothy wine. "Here we are," he said, gulping down the red liquid and setting the empty glass on the table.

"Could you please put some clothes on," Beatrice said placidly.

She watched as the naked man stood confidently before her, then seemed to hesitate, as though the rehearsed moment should have had some other more agreeable outcome.

"As you wish," he said with a note of displeasure.

He clapped his hands and immediately the tall Thunsi maid hurried to him. He looked at her with a smile. "Towel me off." The maid bowed then toweled him off. "Get me my...cerulean blue covering."

She bowed, then hurried back with a blue, silk robe, sweeping it over his naked body, he irritated, waving her away impatiently.

"Now? Better?"

He walked confidently to a chair, pulled it free, then poured another glass of the frothy red beverage. He stared. She stared. His face was long and handsome, hair greased back with blonde and brown streaks of color from the sun. He sipped from his glass. "So, here I am."

He smiled at her. Beatrice was about to speak. "That won't work here," he interrupted and wagged his finger at her.

"What?"

"Oh, silly. You know what." He looked out at the vista

And breathed deeply. "Tell me something marvelous, my dear. It has been...four hundred years."

"What am I doing here?"

"Existentially?"

"More practical?"

"I brought you here, my dear Beatrice. I saved you."

"Where are my clothes?"

"You don't like the ones you have?"

"Where?"

"They should have been burned. Poor dear." He put his hands up in defense, for Beatrice was about to rise. "But they weren't. They are clean, pressed and...dare I say...ready to wear."

"I want them."

"You shall have everything you want, my precious Beatrice, but could you first allow me the courtesy of catching up before you...go to do whatever it is you want to do." He sipped from his cup, a red stain in the corner of his mouth, eyes constant and intense on her. "It was *you* who sought *me* out, my darling Beatrice."

He began to tap his index finger on the table, rhythmically, subtly, a nervousness to it at first, then a slow steady beat.

"I didn't."

"Yet here you are."

He smiled wide at her. So intense, in fact, was his gaze, his smile, his confidence and demeanor, that soft, beautiful tapping that Beatrice nearly forgot what he said.

"Yes," she whispered. "Yes, here I am."

Her head spun and swooped with random images of dancing, celebrating and joy. *It was such a glorious day.* She thought. *It was such a wonderful, glorious morning, indeed.*

"There's my girl, my darling Beatrice," said the man almost to himself. "Would you like tea or coffee?"

"Some coffee, please."

"How delightful," he said.

"What shall we talk about? There is so much to catch up on."

"How did you get...?"

"Oh, how droll, darling Beatrice. Ask me something else."

"What am I doing here?"

"Oh, I love twenty questions. How delightful," he clapped his hands together.

With that, the tall Thunsi Maid hurried over. He shewed her away in disgust, then leaned on his elbows. "That is boring, my dear. So let me start a new game. What are *you* doing here? Did you finally come to see me?"

"No...I was sent."

"Oh, like a letter or a message. How fun! Who sent you?"

"MaMaw."

The man's face cringed like he suddenly tasted something bitter or sour. "Oh, now you're just being mean, honey."

He sipped the red, frothy drink again, then grabbed a grape from a plump mound. "Why would that old rock send you to me?"

Beatrice tried desperately to fight through the powerful thaumaturgy. Just when her mind cleared, it filled with other images of delight and celebration, of dance, a thrumming, humming, sensuous thrill like an electrical charge pulsing through her body.

"You didn't answer me, sweetie. What does that petrified turd want with me?"

"Not you. Christopher. Christopher Dante."

Just like that the spell broke, and it seemed to Beatrice that the beautiful bright sunny day now seemed overcast. The man in the cerulean robe, thin, meek and small, a painted vase that on closer inspection showed the micro cracks of time and use. That was only an impression, for the thrumming, tapping finger, now steady and even like breathing was all she could hear.

"Well, sister, that's a whole other story... If you know what I mean." He sniggered and winked and waved his hand back and forth, and she laughed because she thought that was what he expected. Then he composed himself and became once again earnest. "So, tell me who I am?"

"You're Cyril, of course."

"Of course, I am, honey. And don't you forget it." He tapped her arm in a playful manner. "I'll bet you can't remember the first time we met."

Beatrice concentrated. She began to sing silently, internally, a concert in her mind's eye. Soon she had a foothold in the thaumaturgy that was penetrating every part of her being. She still could not control what was happening to her, her mind a freely giving thing, a faucet opened. Her internal song snatched what information she wanted to protect and distracted and put forth other things mostly harmless or irrelevant. She had only felt such massive power from Christopher, and the seemingly charming, playful being before her stirred up a sense of absolute terror.

"Oh, come on. You must remember. I do. How could I forget?"

She remembered Cyril. The memory was raw and fresh like a deep gash exposed to salt water.

"So much tension. So much need."

Cyril thumped his finger harder and harder on the glass table, then two fingers, then three at a time, the thaumaturgy thick like fog in Beatrice's mind. She tried to resist, to sing her way through it, but it was too much, and she settled back in her seat helpless and defeated.

"Oh, my poor, poor darling Beatrice. So much has

changed. So much has stayed the same." He reached out his hand and touched her face, she powerless to stop him. Quite suddenly everything collapsed. She could hear Cyril snap and grind his teeth.

"What is it, you old shit? Can't you see I'm busy?"

"It's the Mine Bosses, sir," said the old Thunsi servant. "They are impatient and riled up. Apparently, they have three instigators with them and are demanding justice."

He brushed back Beatrice's hair. "Justice? Hmm. I guess I will have to mete it out then." He smiled "A delightfully wicked amount of it."

He concentrated on Beatrice, staring at her, but his fingers stopped, his mind and visage distracted. "There will be time for us later, my darling, beautiful Beatrice."

He turned his attention to the old Thunsi Servant. "Send them to the council room and bring some armed guards with you." He stood, wrapping the loose gown tighter around him and tied it. "She will want for nothing while she is here. Is that understood?" The Thunsi maid bowed. "She'll be groggy for a while. Just leave her be. Prepare for a trip south. There are some issues that need my attention. We leave in an hour."

All Beatrice could do was try to remember that which she knew she had forgotten. She sat in the glorious sun on that glorious afternoon, staring out over that glorious view, and for some reason she could not fathom, no matter how hard she concentrated—she was unable to recall even a snatch of the four-hundred-year-old horror that was Cyril.

Chapter Fifty-two

The Cuy river at its crossing in Kyrnunos was nearly one mile wide with the great snake of water, beginning as runoff from The Black Mountains, gaining volume and current from nearly twenty tributaries and draining out into a basin that expanded over two hundred thousand square miles. The people of Kyrnunos liked to say it drank from MaMaw's teat and shit in the Great Lakes somewhere in the West. It had many names depending on where one lived, and according to myth it originally was called Cuyahoga which originated in a majestic city called Constantinople. Unfortunately, myths like dreams tend to be only partially true and almost always forgotten.

Beatrice, Cyril and the Thunsi maid boarded the private steamer car, a small but opulent train, much like the mansion on the hill—gaudy, shiny, a pastel blot of paint on a monochrome desperate river world. That river world of Kyrnunos had just been made even more desperate due to Cyril's *Grand Statement of Justice*. As Beatrice and Cyril wound their way down from the bluff, as they puffed and chugged to a stop near the docks, it was quite clear what that statement entailed. There, hanging by the neck, like wind chimes swaying and bumping in the river wind were not only the three miners (naked Thunsi males) who were caught in an act of sedition, but also the four Mining Bosses who brought the traitors before Cyril. A grand and macabre statement, indeed.

No Thunsi looked at them. Cyril pronounced it "glorious" like one commenting on new wallpaper. Beatrice gasped and breathed in deeply, all the while whispering an internal song of calming, of peace to keep herself steady and anchored in the fog of Cyril's thaumaturgy.

"They better all be here when I return," Cyril chastened the Old Thunsi. "None of this cutting them down because of your superstitious nonsense. I want to smell the glorious aroma of justice when I pull into the dock."

He nearly sauntered onto the river boat, his overcoat flapping like wings in the stiff breeze.

A middle-aged man in a captain's outfit saluted and bowed to Cyril. "If you want to settle in, my lord. It will be a good hour before we dock. The wind and current are against us today." The Thunsi maid escorted them to the lounge.

"Give her whatever she wants," Cyril said. "I will be in my quarters."

"Yes, Sir," said the Thunsi maid.

"Don't keep me waiting," he said sternly. "Also, don't forget my drink. I'm running low.

The Thunsi maid nodded again and bowed. Cyril departed. Beatrice sat in a seat and looked out over the great gray expanse of flowing water.

~ * ~

It was when they arrived at the dock on the other side of the Cuy river that Cyril made an appearance. He was bright and elegant, waving his arms about. He called the captain to serve him more of his frothy, red beverage. He called the captain again to put on his overcoat.

"Where's your maid?" asked Beatrice.

"Oh, she's busy."

"Shouldn't she accompany us to the mines?"

Cyril stopped and cocked his head. "Why, aren't you just

the nosey Ned. She has some cleaning up to do, honey. She'll catch up when she is able." He walked onto the deck and turned back. "She knows not to be late."

He hurried down the gangway and onto the shore. "I have some business to attend to, darling. Make yourself busy for a bit. Don't stray too far." He shook his finger at the place. "Can be quite nasty."

Cyril left her and at first, she just stayed near the dock. Boredom soon set in and she began to walk. After fifteen minutes or so, she came to the outskirts of town and an old, abandoned shack that smelled of sweat and fecal material. She had seen such shacks before when she and NORM first arrived. She peaked into it, and to her horror saw the chains and shackles bolted to the walls. On further inspection she saw several nearly naked Thunsi squatting in their own filth, silent, pensive, their faces obscured in the shadows.

She put her hand to her mouth, then pulled back and looked around. Such an emotion overwhelmed her that she instinctively began to sing, softly, steady, a chant really, under her breath.

"Come, come, come to me
Silently and without delay
Crawling creature, buzzing bee
Pick the locks and set them free."

She heard a stirring in the shadows, and at first the chained Thunsi struggled and swatted at the intruders. Beatrice commanded the insects into a form, a shadow in a shadow...a manifest god to the Thunsi. *Don't be afraid. I am here to help you. Don't be afraid. When the night comes, go! Go to Christopher Dante. Find Christopher Dante. He will help you.*

Her song was interrupted. "You must leave here, ma'am," said the Thunsi maid. "Sir will not be happy with your here. Please, Miss. Come with me, please."

Beatrice turned with a start to face the maid who quickly shielded her face and began to walk. Beatrice hurried after her, finally grabbing her hard by her thin wrist and stopping her. "What happened?"

"Nothing, Miss. We must hurry. Sir is waiting for us."

"You're hurt," Beatrice said. She saw the bruises on her skeleton arm, snaking around her long neck, the laceration on her face, the black eye. "Did...did *he* do this to you?"

The Thunsi maid turned and pulled away, her force astonishingly great. "We must go, Miss. We must not be late. Sir is waiting."

She hurriedly walked away, the even gait turning into a pronounced limp with every arduous step.

"I've had quite enough of this!" remonstrated Beatrice. "He wants to play games? I've got some..."

"No, Miss! Please!" The Thunsi maid turned almost violently toward Beatrice. "You must not say anything," she hissed. "He will just kill my people. He will just hurt or kill *me*. Please, Miss. It will not do!"

Beatrice stood still and watched the determined Thunsi limp toward the steamboat and the gathering group of Mine Bosses. Then she ran after her.

"There you are," Cyril said sternly.

He paused and looked at the Thunsi maid skeptically, then to Beatrice, then back to the Maid. "Nothing to report, I hope."

"No sir. The Miss got lost."

"That better be all."

"I wandered off, I'm afraid," Beatrice hurried on. "She was so kind to find me."

Cyril watched them both, eyes squinting from the sun or from some internal choice now decided. His demeanor changed like flipping a switch. "It can be an overwhelming sort of place, quite deadly if you find yourself in the wrong hovel."

He motioned and waved his arms spastically as if to say "Now let's go! Let's go!"

Beatrice watched workers load barrel after barrel from the river boat to a train car. The small band of Mine Bosses escorted them into passenger cars linked together to a large steam engine. It hissed, belching out smoke, soot and acrid vapors, lurched forward, once, twice; then in a steady even motion it made its way toward the mineral mines far off in the distance.

Chapter Fifty-three

They never stepped foot into the actual Mineral Mines, the issues had spread even to the miner's camps, and soon Cyril was neck deep in a full-blown insurrection. It did not take long before a sort of terror and desperation undulated out from his council meetings, spreading through the Mine Bosses who then took that message to their workers which resulted in more hangings, more beatings, more and more outlandish "making examples."

At one point on the second week of their stay, the Mine Bosses complained that soon there would not be enough workers to make examples of. Of course, this lead to replacing the seditious Thunsi with the vocal bosses. The complaining stopped. Still, the raids kept coming. Nearly every night, a new group of slaves were freed. The mining city became a fortress city, armed guards everywhere, and the enslaved Thunsi placed in giant holding pens. Still, they escaped. "How? How could malnourished, half dead Thunsi escape even a wet paper bag?" complained the bosses and guards to each other.

At one point the Mining Bosses made a nearly complete human chain of armed guards around the holding pen. Even that did not stop them from escaping!

Cyril was so angry by the third week of their "putting down the rebellion" he demanded a bounty on any Thunsi that may be secretly sending information to this secret enemy. That failed. Money was offered, then violence and money. One of the Mining Bosses proposed a search and destroy mission. Find the nest, kill the serpent in the egg. All agreed, even cheered, for everyone was at their wits end. They gathered their horses, guns, even put up a dirigible for surveillance. No horse, gun, Mining Boss, or dirigible returned.

~ * ~

It was during the end of the second week when the Mine Bosses had determined to place the poor Thunsi slaves in holding pens *for their own safety*—it was on a particular humid evening that Beatrice made her first contact with the enemy. It was quite by accident, really. Hot, and tired and sick of the sand and the grime and the constantly blowing granules that lodged between the fingers and in the folds of skin, nesting in the ear or burrowing deep into the hairline—it was on this evening that Beatrice walked into the Thunsi maid's tent to ask her to fill the bath. She was holding a small, gold compass-like instrument, and next to her was another Thunsi servant, a younger female. Both turned panic stricken, beady black eyes wide. Nobody said anything. The Thunsi maid turned quickly to the younger servant and casually gave her something.

"Mail this as I told you," said the Thunsi maid.

"Yes, ma'am," said the young Thunsi female.

"Alright, go now. Give it to the postmaster. Only the postmaster, like I told you." The young Thunsi stared at Beatrice.

"Go on, Thunsi!" commanded the Thunsi maid. "Go."

She turned to Beatrice, looking at her confidently, directly, eye to eye, as if a sheer act of will would erase what everyone knew had just transpired. "May I help you, Miss?"

Beatrice stared as the young Thunsi hurried past her.

"Miss, are you in need of something? Sir is not here. I believe he will return later tonight."

"I um... Was..."

The Thunsi maid gathered herself, shuffled this and that, pocketing the gold compass, then boldly walked toward Beatrice. "I will make you a bath, Miss. It is so hot right now, don't you agree? A cool bath will feel very nice."

"Yes, yes, a cool bath will be very kind of you."

They walked out of the tent together.

~ * ~

While Beatrice sat in the cold bathwater, the Thunsi maid dowsing her from a pitcher then massaging her scalp with soap, rinsing it, massaging it again—it was right at this time that the Thunsi Maid whispered, "I know it was you."

Beatrice blinked and wiped her eyes. She felt her body tense with an electrical pulse of adrenaline. This tall, formidable Thunsi, hands massaging her scalp, her neck, this Thunsi maid with one twist, could break her spine or cut her throat.

Beatrice breathed out slowly. "I'm sure I don't know what you mean."

She felt the tension building in the Thunsi maid's hands, a slight pressure increasing on her scalp.

"He knows too."

"What does *he* know?"

"It was you."

Beatrice's mind raced to the hanging Thunsi on the dock, the almost nightly tortures in the mining camp like elaborate plays, the terror and sorrow. This Thunsi maid...she had everything to lose. She had been caught. Beatrice walked in on her and caught her giving seditious information to the young Thunsi servant. Now, simply, it had come down to *me* or *her* in the Thunsi Maid's mind. How easy, simple it would be to rid herself of this irritating problem. More strategically, blame

Beatrice as the usurper. The Thunsi maid had too much, just too much to lose in this moment not to act. "What now," Beatrice whispered, her throat dry.

The Thunsi maid grabbed her cheeks with both hands, huge, wide palms nearly wrapping her skull. "Hmmmmmm. I don't care what happens now."

She pulled slightly upward. Was it a threat? Beatrice was helpless. The Thunsi maid released her grip and gently pushed Beatrice forward to massage her back and shoulders.

"I won't...say...anything," Beatrice said, again her voice caught in her throat.

The Thunsi maid chuckled and stopped her massage. She pulled Beatrice toward her. "Of course, you won't." They stared at each other. "He is coming. He told me what he is going to do."

"You could stop him. *We* could...stop him...together."

Beatrice glanced around her for anything that could be used as a weapon. She had not the time to sing any thaumaturgy, the Thunsi maid was too close to her. The Thunsi maid stared at her, the small black beady eyes, unfathomable.

"Why? Why would I stop him?" the Thunsi maid said.

There was a commotion outside. They could hear Cyril pronouncing something in his bombastic fashion, obviously drunk. He was yelling for Beatrice.

"Miss wants to escape, yes?"

"What?"

"He is coming," the Thunsi maid said. "He is coming to save you."

"Who?" Beatrice said bewilderedly.

"Christopher Dante. He is coming for you."

"But...how...?"

"You freed my brother. You told him to tell Christopher

Dante. He did."

At that moment, the Thunsi maid stood suddenly and met the inebriated Cyril at the tent doorway, cajoling him, calming him, promising him this delight and that delight as their voices faded into the night.

Chapter Fifty-four

A week passed without event, but Cyril was pensive and withdrawn. He spent much of the days in his expansive tent drinking the foamy, frothy red liquid from the barrels stacked in the corner. One morning he had a surprise visit by the old Thunsi servant from Kyrnunos. He was tall and strong, his skin like weathered metal. He hurried to Cyril's tent, posted guards outside, and the two stayed in there for an hour. Beatrice could hear Cyril shouting, the old Thunsi servant calming him in low tones. Cyril departed in a huff, then returned several hours later.

She sat in the shadows as the evening sun drifted behind the great Mineral Mines and listened to the old Thunsi servant explain how dire the actual situation had become in the Forest of the Dead. Cyril played down the panic and insisted that "This was the point of the spear." The old Thunsi servant laughed. "The point of the spear you say? Ha! You do not understand the situation," barked the old Thunsi servant. "To tarry any longer here at the Mineral Mines is like fixing a lightbulb on a sinking ship."

Cyril did not respond. In fact, since Beatrice could only hear them, she imagined Cyril nodding his head in deep contemplation. "Well, well, well. This is how it is." There was silence. And, "We will leave immediately!"

No one left anywhere. In fact, the old Thunsi servant took an active but behind the scenes role in walking about, sitting in on Mine Boss meetings, questioning them individually on various aspects of their daily involvement. This went on for another week. One evening Cyril called everyone in the small tent city together. He sat on his throne-like wooden chair before an assembly of Mine Bosses, servants, and even some Thunsi slave leaders and announced they would be leaving for Kyrnunos in the morning.

"Before we go," he said without emotion. "We shall have...a cleansing, a purging if you will." He looked about the gathered group, scanning them, his fingers erratically, irritatingly tapping the armrest.

"We have become a dross-covered sword. We have been...dulled, blunted, corrupted by our complacency. Inured by our mundane systems and routines." He smiled. "Purification and introspection are needed." He began to tap his fingers rhythmically.

Beatrice stood next to Cyril. She had no choice. He positioned her and the Thunsi maid on either side of him as the group gathered before him. All through his speech, she could feel the thaumaturgy building around the space where the assembly stood, like a net slowly closing around a school of fish. She began to sing within her mind, a preventative measure so to initially withstand the powerful onslaught that was about to overwhelm them all. Cyril drank from a large cup, the corner of his lips stained with purple from the foamy drink.

"I think we all should kneel, don't you?"

As he tapped his fingers rhythmically, more intensely, the crowd fell to their knees in unison. "Good. Now, as you all know quite well, we have had some unwanted intruders, a fifth pillar as it were."

He gulped more of his drink, and each time he did, his actions became more manic. "Ha!" he pronounced as he swooped up, his silk gown flowing and flapping in the arid breeze. "Quite remarkable, my man here." He pointed to the old Thunsi servant. "Like a hound dog. Good boy! Good Boy! Come here, boy!"

The old Thunsi servant stepped to him obediently.

"Kneel down, boy!"

The old Thunsi servant knelt before him. Only Beatrice and the Thunsi maid were allowed to stand with Cyril.

"Good boy! See what an obedient and good boy my Thunsi dog is?"

He gulped from the cup, some of the red, foamy liquid sloshing out. He gently placed it on the arm of the chair. With a sudden and great force, he raised his fisted hand and smashed the old Thunsi servant to the ground. One blow, and the old Thunsi servant Wobbled. The second great blow flattened him to the ground unconscious. Blood was seeping from his ears, his nose and the back of his head.

"How dare you speak to me in such a manner, old fool!" roared Cyril like a lunatic. "Fixing a lightbulb! You say that to me? To me! How dare you even look at me when you are in my presence!"

With another savage blow he smashed the Old Thunsi Servant in the head once again. He gulped from the glass then nearly fell into his chair exhausted.

The great assembly of Mine Bosses and servants looked up uncertain. Cyril stared at them like a brooding spoiled child who must pick up his mess of toys. He slapped his hands together twice and the crowd shook their heads and blinked.

"Rise," Cyril said.

They did in unison. The old Thunsi bashed, and bleeding wobbled to his knees, then stood on his long, shaky limbs. His skull face was grossly swollen and a deep gash from Cyril's rings split his cheek and temple. Cyril glanced at him. "Good boy."

He looked out at the crowd, then back to the old Thunsi servant. He jerked his head ever so slightly at him. The old Thunsi servant hobbled and swayed slowly into the crowd.

Beatrice trembled at the sheer erratic violence of Cyril.

Enormous, terrifying memories crashed about her. Four Hundred years she had locked those memories away. Four hundred years, pushed down and buried, forgotten. She escaped from it all, left behind by the chaos and burdens of living in this world. Now, after all this time, the savagery, terror, and suffering of those lost days returned. She watched in horror as the old Thunsi servant wobbled and dragged himself into the crowd, standing right next to the young Thunsi who Beatrice saw with the Thunsi maid. The old Thunsi servant, motioned to the positioned guards to grab her. They did and dragged her before Cyril. She was sobbing now, pleading, crying out for the Thunsi maid to help her.

"Hush, hush, hush, my child," Cyril said placidly. "I am not going to harm you." He looked at the crowd again, still brooding, then at the Thunsi girl. "Do you admit to treasonous acts? Do you admit you have been passing information to the enemy?"

"Please, sir."

"There, there," Cyril said still without emotion. "Answer the question. I will not harm you. Please, tell the truth."

"Yes," she whimpered. "I am sorry, Sir. I am so sorry. I will do anything..."

Cyril raised his hand. "My poor, poor flower." Suddenly, a switch flipped. "For your act of treason, you will be made an example... And..."

"You said you would not harm her!" Beatrice suddenly blurted out. "Those were *your words*. You tell her to speak truth, but *you* don't?"

Cyril looked annoyed, almost with pity at Beatrice. "Of course, I did, my sweet and beautiful Beatrice. A person is only as good as his word. If not, what would we be but savages."

He smiled, then nodded to the old Thunsi servant who grabbed the young Thunsi spy and shoved her down to her knees. "I am a man of my word, every single word, my dear sweet

Beatrice. You will come to understand that in time. Every...single...word."

He suddenly snapped his fingers rhythmically, quickly, a sort of clicking code and pointed his hand at the Thunsi maid standing next to him. Like a possessed thing, a puppet lurching with the strings of the puppeteer above, she stumbled and walked over to the sobbing young Thunsi. "I am not going to take this poor thing's life, my sweet Beatrice. She will."

Quick like lightening, the intense snapping, and a booming pronouncement from Cyril, "Do it!"

The Thunsi maid took the knife from the old Thunsi servant, swept it across the young girl's neck and dropped her to the ground.

"Next time it will be you," Cyril said viciously to the Thunsi aid. "Is that perfectly clear?"

The Thunsi maid cried out, covered her mouth, and nodded.

Cyril clapped his hands with great joy. "Now! Let's pack up! We leave in two hours for Kyrnunos!"

Chapter Fifty-five

It was evening when the river boat with all Cyril, Beatrice, the Thunsi maid and the old Thunsi servant arrived on the northern side of the Cuy River. It had been a tense and silent hour journey across the great plain of moving water, Beatrice hoping to reach the shoreline before Cyril called her. He had been locked in his cabin with the old Thunsi servant and several mine bosses.

Beatrice stood at the railing and watched the setting sun far in the West, it's orange light bright and haunting, the clouds making it shift in appearance. She thought of Caravaggio and his prolific magenta butterflies, scrawling them here and there, A sign of hope, of longing, a terror and warning to their enemies. She found herself engrossed in the shape as it moved now forming one wing, then another, then the long whipping tail... Could it be...? The pattern morphed into something unrecognizable, and she turned away as the first mate called out the depths to the river boat pilot.

The river boat eased closer and closer to the dock. Behind Beatrice she could hear the crew as they prepared the long process of unloading the new cargo.

"Be ready," whispered the Thunsi maid to Beatrice when she walked by. "You must be ready."

With that she and others gathered bags, large crates and carried them down the docking plank. Cyril emerged from his cabin, and by his side limped the old Thunsi servant. He was intense and looking straight ahead. When Cyril walked by

Beatrice, she barely made out what he said. "You will come to my study in an hour."

The crew and the servants gathered and carried and loaded the bombastic colored train cars in silence and whispers.

It was then, when they were least expecting it, that Christopher Dante Struck.

~ * ~

It was like lightening from heaven as the old Thunsi servant would later recall. It was bright as the sun, white hot and focused. A holy beam from the Horned God. It was not a holy beam at all, nor was it from the Horned God. It was a laser set off by NORM's connection to the only Satellite Christopher Dante allowed the AI to access. It was most certainly not *from* the Horned God, for it was directly aiming *at* and tracking Cyril! The laser sliced and smoked through the metal train cars, separating them into molten iron boxes as it made its way toward Cyril. The servants, mine bosses and Thunsi scattered and screamed as barrels of eel oil exploded splattering flames on wood and straw and living things.

Beatrice ran toward NORM who was whirling and beeping. A metal animal now pushed up on two legs for a better signal, now on all fours crab-walking this way and that as it dodged and weaved its enemies. She was halfway to him, when she saw Cyril stand still and raise his hands, then clap them together like thunder. A shockwave of thaumaturgy crackled, spit and sparked, exploding outward in concentric circles. Everything in its path fell like dead things to the ground.

Beatrice sang. She pictured the thing as she cobbled it together, a train car leg and another, a body made of collapsed stone from the nearby wall. A head of loose and abandoned tires. The golem shivered to life and lurched forward. One step, two. It reached down as Beatrice sang it to do so. It lifted another train car in its grotesque hands and hurled it at Cyril who leapt out of the way and disappeared into the shadows. NORM connected to the laser once again and chased after Cyril's last position. Beatrice sang the golem toward Cyril, and now he was trapped, a dangerous animal.

The old Thunsi servant, wounded as he was, snuck over to NORM, and with a ferocious blow from an enormous board, smashed the machine off its legs. It fell over with a thud, whirled, beeped and pulled its vulnerable camera head into the metal chassis. The laser vanished, and Cyril, seeing the opportunity, lifted his hands again and clapped them together in a rhythmic pattern, short, long, long, short, long, long. Over and over, he clapped in that same rhythmical way. The thaumaturgy exploded from him, powerful, steady, a wave racing over the flats of sand as the tide relentlessly comes in. The golem shimmered and wrenched one way then the other. Beatrice lost control, her head foggy and confused. The golem swung toward her. With huge steps stomped and whirled like a dancing bear, closer and closer to her to cut off her escape.

As the hex filled the night air, she saw the great host of the Blodetan emerge and span the entire open bluff far above them.

"You can never have her!" screamed Cyril. "She is mine alone! She has always been mine!"

This was a rage, a shout into a thunderstorm, a bluster of braggadocio from a child shouting at the hurricane.

"Follow me," said the Thunsi maid into Beatrice's ear. "Hurry! This way!"

They ran toward the river, then took a tiny path that followed the bank. "Hurry! You must keep up!" yelled the Thunsi maid as she pulled away from Beatrice, the long lanky strides bounding her forward like a gazelle. Beatrice could hear the

Blodetan howling and hooting as they came upon the town. She could hear the screams of the townsfolk as they fled into their homes for protection. All the while, she recognized the new thaumaturgy she was feeling, familiar, controlled. She cried out with joy and quickened her pace.

By the time she caught up to the Thunsi maid, they ran nearly a mile down the river path, and there before her was an immense bridge spanning the gaping, flowing water. "We must run!" cried the Thunsi maid. "Hurry! They are right behind you!"

Beatrice turned and saw the King of the Blodetan, the crown of bones upon his head. He was down on all fours like a predator, tearing toward her, the others just behind.

She leapt on the bridge and ran. On further inspection, the snippets the mind catches as it patches together a traumatic event in real time, the bridge was rickety and slapped together. It was made from old wood and new iron girders, a collage of materials in the form of a great bridge. One held by some force of will rather than weld or ingot or bolt.

Christopher made this! she thought, but even that thought was so fleeting because the great army of Blodetan now gained the bridge and were scurrying like insects on every surface. The King of the Blodetan howled and screeched commands. That was when Beatrice saw him.

Far behind, a shadow of a figure really, was Cyril, arms stretched to the sky, silk robe flowing out like some absurd cape, his thaumaturgy before the King of the Blodetan like a great and terrible spearhead.

"We'll never make the other side," Beatrice screamed to the Thunsi maid.

"Run!"

Beatrice could not fight the great pulling weight of Cyril and the King of the Blodetan. She began to slow, her will and mind succumbing to the power. The Thunsi maid stopped and turned, and in great bounds came upon Beatrice, snatched her like a piece of luggage and dashed across the bridge toward the other side. Beatrice struggled, then lay limp over the pointy shoulders of the Thunsi maid. She watched as the King of the Blodetan gained on them. That was when she heard it.

At first, she thought it was a clap of thunder from a coming storm, but as she looked into the darkness behind her, she could see what was happening. The Bridge was collapsing! The wood and iron that was held together began to fold, drop away, plummet into the river below. The Thunsi maid raced to the other side, and as she took her last several steps, Beatrice witnessed the terrifying lament and screech of the King of the Blodetan as he fell into the water and disappeared down the river.

"Come," said the Thunsi Maid to Beatrice as she gently put her down. "He is waiting for us. There are a great many things yet to do."

Gods of IMAGO

Greg Belliveau

Part Five

The Forest of the Dead

Gods of IMAGO

Chapter Fifty-six

Lara was uncertain just how her official meeting with Roman would go. She watched Raya fawn and paw at Roman, saying "oh you silly, sweet thing" or "how adorable you are," and erupt with a forced, gleeful laugh at the most awkward of times. He was most receptive to her pandering. In fact, since Roman returned from the coast, they had been inseparable. How many times had she watched him, her once greatest love, bend over Raya's fat and swollen face, gently sweep her cornsilk hair from her forehead and kiss her on the cheek, walking out of the large room with a nod to the old, withered Ruth, but without even a glance to Lara. It was as if Roman wished only to be rid of her, that she wronged him in some way, like all those months together on the mainland never existed. Now, Roman asked for an official meeting.

Roman acquired quite a new reputation after he killed the great eel. After returning from his encounter with the Horned God, he assumed a new authority which both Ruth and Ralph silently acquiesced. As the *Intruder* sailed into port, the eel secured to the side, as it drifted slowly into the tiny inlet, the Thunsi gathered and cheered, crying out, "Roman the Eel Slayer!" "Roman the Great High Priest!" "Roman has returned victorious!" There was a sort of madness to it all, a fervent energy, and for good reason. The killing of the Spring eel always kicked off the most sacred Religious Festival known to a Thunsi, The Gathering.

The Thunsi huddled around the eel, everyone skinning,

cutting, and parceling out all the wonderful parts, everything until only a skeleton remained. It was Roman (and Ralph, Old Bony Root) who skinned and boiled the great skull, dried and painted it for the new ceremony to be held in the Grove of the Horned God when the young Thunsi were born.

The pregnant Thunsi sat in the Purity House, plump and swollen and hormonal, all of them waiting, Raya and Rebecca, Roberta, Rachel, Rita, Raelynn, and even Renilda who brooded and squeaked as the birthing pains began, adjusting her pillow behind her back in frustration.

Lara sat in the corner, legs drawn up, her belly splayed out like she had swallowed whole a great round stone. The old crone, Ruth, sat before her. She was either dozing off or thinking with much consideration what to say next.

"Yes," she wheezed. "Yes, indeed, quite a mess you have caused. I would not be at all surprised if Roman..."

Again, she fell silent, eyes closed. Lara thought perhaps she had fallen asleep. "Well, no matter," the old, withered matron wheezed. "The Horned God has spoken and that is that."

She smirked and stared intensely at Lara. "You better not be late for your meeting."

Lara rolled a new licorice root cigarette. She inhaled deeply as if that would assuage the annoyance and the demeaning tone. She felt the tiny Thunsi kick within her, and she instinctively rubbed her belly through the thin cotton gown. She slowly, and with great effort stood to her feet, then shuffled past the glares and smirks of Raya and out the Purity House door and into the bright spring day. She looked into the deep blue of the sky. A thought settled and clicked into place. Something larger than herself was transpiring, something wonderful, she a tiny bee buzzing, doing and making existing in a hive with no end or border.

When she arrived at the High Priest's dwelling, it had

been the first time since her leaving, she realized Roman made changes. Instead of an opulent, intimidating, gilded room, it was more a great laboratory or study filled with half written papers, stacked, and splayed books, various gas burners and test tubes with rubber hoses snaking here and there. He obviously moved his entire library into this place. In the midst of it all was Roman, goggles pushed high on his forehead, buzzing here and there, hovering over this, jotting down that, a manic spirit about the place. Old Bony Root sat slumped in the corner on a wooden chair. His head was in his hands, bored or dozing off.

She stood in the doorway for what seemed minutes on end, then moved several books from a chair and sat near a table. She glanced at the paper with scribbles and equations. Each paper fanned or dog-eared, some half crumpled, some torn in half—each one crossed out or struck though with ink. This was a laboratory of failures.

After almost ten minutes, Roman in his laboratory coat with back turned to her, she spoke. "You sent for me?"

There was silence, then Roman turned as if seeing her for the first time.

"Oh, you've come."

Lara rubbed her belly, a twinge, a sharp sting of pain making her wince. She repositioned herself. "I had no choice."

Roman scratched his cheek. He noticed he had on his goggles and pulled them from his head, tossing them onto a mess of glass tubes and a microscope. He stood tall and stared at her, rubbing his chest subconsciously. "I called for you?" And "yes, of course I called for you. Yes, of course."

He walked over to Old Bony Root and poked him. "Leave us."

He did it again and repeated himself. With exasperation, he kicked the leg of the old Thunsi's chair, Ralph blinked and looked up. Roman repeated himself. With great care Old Bony

Root pushed himself up, wavered and hobbled slowly with his wooden stick out of the room, closing the door behind him.

"Any day now, yeh?" Roman said.

"Yes."

"It will be spectacular this year," Roman continued cheerfully. "I think something magnificent is happening."

They sat in silence, Roman pulling up a chair across from her.

Lara stared at him in silence. He was not the Roman from early days. The Horned God changed him. The Horned God changed all of them. When she thought back to her experience in The Grove, the encounter in the cave, the desperate winter... And, that Roman in the Salty Sea, the rage and violence, the hatred...toward...her? At that moment, when she looked up from that basket and saw him, harpoon raised to murder... No, Roman was not his own any longer. This was not *her* Roman, the Roman who dreamed, planned, read, and longed to have a future with her. No, he had been chosen by the Horned God, the greatest honor a Thunsi could have, and she was now before...well...a select few, a Holy Thunsi prophet.

Roman reached for an elegant wooden box of licorice root cigarettes and handed one to her and lit it. She inhaled and enjoyed the sensation, the calming, soothing internal hand that suppressed the ferocious hunger.

"I wanted to say," Roman began, but stopped. He rubbed his chest again, then with what seemed like renewed effort, continued. "I just wanted to say how good it is to see you."

Whether it was the raging hormones or the irony of the statement, Lara burst out with a laugh.

Roman looked confused. "I know I have not been...well, it's just...since the death of my father, the strange accident. He looked at her intensely. "Where did you go?"

"What do you mean?"

"I mean. You just disappear, and the next thing I hear, you have been taken out of the Salty Sea."

"I wasn't *taken*, Roman. *You* rescued me!"

"Nonsense," he said and rubbed his chest again, then sucked on his cigarette in frustration.

"You were there, Roman." Lara felt the pangs again in her belly. She rubbed it. "Don't you remember anything? You went to the Cave of the Horned God, Roman. It was you who..."

She stopped. His face was blank, registering only her lunatic words. "Roman? You came to rescue me. You took the *Endeavor*. You came and..."

Roman guffawed and stood up. He walked to the table where several documents lay, a blue liquid popped and bubbled over a gas burner. He flicked it with his fingers several times, then wrote something down. He rubbed his chest. "Well, besides all the nonsense. I seem to be on to something quite spectacular now. I'm not sure what it is, but it just seems that I am close," he said hopefully. He looked up, but there was something troubling him.

Lara remembered his sinister laughing and jabbering. The erratic, manic Roman with the eel skull wheeling Elizabeth to the ravine and dumping her. She remembered him in the darkness of the Cave of the Horned God, the thick smoke of licorice root, the laughing and mocking tone. Quite suddenly, she remembered the great call from Elizabeth, *Find Christopher Dante! Find My Son!* A sharp bolt of pain shot through her abdomen, intense to the point she winced and panted. She rubbed her belly and put out her cigarette. "I must go," she said.

Roman nearly fell at her lap. "I think something is desperately wrong," he whispered. "I don't understand anything. I have these thoughts, but I'm not sure if they are real."

The look on his face was one of horror, of torment. "I think the Mendel Fragment has done something to me. I don't know what is happening. Why can't I remember anything? Oh, Lara..."

Old Bony Root shuffled in, noticed Roman kneeling at Lara and scurried over to him. "There, there, my boy. What is all this nonsense. Get up. Get up now."

He pulled Roman to his feet and walked him over to a chair. "And you," he said with his back to Lara, "you've said enough. Agitating the Great High Priest like this."

He faced her. "Go on! Get out of here! You've caused enough trouble. You're an abomination. I don't care what the Horned God said."

Lara stood up, holding her belly as she did. Roman sat on his chair, head in hands. She hobbled out into the bright blue of the spring day, her mind reeling from the encounter and the more intense, spiking pain that now turned into full blown contractions.

The small Thunsi came that evening in the Purity House, Ruth receiving the little one, a great joy on her old, creased face. She bundled it up and placed it on the exhausted Lara's chest.

"It's a boy," she said. "A perfect seedling. How precious. Praise the Horned God."

Ruth could not stay with her very long. She hurried to Raya who was in the throes of a ten hour labor. Tiny Thunsi cried all around her, as mothers nursed and coddled the slick almost white skeletal infants.

When all of the mothers had given birth, the tiny newborns lined in cribs in the "holding room" of the Purity House—only after the week of prayer and preparation, the careful inspection of every infant Thunsi, every limb and cavity, fold and orifice—after the proper time elapsed, mothers, infants, Roman, Ruth, Old Bony Root, and a crew of sailors prepared the newly fitted *Intruder* for the journey to the coast and to the Cave of the Horned God, and...ultimately...and unbeknownst to the mothers...to the Forest of the Dead for the Great Sacrifice.

Chapter Fifty-seven

Hal walked out from the dark cave and headed into the woods to find something to eat. The day was bright and sunny, and the coolness of spring was beginning to blossom into early summer. He stopped, stretched, scratched himself and looked around. Yep, today was as good as any. He had committed to the plan now, and when he committed to something, few if any could persuade him otherwise.

Oh, Clem had been adamant, calling it outright murder. Yes, he was ending a life, but murder was a bit harsh. Murder was taking an *innocent* life. This was no murder. If you find a malignant tumor, you cut it out, kill it. That was exactly what happened. While surviving the winter in the cave, they found a tumor. Oh, it had a name alright. He knew that specific malignancy immediately, Caravaggio. How ironic! Flee for your life in the dead of winter and hide in a cave only to discover...there in the stone cell, in some sort of stasis with tubes coming from neck and arms, sat that bastard painter. Was he even alive? Some sort of pump sucked his blood out of his big fat body and into wooden barrels on the other side of the cold, damp wall. It was just too good to be true. He looked so helpless and pathetic. He was an obvious prisoner of someone or something. He had half a mind to leave him in his suffering. No, better to end it, and by doing so know that it is done.

One god at a time. First, of course, there was Elizabeth who must have met her doom over the sea. How could she have survived his bomb? Now Caravaggio, a gift packaged and waiting for him. Blow the mountain down around him...forever. After this, Beatrice and Christopher Dante. Together, perhaps. Wouldn't that be sweet. Another god bites the dust. Another one down and another one down....

Clem interrupted his internal rant. "I found something," he whined.

When Hal arrived, it appeared to be a desiccated fox, still with moldered flesh and skin intact. They knelt and hovered, the mycelia sweeping down Hal's arm, spreading out from his fingers and digesting the ruined animal. He had gotten quite used to and even anticipated these meals. Long ago, indeed, were the days of his disgust in the tunnels under the Black Mountains. His body changed. He could sense it rather than see it. It was like his bones, tendons and muscles were reforming beneath the skin. Every time he woke, he understood some other structural adaptation of mycelia strands, strong like iron, flexible like spider webs had been formed. It was taking more and more scavenging to replace the energy from this transformation. His appetite grew two, three, four-fold. He and Clem roamed sometimes for hours in order to find something, anything that was decomposing.

Hal's relationship with Clem changed as well. When they first had met, Clem was all but unintelligible to him. Now, after all these months, what first was a whine and groan, now became clear and understandable. That too had its issues. Clem talked incessantly. What Hal had originally taken for the wind or perhaps some kind of wheezing breathing issue with the mountain ghost was Clem's incessant monologuing. He narrated his life! When he observed something curious, when something that made him sad, glad, or prompted any kind of emotion at all—anything and everything all the time—he just spoke about it out loud. Hal realized this one day as they trudged through the woods searching for a meal. At first, he stopped to listen, thinking that someone else was in the woods with them, voices drifting on the wind. As he crouched behind a tree and homed in on the sound, he began to realize the voices were talking about...*him!*

We are stopping now, squatting, listening. He must hear something, but I don't hear anything, nothing, maybe the wind. Now he's turning, staring at me. He looks like he swallowed a bit of spoiled potato. Hmmm. That is a good question. Why do potatoes spoil? I mean, they are in the ground, basically rotting from the start, then..."

"It's you!" Hal hissed. "What in the hell is wrong with you? Are you some kind of lunatic ghost or something? Are you cracked in the head? Why are you doing that?"

Clem stopped his narration. "You can understand me?"

"Of course, I can understand you, you imbecile!"

"Well, you couldn't yesterday."

"Well, I can now. So, stop jabbering like that."

They stared in silence at each other.

"I am lonely," Clem said.

"Idiot!" Hal blustered and walked away.

That was several months ago when Hawthorn was with them. The tree thing left unexpectedly babbling on about Lara, Thunsi, holes and The Forest of the Dead. And Clem made a point to test the waters every once in a while, which was always shut down with a "I can hear you. Do that somewhere else."

When they returned to the cave, it was late afternoon. "Time we got to it," Hal said.

"There is no reason to do this," Clem said. He floated and shimmered before Hal as they stood by the mouth of the cave. "He is obviously already incapacitated, and you have no justification for murder."

"Again, with the *murder*. It's not *murder*. It's fixing a global issue. It's solving a potential problem before it becomes unsolvable."

"Like Elizabeth?"

"Well, now that you mention it."

Hal huffed and walked by Clem and into the Cave. Clem streaked after him.

For months now, Hal experimented with various types of explosives. He traveled deep into the tunnels beyond. To his amazement he found, Sulphur, and with a little ingenuity made saltpeter (or close enough), after burning wood—combined all of it together to make a somewhat ignitable powder. Who knew? The real kicker, and the tipping point for his latest idea, quite by accident, he discovered the fermented concoctions in the wooden barrels (this *Thunsae Myrrha* as it was labeled) was as burnable as gasoline. With a little luck, the barrels would become a bomb. That bomb would collapse the cave and destroy everything inside.

"This is wrong, Hal. He should be rescued not murdered."

Hal turned violently at the Mountain Ghost. "Say that one more time," he hissed. "I dare you."

Clem stared at him. "Murder."

"I told you once. I told you a thousand times. This guy is a bad apple. I know for a fact he is."

"How?" Clem said forcefully.

Hal stared at him. "I just do. Now if you are through..."

Clem fluttered and shimmered out of the cave. Hal pushed and moved the wooden barrels together, a barricade of flammable liquid waiting for a spark. He laid a line of his homemade gunpowder out of the cave mouth and to the side. He grabbed his flint and steel, chipped it once, twice, three times, and whoosh! He fell back, crawled, crabbed, and rolled. That was when he heard a fissile, the black smoke drifting out of the cave the aftermath of a useless attempt.

"Damnit!" Hal said.

The earth shook, the wave of energy blowing Hal back fifteen feet, the white-hot flash scorching his eyebrows, shirt, hair, the earth around and the fronts of trees. When the cloud of rock dust and smoke settled, the cave was no longer a cave, the very mountain above it had folded in on itself and now lay on the forest floor.

"Damnit," Hal squeaked.

"Murder," Clem said.

Hal stood, brushed his pants off in a defiant gesture. He took a step, wobbled, and weaved, ears ringing, brain concussed—and he lumbered southward into the forest, his jacket still smoldering from the devastation.

Chapter Fifty-eight

"When can I see him," Beatrice asked the Thunsi maid.
"He will let you know. I promise."
Beatrice sat in a chair on the front porch, the great Cuy River expansive before her. A sparse amount of trees dotted the bluff. Once past the small house where she was staying, the forest all but disappeared. It was replaced with arid flatlands and sudden elevations that eventually became The Mineral Mines.
It had been nearly a month since her rescue from Cyril, and she had been quite alone. The Thunsi maid would come with food, would barely stay, then disappear for several days on end. Night was falling, Beatrice was getting impatient. It may have been the wine, but she was once again feeling a prisoner trapped yet again in someone else's unfolding narrative. The Thunsi maid was about to leave.
"Look," Beatrice said. "He called me to the Black Mountains. I went. MaMaw told me to come to Kyrnunos. I did and look how that turned out. I am supposed to meet Christopher. I still, after all this time have not seen or heard from him."
The Thunsi maid smiled. "And here you are." She fidgeted with the tray of wine and glasses, then turned to leave.
"Why...?" Beatrice stuttered. "Why where you with Cyril?"
The Thunsi maid turned back around and stared at Beatrice as if considering something. She sat down on the stone stairs, her long skeletal back to the wooden post. "I wasn't *with* Cyril. At least not at first."

She breathed in deeply then out. She pulled out a small pouch, and from it rolled a cigarette with some sort of tobacco.

"Do you have another one of those?" Beatrice said.

"Oh, Miss, you should be careful with this. It is from my island people far in the north. It's derived from what you would call licorice root. Its effect is quite potent on humans.

Beatrice smiled and held out her hand. It had been a very, very long time since she had been called *human*. "I'll take my chances."

Soon both sat on the broad stone stairs, smoking, and looking out at the river night world.

"My people come from far away north. It is a small island known as Widorexiton."

Beatrice asked several times for her to repeat it, then the Thunsi maid pronounced it slowly, syllable by syllable. "It literally means *Hunger From Within*. I am a Thunsi."

She said this and Beatrice could see her blush, then stiffen. A sort of inner strength and pride taking over. "We are the *Thin Skinned*. An ironic name, for we live so far in the land of winter that it is nonsensical to be made thus."

She smoked the cigarette again, keeping the vapor inside her, allowing it slowly to trickle out her barely perceptible nostrils. "There I was born, Widorexiton, into a slave class of people. I fell in love with the High Priest there, and because of this, he sold me into slavery. That was many, many years ago..." She grew silent, introspective.

"What happened?" Beatrice was bewitched now with the Thunsi maid's tragedy.

"Oh, that was so long ago, Miss. I can barely remember."

They stared at the night. Beatrice could see on the Thunsi maid's face such a sadness, something scarred over and healed, forever impressed into the soul. She had known such sorrow. She and the Thunsi maid were one. "I still don't even know your name."

The Thunsi Maid smiled. "I had one long ago. Cyril took it from me, refused to call me anything. I became, anonymous." This revelation brought a new cigarette to life, and she smoked a quarter of it before she continued. "You see, my people are very simple in their delegation of status. There are only two sounds that dictate class in my culture." She made the sound which had the phonetic properties of R and L. "All who are aristocratic are named with the R. Those, like me, were named with the L. My name is..." The Thunsi maid uttered a guttural sound that Beatrice could never possibly pronounce. She tried anyway. The Thunsi maid chuckled then covered her mouth in embarrassment. "You must never try to say that again. At least not around Thunsi. You have just called the High Priest a son of a whore. Which may be the case, but all the same. You can call me Lucy. That seems to be an adequate enough translation."

Beatrice sipped from her wine. The licorice root cigarette now softening the edges of her tensions, making her feel...just a bit...hopeful. "I'm sorry, Lucy."

Lucy looked up at her. "Why be sorry for something you cannot control?"

"I mean, I'm sorry for your time with Cyril. I'm glad we both escaped."

"I did not escape, Miss," Lucy said. "Well, I did not escape when you did. I have been free from Cyril for ten years."

"You were beaten. I saw the hell you were in."

Lucy sucked in again on the licorice root cigarette and talked out the smoke. "One can endure anything if one chooses to be put in such positions."

Beatrice shook her head.

"I came to Kyrnunos and Cyril many, many, many years ago. I was young then. I was in deep despair from losing... I was in a very bad condition. Christopher Dante rescued me from

Cyril. He restored me, gave me hope that we could save my people, that he had a plan. He sent me back to Cyril. I am a spy for Christopher. I have been gathering intelligence for him, and we rescue as many Thunsi as we can." She sighed. "Everything has changed now. You have come, Beatrice. You have finally come, and with you here now, the last days have begun."

Beatrice pulled back. Once again, she had been snared into the narrative of some other unfolding tale, but this one, this story rang deep within her, the four hundred years of suffering, the disappearance of Christopher—all of it suddenly put into context, defined, a teleological event. "What do you mean, last days?"

"Well, that may be hyperbole. It's a fault of my people. We Thunsi were raised in a deeply superstitious culture. We believe in a Horned God!" She laughed out loud. "Anyway, Christopher has been waiting for you, and now that you are here, we will soon be traveling north. That is what we wait for. The right time to go."

They sat quietly for a little bit, the sound of the river at night now coming to life. "You have met Cyril before," Lucy said quietly. "You obviously knew each other. He said as much."

Beatrice closed her eyes, hard, pushing down the memories that were Cyril, the horror, the violence. She breathed deep, then out, opened her eyes and stared at the river, the calming, flowing, forever river. Like a river, like time itself, she found herself racing down a current she could not control, the landscape of four hundred years forever changing. What was not supposed to happen, what was never supposed to be possible...the river looped back on itself and what should have been a past forgotten suddenly became (once again) the horizon with the same terrifying plot unfolding, the characters all the same, Beatrice, Christopher, and Cyril. "Yes, I knew him. Like you, that was long ago."

She finished the licorice root cigarette, allowed the wine and the toxins in the smoke to settle over her. They were quiet, content.

"One of these days," Beatrice said, "I will get back to my world, IMAGO, see the Crystal Sea, stick my feet in it and look at the great colonies in the clouds. Someday, when this is all gone, I will sing for the sheer joy of it. Singing was my greatest pleasure. To sing to the sea." She sighed. "Someday."

They were quiet again. Happy.

"Someday," Lucy said. "Someday I will go back to my homeland up north. Someday I will see my people kill the great eel again and celebrate the coming of winter. Someday," she whispered. "Just maybe...someday...I will be able to see my daughter."

Beatrice stared at the tall Thunsi, her skin nearly black from the shadow of night, the small candle flame made the lines on her face shift and dance. "I'm sorry," she said. "This was why you were sold?"

"Yes."

"What was her name, your daughter?"

Lucy wiped her eyes. "I must go now. It is so late."

She stood tall and elegant, her sun dress blowing in the soft breeze. She bent down and kissed Beatrice on the head. Beatrice reached out and squeezed her skeletal fingers.

"Goodbye, Miss," Lucy said.

She stepped down the stairs, then turned. "Lara. Her name was Lara. She was *my* great pleasure. She was *my* greatest joy."

With that, Lucy hurried into the night.

Chapter Fifty-nine

Yet another week drifted by, Beatrice piddling around the small house, Lucy coming intermittently, the days warm and overcast. That was when the rains came. At first it drizzled, then low humid clouds fell upon the river world. The surface of the rolling water danced and sputtered with the steady force of it. Thunder rumbled deep in the clouds, followed by white flashes that shook the small house, and the storm-tossed day soon turned into evening. That was when Lucy came for her.

"He would like to see you now," she said softly.

She stood tall like a phantom in the doorway, the hood pulled up on her rain slick, and when Beatrice finally readied, they hurried through the storm, down to the river's edge and to a large river boat, dark and foreboding like some great theater prop.

They crossed the gangway and stopped underneath the second-floor overhang. "When we come to his room, you must sit where I tell you. You must not move from there. Do you understand?" She reached out and touched Beatrice's shoulder. "He has changed since you have seen him. Prepare yourself."

She turned and walked through the first-floor deck and up the stairs.

The stairs were worn and splintered, some risers with sweeping cracks like the river boat itself shifted and run aground. She was reminded of the bridge she crossed so many weeks ago. Like the bridge, the river boat seemed to be put together with an outside will, an eclectic madman who knew roughly what a boat should look like but had not fully completed the research. They stopped outside a large suite made of many rooms. The entire top deck had been reorganized as living quarters. Lucy knocked on the closed door, and it was opened by a tall Thunsi male. Beatrice recognized him immediately as the one chained in the shack, Lucy's brother.

"Miss," he said. "Welcome. He is very weak this evening, so your time will be limited."

He was tall, like Lucy, but broader, thicker, if a skeleton can be thicker. His face was gray and worn, older than Lucy. Several large scars like two tectonic plates converging, ridged flesh, swept across his right cheek and disappeared below the neckline of his baggy shirt.

The room was expansive but very dark, only a small light on a wall illuminated the entire space. Like the ship itself, the room was dingy and used, the bones of it worn, the furniture as if gathered from flea markets and yard sales. She could make out a small kitchen table with chairs near the darkened windows, a kitchen area next to that, a coffee table with a sitting area. They walked past all of this and to a tall door made of wood and metal. Occasionally, the rumble of thunder and the bright flash of lightening exposing some hidden item in the room.

"Sit in the chair near the window," he said. "I will return shortly."

He opened the door and closed it behind Beatrice. Christopher sat near an open window, the wind fluttering leaves of paper held down by what looked like smooth stones. He was tall, so tall, like a Thunsi, his shoulders rounded and pointed through his loose-fitting shirt. His legs where lanky like his arms, fingers spindly as they scratched a pronounced cheek bone. His head was wrapped in a flowing scarf, tied like a ponytail in the back. He smiled at her, an exhaustion across his countenance. "My Beatrice. You have come."

As the image of the transformed man settled on her, she

blinked and placed her hand over her mouth. "I am quite the same as you once knew. I can assure you," he responded. "I'm under a bit of alarming transformation, I'm afraid."

He breathed in deeply, a raspy guttural sound, then reached over to a coffee table where perched a short, stemmed pipe and a jar of what looked like tobacco. When he lit it and puffed the bowl to red embers, Beatrice recognized it as the Licorice Root that all Thunsi seemed to imbibe. "It somehow slows the change," he said. "The properties are quite complicated. On a molecular level..."

"What's happening to you?" Beatrice whispered.

She watched as he shifted in the seat, crossing one of his emaciated legs over the other.

"That's as complicated as this dried concoction, I'm afraid. There seems to be some law in place I have yet to fully understand, some physics principle that is particularly in play with...just me...with my particular...gift...as it were."

"I don't understand. You were...fine when I saw you last."

He puffed on the pipe, a thunderclap and flash illuminating the spartan room. She saw a bed in the corner near the desk, rumpled and unmade. "Ten, fifteen years?" he said. "A lifetime in what I have experienced." He looked at her, a sadness mixed with joy across his face. "Oh Beatrice. You have come. You have found me at last. Tell me everything of your journey."

Beatrice told him about Hal, about the journey to the mountains. He seemed surprised Hal made it to MaMaw, but seemed relieved at this as well, like some great, inevitable wheel so long dreaded had finally begun to turn. He asked what had happened to him, and Beatrice explained they separated, and MaMaw told her to go to Kyrnunos.

"She is a persistent old thing," he said. "What did you think of her...of it...really. MaMaw defies most categories."

The storm raged outside, the drumming on the metal roof sounded like rocks falling, a crash and boom, a flash then a steady down pour. Christopher placed the pipe on the table and rubbed his thighs. They were thin sticks hidden under fabric, and he soon arranged his pant legs in such a way as to hide that fact.

"I didn't understand what you were telling me back then," Beatrice said. "I think I understand more now. MaMaw showed me things, pictures that show a process."

"Probably not as much as you think," he whispered. He fidgeted with the pipe and bowl, chipping out the burnt ash. He placed it down again, picked it up and packed it full and lit it. "Cyril," he mumbled. "I'll bet that was a surprise."

Beatrice pulled her knees up to her chest instinctively. They were both silent. She looked out the window. "I thought I would never see him again."

"I am deeply sorry that you had to. When we came through the IMAGO portal, it would seem many others did as well. What amplified our talents, amplified theirs. My mother never was one for deep analysis. She never did think through consequences. She was always impulsive."

"Did you ever find her," Beatrice said, trying to forget the past, change the direction of the conversation. "Or hear what happened to her?"

"She is tied up with Cyril somehow. I think I have figured it out, the links in the chain...*your process discovered*. Something has happened up North. The Thunsi tell me there has been a catastrophe. Cyril and the Blodetan have gathered there. A great terror is now afoot, and I fear my time has finally come."

She sensed the deep sorrow on his face. It was a settled thing that only now clearly came into focus, a great weight and burden accepted, finally, after incredible resistance. His face was drawn, grooved wrinkles across his brow. She leaned forward. "Oh, Christopher. What are you about to do? How can I help you?"

He sighed and smiled. "It is something that should have been done hundreds of years ago, but because of circumstance, bad luck, personal choices—all of it... Now it is unfolding, just as it must."

"You're speaking in riddles. Speak plainly to me. Tell me what is happening. What is happening *to you*?"

"As to what is happening out there. Well, Beatrice, my darling, Beatrice. Two worlds cannot collide as they have without great changes. My mother was a fool to think she and others could enter that portal without consequence—a free, untethered act. From all that I have gathered, Stutz, your father, told her as much. She was reckless, ambitious. The Ghul validates the wrong done if nothing else. When one culture comes against another, there is always destruction, assimilation, transformation. Two things, after much violence and resistance eventually synthesize. Well, what if there is no synthesis...ever. We have seen it time and again in this world, but never on a dimensional, cosmic scale. What if one just supersedes the other, transforms it from what it was to...something else... well...becomes a tyrant over it? This is what has happened."

Beatrice listened to the rain as it slowed to a steady, even thrumming. She thought of her forever battle with the Ghul in Cogstin, and all of them desperately trying to figure out how that thing had taken such a foothold in this new world. "That doesn't explain The Event. It doesn't explain what happened, only that something *did* happen."

Christopher placed his skinny, skeletal hands together. "I happened, Beatrice. When my power, my true amplified power was unleashed, it was like a transformative pulse that remade this world. All creation has been groaning and struggling against the fallout from that violent act ever since." He stood up with great effort and walked to the window. "It was not done, as perhaps the original had been—an act of love. No, this was a desperate, vengeful release of energy that riddled every change with something...else. You see!" He turned toward her. "I caused the Mountain Folk. I caused the Thunsi. I caused the mess in Cogstin."

She was horrified at his appearance. His clothes hung on him. A stick frame of wood draped carelessly in cloth. The colorful scarf around his head slid back, revealing patches of hair, thin wisps like corn silk. She watched in wonder as he continued, now deep in his head.

"Well, maybe not the mess, not The Ghul, Cyril or The NRM. Not that. Those were compounded consequences from their choices, their actions. You see? When they realized that power in this world was amplified, they chose, and those tyrannical choices caused other consequences. The Ghul subjugated Cogstin to its will. NORM, that was created to open the portal and make first contact was transformed into a broken AI whose fragmented and myopic view subjugated Cogstin even more. It all started, the point of the spear, contact with IMAGO. From that point on—it all rests on my shoulders, my one act." He started to laugh. "In the beginning god created..." He convulsed and coughed from the exertion then gathered himself again and sat back down. "What a terrifying and damning phrase to start a story."

"We are not gods, Christopher. We are...astronauts trapped. We are travelers lost, longing to get home."

She stared at him, her mind racing. She never once stopped to consider this point. She lived all these years battling, scraping and singing to Christopher, finding him, gathering him with the others to open the portal and get back home. Get back to IMAGO. She had not thought of giving up, settling, taking on the new mantel of a new destiny. Madness! This is madness! This is what the Ghul did. This is what Cyril did. They came into this new world not as visitors longing to go back, but as conquerors. It may have been Christopher—through no fault of his own. How could there be fault. It was an act of love, an act of salvation for his mother—it may have been his one act that caused a transformation, but it was those diabolical, selfish choices that caused the tyranny of The Ghul of Cyril of anything else yet to threaten them.

Christopher stared intensely at her. "You believe that don't you? Yes, I can see it. You do believe that."

He reached out to Beatrice and grabbed her hand. His hands were cold, like thin pieces of abandoned metal. She instinctively pulled back.

"Oh, my darling, beautiful Beatrice. There is no *going back* for me. There is only what comes next. I must see it all the way through now."

"You can't go back now, not in this state. Cyril will kill you. It's madness to go back. Wait until you are better. Yes, let's wait until you improve, then we will..."

He reached out and grabbed her hand again. "Beatrice," he said. "Beatrice, my love, look at me."

She stopped.

"The transformation has already begun. There is no going back or starting over. I am leaving in the morning. It has already been decided. It was decided from the beginning. Now is the time. It must be this way. I don't want you to stop me. You could not even if you tried. I want you to go with me. I want to be with you for this. That is my great desire now, my beautiful Beatrice."

Just on cue, Lucy's brother entered the room. He stood over Beatrice.

"This way, Miss. I will show you to your room."

Beatrice stood. They looked one at another in silence. Beatrice bent over and kissed the top of Christopher's head. She turned and followed the Thunsi out of the room, wiping her eyes with the back of her fingers. A strangeness settled on her, something familiar but awful, something she experienced before in The Black Mountains. She smelled it with the Mountain Ghosts. She smelled it in the presence of MaMaw. it was a distinct and frightening scent, oily and persistent long after the encounter. If it was a voice, it would call out, I am decay. I am death. I am forever.

Chapter Sixty

When they arrived at the Cave of the Horned God, it was certain that things went terribly wrong for the Gathering Ceremony now into its fourth day. The plain fact of the matter was simply, there was no Cave of the Horned God.

Roman tried to remember what the actual place looked like, recall what transpired in the grove and inside the cave during his last visit. Before him was a landscape so transformed that his recollections from just a season ago seemed an ancient myth or images from an unreliable dream.

Roman in full High Priest robes stood before the landslide of boulders and gravel, the large eel skull now drooping down so that he had to continually push it up in order to see anything.

"We should go back," Ralph, the former High Priest, said to Roman's back.

"Yes," agreed old Ruth, her feet aching, her back aching, her mind half fogged with dementia and panic from seeing the great collapse. "It is a sign we must return to the Island."

Roman still stood facing the ruin. "No," he said. And more forcibly. "No, we will travel onward."

"Where?" Ruth whined. "Where do we go?"

"To the great forest itself. To The Forest of the Dead."

"Nonsense!" said Old Ralph. "Nobody has ever gone there. Nobody. Not one single High Priest has ever set foot in that sacred place."

"We shall be the first," Roman said.

"You have a duty," said Ruth, now not wanting to go one

step further. "You have a sacred duty to follow in the footsteps of those who came before you. How dare you decide such a foolish thing?"

"We have been called to go," Roman said.

"By whom?" Mocked Ralph, sensing a power shift...finally. "Clearly something monstrous has happened here. The Horned God is angry with you."

He turned more toward the crowd of Thunsi mothers and the ship's crew. "Surly The Horned God has spoken against your usurpation of power!"

Roman turned on the former High Priest, the point of the eel skull now right next to Ralph's forehead. "The circumstances of this situation call us now. Great and terrible events are unfolding. We must follow the call of The Horned God over all else."

"He is silent," Ruth persisted. "Maybe he has revoked his calling. What sign can you give? What sign, I ask you!"

"If no sign invoked, the position is revoked," Ralph semi chanted several times.

Roman sensed the shift now, and he dove deep into his consciousness for any message, no matter how small, from the Horned God. Usually, it was clear, a pulsating, rhythmical possession that demanded everything. Now, his mind ached. His stomach swirled with worry and doubt. He imagined himself vomiting all over both the two old farts.

He pulled the eel skull from his head then muddled through his small pack until he came to the Mendel Fragment enclosed in glass. He rubbed the smooth surface with the tip of his finger. He knew the half equation, the fragment by heart. So, he stood before the crowd of confused Thunsi and raised his hands out to the sky. He recited the fragment, then instinctively began to rearrange it, pronouncing some parts with more emphasis, others haltingly, then rapidly, understanding how the same equation now revealed other more possible, potential meanings, had at times whole phrases speaking out in ways he had never heard them before. From his outstretched hands came a small, blue orb. He did not know what the orb was, what it was supposed to do. In fact, he was as terrified and amazed as his Thunsi audience. "Behold," he said more as a reaction than a pronouncement because he could think of nothing else.

The blue orb grew in diameter and weight, the content within spinning faster and faster, a smoke within the globe, filling, expanding, then suddenly transforming into crystal glass. And Whether it was in Roman's head or broadcast out to the group, he saw Thunsi mothers standing in rows, the great forest before them...The Forest of the Dead.

"Look," wheezed Roman, eyes wide. There in the orb were Thunsi mothers stooped down with their Thunsi infants before... At that moment, the blue orb vanished. Poof!

Roman gasped.

Ralph and Ruth gasped, Ruth catching herself on her cane so as not to do a face plant.

The crowd of Thunsi Mothers with their infants gasped.

The *Intrepid* Crew stood with mouths open.

Like one single organism, all the Thunsi fell to their knees before Roman.

"So be it," he whispered. He continued, in a more authoritative voice, "So be it. We head south to The Forest of the Dead."

Chapter Sixty-one

It was slow, but the trail was wide and clearly marked with the hanging bones and stones and runes carved into the trunks. Soon the forest was laden with fog, like a great cloud lowered onto the trees, and for another day they wandered slowly southward down the trail toward the Forest of the Dead. After several miles they came to a low wall and a stone archway perfectly fitted one to the other, the keystone black as onyx. On the surface was a rune, and not one of the Thunsi doubted what it signified.

"I feel no joy," whispered Rebecca. "Why am I not happy to be here."

"It is a terrible place," said Renilda.

"Hush your mouth, foolish girl," hissed Ruth. Even the old crone's voice was shaky and twinged with fear.

The trail entered through the archway and disappeared into a blanket of fog. Everyone stood still. Roman walked through the gate, and Ruth cried out.

"Open your mouth again, old crone," said Roman, "and it will be your last."

Lara followed Renilda, Raya, Rebecca, and the other mothers through the gate, then the rest of the crew of the *Intrepid* taking up the rear. Onward and onward. Something was happening now inside Lara. A persistent doubt like a tiny grain of sand in between the toes, rubbing and chaffing, constantly calling out, THIS IS NOT RIGHT. SOMETHING IS WRONG. Then, it would dissipate when she looked into her tiny Thunsi's face. She even knew what name to give her when the time came. She did not care if it was proper or not. She did not care if they changed it. She would never change it, ever. This little one would forever be Elizabeth.

The stone wall marked the change. Now great sweeping tubes snaked from one tree to the next and to the next as far as the eye could see. Each clear hose fastened to the trunk with what looked to be iron taps rusted from time and weather, incrusted with a thick orange sap.

Lara placed her hand on her infant Thunsi now wrapped tightly to her chest in a papoose. As they walked, her mind raced back to what she saw in Roman's blue orb. Why were they standing there in a row? Yes, she saw herself specifically. Did everyone see her, or did they each see themselves? After talking to Rita and Renilda, she was not quite sure. Raya was walking with Ruth and seemed at every turn to spite her. Now none of this nonsense mattered. She was with her little one. She had been blessed by The Horned God to deliver a great mystery, and she was excited and expectant to participate in the actual Gathering ritual of which no mother, ever, had been a part.

They walked for miles and miles, the forest thickening, the trunks closer together. A smell of dampness and of places rarely touched if at all by the sun. And the tubes no longer hung from the trees. It was their eighth day from landing on the coast, and Lara noticed how young the trees looked. She wondered what kind of tree would be colored so, a bluish gray tint, tall, straight, like steel posts, some with very few limbs, like arms really. It was when they entered this new section, they realized the Blodetan were following them. That night they could hear the Blodetan surrounding them, the sniffs, a far-off whine followed by a response close by, the cracking of twigs and the rustling of leaves. When she looked, Lara could sometimes make out the vague image of the pale king, his bone crown jutting out irregularly.

It was evening of the following day when they came to the clearing in The Forest of the Dead. Roman was now certainly under the thaumaturgy of The Horned God. The atmosphere crackled and spit with the power. At first, she thought it was the low buzz of swarming insects, but soon Lara realized that it was indeed the music of The Horned God, the powerful rhythmical pulsating beat that entered the ears and soon overtook ones very soul. She resisted it at first, watching others submit willfully, their bodies swaying to and from. She watched Ruth smile in the delight of the sensation, Ralph, Old Bony Root, grasp her and hold her, petting her shoulder and her withered cheek like a bewitched schoolboy.

She saw them standing just beyond, Hal and Clem. They were motionless, like statues of flesh, rigid and awkward in the swaying, moaning mass of Thunsi. She heard a distinct voice unlike any voice she had ever heard. At first, she thought it Elizabeth, but it was rougher, full of suffering. The chant clearer and clearer through the fog of thaumaturgy:

Come, come, come to me
Through the fog and power strong
Cross the ghosts and bones and flee
To your Mother, come and see

Lara did not understand it. She felt it raging against the power that so desperately tried to possess her. It pulled at her. Strong. When she looked up, now clutching her tiny Thunsi infant in desperation and confusion, she saw beyond the clearing several figures racing toward her, and one of them, tentacle limbs stretched out for attack, was Hawthorn.

Chapter Sixty-two

By the time Hal got to the clearing, past the creepy Forest of the Dead, past the trees with hoses, tubes and rusted taps. Past taps; past the bones and stones dangling and clanging and annoyingly consistent in their rhythms; past all of that and to the straight grayish blueish trees with sparse branches like limbs that had now become the creepiest thing he had yet seen in an incredibly creepy woods. By the time Hal got to the clearing, he was more and more convinced of his extermination plan. *Hadn't Christopher Dante caused all of this? Wasn't he to blame for the suffering, sorrow, the bizarre and twisted, evil...yes, let's call it what it was...evil!*

This coursed through Hal's head, looped back again, always focusing on the same equation, Christopher Dante equaled the cause of evil. When he came to the clearing, he had gotten into such a state he was ready for action.

When Hal and Clem walked through the last row of tall, gray, creepy trees...when they stepped into the great open space in the woods, they were greeted by a very odd sight. A giant Thunsi, the same race as Lara and Captain Robert, stood tall and proud. He was old, grayish, and wrinkled, clothed in white trousers that were too short, his baggy shirt open at the chest. Next to him (and this was even more striking) sat a tall human, long face, long arms, legs crossed, and draped in a flowing silk robe of flowers. He smoked a cigarette. He had a Cheshire grin across his elegant face.

"Well, this is unexpected," he said in a delighted voice.

"I love surprises. Who might you be? Come closer. Pease, come closer."

Hal reached for his machete. "Oh, that will not be necessary," said the man in the chair, and he suddenly thrust out his hand and snapped his fingers rapidly. "Come. Approach me, little man... And...a mountain ghost. How delightful."

Hal's mind fogged with the powerful thaumaturgy, his will pulled from him, his mind open like a young blossom. The mycelia on his arm, which now covered most of his chest and shoulders, writhed under the spell of compulsion. He stopped ten feet from the seated man.

"Well," said the man, "you are quite peculiar, aren't you?" He continued the snapping, then stopped. "It seems as though you have had some work done, poor dear. The old rock has done...what...?" The man in the chair waved his hand and Hal's shirt pulled open. "Oh, my!" His face grimaced. "Oh, that's just nasty." He shook his head. "Button that up. Nobody needs to see that. Oh, my poor dear."

Hal obeyed, then hands falling to his side. "Answer me. Chop! Chop!"

He clapped his hands together. Hal felt the wall guarding his thoughts crumple like tin foil.

Something was happening now inside Hal. The mycelial structuring in his body, this network of hyphae now so strong, began to receive the thaumaturgy, absorb, and circulate it, spreading it through itself and circumventing the command. For Hal, what was at first an overwhelming signal, suddenly became intermittent, less powerful, like a strong radio wave at a long distance. His will still wanted to submit to the command, but the mycelia fought hard against it. Hal struggled, then blurted out, "Christopher."

The man in the chair grimaced. Then hesitated. He turned to the Tall Thunsi next to him. "It would be just like him to throw the Old Rock and her minions at me."

The Thunsi nodded.

"So that little arrogant shit sent you. To do what? Come, speak!"

The mycelia pressed and fought against Hal's mind, like a great hand pushing back his thoughts. Hal was strong, and he nearly yelled out, "To kill."

"Oh, how delightful! Christopher Dante has sent a puny little man to do what he could not." Now the man in the chair was laughing, a hearty, full laugh that shook his body.

He once again turned to the old Thunsi, "I had heard that the poor dear was sickly, but this proves how desperate he actually is."

And to Hal. "Well, what is the great catastrophe you caused up here, little human weapon of vengeance?"

The man smiled, but suddenly, the smile dropped into puzzlement, for just now, a large gathering of Thunsi emerged from the tall gray blue trees behind Hal. The man in the chair stood, his silk robe blowing in the summer breeze. He clapped his hands rapidly, vigorously, then in one great movement, he smacked his hands together and stomped his foot. The space filled with a crackling, sparking, spitting energy. Everyone stood still as stone.

The mycelia inside Hal did something it had never done before—it filled Hal's imagination with words, not his words, but words from someplace else. *He is coming. He is coming. Be still. He is coming. Be still. He is coming. Don't be afraid. He is coming. Be still.*

Hal did not know who was coming, why they were coming or what they wanted, but it was clear that whatever was to transpire now was beyond anything he planned.

"Why are you here? You are not supposed to be here! How dare you bring them with you!" The man cried out to a

Thunsi wearing what looked to be a great painted skull. The man's face changed to fury, and he stared at Hal, pointing his finger at him. "What did you do?"

"I killed a god," Hal said and smiled.

Chapter Sixty-three

Beatrice, Lucy and Christopher walked several miles north of the stone wall that separated Kyrnunos from the great forest beyond the river bluffs. NORM buzzed and whirled next them. Christopher connected it to a satellite. That seemed to truly change the digital personality of the odd and awkward AI. It was more like a dog now, following close to Christopher's heels, never allowing him to be more than several feet away. Sometimes it would randomly speak out with observations. "Human joy appears to be a result of hormonal influxes combined with recalled memory." Or "The location of the nearest fresh water source is approximately twenty meters. A human can sustain viability for seventy-two hours without fresh water." And, "The average length of a human male's...."

"Okay already! Shut up!"

She turned to Christopher. "What's wrong with that thing?" Beatrice said finally.

Christopher took the opportunity to rest. He was breathless and even though it was summer, he wore a hoodie. He pulled it down, the scarf covering his head glistened from the sweat in the sunlight. "Well," he said. "I imagine it's like any of us when we discover that the world we have been limited to is much larger than we first thought."

He looked down at NORM. The AI's camera zooming in and out to focus on his face. "It's connected to a source it could not connect with, and it's downloading all manner of information...clearly. The trick is trying to limit that world once the process has begun." He tapped the metal shell. "NORM, Protocol check."

Norm buzzed and whirled, then in a synthetic voice, "Dante Protocol functioning properly."

"Good," Christopher said.

"Connecting to the satellites caused a disaster in Cogstin. How can you trust it?"

"It's not trust, Beatrice," Christopher said. "I don't trust NORM. Just like I don't trust anything and anyone in this world. I must, however, have it connected. We will need it when we get to The Forest of the Dead and Cyril. NORM's connection to the only remaining telecommunication satellite will be invaluable to us. Quite frankly, after the fall of The Ghul, I don't think there is anything else up there."

Beatrice looked up in the sky as if she would be able to see the metal transponder hovering in the deep blue of the day.

Lucy came back from her reconnaissance. "There is quite an elevation ahead. I think I have found a path around."

"No," Christopher said. "We don't have time to go around. I can make it. Let's keep moving."

The forest floor began to rise, rocks and small cliffs gave way to steep ravines. They struggled up the soggy, leaf-slicked precipices and slid down the other sides as the ground eventually evened out. Soon the canopy above them turned to a deep green of rustling leaves, and the spaces between the trunks drew closer together. It was nearing evening when they decided to make camp for the night.

Christopher set up a perimeter with NORM as patrol. The three of them sat around a small fire listening to the night animals stir and go about their way. After a small, sparse dinner, Christopher stood up and consulted with NORM in the dark. Beatrice and Lucy sat smoking the licorice root that Lucy brought with her. When Christopher returned, he was unsettled. He looked even more gaunt and sickly then Beatrice had yet seen. His hood was pulled over his head, and he sat down facing the fire, knees drawn up, his thin arms snaking around them.

"Do you remember the first time we met, Beatrice?"

"Of course, I do," she said now staring at him with concern.

"You were...well, let's say you were a hardened shell."

"Still am," she said with a smile.

"Yes, yes you are," Christopher chuckled. There was silence. "You have a soft middle."

"My people say," said Lucy, "to get to the eel's blubber, you must first go through the teeth."

She laughed, and Beatrice found her presence, her stately, tall, proud demeanor comforting in the darkness of the forest.

"So now I am blubber?"

"Sweet to eat and satisfying all day," laughed Lucy. She reached her long spindly Thunsi arm around Beatrice and pulled her close.

There was silence again.

"Why did you ask me that?" Beatrice said.

"Memories are all that remain sometimes. They can be more powerful than being in the present. I hope you never lose them. I hope you will always remember me." He looked directly at her. "Will you remember me, Beatrice?"

"Of course, I will."

"Good. That is good. You will know what to do then."

They sat and chatted about their childhoods. Lucy remembering the Salty Sea, the first time she sailed out into it, the great wonder of the open space. Beatrice remembered something she had long forgotten. She was young, and she was sitting with...Christopher. Yes, it was Christopher! They were sitting on a stone wall staring up into the dim, cold day, the dying sun orange in the distance. They were bundled thick and warm and sitting staring out over the great crystal ocean, the cloud colonies high above in the distance. They were laughing...that was when Cyril came. Beatrice blinked and stirred. Christopher was staring at her intensely. Lucy was dozing off to the side.

"Will you remember the good of me, Beatrice?" Christopher said.

Beatrice stared at him. His sunken eyes now even more pronounced in the shadows of the fire. "You know that I will. Always and forever."

"The good is so hard to remember," he said, "when there is so much evil in the world."

"Why are you speaking like this?" Beatrice said.

"I'm just so tired, my love."

She sat up and hurried to him, holding him, his head in her lap, she caressing his cheek.

"I'm afraid, my love. I'm so terribly afraid," he said.

"Shhhhhh," she calmed him, stroking his cheek, removing the silk scarf, and caressing his patched, balding scalp. She closed her eyes to stop the tears. "I will remember you," she whispered. "I love you...I will love you...forever."

~ * ~

In the morning Christopher and NORM were gone. Beatrice and Lucy searched for them all about the small camp, but there was no sign. It was as if they had just flown away.

"We will head north," Lucy said. "Maybe he has gone before us."

"He's in deep trouble," Beatrice said and stuffed the last of the camping supplies into her pack. "He is going to do something foolish."

"Hurry!" said Lucy. "We may catch him still."

They ran north further into the great woods.

~ * ~

A mile from camp, they came face to face with such a strange creature, neither knew what to do. It flung its tentacle-branches this way and that and blocked any way they tried to go.

"Stand aside, tree!" bellowed Lucy, her iron fist raised to strike."

"No, no, no, no hit Hawthorn. Hawthorn no tree! Hawthorn come for you! Hawthorn no hurt Thunsi. Lara Thunsi! Captain Robert Thunsi! Roman Thunsi! Me no hurt Thunsi. Me come to help Thunsi."

"What did you say?" Lucy stood dumbfounded; hands outstretched to calm the crazed creature. "What did you just say?"

"Me no hurt Thunsi. Me love Thunsi. Me know Thunsi. Me come to get Thunsi and little one." Hawthorn pointed a tentacle branch at Beatrice.

"Little one?" Beatrice blustered. "I'll show you *little one*."

"Wait!" Lucy dropped her hands and walked to Hawthorn. "Repeat what you said just now."

"Hawthorn say he like Thunsi?"

"Before that."

"Me know Thunsi?"

"Yes! Yes! What Thunsi did you say?"

"Me like Thunsi. Me no harm Thunsi. Me like Captain Robert Thunsi and Roman Thunsi...."

"Yes, yes, yes," insisted Lucy. "There was another."

Hawthorn scratched his root ball head. "Lara. Me love Lara. Lara the best Thunsi. Lara is my friend."

Lucy began to cry. "You have seen Lara? You know Lara, my Lara?"

Hawthorn was now in uncertain waters. He did not know if the Thunsi was going to kill him or hug him. He stepped back. "Yes, Hawthorn take you to her. Hawthorn told to find Lucy the Thunsi and little one. Me find you."

"Who told you to find us?" Beatrice interrupted.

"Christopher Dante told Hawthorn. Follow me. Follow me. I bring you to Lara and Christopher Dante!"

Just like that, the strange creature rushed off into the woods. Lucy leapt after it, Beatrice struggling with all her might to keep up with them.

Chapter Sixty-four

Night was falling on the clearing in the Forest of the Dead. Lara stood and watched Roman walk from the line of Thunsi mothers with their infants and step to the tall man and his old Thunsi servant. She could not hear what was going on, nor did she really care, for the power of the thaumaturgy was so strong, that her head filled with a rapturous hope and celebration. All she really wanted to do at this point was dance. The line of Thunsi shifted back and forth, swaying to unheard tunes.

That was when she heard that strange incantation.

Come, come, come to me
Through the fog and power strong
Cross the ghosts and bones and flee
To your Mother, come and see

No matter what she *wanted* to do, all she *could* do was sway and slowly move to the sensuous, pulsating rhythm of the Horned God. Now that she thought about it...The Horned God was actually...the tall thin man standing before Roman. "Yes, yes, you are here, my beloved, oh my beloved."

~ * ~

Lucy and Hawthorn made it to the clearing in the Forest of the Dead first, and that was to their disadvantage, for Cyril was now the conductor of a terrifying orchestra of destruction. With one hand he moved Roman and the Thunsi mothers, like a child playing with toy soldiers on a pretend battlefield. Roman lead them all, mother Thunsi and infants, a straight line following him down a great empty row that edged the clearing. He stopped. They stopped. Before each mother were large holes dug into the soft earth. Beyond the holes, thousands of young trees one after the other, row upon row as far as they could see. They stood, statues before the holes, the small bundled Thunsi infants grasped tightly into their long spindly fingers. And still their bodies moved and swayed to the pulsing, thrumming music of the Horned God.

When Cyril saw Lucy and Hawthorn enter the clearing, he swept up his hand and turned them stiff as stone. On one side now stood the row of Thunsi mothers with their Thunsi infants. On the other, he moved Ralph, Ruth and the rest of the *Intrepid* crew along with Hawthorn and Lucy. Two parallel lines, the energy crackling with the power of the Horned God, a low chant from everyone in celebration and expectation.

~ * ~

Hal's sardonic smirk soon disappeared when he saw the rage in Cyril's face. Cyril clapped his hands together and Hal fell to his knees, Clem beside him, the mountain ghost now crystal clear and trapped just as Hal was. "Oh," chortled Cyril, "I have a special task for you, my mycelial friends." His voice was wicked, seething, delighted in the terror he was causing. "Behold!" He nearly screamed, and as he did, he placed a crown upon his head. It was a wreath with two great horns looping up into the darkness. Cyril's silk robe fluttered in the night breeze, thaumaturgy now crackling blue, now green, now a flash of pure light. He raised both hands high as the crowd moaned with delight. From the darkness of the Forest of the Dead came the Blodetan King with the crown of bones on his head. Behind him, hunched, lurching, sniffing, and yelping were the horde. High in the air they lifted the emaciated body of Christopher Dante.

Chapter Sixty-five

Beatrice saw the trap before Hawthorn and Lucy did, and she pulled back into the woods and crouched behind a large oak. She knew no one in his presence could withstand his power. She knew that power all too well in IMAGO. She knew the wickedness that was Cyril those first days in this new world, and she knew full well the hatred he had toward Christopher. She watched from a dense thicket how Cyril moved his pawns about. She had one chance, and that was to find Christopher before Cyril did. Find Christopher.

So, she ran and skirted the great clearing in the Forest of the Dead, and there she discovered NORM. His legs were straight beneath him like a table, camera-head pulled low, a red light blinking in rhythm.

"NORM, where is Christopher?"

"Dante Protocol activated," said the synthetic voice.

"NORM, I must find Christopher. NORM!"

"Dante Protocol activated."

She heard a howl, yapping, like animals that discovered a kill. She ran. As she swept past the low limbs and stumbled over surfacing roots, she recalled the strange conversation with Christopher around the fire. "What have you done? Oh, Christopher! What have you done?"

She crossed over a small stream and raced up the slick ravine, then fell flat to the damp earth. There in a great mass was the Blodetan. Before them, tall, slightly stooped, gangly, the hood pulled high over his head—there stood Christopher. He did not fight. He did not speak. Everyone was silent. The king of the Blodetan stood before him, the bone crown pronounced and tall and sharp upon his head, and with a savage blow, fingers like daggers splayed out, he struck Christopher to the ground.

Beatrice yelped, her hands to her mouth, "No. Oh no. Do something. Why don't you do something?" Her voice was caught in her chest, and she watched in silent horror as the King of the Blodetan raised Christopher by the throat and swept him effortlessly onto the backs of the horde. The horde screamed, whined, and gnashed their teeth. The King of the Blodetan cocked back his head and howled. The macabre army marched hooting and hollering toward Cyril and the great clearing in the Forest of the Dead.

Chapter Sixty-six

Lara stood with all the other Thunsi mothers holding their Thunsi infants, the strange, perfectly round holes opening before them. They faced the clearing now, backs to the young, tall, nearly limbless trees beyond. Roman stood before the Horned God who in the darkness of the night looked monstrous and terrifying with the great horns jutting up. Roman and the Old Thunsi Servant erected an immense bon fire. It roared and crackled orange against the darkness and the energy of Cyril's thaumaturgy.

Soon all but the Thunsi mothers and their Thunsi infants gathered in the light of the fire. Hundreds of Blodetan stooped and swayed with their king to an unheard melody. There were pale, thin, hunched things growling and sniffing, their eyes nearly invisible in the darkness. In the middle of them all stood the Horned God and kneeling before him, the mythical Christopher Dante.

The Horned God was in the middle of some tirade, Lara could barely remember any of it. All she wanted, longed for was her precious beloved, his hands touching her, his beautiful voice like falling water. Gnawing at her was the strange chant, a song really, chipping away at the powerful spell.

~ * ~

Hal stood before Cyril. Next to him was Clem, and next to Clem, lined up in a great row were the strange, tall Thunsi women with their babies. *What were the holes for?* He felt the power of the thaumaturgy, and it was like a strong current, sweeping around him, immobilizing him. The Mycelia structure in his body, the network of hyphae sparked and pulsed electrical currents of their own, gathering in tiny hubs of woven fibers, a body within a body, and Hal recognized all of this, but his mind was concentrating on one thing, Christopher Dante. The words of Cyril pierced and prodded his thoughts, like a fiery preacher pronouncing judgement and condemnation on a recognized sinner. Though he tried to concentrate on the words, he continually was sidetracked by another voice, a whisper really. It was subtle like a soft breeze, the rustling of leaves in the springtime: *Don't be afraid. Don't be afraid. I understand. Don't be afraid. It must be. I am with you still.* It made no sense because he wasn't afraid, and he certainly wasn't afraid of this Cyril with the stupid horns on his head. *One more asshole god to remove*, Hal thought. He was the god killer. *Let them kill each other, and I will finish the one who is left.* Through the terrible scene unfolding, Hal suddenly smiled.

~ * ~

It was just after the Horde brought Christopher Dante before Cyril that Beatrice was summoned.

"You cannot stay out there, my beautiful flower, Beatrice," cried out the horned Cyril to the night. "You won't be able to see out there. You need a front row seat!"

He suddenly turned behind him and stared into the darkness of the forest. "There you are, my sweet."

He snapped his fingers in such a strange cadence, so quick did the sound penetrate her mind, that Beatrice had no time to react. She stood, like a marionette moved by the puppeteer, then walked stiffly into the clearing while Cyril patiently waited for her. "Here we are again," he said as she stood next to him. "How can we have a play without the most important member in the audience?"

Cyril nodded to the Thunsi servant who pushed Beatrice down onto the chair that Cyril used earlier. She was surrounded by the Blodetan who sniffed and whined around her. *Why was he not doing anything? He had the power to transform the world! He had the power to annihilate Cyril and the Blodetan with some simple thought. He WAS a god! If anyone could be called such a thing. And yet...* She looked at the defeated Christopher, head down, bleeding, his jacket slashed and torn from the journey to the clearing. What was happening? Beatrice began to sing within her head. She knew what was coming, and with all her gift, she began to form a song, spontaneous, powerful, something to match, somehow, Cyril, the great and terrible Horned God.

Chapter Sixty-seven

"Our play begins with a prologue," pronounced Cyril in full theatrical mode now. "All great plays begin that way. We shall begin ours with the greatest opening known to this world. In the beginning god created..." He chuckled. "Well, no, that just does not fit our tragedy at all. Let's start with, Dearly beloved, we are gathered here today to..." Cyril shook his head and laughed again. "No, no, no. That most certainly won't do. Fitting, indeed, but does not set the right tone for our play." He stood tall and ominous before the kneeling Christopher whose head was hooded and lowered. "This one is more befitting to this night, this moment. Once upon a time... yes...once upon a time there were two brothers noble born who wanted something only one could obtain—the princess of the castle. The younger one, a lonely boy, he spends his days wandering the woods and spying on the princess. Day after day, week after week he would stand far off and watch the beautiful princess and his brother play and laugh and dance and sit on the stone wall in the sunlight on the shores of the Crystal Sea. 'Oh,' thought the young boy, maybe someday I will marry the beautiful princess.'"

Cyril walked over to Beatrice. He cupped her cheeks with his hands and kissed her on the head. "What a foolish thought to have such a one as the princess for his own. Why, may you ask? Well, she was secretly betrothed to the older brother, the family patriarch had already decreed it. Unite the two families, carry on the sacred bloodline. There was a problem, like all good stories, and this one was a doozie! The planet of IMGO was dying. It was a famine and plague and violent planet of war and blood, and it had run its course. The boy's mother was smart, and selfish, and when she could find no exit, she made one. Even that had a catch to it. There is always a catch when you dance with death. She could only take twelve to this new world.

"Not a lottery. Not an intentional plan. Save yourself, save the ones you love—leave the rest. One day the younger brother awoke to an empty house, abandoned. He was a tricky, tricky rascal, that younger brother, and he found his own way, a darker, more perilous way in the end."

Cyril stopped and pulled Christopher's head up by the hood. "How am I doing so far? You remember this story. Its plot is as old as time, love, betrayal, the murder of a brother." Cyril violently grabbed Christopher by his hood. "You remember, don't you...brother."

Cyril turned to the Blodetan and raised his hands. They howled and groaned. He turned to the Thunsi mothers with their Thunsi infants. They swayed and moaned with delight. "Oh, brother, this will be a night to remember. The ending to this story, dear, dear brother, has been four hundred years in the making."

Chapter Sixty-eight

Hal was deep in his head when he noticed Beatrice (who was sitting in the chair) mumbling something. *Was she singing? She was singing!* She was going to ruin everything if she interfered now. *Christopher must die. Who cares who kills him. He must die! And Cyril And Beatrice... All of them.*

He was the god killer now. This was his mission, and such a hatred filled him, such a focused will, that when he stared at Christopher kneeling on the ground, he did not at first understand that he, Christopher Dante, was staring back at him. It was not a face of hatred and revenge. It was one filled with sadness, like a great weight had been placed upon his shoulders, a choice that needed to be made—now made.

At that moment, through the spinning vitriol, the storm of hate thundering and booming inside Hal's head, he heard a still small voice. *Don't be afraid. Don't be afraid. I understand. It's okay. This is how it must be. I forgive you. Don't be afraid...*

Hal blinked and shook his head to rid himself of the voice, but it persisted. He turned away and tried focusing on Cyril who was now in a complete rage.

Cyril pulled Christopher to him and screamed, "After all this time! After four hundred years, after we solved the problem called Christopher Dante. Yes, we solved the problem *you made!* After all this time, you have the nerve, the gall, to come back and destroy the systems the rest of us put in place!" He swept his fist down again and smashed Christopher to the ground. Then again and again and again, emphasizing the words with every blow,

"You sanctimonious...piece...of...shit!"

A voice inside Hal clapped and cheered, "Y*es! Kill each other! Kill them all!*

~ * ~

Beatrice knew she could never match Cyril's power. You can't topple a building with one blow, but you can take out a foundational block... then see what happens. So, she looked for one...and found it. Of all the Thunsi Mother's standing with their Thunsi infants, swaying back and forth completely consumed by Cyril's enchantment—out of all of them, she saw one who seemed a bit confused, seemed to fight what was happening to her.

She focused her attention on her, concentrating the internal song like a radio beam, a condensed energy with the single intention of complete disruption. She sang, silently, internally, chanting the phrases over and over, coalescing strands of diverse themes, weaving them, and directing them at the young Thunsi with her infant.

Come, Come, Come to me
All the beetles, spiders, bees
Stir from slumber, shiver, and shake
Young Thunsi with her daughter awake!

While Cyril began to rage and take out his fury on Christopher Dante, a swarm, an army of creeping things emerged. They gathered, climbed, buzzed, bit, pinched, tickled the young Thunsi with her infant. So annoying, irritating and confounding were the insects that the Thunsi with her infant twitched. They attacked again, and soon she was slapping the intruders while holding her young child. She shook her head as if reeling from a sudden blow. The swarm vanished. She blinked and looked around her, a startled animal before the hunter's bow.

Chapter Sixty-nine

Something confusing and terrifying was happening to Roman, the High Priest of Widorexiton. He stood in the gathering, the great bonfire blazing, the light dancing and shifting as the shadow play unfolded before him. He was deep in the Thaumaturgy now, and he knew that this apostate Christopher Dante, son of the cursed Elizabeth Dante—the one most hated by Horned God—this being must suffer and die.

He also knew Christopher Dante was a destroyer of their whole belief system. How dare he come here and pronounce the end to this...this holy, glorious cycle of birth and renewal?

There was another voice deep inside him, a skeptical voice whispering and pointing out the disparities of what he believed. Of what he was watching. Sure, he was the most powerful Thunsi now. He was The High Priest of Widorexiton. He was the only one allowed to go to the Cave of the Horned God. He was the only one the Horned God called, but who were these others? There was another Thunsi standing next to The Horned God, and he never saw him before. Who, indeed, was this old raggedy, crinkled up Thunsi? Obviously, a place of high honor... of higher honor than his?

There were more fundamental things happening before him, foundational things, things of myths and legends, ancient histories long forgotten—they were here. The Horned God was here! Christopher Dante was here! The very systems built around the sacred God...all of it seemed...well, stupid now. The Mendel Fragment? Now that Christopher Dante was before him...well, that seemed a child's scribbling, a simple, pathetic half-witted utterance. He felt ashamed, mocked, even angry. Everything he believed to be true seemed to crumble into powder, ash, the aftermath of an all-consuming fire. Two gods battled it out before his eyes, and he knew he was being asked one terrible, awful question. Who do you choose? You must choose. Who do you choose? As the Horned God raged before him, he looked over at the Thunsi mothers with their Thunsi Infants all standing before those holes. What was happening here? "This has always been the way, the mysterious and secret way," said a voice in his head. "You knew there was a price to pay. Did you not think there was a cost? The Horned God demands everything...everything from you." *Choose!*

~ * ~

Christopher Dante's voice was almost a whisper, but when he repeated himself, the blood dripping from his nose and face—when he repeated himself, the whole assembly seemed to hush.
"You are a murder," he wheezed. "You are no god. You are nothing but a murdering slave trader." He wiped his mouth and spit a coagulation of phlegm and blood onto the ground. "Tell them about the Thunsi slaves in the mines. Tell them how the Thunsae Myrrha is made. Tell them what the Forest of the Dead really is." He paused, nearly crying. "Tell these mothers what will happen to their precious babies." He coughed up more blood, then screamed, "Tell them!"
Cyril did not wait for those words to register on anyone. He clicked his fingers rapidly then clapped his hands in a strange uneven rhythm. "Stand before the Horned God!" He commanded.
Christopher stood, his legs wobbly beneath him, hood pulled back, face swollen and bleeding. The Blodetan began to howl and chant. The Thunsi Mothers held their Thunsi Infants and knelt before the holes before them. The bonfire raged, shooting up as if to topple the tallest tree. From behind Christopher Dante the King of the Blodetan stepped from the

Horde, the crown of bones on his head, and in his hand he held a great polished bone knife that gleamed in the firelight. The Horned God pronounced, "behold your god!" The King of the Blodetan swept the blade into Christopher Dante's back, and he dropped face down to the cold ground.

~ * ~

Beatrice screamed in horror, and as the bone knife came down, a single sentence blew through her mind, *I love you. I have always loved you.*

~ * ~

Hal smiled. *One down, two to go.* That voice was superseded by another, looping over and over, *I forgive you. I forgive you. This is how it must be done.*

~ * ~

Lara saw the King of the Blodetan rise from the horde, and she was truly terrified, but all she could think about was the strange questions the mythical Christopher Dante asked. She thought of his mother, Elizabeth, how she would have reacted to seeing her children killing each other? A fire sparked and sputtered, a small flame igniting the expansive planes of dried grass, a smoldering, expanding, all-consuming inferno within. *Nobody harms my baby! Nobody!* The true and pure anger erupted, the violence of a mother protecting her child, a fierce white-hot explosion of unpredictable rage unleashed. As she watched Christopher Dante gasp and crumble to the ground, watched as the Horned God turned to Hal and the Mountain Ghost Clem—as they were summoned before him—it was then that she acted.

Chapter Seventy

Hal's smile of triumph evaporated as he and Clem were compelled to stand before Christopher Dante's dying body. He could see the great wound in his back, the dark maroon patch expanding across his shirt, pooling under him, a great ocean of blood, Christopher's eyes open wide staring at...Hal. Again, the voice, *Don't be afraid. I forgive you. I forgive you. This is how it must be done. It is the only way.* Cyril was clapping his hands now and pronouncing something to the gathered crowd.

"Four hundred years of ritual and rite. This is the way, the only way. I am The Horned God. Bow before your god, your only god!"

The Blodetan fell to their knees. The Thunsi Mothers with their Thunsi infants fell to their knees before the holes. Hal and Clem fell to their knees before Christopher's dead body, the blood viscous and blackening, Christopher's eyes now open, empty windows void of life. Beatrice sat in her chair, sobbing uncontrollably, watching the motionless body of her beloved, the internal song strong in her head, building like a recharging weapon.

And the unthinkable! Hal felt a sensation building within. It was familiar, a recognized, profoundly powerful, unstoppable urge. "No," Hal screamed. "No, please no!"

Clem, resisting, straining with great effort but to no avail, was already stooping over the dead body of Christopher Dante.

"Oh, yes, my mycelial friend," chortled Cyril. "Oh yes, indeed."

"Please, no! Please."

Cyril raised his arms like pronouncing a blessing, and clapped his hands in quick successions, a powerful, explosive wave of thaumaturgy released. "Begin!" His voice boomed.

Hal felt the hunger overwhelm his body, the mycelial strands surging down his arms, alive, vibrant ferocious things. His hands fell to the cold husk of Christopher, and the mycelia strands reached out like great webbing and began to feed. Clem's mouth was open wide, his hands also on the dead body of Christopher. Hal sobbed, convulsed, and closed his eyes in humiliation.

~ * ~

When Hal and Clem stooped over the dead body of Christopher, Lara along with the mothers with their young Thunsi infants knelt before the holes. Cyril's music was strong and thrumming, a pulsating urge to obey. To her horror, the mothers reached down with the wriggling and crying infants and placed them into the holes. Lara fought the urge to obey and held her little Elizabeth to her chest. "No," she screamed. "No. I will not!"

Cyril turned from Hal and Clem, a ghoulish grin of satisfaction across his face which soon dropped into confusion. Lara pushed herself up from her knees, as the Thunsi Mothers under the terrible spell began to pull the dirt over their crying babies. "No," Lara said again, but this time she was not alone.

~ * ~

When Beatrice saw Hal and Clem hover over her beloved, she cried out, but something deep within her, some foundational truth, something from the very beginning was now at work. In this horrifying moment, she recalled what MaMaw showed her so long ago. This was unfolding just as it was supposed to, and although she did not understand it, she knew she still had a part to play. Christopher was gone. The great river of the event called Christopher Dante of IMAGO flowed by, and she was now left with only the present moment. She acted.

As Cyril turned to the defiant young Thunsi mother with her Thunsi infant, Beatrice saw Lucy break free from her trance and rush at Cyril, and at that very moment, Beatrice yelled out her gathered song, a chorus so strong and violent that Cyril's thaumaturgy shuddered and like the fog exposed to the noonday sun, it vanished. It was for only an instant, but that was all that was needed. It was at that moment that the great army of the Thunsi slaves stepped into the clearing.

~ * ~

Lara screamed to Raya who was beside her. "Stop! Wake up! Raya! Wake up!" Raya twitched, shuddered, and blinked at Lara. She heard her young Thunsi infant cry, turned and gasped, hurriedly scraping away the layer of dirt. Lara ran to each mother and shook her out of the spell, turning to Old Ruth, "Help them! Help them now!"

~ * ~

It was Hawthorn who created the massive distraction, for when the thaumaturgy evaporated, he was in full battle mode. With great speed and violence, he rushed into the Blodetan horde and began smashing and mashing and crushing, breaking bones and taring flesh, a whirling hurricane of vengeance.

~ * ~

Beatrice stood, then watched Cyril sidestep Lucy, throwing her to the ground. He looked up past the Blodetan and saw hundreds of Thunsi, tall, armed with spears and machetes, a tall shadow army rushing into the clearing from the south. She saw the King of the Blodetan howl and ready for the attack, and she stooped down and sang:

Gather, gather, come to me
Bark and branch and leaf and tree
Gather, bind, wrap and weave
Into a mighty golem be

The Forest of the Dead shuddered, a great wind ripping through it. There a mass of fallen logs, branches, desiccated carcasses, rocks, earth and forgotten things from the ancient of days, gathered into a great animated beast with a log head as well as branch hands. A thunderous, heavy terror, and it pounced on the King of the Blodetan. Beatrice turned to find Cyril, but he vanished.

~ * ~

When the spell from Cyril broke, it did not really matter, for Hal, Clem and their mycelia bodies finished feasting over the corpse of Christopher Dante. He was gorged, revolted, sobbing and shaking, a traumatized, terrified child. Again, he heard that voice, that still small voice. *Don't be afraid. I forgive you. I forgive you. This is how it must be done. It is the only way.*

When he did finally open his eyes he stared in disbelief. Before him was not a corpse of the dead Christopher Dante, but a blanket of indigo fungi glowing in the darkness of the night, an electrical, living thing. For all the world, whether it was from his deep humiliation or from some deep desire, he would swear the rest of his days it was in the shape of a beautiful butterfly.

Chapter Seventy-one

The Blodetan scattered into the dark woods when the great King of the Blodetan fell, his bone crown smashed under the weight of the now defunct golem.

Lara calmed the Thunsi Mothers – pulling Renilda to her feet, helped Rita wipe the dirt from her infant's mouth. Rebecca and Roberta were not so lucky. They still held the lifeless infants in their arms. Ralph, Old Bony Root, had stumbled over to them, consoling them, pulling them aside and speaking to them in whispers, pointing at the holes.

The night grew cold and the mass of Thunsi collected and pooled around fires, rotating huddling close, then pulling away to allow others to warm themselves. The Thunsi from Widorexiton and those from the Southern mines greeted each other, spoke in low whispers, delighting in the strange but familiar dialects of the other. Occasionally, there was a howl or cry somewhere in the scattering, but that soon was replaced with a chuckle, a shout of recognition.

~ * ~

In the morning a fog of confusion and malaise hovered over the large group. There was a disturbance near the woods. Lara walked over.

"You must, my children," wheezed Old Bony Root to a huddled group of Thunsi's from Widorexiton. "We are the only ones now who can keep the ritual alive."

"What is this nonsense," Lara interrupted. "Don't listen to this liar."

"You may say such things now," the old Thunsi said, "in the company and power of this...this rebellion you have started. These young flowers will not be part of your apostasy."

"There is no Horned God," Lara belted out to the two young suffering Thunsi Rebecca and Roberta. "It's all a lie. It's always been a lie. This... Him (she nearly punched Old Bony Root), all of it... It's nothing but a cycle of death, of slavery, oppression, and death." Lara realized all the other Thunsi were listening to her now, the slaves from the south had gathered as well as some crew members from the *Intrepid*.

"Hawthorn tried to tell me. Hawthorn knew all about it, and he tried so hard to tell me."

Hawthorn, who was scraped and slashed, some tentacle-limbs hanging limp—pointed at the holes and to the tall gray trunks beyond them with their few branches like limbs and jabbered and howled.

"Yes," Lara interpreted. "Yes, it is all a lie. Four hundred years of lies! What is the Forest of the Dead? Tell them, Old Bony Root! Tell them, Ruth, you old crone! Tell them what The Forest of the Dead and Thunsae Myrrha is! Tell them!"

Ruth trembled, and whether it was from all the excitement or the sudden terrible question put to her, she fell back so that one of the *Intrepid's* crew caught her and steadied her to her feet.

"I'll tell you!" Lara rumbled on. "The Forest of the Dead...is You! Four hundred years of ritual killing, planting, and we...*we* all are culpable for this shame!" The Thunsi grumbled and murmured amongst themselves.

"Who do you think you are, peasant Thunsi?" Ralph, Old Bony Root, bellowed. "I should banish you for high treason, such blasphemy!"

The great gathering of Thunsi slaves from the south moved forward, Lucy and her brother leading them.

"Get out of here, old fool," Lucy said, and her voice was full of authority. "Go and bury your dead beliefs with your own dead. Go! Do not ever bring your evil back to this land...or our island!"

Ralph walked over to Ruth and stood. "Where will we go?" asked Ruth. Her voice was shrill and weak and old.

"Come. Come," Old Bony Root said. "Let us go. We shall seek out The Horned God. We will ask him for direction. We will cast down these blasphemers, and his wrath will justify the righteous. Come."

"Wait, please wait for me," Raya suddenly blurted out.

She stopped in front of Lara. "You were never one of us. You will pay for your heresy, peasant. Roman and I will see to that."

She hurried to the two old Thunsi, followed immediately by the mourning Rebecca and Roberta still holding their dead infant Thunsi. Several of *Intrepid's* crew left with them as well.

Lara watched the ragged group disappear into the forest, the coming morning now nearly upon them. A tall Thunsi stepped up to her. She was beautiful, strong. She placed her hand on infant Elizabeth's cheek, then looked at Lara.

"You are so strong, young one. I am proud of you." She stared at Lara until Lara felt uncomfortable. "My name is Lucy. What is your little one's name?"

"Elizabeth," Lara said.

Lucy smiled. "I knew an Elizabeth once. That is a powerful name. A beautiful and fitting name."

Lara looked up, the face before her, elegant, long suffering. It was for only a moment, a synapse of electricity perhaps, but she felt known by this beautiful, strong Thunsi. Lara turned when Old Bony Root pronounced a curse upon those who would not follow him. She barked and hurled abuse with the others as they walked into the forest. When she turned back, the tall Thunsi woman had gone.

Chapter Seventy-two

Beatrice searched for an hour, but she could not find any sign of Cyril's fleeing. She recalled him running with the tall old Thunsi servant at his side, and she thought there was another one, one carrying the painted skull of an eel but her mind was still jumbled from the night's events. Frustrated and tired, she walked back to the clearing in the Forest of the Dead. There she sat, alone in the dark night, the weight of Christopher Dante's death suddenly crushing, something so profound and heavy that to focus on the event was to end her being.

Morning broke, and the sun was now rising in the east, the rays casting down upon the clearing and in the spaces, it could find through the dense canopy above. Her mind drifted back and back, trying to piece together how the now completed road had led to so great a tragedy. Question after question surfaced, like great heads of beasts. How did the Thunsi from the mines know how to find them? At just the right time, they appeared.

She remembered in the heat of the battle—there was NORM. She came across him by accident. There he was anchored to a spot in the woods, continually repeating *Dante Protocol initiated*. Christopher must have used its satellite capabilities to guide the Thunsi slaves.

That lead to something else quite disturbing. NORM connected to the satellite! What did that unleash? Why did Christopher break his rule? As she pondered this, these strategic moments—his strange words the night before, his disappearing with NORM that morning, the complete submission to Cyril when she knew damn well, he had the power to wreck the very world into ash. She sat in silence, head spinning.

He was not some helpless insect caught in a web, no, he was the spider all along. It was Cyril, Beatrice, and Hal, all of them—they were the ones caught in *his* web. He was not fleeing from anything. No, he was running ahead and pulling them all toward...what?

A sense of hope surfaced for a moment, but it was soon eclipsed, snuffed out by the horrifying scenes of his slaughter. No, Christopher Dante was dead. She saw him fall. She saw the horror of Hal and Clem over the dead body. She closed her eyes and shook her head to banish the terror.

Hal found her still sitting there. It was now late morning. Clem, the Mountain Ghost, was by his side. They had just ended a heated conversation which she caught only bits and pieces. His attitude changed when he saw her. He sat next to her, nobody saying anything. Finally, Hal said, "I didn't know. I'm so ashamed."

Beatrice looked at the Thunsi who were dragging their dead into great rows for burial. She looked at Hal, his worn and weathered face; the deep humiliation, and uncertainty. "None of us did. I think the only one who knew was Christopher, and now he's gone forever."

They sat in silence. "I killed them," Hal said.

"Who?"

"His mother. I blew her out of the sky. And Caravaggio. I killed them both." He wiped his face with his grimy hands. "I think Christopher knew that. Why else...?"

"Why else what?" Beatrice said. She looked at him, hopeful for some artifact found that could make sense of it all, but there was nothing. He was exhausted, defeated, empty. "Nothing. It's nothing," he said.

They both rested with their backs to the large, strange tree and watched the morning turn into afternoon. They helped the Thunsi bury their dead.

They ended up staying in the Forest of the Dead for nearly three months. Each day they would wake to venture further and further into the woods. They lovingly and carefully, gently spent the hours pulling the terrible taps with the coagulated orange foam—pulling them free, salving over the deep wounds with a thick tar poultice. Each time they did, there seemed to be a sort of joyous shiver that shook the leaves and twitched the limbs, as if the tree itself was welcoming the act.

It was mid-summer when they parted company. Lara, Beatrice, and Hal, Clem and many Thunsi headed north. Lucy and her brother traveled south. So much was to be done. So much to rebuild, prepare for what was coming. They promised the others to gather the very next year to memorialize all that transpired.

Lucy said nothing to Lara, a sense of intrusion, of chances missed, a tragic inevitable parting.

Chapter Seventy-three

The large group separated once again, Lara and her young baby along with nearly a hundred Thunsi left for the coast and there to sail back to Widorexiton. Beatrice watched them leave, her heart heavy for the young Thunsi and her child, a sense of doom she could not shake. Their fate was tied together now, inevitably bound.

"Wait!" She screamed and ran to Lara.

A world of hope and doubt and joy rushed and swirled in her chest. All she could manage was, "Be careful."

"I will be." Lara smiled. "I will see you again." She turned and hurried toward the disappearing crowd.

Now Hal, Beatrice and Clem stood before a small Cave. The rock mouth and tunnel Hal and Clem took through the Black Mountains and to the Forest of the Dead. Hal put his hand on Beatrice's back. "This is the way through."

They entered the mouth of the small cave and walked deeper into the mountain until coming to another passage that branched off to the right.

"That was where the Horned God lair is. That's where Caravaggio was killed. There's fifty tons of rock on everything back that way."

As Beatrice stood there, she felt something she had not felt in years. At first it was a sensation, something delightfully remembered that was forgotten. "Wait," she said.

"I'm telling you. It's rock and ruin back there. Let's go. There will be enough pain ahead, I can assure you."

Now Clem hovered next to Beatrice, an electricity of excitement flittering and fluttering about him.

"What?" Hal remonstrated. "Not you too?"

Beatrice ignored him and walked into the darkness of the tunnel beyond. "I'm telling you! There's... Well, damn it! Wait for me!" He hurried after them.

They walked slowly at first, hesitantly, blindly with hands stretched out. Now even Hal could feel something changed. There was not the creepy, eerie feeling of despair he and Clem felt when they came across it so many weeks earlier. No, there was no Horned God waiting for them this time. There was something else here now.

Beatrice cried out and dashed down the tunnel. Hal raced after. He turned with the tunnel and came to a wide opening, a bright fire roaring, illuminating the great expanse. No longer were the stone walls covered in the terrible runes of the Horned God, but bright murals of lush forests. Of Thunsi and eels. Of the great battle in the clearing of the Forest of the Dead. So, life-like were they, that Hal secretly believed he stepped into some new thaumaturgy. Perhaps he had, so glorious, powerful, and moving! "I don't understand," Hal stumbled and stuttered.

"What's not to understand, Pal?" Said a booming, stentorian voice from the shadows. "If there's one thing, I have learned in my four hundred years of shit and hell, brother... It's that it's tough to kill a painter." The great bearded man stood up. "There is no doubt, Pal, the last year or so was tough. There is going to be hell to pay for the idiot who did it to me."

Beatrice ran to Caravaggio and hugged him so tightly.

"What's all this now?"

He pushed her back, gently, kindly. "You're not getting a heart suddenly? We wouldn't want that. Not with the shit coming down around us."

Hal stumbled and stared then stood, statue-like, eyes

wide, mouth ajar.

"A lot of water under the bridge since the ole birthday bash, eh Pal?"

The great bear of a man stepped up to Hal and grabbed him by the shoulders. "I underestimated you, Pal. That won't happen again."

He turned and pointed to a kettle of stew on the fire. "Help yourself. I have more to work out over here." He rubbed his beard in contemplation. "Go on! You're wasting time, and time is what none of us seem to have now."

He walked over to the wall and began to draw immaculate pictures of what looked like Cogstin in its glory. Of things flying and moving in the air about the great city. To the right, a great army of Thunsi marching across the land bridge connecting the Salty Sea to the Great Lake where they entered an armada of ships as far as the eye could see. It was stunning in its detail, like living breathing events unfolding before them.

Hal walked over to a large boulder and sat down near Beatrice. He could not focus on Caravaggio as he spoke of doom and coming events. He concentrated again and again but even with the great man's gesticulating arms, his bushy, wiry beard and awe-inspiring cave paintings, Hal's mind was swarming with something new transpiring within him.

At first it seemed just a voice, maybe a memory from the past, but soon he was quite sure that the mycelial hyphae within him had connected to some sort of network. It was very disturbing. He heard millions of voices in that network, but one very much in particular was present. He knew it could not be, but still the voice persisted, familiar, but now...excited, full of energy. As he tried to focus on Caravaggio's words, allowing himself to fully understand what he was saying. That a new and terrible alliance was forming somewhere outside of Cogstin—as those words settled, another voice superseded them all, *Yes. I told you. You are forgiven. Just as I said. You raised me, Hal. My precious, precious Hal. You are my vessel. Now Listen carefully, I have much to say.*

Chapter Seventy-four

Lara sat on the edge of her bed and stepped softly over to the small crib where Elizabeth lay sleeping. She pulled the covers over her, grabbed her small shawl and walked into the fall morning. She could not sleep these days. When she did it was short and restless. Each night she seemed to have formed a routine. It was cold and brisk, the coming of something unexpected. She loved the fall, the changing of the leaves, the last chance to prepare for the harsh winter to come. There was also a sense of sadness. She lived close to the Harbor now, and with a very short walk, she found herself standing on the pier looking out at the great Salty Sea.

Like all the mornings past, she found herself thinking of Roman. Would this be the day she would see his ship on the horizon? Would this be the moment she would see the mast breaking the line of the horizon? She imagined, like she did every morning, him waving, the absolute joy she would feel, the great expansive relief of something wonderful and new swooping down upon her life, a hurricane of joy and happiness.

She would present Elizabeth to him, his child, their child together. He would grab them both with such joy, such pride. As she watched, all that appeared was the reddish hue of the sun blast over the great waters, the god of day. She heard Elizabeth squeak behind her, the chirp, then cry out, and she hurried back to the small house and to the new life waiting expectantly for all that she could offer.

Chapter Seventy-five

Roman stood in the darkness. If it were not for the strange blue light emanating from the metal box with legs, they would be in complete night. Why had they come here, to this ruined city, to the tunnels under the earth that smelled of death and ancient forgotten earth? He was exhausted, and his stomach hurt.

"Where is it?" said an impatient Cyril.

The metal box with legs whirled and buzzed.

"Geological interference detected," it said in its synthetic voice. "Current S-Value of 3."

"Yes, yes, of course the signal is diminished. Are you still connected? You said you have access to all the satellites. Well, do you, or don't you? Where is it, damn you?"

"Processing. Rune located. Two hundred meters ahead."

Roman was confused, felt a third wheel, as these two beings, both strange gods (one known, the other some sort of metal box with a brain) bickered and searched in the tunnels under the mythical city of Cogstin. That too was a disappointment. After all his readings and dreaming. The place was nothing but rubble, wind, and noxious dust storms. It seemed they searched for days, and he had run out of licorice root. A great hunger beginning to take hold of him. He was afraid that something was beginning in him that he could not now stop.

The Horned God, if Roman was honest with himself, was also a disappointment. Yes, he had power, but after the murder of Christopher Dante, well, he seemed small and petty. Cyril was now not so much a god but a demanding diva. Irritating but

threatening at the same time.
Why am I here? Thought Roman.
Again, he grimaced as the hunger began to crawl up his throat, pulsing, cramping. For some reason he thought of Lara, that wonderful and strange day when he showed her the Mendel Fragment, and a great sorrow overwhelmed him. He desperately wanted something, something to fill the terrible void left when his religion crumbled, but he could not think of what that might be. He watched Cyril hurry down the tunnel, then give out a delighted schoolboy cry. NORM carefully crab walked around the cascading rocks and broken cement blocks. Roman scrambled behind.

"Quick. Bring the Fragment. Bring the Fragment." Roman pulled out the glass piece and held it out in the light from NORM. "Hold it steady, you idiot."

While NORM scanned and buzzed, while Cyril pronounced the fragment equations into the night, finally grabbing the glass and holding it himself—while the incantation was beginning, Roman suddenly convulsed and fell to the earthen floor of the tunnel. He was now so wracked with pain that he lost where he was and what he was doing. He saw in his imagination, like a cloud that slowly dissipates, an image of Lara, they looking out at the Salty Sea together. he could not now recall who she was or why they were there. A flash of red light came from the strange rune on the wall and all was darkness.

"Did It work?" Cyril screamed. "Is It free? Where's the damn light? We need light!"

NORM buzzed, seeming to reboot, and Cyril smacked the side of its metal chassis. A sensor popped out with a small bulb at the end, a dim beam shining on a hole, like a chip of stone had broken free.

"It did work! It worked!"

Cyril hesitated, then stooped down to Roman who had

utterly transformed. He was pale and white, his eyes nearly disappearing into the large oblong sockets. Roman sniffed, then sniffed again. "You must be so hungry, my poor, poor dear," Cyril mocked. "Let's see if anyone in the city is home for dinner."

Cyril walked into the darkness of the tunnel. NORM scurried after. Roman watched them walk away through the sunken eyes of his new world. He sniffed several times to locate them. Then he took the painted eel skull and smashed it on a stone, the outer parts now shards and splinters of bone. He placed it on his head, leaned his head back and howled. Like a called animal, he ran after his new masters.

Also by the author
at
Rogue Phoenix Press

IMAGO

Chapter One

I see the room and hear the voice. It is the same every time. The room is white, white cushioned chaise lounge before wall-to-wall glass, and behind the glass...a deep blue horizon-less expanse of water. The voice booms out. The voice? Well, I wake to the voice, like an alarm, and it too is the same, same words in the same order, *Sing to me, oh muse.* The image of the white room, the white chaise lounge and the deep blue water behind the wall-to-wall glass...vanishes. It's a code, this voice, a complex equation, something other than words but words all the same. I have stopped trying to make sense of this, stopped trying to be surprised or afraid or panicked or even intellectually inquisitive.

Every day I can remember, since the first time I ever woke up, Pow! The vision of the white room and the blue water followed by the voice, it's once again morning. I am once again shoved back into *the world of men, time, and things*. That's not original. It's a phrase I discovered sprayed across a crumbling brick wall in the middle of Cogstin.

I was pulling copper in the evening with my uncle Hal, working as a scrapper, ripping out pipes and tearing up old wooden planks in the abandoned parts of the city when I stumbled on it. It was multi-colored and beautiful. At the end of the last letter of the last word like a wondrous punctuation mark: a butterfly. The image triggered something deep, but of course that feeling was soon Reduced Down, that sense of astonishment, of wonder, was disassembled, deconstructed into its component parts: physical, molecular, binary levels, distilled into meaninglessness 1-0-1-0-1-1-0, etc...a habit formed, molded from an early age, like breathing or walking. I can still see the symbol of the butterfly, the magenta outlined wings. I say nothing to Hal, just open the imaginary chest of things I don't understand and place it inside.

I work for my uncle Hal, my legal custodian, at times my shadow, keeping watch, keeping me under control, a barrier between me and Agent Smiley of the NRM Bureau of Corrections who waits for me to break parole, the wrong place at the wrong time, sitting sober with the drunken Hal and Max or perhaps leaving a piece of metal art carelessly lying about. Agent Smiley is not his real name. I have no idea what that is. His smile is so large, and he's about as creepy as a human can be...so Hal and I make fun of Agent Smiley. Hal says, "Listen, Stretch, you know how it is. They're look'n for a reason is all. Bloom where you're planted. What choice do you have? Show me a man's choices, and I'll show you a man's future." Hal's an alcoholic with a good heart. "You're a fine scrapper, boy. Embrace your life, don't run from it."

I have known Hal since I can remember. I actually thought he was my dad at one time, but he explained I was orphaned, abandoned on his doorstep. The mythology of this event, much like most of Hal's stories, have an underpinning of fable, of telling the tale too many times so it becomes something altogether different than probably what actually happened. He's not my father, but the only father I know. Hal is all I have, and he is enough.

I asked him about the voices one time. His large brow

crinkled, puffy eyes squinting as if he was trying to see through into my head. He trundled his lips with his sausage-like fingers and said, "What voices?"

I stared up at him, a man mountain, hands on his hips, overall bib pulled taut across his enormous stomach like a canvas tarp pulling back the moon, work gloves dangling from his back pocket, fingers splayed out like a rooster's cockscomb. "Can I have some more eggs?" I said. He seemed relieved with the deflection, still his face soured like when he missed some good copper or being awakened after falling asleep on the job site after an all night bender. He never asked about it again.

My job is temporary, working for Hal at U-Salvage, and that's not just wishful thinking on my part. I know that letter is coming. I know my life will finally begin, time served, literally. The NRM can't keep me under observation forever. It's just how it is. Every male child is monitored until the powers that be verify you are not some sort of miscreant. I've been waiting longer than others.

"Just bad luck," Hal says. "Sometimes the big guy has to show the little guy who is boss."

I grew up with the inspections. I grew up with the salvage yard. This, like Hal, is all I know. "The NRM checks everyone," Hal says. "It's just the way of things. But there will come a time," Hal says and smiles. He pats me on the shoulder. "The letter will come, and when it does... You'll pack your bags and say adios to me, to Max, and to this Universal Salvage Company forever."

He grabs me by both shoulders and puts his nose nearly touching mine. "The past is the past, Stretch. The future means new beginnings. Change is good."

Well, change may be good, but Cogstin will never change, it's beyond changing, more like a ghost city, a dead city, a city of ashes. Yes, I discovered that phrase too, sprayed across a cement archway under an overpass: *City Of Ash, Awake!*

Today and the rest of the foreseeable future is about

inventory. Hal is under a lot of pressure to make sure all his ducks are in order, and all his ducks are actually ducks. He and Max have been selling scrap on the side. That has raised some eyebrows somewhere above. Hal is beside me, as we walk around the large metal-sided out-building which holds the dump truck, the backhoe, the metal cutting torches and skid steer, all the tools to scrap in Cogstin. The sun is just coming up over the horizon, a red hue above the walls to the yard. I hear yapping and yelping in the distance.

Hal grumbles, "Time for another hunting trip with Max."

He stops, grabs the straps to his overalls, forearms resting on his enormous gut. He is three hundred pounds of sheer pride, legs apart, a slight smile on his face as he surveys the vast racks of stacked corrugated sheeting, coiled wire, layers of reclaimed bricks, lumber, everything that can be taken, everything pulled and popped and sheered from the abandoned city of Cogstin. I must say the cool breeze, the red hue and the vast expanse of metal walls, does have an effect.

"Inventory, boy. Today is all about inventory. Keep those nosey Neds out of our business. You know the drill."

I nod my head. "What's there is there, and what's not there that should be...is still there."

"Good lad," Hal says and slaps my back. "Max and I will work on the dump truck in a bit." I watch him wobble to the storage building, and understand full well that "work on the dump truck with Max" means drink vodka and talk about old times until both are napping.

I use the lift to move slowly up and down the rows, the hydraulic whine as the metal platform raises high into the air, then slowly down in fits and halts. I count the scraps we have, check the numbers they have, make sure they match, and make a note of what we need to scrap next time in Cogstin. I do this until lunch. After lunch, I do it again. It is monotonous and lacking in any mental acuity whatsoever. I find myself distracted by the red plains beyond the scrap yard walls.

These are the Great Sand Flats that sweep as far as the eye can see. I lift myself just above the wall, stop for a moment to listen for Hal and Max, the radio, all is calm. I turn to view north, the dead city of Cogstin rising up into the hazy cloudy horizon. I turn to the south and rest my arms on the four-by-four beam framing the metal wall. They are red, the flats, red sand blowing and drifting, gathering in great clouds, settling upon everything exposed. Far beyond them are the mineral mines, of which I have only heard about. I think how dry, vapid and lonely is such a place, so similar to the ruined world of Cogstin, and immediately I think of the white room and the white chaise lounge with the great blue water beyond the glass. My head aches and my stomach aches with the resonance, and I feel an inexpressible sadness. My talkie buzzes. It chirps again. It's Hal. "Stop lolly gagging out there, boy. Time for some steaks."

When I make it to the house, Max has already made drinks and Hal is standing over the sizzling meat with a set of tongs.

"So, we even out today, Stretch?"

I take my drink and sit next to Max who has to lift his large nose in the air to sip from the martini glass. He wipes his thin caterpillar mustache in satisfaction. We talk about the inventory. About Max's garage and what cars he is currently working on. We eat and drink and laugh. All the while I see the great sand flats juxtaposed to the white room and the blue water. After dinner, the sun nearly completely down, a cool and comfortable breeze ruffling the large umbrella, Hal leaning back with contentment. Right then, I suddenly ask, "Have I ever been in a white room with ceiling to wall glass?"

Hal is motionless like he's asleep, but I know he is not. Max chortles, "I don't know, have you?"

"I was just curious," I say.

"Not unless you have one hidden in the salvage yard,"

says Max.

He toasts the air and laughs. Hal is sitting up now and staring at me like he's going to draw me. "That's an odd question, Stretch."

"It's just, well...have I?"

"Anyone for another one?" Max says and stands up.

Hal blinks several times, like something is in his eyes.

"You want to come with me to make the drinks, Hal?" says Max nudging him.

"No, I'm fine. Go ahead. A round for all of us," but his voice is a whisper, like he's somewhere else.

Max walks into the house. "A white room," Hal says, mumbling. "A white room."

"Have I been there?" I say. I am leaning forward now, intense. "Have you seen it?"

Max comes hurrying over with new glasses filled to spilling. "Sorry for the wait, gents. Here we go."

He looks at me, then Hal. He puts the glasses down and kicks Hal's boot. Hal comes back from where he went, smiles broadly at the liquor and toasts Max and me.

I sit back in my chair frustrated. I watch them laugh and talk about the same things they have laughed and talked about since I can remember. Max brings up the drudgery of inventory. Hal pauses, toasts the air and tells the story of how he and Max switched the rack numbers on the NRM U SALVAGE Director just as he was about to scan the barcodes...and... "You should have seen his face, boy." rumbles Hal, slapping his thigh. I think in my head simultaneously as he says, "Ducks to Dimes, did we get a talking to after that, eh Max?" Max toasts the air and gulps his drink. I'm not sure why this bothers me so badly on this particular night, but I walk out of the kitchen and head to the little shack behind the metal out-building in the scrap yard.

About the Author

Greg Belliveau is an award-winning novelist and author of the Science Fiction Dystopian novel *Gods of IMAGO* (Rogue Phoenix Press, 2023) and *IMAGO* (RPP, 2019), as well as *Go Down To Silence* (Multnomah Publishing: a Division of Penguin Random house, 2001) which was a Christy Award Finalist for Best First Novel; and a collection of creative nonfiction entitled *Seeds: Mediations on Grace in a World with Teeth* (Crosslink Publishing, 2017). He is currently working on the TV series *Go Down To Silence* based on the novel of the same name. He is a Christopher Isherwood grant recipient and teaches Writing at Antioch University and Capital University.

FOR THE FULL INVENTORY OF QUALITY BOOKS:
http://www.roguephoenixpress.com

Rogue Phoenix Press
Representing Excellence in Publishing

**Quality trade paperbacks and downloads
in multiple formats,
in genres ranging from historical to contemporary romance,
mystery and science fiction.
Visit the website then bookmark it.
We add new titles each month!**

Printed in the USA
CPSIA information can be obtained
at www.ICGtesting.com
LVHW010032290524
781600LV00004B/173